LOVE AD LIB

EVIE ALEXANDER

EMLIN PRESS

First Published in Great Britain 2023 by Emlin Press

ISBN (eBook) 978-1-914473-26-5

ISBN (Print) 978-1-914473-27-2

ISBN (Audiobook) 978-1-914473-43-2

A CIP catalogue record for this book is available from the British Library.

www.emlinpress.com

For Chester and Joy

ALSO BY EVIE ALEXANDER

THE KINLOCH SERIES

Highland Games

Hollywood Games

Kissing Games

Musical Games

Wedding Games

Christmas Games

※

THE FOXBROOKE SERIES

One Night in Foxbrooke

Love ad Lib

An Unholy Affair

The Upper Crush

The Love Position

Christmas off Script

One Night Only

Righting Mr Wrong

Under the Influencer

Foxbrooke Extras

※

By Evie Alexander and Kelly Kay

EVIE & KELLY'S HOLIDAY DISASTERS SERIES

Cupid Calamity

Cookout Carnage

Christmas Chaos

Get Evie's books in all formats as well as special offers, early releases, and exclusive deals direct from her website:

www.eviealexanderbooks.com

EMLIN
PRESS

PROLOGUE

Lord Henry Arthur Fitzwilliam Foxbrooke, Viscount of Nobbury and heir to his father's title and estate, stood in the entrance hall of his family home and seethed.

In front of him, a woman in a red latex crotchless catsuit squeaked across the tiled floor. A naked man crawled behind her, led by a dog leash attached to a studded collar. The man glanced at Henry and barked. The sound bounced off the panelled walls, colliding with peals of laughter and groans of lust that echoed from elsewhere in the house.

Henry ground his teeth. One of his father's infamous soirées was in full swing.

Whether it floated your boat or sank your ship, as long as you were a consenting adult and left your pets at home, every sexual proclivity was catered for at Foxbrooke Manor. The parties had been running for decades ever since Henry's father, Arthur, unexpectedly acceded to the title of Duke and turned the ancestral seat from a stuffy stately home in Somerset to a go-to destination for high-class hedonists and their hangers-on.

The affairs had started out small, but once word got out about the smorgasbord of sex and other stimulants on offer, they engorged. The *Daily Mail* newspaper was one of the most voracious critics, working itself up into a frothing frenzy of self-righteous indignation as it sought to lay the lassitude of youth, the decline of 'British' values, and the rise in house prices firmly at the door of Foxbrooke Manor.

The fact that the Duchess of Somerset, Henry's mother, was a Black American model and movie star was unusual enough. However, a year after producing Henry and his twin sister, Estelle, Vivienne Camille Boucher-Foxbrooke began an affair with an Irish single mother from the village and introduced her to the Duke. Three months after that, Dervla O'Sullivan married the Duke and Duchess of Somerset in a pagan ceremony, and she and her infant son took the Foxbrooke name.

The three adults may have been happy in their unconventional relationship, however the mainstream media was not. The *Daily Mail* spearheaded a letter-writing campaign to show the Foxbrooke family just what the Great British Public thought of them and their lifestyle.

Arthur, Vivienne and Dervla responded by creating a pyre and burning every piece of correspondence in the centre of Foxbrooke village on a Saturday afternoon, surrounded by their young children.

Life was never the same again.

'Henry! My boy!'

Arthur George Edward Foxbrooke was descending the wide staircase, a champagne flute in one hand, a lit cigarette in a holder in the other. He was dressed only in a patterned gold silk dressing gown that stretched over his tummy, and a pair of old carpet slippers. His salt-and-pepper hair stuck up in all directions and his cheeks were flushed. If Holly Golightly, Henry VIII and Hugh Hefner had indulged in a three-way, the Duke of Foxbrooke would be their love child.

'Perfect timing,' his father said, drawing him in for a hug.

Henry stood stiffly, his overnight bag clutched to his side as the smell of patchouli punched him in the nose.

His father disengaged with a satisfied smile. 'I've just finished servicing your mam.'

Henry repressed a shudder and brushed his jacket as if to remove the scent of his second mother, now clinging to him like an unwanted hug. 'Dad—'

'I wish your mom was here,' his father continued, his brow furrowing. 'The sooner that fashion shoot thingumajig is over, the sooner I'm back between her—'

'Dad!'

His father blinked, as if woken from a dream.

'Your message said there was an emergency,' Henry snapped.

Arthur took a drag from his cigarette, ash dropping to the floor. The sight and smell made Henry's skin itch. Sod staying the night. He wanted to get back to London on the next train and dump everything he was wearing at the dry cleaners.

'Yes.' Arthur fixed his pale blue eyes on his son's brown ones. '*You're* the emergency.'

'What?'

His father glugged a mouthful of champagne and unsuccessfully stifled a burp.

'Dad?'

'Come with me. I've got something for you.' He turned on his heel and beckoned Henry to follow.

Henry's heart sank. He should have cross-checked with Estelle or any of his other siblings if there was *actually* an emergency before setting off. However, any conversation with his family always ended with them asking him the same question, to which he never provided the answer they were looking for. He figured it was better for everyone if he minimised contact rather than continue to disappoint them.

He focused on the slap of his father's slippers as he strode through the Manor. His dad didn't believe in throwing anything away that still functioned, so his slippers were dirty and threadbare. They'd been used as chew toys by the family dogs, had holes from his big toenails, were stained from cooking accidents, and were shiny inside from sebum.

Each Christmas, Henry bought him a new pair, and each year they were re-gifted to one of his brothers or given to the village charity shop. But Henry refused to give up. If he could convince his father to condemn his slippers to the interior of a biohazard bag, maybe there was hope that one day the rest of Arthur Foxbrooke could be moulded into some sense of normalcy.

His dad stopped at the entrance to the long gallery. The floor was a chequerboard of black and white tiles ground down by the passage of footsteps across time. The walls were panelled in dark wood, and suits of armour stood sentry by the many doors. Halfway down the space stood a couple wearing high-vis jackets and safety shoes. By their rigid posture, Henry guessed they were attending the party for work, not pleasure.

'First-aiders,' said Arthur out of the corner of his mouth. 'You never know where a vegetable may get stuck.'

Henry blanched as his mind vomited a medley of unpleasant images.

'I'm joking,' his father chortled. 'But this *is* what I'm worried about.'

'Vegetables?'

'*You*. I'm worried about *you*. We all are.'

Give me strength. Henry took a big breath. '*You're* worried about *me?*'

His father's eyes creased with concern. 'Yes—'

A door banged open ahead of them, and a couple of women slid into the corridor. They were naked and glistening, holding onto each other to stay upright as they cackled. Henry stared pointedly at the wood-panelled ceiling as they stumbled towards them.

'Enjoy the jelly room?' his father asked.

'OMG yes,' one replied. 'And you made them with vodka! You're a total legend, Foxy.'

Henry stiffened at the pet name. The media had recently transferred his father's moniker to him, and he hated everything about it. How could they think he was anything like his dad?

'Have you tried any of the other wet play areas?' Arthur continued. 'Our latest addition is the lube room. We've got water blasters locked and loaded with every flavour of the rainbow.'

'Such fun!' the girl squealed.

Henry swallowed to keep the bile from rising. He needed to get out of there and back to the safety of his controlled life in London. Even though his eyes were still glued to the ceiling, the scent of raspberry jelly was closing in. He flinched as someone touched his arm.

'OMG, it *is* you. Cass, look. It's Foxy junior!'

'Eek! Excited face! Wanna come and play?'

Gritting his teeth, Henry shook his head.

'Maybe later,' his father replied. 'Why don't you two run along and have fun. There's a champagne fountain in the library, and at eleven you can play "hunt the marshmallow" in the billiards room.'

The women slipped away with shrieks of excitement and Henry let out a breath.

'Dad, I'm leaving now.'

His father took his hand. 'Dear, dear Henry.' He sighed. 'I so desperately want you to be happy.'

Arthur looked genuinely pained and something inside Henry's chest tugged. How could he say that what stressed him out the most were the antics of his father and a family legacy he wanted no part of?

'I *am* happy, Dad. I like my life in London.'

Arthur lifted the cigarette holder and took a drag even though it had burnt out. Henry knew the action was designed to give his mouth something to do rather than badger his son to come home permanently.

'Love,' his father finally said. 'You don't have love in London.'

Henry opened his mouth, but his brain couldn't find the words to fill it.

His father squeezed his hand and led him towards a door. 'Just give them a chance, okay?'

Them? 'What have you done?' His heart rate spiked, adrenaline rushing through his veins.

'Just talk to them. Kick back a bit and relax. They're lovely ladies. And very excited to meet you.'

Arthur opened the door to around twenty beautiful women. They looked up expectantly.

Henry shut the door. 'Dad! Just no. Jesus Christ, that is not what I want.'

His father didn't seem perturbed. 'Okay, my boy, not a problem at all.' He led Henry farther down the long gallery and opened another door. 'This should be more suitable.'

Inside were a group of good-looking men who smiled with undisguised interest as they met Henry's gaze.

Henry slammed the door and turned away, trying to control his breathing. His father had lost the plot.

'Dad, this is…' He scored his fingers through the tight curls of his short hair. 'Look, you don't have to set me up. I can sort out my own love life.'

'But you've never had a relationship—'

'Yes, Dad, I have.'

'Not that we know of. You've never brought anyone home before—'

'And why do you think that is?' he exploded. 'Jesus Christ. I want to bring someone home to meet a *normal* family.'

His father guffawed. 'No family is normal. You just mean boring.'

'I'll take boring a million times over this.'

'But—'

'And I've got a girlfriend.'

His dad perked up. 'How wonderful! What's her name?'

'None of your business,' he snapped. Lying didn't come easily to him, and he was beginning to sweat.

'When can we meet her?'

Henry started down the corridor. 'I'm leaving.'

'Henry, hang on…'

But he was done.

'Careful of—'

It was too late. As his front foot made contact with the jelly, it slipped from under him. Henry windmilled his arms to stay upright, his other foot stepping in the gloop. Gathering speed, he slid at an angle along the tiled floor. He reached for a suit of armour to steady himself, but it detached from the wall. For a moment their spin could have been considered dancing before all balance was lost, and the pair crashed to the ground in a jumble of human and metal limbs.

The two first-aiders rushed to his side, seemingly eager to help someone who was fully clothed.

'Are you okay?' asked the woman as her colleague removed the pieces of armour.

'I'm fine,' Henry spat, getting to his feet and surveying his ruined suit.

His father was bent over, wheezing with laughter. 'Oh Henry, I wish I'd got that on film. Do you want to borrow some of my clothes?'

Henry shook his head and grabbed his bag. He needed to get back to London immediately. He could control everything there.

❧ I ❧

Henry stared at the contents of his desk drawer. Hundreds of paperclips were strewn haphazardly, a chaotic mess on top of the neatly placed notepad and pens. He picked up a paperclip. It had been bent out of shape. He lifted another, then another. Each one had been fucked with.

James Hunter-Savage.

Henry was usually the last to leave work each evening and the first to arrive the next morning. This had happened during the night. He'd never considered himself a violent person, but the urge to punch his colleague into next year was intensifying daily.

He replaced the paperclips into their box, swapped it for a new one in the stationery cupboard, then turned on his computer. He was in the middle of brokering a huge deal on behalf of an international steel conglomeration and couldn't afford to make any mistakes. The commission was worth tens of thousands of pounds, and he needed every penny.

'Oi, oi, Foxy!'

Henry glanced at his watch. Seven a.m.

Essex boy Carl swaggered into the open-plan office, his hair still damp from the shower. He threw his jacket on a desk and flexed.

'Guess who just benched more than Jamesy-boy?' he asked with a grin.

Henry raised his eyebrows at the rhetorical question.

Carl threw his arms wide. 'Me, baby! There's a new king in town.'

A man sauntered in behind him. 'Only because I've been up all night drilling your sisters. Tomorrow, I'll put you back in your place.'

James Hunter-Savage had arrived.

Tall and muscled, James had his suits tailor-made, his tousled black hair trimmed weekly, and his shave executed by a Turkish barber wielding a cut-throat razor. James had over two years and two inches on Henry and seemed compelled to mention these facts at every opportunity. He was the most successful broker at Conqueror and produced enough testosterone to supply the bulls at Pamplona.

Henry hated him.

James had been three years ahead of him at Eton. He was confident and brash and excelled at sports, whereas Henry was shy and finished growing after leaving school. They both rowed, and their paths crossed again for a year at Oxford University. At only six foot two, Henry lacked the height and bulk to make the top tier. James, on the other hand, rowed Oxford to victory in the boat race.

Just the sight of his face rubbed Henry up the wrong way. And when was Carl going to shut up? He flicked his attention back to the computer screen as an automated reminder pinged in from HR.

Reminder. Mandatory attendance this morning at the experiential training session. Arrive 09.50 for a 10.00 start.

Wasn't there an email about this a few weeks ago? He scrolled back until he found it.

From: Lorna Ferguson

To: Henry Foxbrooke

Subject: Training Workshop

Dear Henry,

At Conqueror we are keen to strengthen interpersonal connections between colleagues and foster a spirit of collaboration. The Industrial Brokerage team has been identified as a department that could benefit from additional support in building communication skills, so we are bringing in a facilitation company to run an experiential training session.

Please find all the details in the attachment.

Kind regards,

Lorna Ferguson

Henry ran his hands over his face. More HR bollocks and a total waste of time. No matter how many PowerPoint presentations he was made to endure, no productivity graph or pie chart was going to convince him to sit down and break bread with Hunter-Savage.

Brokering deals was a relentless treadmill. Week in week out, he slapped on a confident and gregarious mask and schmoozed and charmed the owners of London's most exclusive nightclubs to gain access for small men with big wallets. He didn't have the energy or desire to maintain the performance with his colleagues. They weren't his friends now and certainly wouldn't be after this morning's event.

At nine forty-five, Henry lined up his keyboard with the bottom edge of the desk and placed his mouse two and a half inches to the right. He pushed his chair in, leaving his jacket over the back, then took the stairs to the top floor of the Conqueror building and the biggest conference room.

The tables and chairs had been pushed to one side, leaving most of the floor space clear. He didn't have time to clock anything else, as a young woman appeared in his face.

'Hi! I'm Libby!' She took his hand, squeezing tightly. 'So fantastic to meet you! What's your name?'

'H-Henry,' he stuttered, taken aback by the energy of her welcome.

'Awesome. It's so great to meet you, Henry. My full name is Liberty, but only my mother calls me that if I've done something wrong. Most of the time everyone just calls me Libby, which is cool too; I like it and it's a bit like a version of Elizabeth, which was my grandmother's name. What's the story behind Henry?'

She was still holding his hand. He broke her clasp and rubbed the back of his neck. 'Er... I was named after my uncle.'

'Amazing! Are you close? Tell me about him.'

It was like being assaulted by a sunny day. Her bright blue eyes held his, and his peripheral vision told him she was wearing yellow. Even her bobbed auburn hair seemed to glow.

He cleared his throat. 'My uncle died when my mom was pregnant with me and my sister.'

Her face fell and she clutched his hand again. 'I'm so sorry. That must have been awful for her.'

'Um, she didn't know him very well. He was my dad's older brother.'

'Such a shock for your family. Does your father talk about him much?'

What the fuck was going on? 'Not much, but my grand-mother does.'

'Oh! I'm sure she would have shared so many wonderful memories of him with you. Do you remember any of your favourites?'

The more sensible part of Henry's brain was yelling at him to extricate himself from this overly personal conversation immediately, however a part of him that had lain dormant for years was utterly disarmed. Words fell out of his mouth before he could stop them.

'She said he was thoughtful and polite, sensible and kind.'

'And does she think the same of you?'

Heat ran up his neck into his cheeks. Her smile was so encouraging that before he was aware of doing so, he nodded.

She beamed at him. 'I think that's glorious. The world *needs* more thoughtfulness and kindness in it.'

The fire in his face intensified.

'And politeness and sensibleness.' She frowned, still holding his hand. 'Is "sensibleness" a word?' She laughed and everything about her seemed to shine even brighter. 'I try to be thought-ful, kind and polite, but I don't think I'm particularly sensible. What's your top tip for improving my sensibleness?'

His mind blanked. 'Er, bulk buy toilet roll and keep one hidden in case of emergencies?' he offered, not knowing where the thought had come from and internally cringing.

She let out a peal of laughter so warm and generous he knew she wasn't laughing at him. 'That's perfect advice and one my housemate would do well to remember.' She released his hands and clapped hers together. 'Henry, it's such a pleasure to meet you. We're going to have a great time this morning. *I* promise to remember who you are, but Claire hasn't met you yet, so please can you stick a label on your front with your name on it? They're on the table over there.'

Henry nodded, utterly side-swiped by the encounter, and wandered over to the table. He stuck his name to his chest, then surveyed the room. Libby was greeting Carl like a long-lost friend, and Carl looked as if he didn't know whether to pat her on the head or start flirting.

There was another woman in the room, greeting other team members with the same enthusiasm as Libby. This must be Claire. She was pregnant, wearing a bright green wrap dress and Wonder Woman Converse trainers.

Henry's gaze slid back to Libby. On her feet were Dr Martens boots. Her dress was smart but utterly out of place in the environment of Conqueror. It was as yellow as a buttercup on a summer day, flaring out from the waist and ending just above her knee. In a room full of blacks and greys, the two women looked like pixies who'd slipped in through the window on a sunbeam.

Claire glanced at her watch and clapped her hands. 'Okay, everybody, thank you all so much for being here today. Let's form a circle.'

Henry shuffled into place with his colleagues, reminded of being back at Foxbrooke Primary School as a child.

'I'm Claire, and this is Libby.'

'Hi!' Libby made eye contact with everyone as she waved.

'I think we're almost all here,' Claire continued, 'so, let's make a start. Over the next couple of hours, we're going to work on strengthening the interpersonal connections you have with the other members of your team.'

The door opened, and James entered. Libby broke away from the circle to greet him. Her voice was low, but her body language was enthusiastic and loud.

'This workshop is about breaking organisational silos, collaborating, responding to change, and supporting one another,' Claire continued as James joined the circle. 'Our mission statement is "helping people be better versions of themselves".'

James pointed at his chest. 'Can't improve on perfection.'

A ripple of laughter moved through the group.

Claire smiled. 'So, we're going to start with passing the clap—'

'Carl had better sit this one out then,' interrupted James. 'You don't want the clap he's got after that weekend in Amsterdam.'

Claire ignored him. 'This game is also called "zip, zap, boing". If I pass my clap left it's a zip; right, it's a zap, and if I pass it across the circle then it's a boing.'

Henry felt awkward and out of his depth. Where were the PowerPoint presentations he could fall asleep to?

Claire clapped to the person on her left. 'Zip.'

They passed the clap on.

It made it back to Claire. 'Zap.' She passed it to her right. The clap was halfway around the circle when she pointed her hands and her gaze at Henry and clapped. 'Boing!'

What on earth was he meant to do? He caught Libby's eye. She smiled encouragingly at him.

'Boing!' He clapped at Libby.

She jumped with excitement. 'Boing!' She threw the clap at Carl, who threw it to someone else.

Now they were dealing with a clap going one way around the circle and another travelling randomly across. Henry was keeping track of them all when Libby yelled, 'Zip!' sending another clap running off in the opposite direction to the first. Now there were three to keep track of.

'Boing!' Claire set off a fourth one.

Claps, yells of 'boing', and grunts of concentration filled the room as everyone tried to stay on top of four claps doing completely different things.

Suddenly all four claps converged on Henry and he leapt back, throwing his hands in the air. 'Fuck!'

Everything stopped.

Shit. He'd messed up the game.

'Go Henry, go Henry!' Libby and Claire jumped up and down, punching the air like soccer mums celebrating their kid's first goal.

What?

'Henry wins the prize!' Claire yelled as Libby continued chanting his name.

'But he cocked it up!' James protested.

'Congratulations to Henry!' Claire continued. 'Winner, winner, chicken dinner!'

'But—' James started.

'Let's go again,' said Claire. 'But this time, Libby and I are both going to start, and we want you to be as quick as you can.'

'On your marks...' Libby bent her knees as if preparing to race. 'Get set—'

'Zip!' Claire cried.

'Zap!' Libby replied.

'Fuck!' most of the men yelled.

The claps were fast and furious. Just as Henry felt they had it under control, Libby or Claire added in a boing, or another zap. Within a few seconds, the circle disintegrated into random clapping that Claire and Libby turned into applause.

'Whoop whoop! Let's hear it for all of us fucking it up!' Claire cried as everyone but James laughed.

'I got it right,' he interjected.

Everyone ignored him.

'Let's go again,' said Claire. 'Three... Two—'

'Boing!' Henry threw a clap to Libby.

She whooped and threw it to Carl who acted like he'd been tossed a live grenade and threw it over his shoulder.

'Zip, Zap, Boing!' Claire set claps running and flying.

James put his hands on his hips. 'Come on, guys. Do it properly.'

But nobody seemed to care about getting it right. Men with egos even bigger than their bank balances were shouting, laughing and having fun.

As fast as Carl threw claps out of the circle, Henry, Claire and Libby started more going. Henry no longer had the head-space to analyse what was going on. He was in the moment and loving every second.

When the circle disintegrated into chaos once more, Claire and Libby whooped and ran around the circle high-fiving everyone. Henry couldn't remember the last time he'd felt so exhilarated.

'That was awesome!' said Libby. 'Top job, everyone! Now let's get you into pairs.'

Before any of them could think about who they might or might not want to be paired with, Libby grabbed Henry's arm and put him with Troy, an American who'd been with Conqueror for about six months. Henry raised his eyebrows as if to ask what was going on. Troy shrugged and grinned in return.

'Okay,' said Libby. 'You're going to create a story together. It's one line each so you have to collaborate. The only rule is that you have to start your sentence with the words, "yes, and".'

'On your marks,' Claire began. 'Get—'

'Go!' Libby yelled.

Troy and Henry stared at each other, eyes wide.

Henry leapt. 'Once upon a time there was a magical kingdom.'

'Yes, and there was a little boy called—um, you!'

Henry smiled. 'Yes, and "You" went out one day, er, for a walk.'

Troy grinned. 'Yes, and he met a man with a pig.'

'Yes, and this pig was special because it could fly.'

Troy snorted, which set Henry off. 'Yes, and You bought the pig from the man for five magic beans and set off on an adventure.'

'Yes,' Henry continued. 'And then a dragon appeared beside them in the air and said, "fuck me, a flying pig".'

Troy snorted again. Had he ever heard Troy laugh before? 'Yes, and the pig replied "fuck me, a talking dragon".'

'Okay, great everyone!' Libby interrupted. 'We're going to go again, but this time you have to start every sentence with the words "yes, but". Off you go!'

'Once upon a time there was a magical kingdom,' Henry began.

'Yes, but the magic had run out.'

Henry paused. 'Yes, but they had a special well full of back-up magic.'

'Yes, but, er, it had been a really hot summer so the well had run dry.'

'Yes, but it was a magical kingdom so they went to the magic shop to get some more.'

'Yes, but it was shut.'

'Yes, but they had a key so they went in.'

'Yes, but all the shelves were empty.'

Henry looked at Troy, seeing his own frustration mirrored back at him.

'Okay!' Libby called out, silencing the room. She strolled between the groups. 'So, how did the two exercises compare? How did they make you feel?'

No-one spoke, despite her encouraging expression. Henry

had the overwhelming urge to jump in and save her even though he knew full well she didn't need any help.

'The first one was fun and the second frustrating,' he said.

You'd think he'd invented a cure for cancer by Libby's response.

'Yes!' she exclaimed as she high-fived him. 'Go, Henry! That's exactly right! "Yes, and" builds, opens and affirms the other person, however, "yes, but" negates what they have to say and closes the discussion down.' She threw her arms wide. 'This is "yes, and",' she said and then brought her hands together as if squeezing the air into nothingness. 'And this is "yes, but." What kind of person do you think you are? How do "yes, and" and "yes, but" work in your life?'

Silence.

Henry had the sudden and horrifying thought that he might be one hundred per cent a "yes, but" person.

'Yes,' James began. 'But—'

Carl laughed.

James scowled at him, and turned back to Libby. 'You can't say yes to everything.' He looked at Carl. 'Unless you're Carl's sisters last night.'

'Fuck off,' Carl replied.

'Yes,' Libby replied. '*And*, James is right. Sometimes you need to be a "yes, but" person. If you're a surgeon, there might be moments when you have to shut down an idea. But if you're trying to build something and inspire collaboration and creativity you need to be a "yes, and" person to get things going.'

'This morning,' Claire continued, 'we're practising taking risks and being comfortable when we're vulnerable. Once we remove our filters, we get to be creative and express our authentic selves.'

Henry wasn't entirely sure he knew what his authentic self

was. He'd spent most of life with more filters than a social media app as a direct response to parents who didn't seem to possess any at all.

Libby shifted a table into the middle of the room. On top was a cardboard box decorated with coloured stars and sequins. It had a hole in one side.

'Ta da! Welcome to the box of infinite possibilities!' She lifted it to show everyone there was nothing inside. 'Gather around, marvellous people. Now, you're going to take it in turns to reach inside the shiny box and have a feel around—'

'Said Carl's sister,' interrupted James, prompting laughter.

'Then take something out and tell everyone what it is,' she continued. 'You don't have to be clever—'

'You're safe then, Foxy,' James added.

'Just whatever comes to your mind,' Libby finished with a smile as if James didn't exist. 'Troy!' She took his hand. 'You start us off.'

Troy reached inside the box. He looked unsure as his eyes met those of his colleagues. He pulled out his hand.

'It's the proposal from HR about the new commission scheme. Ha ha.'

'Fantastic!' Libby enthused. 'And now I want you to pull out five things really quickly. Go!'

He reached back in. 'Er, a tuna sandwich, a pen, erm, my desk, er, a holiday... Fuck! Er, my mom!'

'Go, Troy!' Libby yelled, high-fiving him as the room dissolved into hysterics. Troy looked relieved.

'Fuck your mum?' James said. 'Already have, mate.'

'Carl!' said Libby. 'Up you come. Now you have to pull out six things as fast as you can.'

He thrust his hand in the box and pulled it out. 'A pen, my chair, my desk, my jacket, my shoes, my car.'

'Six more!' yelled Libby.

He stared at her, his face paling. 'Um, you.'

Everyone started laughing.

'Go, go, go!' she cried.

'Aghhh! Erm, a cloud, erm, a sheep. Er, shit.'

'Shit will do! Three more!'

'Erm, a toilet, a banana, and er, James.'

Carl's face flushed as he finished to applause and cheers.

'James! Let's have you next,' said Libby.

James shook his head. 'This is bullshit. I've got more important things to do.' He turned on his heel and stalked out, slamming the door behind him.

Libby didn't miss a beat. 'Henry! Let's go! Seven items!'

Fuck! He put his hand inside the box. What could he feel? He looked at Libby and pulled it out. 'Buttercups on a sunny day.'

She clapped. 'Love it! Now go, go go!'

'Um, the river, Fox—Thames, um, disappointment. A blue sheep. A whoopie cushion. A chicken madras, and er, the complete works of Shakespeare.'

Everyone clapped and cheered.

'That's awesome! Love it!' said Libby. 'Gaz, you're next. Eight items. Go!'

The laughter got progressively louder as everyone took their turn. Henry felt lighter than air. Despite his initial panicked urge at the start of the session to leave via the nearest available exit, he was now genuinely enjoying himself. Thanks to two women who added fairy dust and sparkles to everything they touched, he'd gone from suspicious to sold.

'You're all amazing!' said Claire as Libby moved the box and table back against the wall. 'Now it's time for one-minute life stories. Partner up with the person nearest to you.'

Because James had left, the numbers were uneven and Henry was on his own.

Libby came to his side. 'I'll go with you, Henry.'

'Awesome,' said Claire. 'Now, this is a listening exercise. One of you has a minute to tell your entire life story. All the other person has to do is listen. So, choose who is going first.'

'You go first, Henry.' Libby beamed.

He blinked as if he were standing by a waterfall, the sunshine turning the spray into rainbows. A tug in his chest pushed him to leap into the light.

'Three, two one, go!' cried Claire.

He held Libby's gaze and took a deep breath. 'My name is Henry Arthur Fitzwilliam Foxbrooke. I have five siblings, a dad, and, er, two mums. My father is, um, a bit of a hippie? He met Mom, my birth mother—she's American—in Paris when she was acting and modelling.' He drew a quick breath. 'So, er, just after she became pregnant with me, my grandfather and uncle died in a car crash, and my father became the Duke of Somerset. He and Mom got married and came back to live at Foxbrooke Manor. That's the family home. Mom then started an affair with my mammy, er, Dervla, my other mother. She's originally from Ireland. She had a son at the time, Connor. He's, um, the same age as me and my sister. I have a twin, Estelle. Did I say that already? Then Mammy, well, fell in love with my father as well as my mother and, um, moved into the Manor with Connor.' Was he really telling her all of this?

Libby nodded, encouraging him to continue.

He cleared his throat. 'Dad and Mammy had three children together: my brother, Leo, and my sisters, Willow and Summer. So, we've all grown up with a father, um, and a mom and a mammy.' He shook his head. 'I know it's nuts. Anyway, where was I? Oh, yes. My dad ran these wild sex and drugs parties at the Manor. He still does. But back then it all went terribly wrong, as you can imagine, and we were—'

'Time's up!' Claire cried.

Henry blinked. Why had he just shared his family secrets with a stranger?

'Now,' Claire continued. 'The person who listened has a minute to tell the rest of the group their partner's life story. Libby, you go first and tell everyone all about Henry.'

His stomach turned and his mouth ran dry. He stared at Libby in horror.

She took his hand and squeezed, then dropped it and faced the group.

'Hello everyone, I want to introduce you to Henry,' she began. 'He was born the perfect number of years ago. He grew up in Somerset, which is the home of cider, the Glastonbury festival, Morris dancing, Jane Austen, the Roman Baths, Cheddar gorge, Cheddar cheese, England's smallest city, and the Wookey Hole caves. He has never been to the Glastonbury festival, but he does enjoy the odd pint of scrumpy and mature cheddar with his ploughman's on a hot summer day...'

Henry started breathing again, relief and gratitude moving in waves through him.

'... and that brings us to Henry's school life—'

'Time's up!' Claire said. 'Carl, you go next. Tell us all about Gaz.'

'Thank you,' Henry murmured to Libby as Carl started talking. She smiled at him and gave his hand another squeeze.

When they'd gone around the group, it was time for Libby to tell him about her.

'You must have got this bit sussed,' he said.

She grinned. 'There's not a lot you can say in a minute, but I'm good at talking fast.'

'Okay, go!' said Claire.

'Hello Henry, my name is Libby Fletcher and I'm twenty-eight. I was born in Hollywood.' She paused and grinned at his response. 'Hollywood, *Birmingham*. It's about eight miles south of the city centre. Growing up in Hollywood I had two career choices: acting or being a professional chef at an Indian restaurant. My father was *naan* too happy when I did a drama degree at university, however I *curry* favour with him when I pop-*padum* home as I never pass-*anda* up the opportunity to make his favourite dish, which *kormas* him right down.'

Henry snorted with laughter.

'I also *raita* my own jokes,' Libby continued, winking. 'So, where was I? Oh yes. After uni, I started a small theatre group with friends. We were wildly unsuccessful and critically ignored, but had lots of fun taking plays into schools and begging tourists to watch our show at the Edinburgh Fringe. I met my work wife, Claire, at an improv night a few years ago, and it was love at first laugh. We run a regular improvisational comedy show in Covent Garden and during the day, workshops like this one for your company. In my personal life, I have a wonderful—'

'Time's up!' Claire called out. 'Henry, start us off and tell us about Libby in three, two, one, go!'

His mouth opened but nothing came out. *Think!* 'Er, this is Libby and she's the nicest person I've ever met.' He felt heat spreading up his neck again. 'Erm, she really likes curry and went to drama school. I mean she likes cooking curry for her dad, and er, she studied drama at university. Oh, and she went to Edinburgh for the fringe festival. Now she works with Claire running workshops and a comedy night in Covent Garden. Um, oh! And she's originally from Hollywood.' He couldn't think of anything else to say.

'That's fantastic, Henry! Great job! Next up, Gaz, tell us all about Carl.'

. . .

HENRY LEARNT MORE ABOUT HIS COLLEAGUES IN TWO HOURS than he had in all his time at Conqueror to date, and his cheeks were hurting from laughing so much.

'Thank you all so much for taking part in the workshop today,' said Claire. 'Libby and I have a regular improv night every Tuesday above the Spread Eagle pub in Covent Garden.' She handed out business cards. 'Joining in is entirely optional, however having a good time is mandatory.'

Henry looked at the card in his hand.

'Do you think you might come along?' Libby asked him.

A tiny spark of excitement lit up the inside of his chest before he put it out.

'Thank you for the offer. But I don't think it's really me.'

Her smile didn't waver. 'Well, if you ever change your mind, you know where to find us. Lovely to meet you, Henry.'

'You too, Libby.' He smiled back, feeling a small ray of her sunshine still left inside him.

‘Y ou sure you don't want to come back to mine for a bit?’ Claire asked Libby as they exited the Conqueror offices. 'I've got a crib that needs assembling, and I can't be arsed to work it out on my own.'

'Won't Ritchie have a go later?'

Her friend pulled a face. 'He thinks instruction manuals are for people with no imagination. I'm not letting him anywhere near it.'

Libby grinned. 'Fair enough. Can it wait until the weekend? I'm cooking for Lucas tonight.'

Claire looked at her watch and raised her eyebrows. 'Holy shit, Libby. It's one p.m. You'd better get a move on.'

'Ha-de-ha. I need to go shopping first.'

'Ah, yes. I forgot how far you have to travel to buy food in London.'

Libby gave her friend a hard stare. 'His big show is coming up soon and he keeps forgetting to eat. I want to support him.'

'Support is a two-way street, Libby. That man does not deserve you. Or your amazing food.'

'I'll cook for you and Ritchie on the weekend?'

'No, darling. *We'll* cook for *you*.'

Libby hesitated. She wanted to ask if she could bring Lucas with her, but wasn't sure it was the right moment to make that request.

Claire hugged her. 'I'll see you on Saturday. Don't bring anything with you except for yourself.' She stood back and held Libby's gaze as if about to impart life and death information. 'We did great today. Be proud of yourself. You're amazing.'

'*We're* amazing.' She high-fived her friend. 'Go team Awesome Aston-Fletcher.'

'Go team Awesome A.F.,' Claire replied with a grin.

'Hiya, only me,' Libby called out as she staggered into the hallway of the flat she shared with India Markham, a woman she'd met in rep theatre.

India poked her head around the living room door. 'Ooh! Curry?'

Libby nodded. After a twenty-minute walk from the City to Taj Stores on Brick Lane to pick up the best ingredients for Lucas, followed by the three mile walk home, she was knackered, but there was no time to rest.

India helped her carry everything into the pokey kitchen at the back of the flat. Most of the floorspace was taken up by an old wooden table, currently covered with balls of wool.

'I'm preparing for that indie film in Morocco in a few weeks,' India said, pushing them to one end.

India's parents had not only bought their daughter the ground floor flat in an 1920's house, but also gave her an allowance so she could take low-budget film roles that usually only covered expenses.

'With wool?' Libby asked, unpacking the bags.

'Apparently everyone in Hollywood is knitting on set these days. Kirsten Bjorkstrom created a poncho out of qiviut when she was filming the lead role in the *Rambo* reboot. She modelled it for *Vogue* last month.'

'Qiviut?'

'Muskox wool. It's softer than silk and more expensive than saffron.'

'Is that what you've got there?'

India sighed. 'Sold out, so I've got Alpaca instead. Ooh! How was the workshop today? Which of the Pride and Prejudice boys did you have? Please tell me you had at least one Mr Darcy?'

Libby laughed. This was one of their favourite topics of conversation: trying to find real-life versions of their favourite Jane Austen characters.

'It was a City brokerage firm,' she replied. 'So they're all a cross between Darcy and Wickham.'

'No Bingleys?'

Libby's thoughts jumped to Henry. There was something in his initial reserve and aloofness that had reminded her of Darcy, but he had the shy sweetness of Bingley.

'There was one who was fifty-fifty.'

'Mr Bincey? Or Mr Dangley?'

Libby shrieked. 'Oh god, I couldn't call him that—he was far too nice.'

India raised her eyebrows. '*How* nice exactly?'

She turned her back on her housemate and started mixing the dough for the naan bread. 'He was sweet and kind, that's all.'

'Cute?'

She shrugged. 'I guess...'

'Name?'

'Henry.'

'God, this is such hard work. Henry what?'

'Foxbrooke,' she replied, kneading the dough.

There were a few moments of silence.

'Oh. My. God. *Foxy* Foxbrooke?'

Libby whipped around.

India was staring at her phone. 'He's fit as fuck, Libby-Lou! Please tell me you got his number?'

'What? No! Oh, please don't google him! I should never have told you his name. I've broken data protection, his privacy, everything!'

'Don't be daft, it's only me. I won't tell anyone.' India smirked at her. 'Did you touch him? What does he smell like? Sex? Money? Trees?'

Libby couldn't prevent a giggle escaping. 'Trees?'

'All the best men smell like they've used their enormous chopper to fell a forest, rolled around in pine needles, then built a fire hot enough to melt your underwear.'

'India! He was too well put together for any of that. He's a City gent.'

Her friend had a devilish grin on her face. 'Oh, go on, Lib, just imagine Henry Foxbrooke shirtless, with an axe.'

Libby did, and an unexpected wave of heat pulsed through her. She turned back to the bowl, punching the dough and the feelings away. 'Lucas is coming around for tea tonight.'

Silence.

India cleared her throat. 'What time? I've got to go out for a bit anyway, so I'll leave you to it.'

'About six?'

'Cool. I'll be back around seven so I'll see you when he's gone.'

'Oh no, he's staying for the whole evening.'

'Hmm, okay.'

Libby bit her bottom lip. Why weren't her friends more welcoming to Lucas? Why couldn't they see what she did?

India came up behind her and ruffled her hair. 'Save some for me, Libby-Lou, no-one loves your curries more than India.'

BY FOUR O'CLOCK THE MEAL WAS PREPPED AND THE FLAT WAS tidy. By five p.m. Libby was freshly showered in a dress that Lucas had once called 'cutesy'. By five-thirty, scented candles were lit in the kitchen and living room in defiance of the summer sun streaming in from outside.

At five fifty-five the bell rang.

Libby checked her cleaned and flossed teeth in the hall mirror and opened the front door, her heart pitter-pattering.

Lucas Butler was lounging against the wall outside.

Lucas was an artist on the cusp of his big break and had an ethereal beauty about him. His blond hair was bed-head dishevelled, his fingers were eternally paint-stained, and his skin was the perfect pale of a Pre-Raphaelite with consumption.

He looked at her through his long hair, one corner of his mouth turning up. 'Hey, Lib-Lob.'

She grinned back manically.

He held up a four-pack of beer. 'You gonna invite me in?'

'Oh yes, sorry, long day, come in, come in, let me take those from you,' she said, walking backwards.

Libby's job may have involved being creative with words, but since her ex, Giles, had shattered her confidence, she was either tongue-tied or babbled with men she liked. Lucas shared her working-class background and supported her career choices, so was the polar opposite to her ex. However, she didn't have the courage to tell Lucas how she felt, and he seemed unaware that she was dying for the day he would declare himself and make her his muse.

Lucas pushed himself upright and ambled in after her as if filled with so much ennui it was difficult to find the energy to move.

His aquiline nose lifted to sniff the air. 'I hope it's my favourite.'

'Of course it is, and I've made fresh naan bread.'

'That's my girl,' he said with a smile. 'I'm bloody starving.'

'That's because you aren't looking after yourself,' she scolded as they entered the kitchen. 'Sit down and start on the poppadoms and pickles. Let me open a beer for you.'

'What would I do without you, Lib-Lob?'

Her heart thudded in her chest. No one knew better than she how difficult it was to make ends meet if you were a performer or artist, especially in London. Lucas supported her dreams, and she used her savings and overdraft to help him realise his.

To make every penny count, she'd stopped drinking, eating out and using public transport. She was helping Lucas and improving her health and fitness at the same time. Everyone was a winner, and it was no-one's business but theirs that she'd been paying the rent on his studio for the last six months.

'How's the preparation for the show going?' Her voice was fast and breathless.

'Have you got that beer?'

'Oh, yes, sorry.' She popped the cap. 'Do you want a glass?'

'The bottle's good enough for a working-class lad like me. I'm not some posho like your mates.'

She passed it to him. 'Claire's not posh.'

'Fancy flat in St. John's Wood? You can't afford a place like that teaching bankers to play kiddie games.'

Libby ignored the prickle of hurt in her throat. 'They could afford it because Ritchie's mum died.'

Lucas rolled his eyes. 'But his mum still had pots of dosh, didn't she? They're not like us, Lib-Lob. We know what it's like to grow up on the other side of the tracks. We know about hard graft.'

She put the naan bread under the grill. 'How's your painting going? Are you ready for the show?'

He leaned back in his chair and ran his hands through his hair. 'It'll be tight. The gallery owners don't know their arse from their elbow. They know money, but they don't understand the creative process.'

'Can I help at all?'

Lucas shook his head and loaded a piece of poppadom with onion relish and mango chutney.

'You know,' she began, tentatively. 'I haven't seen any of the pieces you're working on. I'd love to visit the studio.'

He held up his hand to stop her whilst he finished his mouthful.

'I can't be disturbed, even by someone as lovely as you, Lib-Lob.'

She nodded. They were both creative people. She understood.

'Do you think you would be free on Tuesday night to come and see our show?' she asked. 'We've been working on new material, and it'll be done by eight. It won't take up your whole evening.'

He raised his eyebrows as if she was mad to have asked such a question, then shook his head.

She turned to the grill to hide her disappointment, accidentally touching a finger to the hot metal tray. 'Aghhh!'

'You okay?'

She pasted on a smile. 'Yes, fine—just burnt myself a bit.'

'Thank fuck.' He puffed out his cheeks. 'If I didn't have you feeding me up, I'd waste away.' He glanced at the clock on the wall. 'Do you need any help? I'm not being much use.'

'No, no, you're fine.' She placed the rice and curry dishes on the table. 'Help yourself. I'll just grab the naan bread.' She put them on the table, then ran her finger under the tap.

Lucas groaned with his first mouthful of food. 'Lib-Lob, you're the best.'

As usual, she'd gone to town with all his favourite dishes. There was chicken tikka masala, mutter paneer, saag bhaji, tarka dahl, tandoori lamb chops and a raita. She wanted to try making different dishes, but once Lucas had found his favourites, he didn't want anything else.

'Talk to me,' he said as he chewed. 'Tell me about your day. I like your voice. It's comforting. Like white noise.'

Libby let the cold water flow over her burn as her mind took the best bits from his sentence and discarded the bits that didn't fit her fantasy. She told him about the workshop in a vague way, how Claire's pregnancy was going, the ideas they had for their improv show, and news of her siblings from home.

'And my parents were asking if they could come to the opening night of your show?'

Lucas continued shovelling food into his mouth. After a few seconds he looked up.

'Sorry, love, what was that last bit again?'

'Can I get tickets for my parents so they can come to the opening night of your show?'

He took his bottle of beer and finished it, then placed it back down, flicking at the edge of the label with his paint-spattered thumbnail.

'Lib-Lob, you know I would get them in if I could, but that decision's not mine to make. I only wangled a ticket for *you* because you're going to help serve the drinks.' He sighed. 'Come here.' She went to his side, and he took her hand, rubbing his thumb in her palm. 'It's out of my hands, Lib-Lob. I'm just one of the proletariat. I don't get to make those decisions.'

'Yet.'

'That's my girl. You've always believed in me. Next stop, the Turner Prize.'

He held her gaze, and she held her breath. Her hand was still in his. Was this it? He looked over her shoulder and jumped to his feet.

Disappointment drenched her. 'Are you leaving already?'

He looked penitent as he nodded. 'I've got to get back to the studio. One of the models is coming in later. It's the only time they can make.'

He pulled her in for a hug and she smelled the combination of white spirit and body odour that had always seemed so perfect for an artist.

'You're the best, Lib-Lob,' he murmured into her hair. 'The show will be done soon.' He released her and picked up the two bottles of beer that had remained unopened. 'No point in leaving these for India. Nobs like her only drink Bolly.' He winked as if they were in some secret Marxist scheme to destroy the establishment, then wandered out towards the front door.

She followed him.

He turned. 'Lib-Lob?'

'Yes, Lucas?' Was this finally the moment when they transitioned from friends to lovers?

'You don't have any of your sourdough left, do you?'

'Er, no, I gave the last of it to you the other day.'

'And you haven't made any more yet?'

'I've been a bit busy.'

'Well, let me know when you do. There's nothing like it in the whole of London.' He lifted her chin with his finger and thumb. 'And nothing like you, either, my Lib-Lob.'

He winked at her and strolled out of the door with a wave.

She shut it behind him and went back to the kitchen. Her plate was still clean and empty. She glanced at the clock just in time to see it strike seven.

❊ 3 ❊

TWO DAYS LATER

Henry's mobile rang. He looked away from his financial calculations and squinted at the screen. *Mom.* He turned the ringer off and put it back on his desk. This deal was complicated and he needed to focus. The desk phone chirped to life. He lifted the receiver and slammed it straight back down.

Five minutes later, a throaty laugh cut through his concentration as it danced towards him from the far end of the office.

He glanced up. *Oh God, no.*

Strolling towards him was his mother. Arm-in-arm with James Hunter-Savage.

'Foxy!' James crowed. 'I can't believe you hung up on your own mum.' He shook his head. 'Especially one as incredible as Vivienne Boucher.'

Vivienne released James's arm. 'Boucher-*Foxbrooke*.'

James gave a little bow. 'And the most stunning duchess our humble shores have ever been graced with.'

She pointed a perfectly manicured finger at him, her eyes alight. 'You are a very naughty boy.'

He winked. '*Man*, my lady—I'm all man.'

Henry grabbed his jacket, phone and wallet, and pushed past James as if he were invisible. Leading his mother out of the office, he ignored the silent faces watching the exchange from their desks. When they reached the bank of lifts in the corridor outside, his breath came out in a rush.

'Mom, what are you doing here? I'm at work.'

She called the lift. 'And it's lunch time, honey.'

He rubbed his forehead. 'Aren't you meant to be in Paris?'

'That was last week.'

The lift doors opened and he followed his mother inside.

'Simone and Laurent say hi,' she continued. 'Apparently your cousins can't wait for your thirtieth. Camille and Olivier haven't visited since they were teenagers. Can you believe it?'

Henry's stomach knotted. The party had been in the planning for years, but he would do anything to get out of it.

'Are you sure you don't want more input?' his mother asked. 'Anything *you* want to do?'

He shook his head. The only thing he wanted was for his birthday to pass without incident. It was impossible, however, to get out of the triple celebration: Estelle's and his thirtieth, and their grandmother, the Dowager Duchess of Somerset, turning eighty.

'I'm sure that between you, Mammy, Estelle and Gram-Gram, you've got it covered.'

They reached the ground floor, and the elevator opened into the spacious lobby.

'Of course we do, honey, but it's like you don't want to be there.'

Henry gave his mother a look as they started towards the front of the building. 'You know I don't want to be there.'

She gifted him one of her thousand kilowatt smiles in return. 'You never know, you might enjoy yourself?'

He rolled his eyes and held the door open for her.

Outside, the streets were filled with City suits, barking at each other or into a phone. Everyone gave them second glances. Henry tried to fit in, and most of the time, succeeded. However, his mother had made a career of standing out from the crowd and revelled in the attention.

Today her hair was styled in neat braids. Her cheekbones shimmered with a dusting of gold, and her lips were painted a deep, sensuous red. She was wearing a pure-white cashmere coat over a designer sheath dress, and her heels took her almost to Henry's height. Vivienne Camille Boucher-Foxbrooke was even more beautiful in her early fifties than she'd been in her late teens when she'd started modelling in Paris. And she knew it.

He steered her into the nearest restaurant but lost the battle when it came to where they were seated. Both the Maître d' and Vivienne knew that the best place for a beautiful and titled celebrity, and her handsome and titled son, was by the window for all the world to admire.

'Avez-vous une bouteille de Perrier-Jouët?' His mother asked, sparking an animated conversation in French with the Maître d' who was now falling over himself to get Vivienne anything she wanted.

'Mom, I can't drink, I'm working.'

She waved her hand dismissively. 'You need to live a little.'

He bunched his hands into fists under the table, then forced them to relax. *Just one lunch*. He could work late again that evening. After they'd ordered, she lifted her glass to chink it with his, a mischievous glint in her eye.

'So...' she began. 'Tell me all about your girlfriend.'

He tensed. 'It's early days.'

'And?'

He shrugged.

'What's her name? How did you meet?'

Fuck, fuck, fuck! He was totally unprepared for this ambush. He had a second date lined up for next week with a lawyer. She would have to do.

'Elizabeth,' he replied. 'But that's all you're going to get.'

'Aw, c'mon.'

He shook his head.

'One more thing, please, honey? Where's she from?'

Libby's bright face popped into his mind. 'Hollywood,' he said without thinking.

'Oh, really? Now that sounds like something you don't just make up on the fly. I can't wait to tell your father.'

'What?'

'That you didn't invent her. We're all convinced she doesn't exist.'

'Excuse me?' he spluttered.

'Are you bringing her to the party?'

'No, absolutely not.'

'Then she's not your girlfriend.'

'How does that make any sense?'

'It's your thirtieth. If she's going to be the most important person in your life, then she should be there by your side.'

'Mom, I told you, it's early days. I don't want to scare her off.'

'Honey, we can behave.'

Henry fixed her with a look, and she held up her little finger.

'Pinkie promise?'

He shook his head. 'Can we change the subject?'

She pouted. 'Okay.' She took a sip of champagne and eyed

him over the top of her glass. 'Simone spoke to me last week about her fall collection.'

Simone was Vivienne's older sister and had left America to study fashion in Paris in her early twenties. Now a successful designer, she was married to a Frenchman who was also her business partner.

'Hmm?' He was dreading where this innocuous sentence might lead.

'She wants the two of us to front the campaign. Estelle too, but, well...'

'Mom!'

'What?'

Growing up, their mother had wanted him and Estelle to model and act, as she'd done. Neither of them wanted to. Taking himself off to boarding school at thirteen had insulated Henry to a degree from his mother's ambitions, but Estelle had borne the brunt of them, especially when it came to her size.

'Estelle is a perfectly healthy weight. You promised you would drop this.'

'I won't say anything. It just pains me when you're both so beautiful. It's a waste.'

'Neither of us wants to be on the cover of a magazine or in the cinema. You know this.'

His mother leaned forward, her voice lowering. 'But the money? The freedom? The excitement? I don't know what you see in all this—' She waved at the sea of black and grey around them. 'Monotony. It's all so pedestrian.'

Henry sighed. 'Without the financial sector, society as we know it wouldn't exist. Simone wouldn't have her fashion house, you wouldn't have your career, and we wouldn't be sitting here now. I happen to like structure, routine, and order, and I'd rather work fourteen-hour days at Conqueror than ponce about getting paid on the basis of what I was born looking like.'

He paused, realising in horror what he'd just said about his mother's career choices.

Thankfully, she laughed. 'Oh, Henry, honey. Poncing about isn't as easy as it looks.'

'I'm sorry, Mom. That came out the wrong way.'

'No offence taken. We just want you to step out of your box a little. Take some risks. Live life to the full whilst you're still young.'

'I do—'

'I bet you won't try anything new between now and your birthday.'

'I will. I'll... I'll take up golf.'

'Puh-lease. Golf, schmolf. Something interesting. Something out of your comfort zone. Your father's right. The vicar's pigs are gonna fly before you take any risks with your life.'

EARLY THE NEXT MORNING, HENRY WAS BACK AT HIS DESK. He stared at the photo on his phone of Elizabeth Lockwood, his date for next week, as he mulled over his mother's words. Weren't romantic entanglements a risk? He wanted a girlfriend in his life but in the same nebulous way one might think forward to a future containing a house in the country or a visit to Machu Picchu.

His dating history hadn't been an abject disaster, but it wasn't something to write home about either. His parents' open attitude to sex had closed him off more. And spending his formative years at a boys' boarding school had limited the opportunity to get to know girls his own age that he wasn't related to. At university, when he did start dating, he was stilted and awkward. His confidence had grown over the years, but none of his relationships had ever felt right. They lacked the ease he saw between his father and his mothers.

Things would be different with Elizabeth. She ticked every box: a year older than him so their ages roughly matched, focused on her career as a lawyer, so she understood the hours he worked, pleasing appearance with a tidy blonde bob and smart dark suits. And, most importantly, her parents were landed gentry, so she was unfazed by Henry's title. After meeting via a dating app for City professionals, they'd had one lunch date, though it was more like a job interview than a romantic encounter. But that had suited him just fine. He knew where he stood and everything was under control.

He glanced at the time, then around the empty office. It was six forty-five a.m., but Elizabeth would be at work. She was handling the legal paperwork for the merger of two companies and her team was working around the clock as the deadline approached. She'd been told to clear her diary and be in the office all weekend, so he'd arranged to meet her for their second date on Tuesday evening, once the final documents had been submitted. He could have texted the details, but a phone call was more personal.

She picked up after two rings. 'Hello, Henry.'

'Good morning, Elizabeth. How are you?'

'Fine, we're on the home straight now. We'll probably have to pull an all-nighter on Monday, but we'll get it done.'

'Are you sure you still want to meet on Tuesday? We could always re-arrange?'

'No, it'll give me something to look forward to. We should be finished by the afternoon, but if anything last-minute comes up, our final deadline is eight when Wall Street closes. I can grab a taxi and be with you around eight-thirty, depending on where we're meeting.'

He smiled. After weeks of effort, he'd finally got into

Imperium, London's most exclusive new restaurant. Everyone at Conqueror was trying to gain access for their clients and he'd got there first.

'I've booked us a table at Imperium.'

He heard her gasp.

'No way! Only the partners here have been, and they said it's fantastic.'

'It's in Soho, so if the tube strike goes ahead and there aren't any taxis, it's only a short walk from your office.'

'That's great. I can't believe you got us in.'

'Yep, Imperium.' He grinned. 'I'll see you there next week.'

'Looking forward to it, Henry. Got to go now.'

'Good luck with the—'

But she'd hung up.

'Imperium? How the fuck did you get in there?'

The scowling face of James Hunter-Savage loomed over him.

'By being good at my job?'

'Or by using family connections?'

Henry bristled. That was something he'd never do. He wanted to distance himself from his family, not use them to his advantage.

'No.' He turned back to his computer.

'When are you going?'

'A week on Friday,' he lied.

'Hmm. I bet I can get in before then.'

Henry didn't respond. Something landed on his desk as James walked away. A bent paperclip lay askew in front of him as if its limbs were broken. Right now, he wanted to do the same to James.

❧ 4 ❧

Henry swivelled in his chair, turning his back on the computer screens, his foot tapping on the floor. He couldn't concentrate. His date with Elizabeth was in a few hours and his insides were itchy and irritable. The one-day tube strike had gone ahead, so he'd walked three miles from his flat in Canary Wharf to the Conqueror building in the City, then changed and rowed for an hour in the office gym until the pain of exercise blotted out everything else in his brain.

But the unease had returned. He kept looking at pictures of Elizabeth, reminding himself of all the reasons they were perfect for each other. However, instead of feeling excited about their date, he felt dread.

He shoved his hands into his trouser pockets and touched the edge of a business card, pressing one of the corners into the pad of his thumb. The sharpness was a welcome distraction. Still another four hours until his date. Could he go back to the gym?

Pulling out the card, he stared at the names. Claire and

Libby. His mouth turned up and his foot stopped tapping. The workshop had been the most bizarre and uplifting two hours of his life. And that was saying something with parents like his.

He flipped the card over, reading the details for their improv night in Covent Garden. Tonight. A half-hour walk from the Conqueror office. It finished at eight. Imperium was ten minutes further. He could watch their show and get to the restaurant for his date with twenty minutes to spare.

The dread in his stomach swirled into excitement. He'd told his mother he would do something new, and this was it. He was going to attend an improvisational comedy show.

At six fifteen, Henry stood outside the Spread Eagle pub. Second thoughts fought with first ones for control over his feet. Libby and Claire's workshop had been exhilarating, but had been in a familiar environment with familiar people. This was a roomful of strangers. Would they expect him to join in? Second thoughts dealt his idea a killer blow. This was a mistake. He would go early to the restaurant and wait for Elizabeth there.

'Henry?'

He turned and there was Libby.

'You came!'

'Er, um, not exactly. I've got a date later and I'm a bit early, so, er, I...'

'What time is your date?'

'Eight thirty.'

She squealed and clapped her hands together. 'We finish at eight, so there's plenty of time.'

Taking his hand, she pulled him into the pub. Her auburn hair sparked off her red dress, her movements filled with energy and vitality, lighting the dark interior like a beacon of fire. He was a moth, dragged against his will and better judgement towards her.

'Come on,' she said. 'We're upstairs. You can help me set up.'

He followed her up a narrow flight of stairs to a room with a tiny stage at one end. She started moving small round tables into place.

'Claire drove because of today's tube strike; she's trying to find a parking space. It's a bit too far for her to walk from St. John's Wood with her bump.'

Henry helped place chairs around the tables. 'How far did you come?'

'Islington. It's only three miles and I walk fast.'

'How are you getting home?'

'Claire's giving me a lift, but I'm fine to walk. I'm used to it.'

Within a few minutes the space was ready.

'Thank you, Henry. You've made my life so much easier.'

He rubbed the back of his neck. All he'd done was move a bit of furniture.

'So, what made you change your mind about coming?' she asked.

He paused. 'My mom... she seems to think I don't step out of my comfort zone and couldn't believe that I would try something new before my birthday. So...' He shrugged.

'Are you going to take part tonight?'

He held his hands up and took a step back, colliding with a chair. 'I'm just here to watch.'

She tilted her head to one side. 'That's not exactly stepping out of your comfort zone?'

'I'm moving slowly towards the edge.'

'One day, Henry, we'll get you to leap.'

He blinked at the brightness of her smile. What would it

feel like to be as brave as she was? To leap without knowing where you would land?

'Henry?' Claire was puffing up the stairs carrying a guitar case.

He rushed forward to take it from her and offer his arm.

'Thank, you,' she said, smiling at him. 'I'm so happy you've come to our show.'

'How are you doing?' Libby asked, concern etched on her forehead. 'Did you find somewhere to park okay?'

Claire fanned herself. 'Yes, thank god—the car's so small, I found a space around the corner. I've felt like shit all day.'

As the room filled up, Henry migrated farther and farther back from the front until he melted into the shadows. He wasn't the only one in a suit, but still felt awkward and out of place.

At seven, Claire stepped onto the tiny stage with Libby by her side.

'Good evening, everyone!' she cried. 'My name is Claire Aston.'

'And I'm Libby Fletcher.'

'And every Tuesday night we run our self-help group, "Improv yourself with Claire and Libby".'

Henry clapped with the rest of the audience, a grin spreading across his face.

'We'd like to start with a story and a song,' Claire continued. 'About a poor creature on the brink of annihilation.'

She strummed a minor chord on her guitar, and Libby moved to the side of the stage.

'Once upon a time,' Claire spoke, 'a beautiful woodland creature roamed the land.'

Libby stepped centre stage, her nose twitching, her hands resembling paws in front of her chest.

'It was sweet, it was gentle, and its colour was red.'

Libby pointed at her dress and her hair and winked at the audience.

'They lived in harmony with nature,' Claire continued. 'Until—' She strummed the guitar forcefully. 'The greys arrived.'

Libby ran around the stage, her expressions cycling through various states of terror. Henry's eyes hadn't left her face, and his smile hadn't left his.

Claire picked out the opening notes from *The Twilight Zone*. 'Nothing would ever be the same again.'

Libby went to her side. 'And who were these invaders?' she asked.

Claire launched into hoedown music, and the two of them sang an upbeat country song, bending their knees and bobbing up and down in opposition to each other.

'They're grey, they're vicious, they're rats with fluffy tails.

They steal your seeds, chew on your wires, they're hard as fucking nails.

They eat tiny baby birds, right out of their nest.

They're mindless psycho killers, yes, grey squirrels are a pest.'

The crowd roared and Henry laughed out loud.

'So, we at the Red Action Trust for Squirrels, also known as "RATS",' Claire continued, 'have put together a white paper, detailing our proposal for halting the grey menace and reinstating the red one.'

Libby pretended to put on a pair of glasses and look at a sheaf of papers in her hand.

'Suggestion one,' she said. 'We round them up and ship

them off to Australia as this policy has worked so well in the past with pigs, cats, dogs, rats, foxes, rabbits, and cane toads.'

'Don't forget the fecking camels,' an Australian voice rang out from the audience.

'Ah yes.' Libby pretended to add the word to the list. 'Thank you, Mr... Bruce?'

'Yeah, that's me,' he replied. 'Bruce Bruce. The third.'

Henry put his hand over his mouth as he snorted.

'Suggestion two,' Libby continued. 'We undertake an extensive marketing campaign around sustainable, locally sourced, high protein meat, and champion the use of "Squicken" in our diet.'

Claire leaned towards the audience and played an upbeat jingle on her guitar. 'Squicken! Like chicken, but grows on trees!'

'Because, at the end of the day...' Libby looked bereft. 'Without the work of RATS, our beautiful red squirrels will be no more. And we cannot allow this to happen, because...'

Claire started the hoedown music again and they sang together.

'They're red, they're chirpy, they're endangered little mites.

They're on the run, they're dying out and don't know how to fight.

With no-one to save them, you need to join our quest.

They're cute, they're fluffy, yes, red squirrels are the best!'

'Everybody now!' Libby held up the words for the last chorus on a big sheet of paper. The audience sang with them.

'Now on your feet!' yelled Claire.

Everyone stood, singing and stamping as they sang one more time. At the end, Claire and Libby bowed and the audience went wild, cheering and clapping. Henry put his fingers in his mouth and whistled loudly. Libby caught his eye and grinned.

Claire strummed another chord. 'Now then, ladies, gentlemen and Australians, let's have some audience participation!'

Henry shrank back against the wall.

'Claire and I are keen to sell our jingle and tagline writing services to the highest bidder,' said Libby. 'But we need a bit of practice. So how about you give us some suggestions and we'll give you a jingle or a tagline to match.'

People started shouting ideas.

'What was that?' asked Libby. 'A vacuum cleaner? Hmm.' She looked at Claire. 'I feel a jingle coming on.'

Claire picked out a tune, and Libby threw back her head as if she was a singer from the sixties hoping to send her voice into the seventies.

'It sucks so good, it sucks so hard, it sucks all through the night. Yeah, yeah, get the carpet muncher. It's the mother-sucking best!'

'Funeral directors!' A voice yelled over the laughter and applause.

Libby put her hands in a prayer position and bowed.

'We deal with your skinsuit,' Claire said, solemnly.

Henry snorted as someone else yelled, 'A zoo!'

Libby looked up. 'Learn about the natural world through your senses. Come and smell two hundred different kinds of poo.'

Claire put her guitar to one side. 'How about "world's worst"?'

The crowd whooped and Bruce Bruce called out, 'Santa!'

Libby's body became loose and sloppy, and she staggered around the stage as if drunk. Claire stared hopefully at her, hands clasped in excitement.

Libby stumbled closer, pointing her finger. 'It's always about you, isn't it. What about me? Where are my presents, eh?' She pretended to rummage in a pocket and presented something to Claire. 'Here's a five-pound gift card. I'm only here for the booze and mince pies.'

People laughed and clapped, and someone else yelled, 'World's worst reality show!'

'And now,' Libby began. 'Welcome to "Om Island", where we're going to follow a group of sexy young monks as they meditate, fully clothed, in silence for ten days.'

'Household product!'

Claire wiggled her eyebrows. 'Mopeoke. Fifty per cent mop, fifty per cent karaoke machine, and one hundred per cent destined for landfill.'

'World's worst best man!'

Libby continued her drunk act, but this time she seemed to embody Henry's work colleagues at the end of a big night out.

'Hi, er, yes, sorry about, er, being a bit late for the wedding, and losing the ring.' She burped loudly. 'Oh, and the accident in the font. Oopsies. But, um... yeah... congrats, mate, for marrying Lara. Me and the other groomsmen all agree she's a top shag.'

As everyone laughed, Claire turned her back to the stage.

'Plastic surgeon!'

'So, sir,' Libby began. 'Do you want to use polycarbonate, polystyrene or polyethylene for your procedure today? They're all BPA free!'

Claire was now leaning her hands on the back of a chair.

'Midwife!' yelled Bruce Bruce.

Libby scrunched up her eyes as if she were having trouble seeing and went to Claire's side. 'Hello deary... remind me which hole baby's coming out of today?'

Claire screamed.

Libby put her hand to her ear and frowned. 'What did you say? I didn't quite catch it.'

Claire cried out again, and water ran down her legs onto the stage.

'Oh my god!' Libby yelled.

Henry pushed his way to the front and helped Claire to a seat, kneeling by her side.

'I'm fine, I'm fine,' she panted. 'Just get everyone out.'

He leapt up. 'Okay everyone, slight change of plan. If you all could please go back downstairs.' He took as much cash as he had in his wallet and handed it to the Australian. 'Mr Bruce Bruce is going to buy most of you a drink and explain why he thinks Australian lager is superior to British.'

The Aussie nodded and led everyone away.

Henry returned to Claire's side. 'What can I do?'

She was leaning on Libby's shoulders, breathing heavily.

'Call an ambulance,' Libby said.

'Ritchie,' Claire moaned, 'I need Ritchie.'

'I'll call him,' said Libby. 'But with the strike on today, the buses are going to take forever and it'll take him too long to walk.'

'Claire,' Henry said. 'Let me take your car, and I'll go and get him. Okay?'

She nodded. 'Keys. In my bag.'

He grabbed it and took them out. 'Libby, I'm going to give you my number. Text me the address and Ritchie's number. When I've left, ring him and tell him I'm on my way.' He put his hand on Claire's shoulder. 'What car do you drive and where did you park it?'

Claire muttered the details.

He gave her shoulder a gentle squeeze. 'I'll bring him back as soon as possible.'

Outside, it was still light and he sprinted around the corner of the pub to Claire's car, his heart racing inside his chest. *Fuck!* He had to hold it together. A series of texts came through from Libby. He plugged the destination into his maps app, pushed the seat back to accommodate his larger frame, and set off.

He didn't care about the speed limit or cameras. With no points on his licence, he could afford to take risks. Within half an hour he screeched to the side of the road and let a harried man, three bags, a baby's car seat and a Moses basket into the car.

'Hi, I'm Ritchie,' the man said as Henry pulled away.

'Henry.'

'She's not due for another month.'

Henry cleared his throat. 'I'm sure she'll be okay.'

Ritchie made a call. 'Claire bear? I'm on my way. Hang in there, love. Can you pass me to Libby?'

Henry weaved in and out of traffic.

Ritchie rubbed his forehead. 'Libby, have you called an ambulance...? Seriously...? Fuck!' He looked at Henry. 'They can't get one to her for at least an hour.'

'I can drive you to St. Bart's. It's only about a mile from Covent Garden.'

'Lib, did you hear that?' Ritchie asked. 'I'll ring you when we're five minutes away and you can get her outside.' He got off the call and hung his head.

Henry put his foot down.

HENRY PULLED UP OUTSIDE THE PUB, AND RITCHIE LEAPT out to help Claire into the back. Libby sat in the front with their bags and Claire's guitar.

'When we get there,' said Henry over his shoulder, 'you both just go. I'll find somewhere to park the car and give the keys to Libby so she can bring them in for you.'

Ritchie nodded. 'Thanks, mate.'

Claire was now on all fours in the back, moaning and swaying as her husband tried to soothe her. The traffic was heavy and Henry gripped the wheel tighter. After what seemed like forever, he pulled up outside the hospital and Ritchie and Claire got out.

'Go!' yelled Libby. 'I'll bring the Moses basket and the rest of the bags.'

A porter noticed Claire and rushed forward with a wheelchair. As the main doors shut behind them, Henry let out a held breath at the same time as Libby. They looked at each other and laughed with relief.

'That's not normally how one of our shows goes down,' she said.

'Baptism by fire?'

'Something like that.' She blew out her cheeks. 'Fucking hell. I hope she's going to be okay. The baby isn't due for another month.' She gulped in a breath and held it, covering her face with her hands, her shoulders shaking.

He touched her shoulder. 'I know it doesn't help right now, but she's in the right place. As soon as I park, you can go and be with her.'

She nodded and wiped her eyes. 'You're right. I'll find a place on my phone.'

Fifteen minutes later, the car was parked and they were back at the hospital entrance.

'You've got my number now,' said Henry. 'Will you let me know how it goes?'

Libby nodded. 'Yes, of course.' She took his hand, her eyes still damp. 'Thank you, Henry. You've been incredible. I owe you a life debt for this one.'

He shook his head. 'Nonsense—'

'Yes, I do. If there is ever anything you need in the future that I can help with, anything at all. Promise you'll ask?'

He smiled. 'There won't—'

'Promise?

'Okay, Libby.'

She squeezed his hand. 'Thank you.'

He released it and took a couple of steps back.

She hesitated, as if she wanted to say more.

'Go!'

She ran up the stairs, pausing at the doors to give him a wave, her red dress lit up like a flame from the lights behind her.

He held up his hand, only dropping it when she disappeared from view.

Well, that was a night. Henry turned to face the traffic and the realisation landed on him with a sickening thud. He looked at his watch. Nine fifteen. He was nearly an hour late for his date with Elizabeth.

'Fuck!' He called her but it went to voicemail. He left a message and sent a text, then ran back up the main road towards Soho.

Twenty minutes later, sweating and out of breath, Henry entered the restaurant. It was packed. Looking around, he recognised the back of Elizabeth's blonde head as she stood by the bar. His shoulders relaxed. She was still here. He ran his hands over his face, straightened the jacket of his suit and weaved through the crowd towards her. She turned slightly to the side. She was laughing, a cocktail glass in her hand. She'd found someone to talk to. This was good.

'Elizabeth?'

She turned to him and her smile disappeared.

'I'm so sorry I'm late.'

'Late?' a voice cut in. 'It's been over an hour.'

James was standing next to Elizabeth, a look of disdain on his face.

'What the fuck are you doing here?' Henry snapped.

'Fuck you, Foxbrooke.'

'No, fuck you—'

'Hey!' said Elizabeth. 'James has been keeping me company. I would have left ages ago had he not been so chivalrous.'

'Chivalrous? *Him?*' Henry spat.

'Yes. And where on earth have you been? You didn't call or text.'

'I did, as soon as I finished helping get a pregnant woman to hospital.'

James snorted. 'And I'm Father Christmas.'

'Really?' asked Elizabeth, disbelief evident in her tone.

'Yes, I was at a comedy show, and one of the performers went into labour. I went to get her husband, then took them to St. Bart's.'

Elizabeth sighed. 'That sounds ridiculous.'

Henry addressed James. 'It was Claire, the woman from the training session at work the other week. You remember? She was heavily pregnant? It was her I took to the hospital.'

Elizabeth looked at James, her eyebrows raised in question.

James shrugged. 'Don't know what you're talking about, mate.'

The only thing stopping Henry from launching himself at James was the fact that Elizabeth was in the way.

'You fucking arsehole,' he spat at James before turning to Elizabeth. 'Look. Libby, Claire's friend, is going to text me to let me know what happens. I can send you the messages when I get them. I'm not lying.'

Elizabeth shook her head. 'I think you need to come up with better stories in the future. That, or phone a woman if you're going to be late.' She glanced at James. 'Did you manage to get us a table?'

James smirked. 'Yes, one just became free.' He put his arm around Elizabeth and led her away, the hand on her back flipping Henry the bird.

❧ 5 ❧

Henry couldn't sleep. The events of the previous evening circled in his head on endless repeat. He kept checking his phone for messages from Libby, but there was only one, sent just after they'd parted.

> Libby: Don't forget, I owe you one. Claire has a delivery room and is being looked after. I'll message you as soon as I have news! I realised when I got in that you were late for your date. So sorry! Hope it went well! Big hand hugs, Libby x

Was a hand-hug when she squeezed his? She was good at them. She was good at everything. Henry pictured her on the tiny stage. Libby possessed the confidence and self-assurance he'd never managed to achieve authentically. She reminded him of his youngest sister, Summer, only way more mature. Twenty-one and at the end of her third freshman year at university, Summer was still trying to find a subject she liked and Henry was praying she would stick with this one. He'd been bankrolling her education for the last eight years and it was breaking him.

He turned over in bed, his sheets a tangled mess. Summer had been messaging him more than normal. It usually meant she was building up to ask him for more money. As soon as the deal he was working on was signed, he'd get a bonus big enough to pay for whatever she wanted and keep his head above water for the next few months. He was too proud to ask his parents for help. The subject would only open massive wounds that had been gouged nearly twenty years ago.

Around five a.m., when he was contemplating getting out of bed and walking to work, tiredness took him. He awoke at nine-thirty to the sound of his phone and answered it, confused and still half asleep.

'Hello?'

'Viscount Nobbury?'

He pinched the bridge of his nose. 'Unfortunately, yes.'

A melodious laugh sounded on the other end. 'Good morning, my Lord. My name is Catriona, and I am the owner of Bullington's.'

Huh? Some kind of club?

'Your Grandmother, the Dowager Duchess, has bought you a membership for a year or until we have fulfilled our end of the contract.'

'What?' He got out of bed. He was already three hours late for work and had no inclination to join a club and hang out with the kind of men he'd been at school with.

'I assure you, my Lord, discretion is our by-word, and every client has been fully vetted.'

He rubbed his hand over his hair. 'Ms Bullington—'

'Catriona, *please*.'

He bit back a sigh. '*Catriona*, you must excuse me, but I have no idea what your club is, and I'm really not interested.'

'Bullington's is not a club, my Lord. It's a matchmaking agency for the top tier of society.'

The sigh rushed out. 'I don't need that.'

'In my experience, that is what most of our clients say.'

'I have a girlfriend,' he said through his clenched jaw, remembering the look on Elizabeth's face as she walked away with James.

Catriona clearly didn't believe him. 'I'm going to email over some more details for you to peruse at your leisure, and we can chat again in a few days.'

'Look—'

'Have a wonderful day, Viscount Nobbury,' she replied, ending the call.

'Fuck!'

Henry threw on his clothes, infuriated with his meddling family and ready to murder James. His head was splitting, but there was no time for coffee.

Striding past Limehouse, the Thames on his left, he breathed in deeply, hoping the air coming off the water would clear his head. It stank. He thought of his grandmother, the scent of sweet peas in her house. He rang her.

'The Dower House.' Marie, his grandmother's live-in nurse and companion, answered.

'Marie, it's Henry. Is Gram-Gram awake?'

'Good morning, Henry. Yes, she is, I'll put you through.'

There was a pause, then his grandmother spoke. 'Henry, my darling boy. I take it Catriona has been in touch?'

'How—'

Her laugh was deep and throaty. 'My dear child, why else would you be ringing on a Wednesday? Our calls are always on a Sunday afternoon.'

'Gram-Gram, I don't need help finding a girlfriend.'

She sniffed. 'Well, that's patently untrue. You're nearly thirty and still single. Your father was married with a brood of children by that age, as was I with your grandfather.'

'Things are different now.'

'Really? Has the human race modernised so dramatically that procreation is no longer necessary?'

'I haven't really thought about kids.'

'Clearly,' she replied, her tone acidic enough to burn through lead. 'However, it needs to be at the forefront of your mind. If you don't produce issue, your cousin Rupert will inherit your father's title, and you know what I think of that prospect.'

The Dowager Duchess had her favourites amongst the grandchildren, and Rupert was not one of them.

'Gram-Gram. You can't say that.'

She sniffed again. 'Why not? I'm nearly eighty. I can say what I like.'

He couldn't stop the corners of his mouth twitching upward. 'That's true.'

'Darling, let Catriona do her job. You need to find a partner in life.'

'Why does no-one believe I have a girlfriend?'

'Ah yes, *Elizabeth*. Did you use my name in a panic because no others came to mind? If she does exist, then you must produce her.'

'I will.'

'When? Once Eveline's pigs start flying over the church?'

'I'll bring her when I next visit,' he replied, knowing that it would be months away, most likely Christmas.

'Splendid. For the entirety?'

Entirety of what? 'Er.' He could hear distant cries coming from a piece of information he'd left at the back of his mind.

'Marvellous. We'll be seeing you and Elizabeth for the dura-tion of our birthday celebrations in nine days' time.'

Oh god. Oh god, oh god, oh god.

'See you then, my darling boy, and give my fondest regards to Elizabeth,' his grandmother said before cutting the call.

He stared at his phone. What the fuck was he going to do now? Could he ring Elizabeth and beg her to come with him? He dismissed the idea immediately. Could Catriona find him someone at short notice? *No.* His grandmother would find out. His phone pinged with a message.

> Libby: It's a girl! She was born about an hour ago in one of the pools so she's officially half mermaid. If she'd been a boy, I think they would have called her Henry, but she's called Harper, which is close enough. Claire's knackered but doing well, and Harper is so adorable I think I'm melting. Ritchie can't stop crying, which is super cute, but I think it's due to severe sleep deprivation on top of becoming a daddy. Anyway, thank you again! Photo coming up now xxx

A baby with a scrunched-up face and pink bobble hat appeared on the screen. Another picture followed of Libby holding Harper, her eyes shining.

Henry smiled back. This was the best news. Amongst all the stress of his family, his work, Elizabeth, here was some-thing pure and beautiful and perfect.

He thought of the previous night, how Claire went from singing a song about squirrels one moment, to becoming a mum the next. The thought stopped him in his tracks. Would Libby carry on their business without her? Could she do it on her own? Presumably they had a plan, but it had just been brought forward a month. Did this mean they would have to cancel work? Was Libby out of a job?

Before he could second guess himself, he called her.

'Henry! Did you get the photos?'

'Yes, she's beautiful. You must give my very best to Claire and Ritchie.'

Libby yawned. 'I will. And thank you again for last night.'

'It was nothing.'

'Ooh! Did your date work out okay?'

'Not really, but it's probably for the best.'

'Oh no! I'm so sorry.'

'It's okay. Honestly.'

'Oh. If you're sure?'

There was silence. How could he segue into the question that now seemed so ridiculous he couldn't believe he'd even thought of it?

'You still there?' she asked.

'Um, yes. Yes, I'm still here.'

More silence. He stared across the brown water of the Thames as gulls swooped and dipped.

'Are you alright?'

He cleared his throat. 'Forgive my intrusion, but what are you going to do for work now that Claire has given birth to Harper early?'

Now it was her turn to be silent.

'Are you there? Libby?'

'Yes, sorry. It's just been such a crazy few hours that reality hasn't sunk in. I'm not sure, to be honest. I think I need to sleep, then come up with a plan.'

Come on! Ask her!

'Why?' she asked.

He rubbed his hand over his face. 'Um, there's a job I need

an actress for, but I don't really know any apart from the two of you. And you're really talented. So, er, I wondered if you were free around the eighteenth for four days.'

'Of June?'

'Yes.'

'*You* need an actress?'

He pulled at the collar of his shirt. He was sweating despite the breeze coming off the river.

'Go on then, Henry. What's the job?'

'I'd pay you. Um, five grand. And I'll cover all your expenses.' *Fuck!* He was going to have to get another credit card.

'Oh my god! Are you serious?'

'Yes.'

'Bloody hell. What on earth is the job? And where is it?'

'It's in Somerset, just south of Bath.'

'Ooh! Jane Austen land. I've always wanted to visit Bath.'

He didn't know how to reply.

'Go on then,' she continued. 'What is it? What do you need an actress for?'

Oh god.

'Henry?'

He took a big breath. 'I need you to pretend to be my girlfriend at my thirtieth birthday celebrations.'

Silence.

'It's not what you think, I promise,' he said quickly. 'We'd have separate bedrooms, no physical contact, and I'll draw up a contract to protect you—'

'Protect me? From what?'

'Er, me?'

'Are you going to leap on me when I'm unawares?'

'God, no.'

'Are you dangerous? Unhinged?'

'I'm not dangerous, however I'm now thinking I might be a bit unhinged. Sorry.'

Libby laughed. And laughed. And laughed. 'I think I'm a little delirious from lack of sleep,' she finally said. 'So, tell me, Henry. Why do you need a fake girlfriend?'

Ah. He cleared his throat. 'My family have, er, been rather forceful in their, erm, *encouragement* of me to have a girlfriend.'

'Forceful? What did they do? Lock you in a room full of women until you'd chosen one?'

'Erm...'

'Oh my god, Henry! They didn't, did they?'

'It was my father. But, in fairness, the rooms weren't locked.'

'Rooms?'

'He'd also provided one filled with men.' Henry squeezed his eyes shut and pinched the bridge of his nose. He hadn't told anyone else what had happened that night.

'Oh, Henry.' Libby's voice was so full of empathy and understanding, it pierced his heart. He needed to get off the phone.

'Look, I know it's a lot to take in. I want you to go away and think about it, and I'm sure you have a boyfriend, so I want you to talk it over with him as well. It's also imperative I meet him to explain everything and reassure him that this is completely above board. I'll draw up a contract, and you can both check it over. We can all meet for a coffee in the next couple of days?' He didn't wait for her to respond. 'I've got to go into a meeting now, but we can speak soon. Okay? Thanks. Erm, bye.'

He ended the call and stared at the phone as if it was the cause of his discomfort, not the words that had just come from his mouth. He quickly typed out a text.

Henry: You don't have to do this. Sorry for putting you on the spot like that.

A reply came through almost immediately.

Libby: It's okay. I'll have a think about it.

6

Libby gulped from the mug of instant coffee, hoping it would bring her clarity. Sat in the hospital café, she was exhausted and still had to walk three miles home. With Harper arriving ahead of schedule, the moment she'd been in denial about for months had suddenly hit.

What was she going to do?

She'd assured Claire she'd find someone to take her place for the workshops and comedy nights but hadn't approached any of her contacts. Improv required a certain level of trust and experience, and no-one had seemed an adequate replacement for her best friend.

The only option currently on the table was the offer she'd just received.

Poor Henry. During the session at Conqueror, she'd made sure to hide her reaction when he told her about his family. That night she'd googled the Foxbrookes. Within a minute she was thanking her lucky stars for her exceedingly normal parents and siblings, and was filled with empathy for him.

The flickering strip light above her sparked a thought.

What would his proposal mean for her relationship with Lucas?

Would this be the red rag that prompted him to realise and declare his feelings? She imagined his righteous indignation. *'Pretend to love someone else? But Lib-Lob, you're mine!'* Lucas was going to be every Jane Austen hero rolled into one.

Lucas might not be awake yet, and he often took hours or days to reply to her messages, so she sent him a series of texts.

> Libby: Morning! Claire just had her baby! A little girl called Harper! So cute. I'll send you a picture xxx

> Libby: [Picture of Harper]

> Libby: Btw I just got the weirdest job offer.

> Libby: One of the guys I did the workshop with at Conqueror wants to pay me to be his fake girlfriend at his thirtieth birthday celebrations. Can you believe it?

She waited for five minutes, dunking a stale croissant in the remains of her coffee. Was he even awake? Maybe a few more would prompt a reply.

> Libby: His family have been hassling him to get a girlfriend, so he told them he did have one to get them off his back, and now he has to find one in a hurry lol x

> Libby: The job would be for four days x

> Libby: His birthday celebrations are lasting that long x

Still nothing.

She took her tray to the cleaning station, checked directions for the walk home, then sent one final message.

Libby: His name is Henry Foxbrooke.

Her phone rang before she'd reached the front doors of the hospital.

'Lib-Lob, babe, what the fuck?'

Libby tried not to squeal. Lucas's voice was the sexy growl she was hoping for.

'Sorry, did I wake you up?'

'Yeah, I had a late sesh last night. Still in bed.'

Her heart leapt as she pictured him on the double bed that was parked in the corner of his studio. Lucas had been living there for the past year after a disagreement with his previous landlord.

'Did you see the picture of Claire's baby?' she asked.

'Yeah, that's cool. But are you serious? Foxy Foxbrooke wants to pay you to be his girlfriend? Lib-Lob, I can't see you putting out for him. You're not like that.'

'No! God, Lucas, no! There'll be separate bedrooms. And he wants to draw up a contract to protect me.'

'Good. No-one takes advantage of my girl.'

She put her hand to her chest and closed her eyes for a mini swoon.

'How much is he paying you?'

Libby hesitated, then remembered they were friends and didn't have any secrets.

'Five grand.'

He whistled. 'Fucking hell, *I'd* suck him off for that.'

'Lucas!'

He snickered. 'Sorry, Lib-Lob, I don't mean it. Why does he need you to be his fake girlfriend? What's wrong with him?'

Her swoon was rapidly disappearing. 'There's nothing wrong with him. I think he's just shy. His family want him to get married, and he told them he had a girlfriend to stop them from interfering.'

'Do you know who they are?'

'I know his parents are the Duke and Duchess of Somerset and their lifestyle is a little, er, eccentric.'

He snorted. 'They're over-sexed nobs. They're so inbred they'd shag a horse hoping it was their cousin.'

'Lucas! Henry's not like that. He's a really sweet guy. He even said he wanted to meet my boyfriend to explain himself.'

'What boyfriend?'

'I know I don't have a boyfriend. Henry just assumed I did, then got off the call before I could correct him.'

'Humph.'

This was it. She'd given him the perfect opportunity. *Come on!*

'When are you meeting him?'

'We haven't arranged it yet. A couple of days maybe? Enough time to draw up the contract I suppose.'

'Okay, I'm coming with you. I'll be your boyfriend.'

OMG! YES! 'Are you sure?'

'Yeah, yeah. I want to make sure your interests are protected. And if some posh git can fake it with you, then so can I. I'll text you a time and a place and you can let him know.'

Libby: Hi, I spoke to Lucas and he wants to know if you can meet us midday on Friday at Coffine House in Soho?

Henry: Yes, of course. I'll be there. Thank you.
I really appreciate the two of you giving me
the time.

AT ELEVEN FORTY-FIVE ON FRIDAY MORNING, LIBBY MET
Lucas around the corner from the coffee house. She was
wearing the dress she believed was his favourite and a clip with
a red bow holding back one side of her hair. She was so
nervous she hadn't been able to eat since the previous night.
India guessed something was up, but Libby didn't want to
break Henry's confidence, so told her housemate she was
worried about what to do now that Claire had given birth.

Lucas sauntered towards her, wearing a knock-off Ramones
T-shirt, his jeans splattered with paint, and held out his arms.

'Girlfriend?' he asked, cocking his head to one side.

She blushed and stepped towards him at a speed that was
intended to be casual but ended up being halfway between a
skip and a jog.

Lucas hugged her and took a deep breath.

'Mmm, I love that smell.'

OMG, OMG, OMG!

He disengaged, taking a bag off her shoulder and
opening it.

'You bloody star, Lib-Lob. No better smell than your sourdough.' He held out his hand. 'Shall we?'

She took it, swallowing her disappointment. Once again,
her cooking seemed to excite him more than she did.

'Lucas, shouldn't we get our story straight before we go in?'

'Do we need to?' he asked, scrunching his nose.

'What if he asks us how we got together?'

Lucas laughed. 'Then we tell him the truth. How we met at

that party ages ago and blah, blah, blah. Don't sweat it, Lib-Lob. He won't give a shit about how we met. He just needs my approval.'

'But, um, what if we need to, er, look authentic?'

He frowned at her. 'Authentic?'

'Maybe we should, er, practice kissing?'

'Fuck me, we're not giving him a sex show.' He snorted. 'Calm down. I've got this.'

He pulled her towards him and kissed her quickly on the lips. Libby was too shocked to register if it had been pleasurable or not.

'See? Easy peasy. Now, come on. We don't want to keep Lord Fancy-Pants waiting.'

COFFINE HOUSE WAS DESIGNED TO LOOK LIKE A FUNERAL parlour from the Victorian era and was staffed by men with facial hair to match. Henry was sitting in a booth near the back and stood as they entered, his face strained and serious. Lucas dropped her hand and strode ahead, extending his arm.

'Lucas Butler,' he said, shaking Henry's hand. 'Good to meet you, buddy.'

'Henry Foxbrooke. Thank you both for meeting me.'

'No problem,' Lucas replied, sliding into the booth.

Libby smiled tentatively at Henry. 'Um, do you want a coffee or anything?'

'Let me get it,' he replied. 'What would you like?'

'I'll have a double espresso,' Lucas interrupted. 'I'm a man of simple tastes.' He beckoned her towards him. 'Sit down, babe.'

'Libby?' Henry asked.

'Um, just an Americano please,' she replied, her face flushing with heat.

'And I'll take a cronut as well,' added Lucas.

'Libby?'

She shook her head. 'Nothing, thank you. I'm fine.' Sitting next to Lucas, she tried to get her breathing back under control.

He leaned closer and whispered in her ear. 'See, Lib-Lob, piece of cake.'

HENRY RETURNED AND SERVED THE TWO OF THEM. DESPITE the paralysing panic Libby sometimes felt when about to perform improv, nothing was as nauseatingly uncomfortable as sitting next to one fake boyfriend, with a potential one sitting across from them.

Henry cleared his throat. 'So—'

'Look,' Lucas interrupted. 'Let's just lay this out on the table, mano-a-mano, eh? I need to know you'll look after my girl, but everything has to be kosher, okay?'

'Yes, yes, of course.' Henry nodded. 'I want to assure both of you of my intentions and behaviour. I—'

'Buddy, we can't ignore the elephant in the room here. I don't want Lib-Lob drawn into any of the sex shit your family's got going on. Capiche?'

Capiche?

Henry looked stricken.

'Lucas—' she began, but Henry raised his hands.

'Libby, your boyfriend is right. I need both of you to know that, er, that side of my parents' life will not be in evidence during our stay at Foxbrooke Manor. I have five siblings who are, erm, more like me, and the celebrations will also involve my grandmother, who is extremely conservative.'

Lucas nodded. 'But what if you need to seem *authentic?*' His leg knocked against hers under the table, and he took a big bite of his cronut.

Henry coloured. 'I haven't brought a, ahem, girlfriend home before and have a reputation amongst my family of being quite, erm, restrained in my behaviour. There will be no need for any physical contact, beyond the odd hand-hug that Libby may choose to initiate in public if she feels comfortable doing so.'

'"Hand-hug"?' Lucas asked, his mouth full. Powdered sugar sprayed onto the table.

'You know,' Libby said. 'When I squeeze your hand like this?'

Lucas shrugged.

Henry reached into a bag next to him. 'I've drawn up a contract for you both to look at. It includes all the assurances about physicality as well as a get-out clause for Libby if at any time she feels uncomfortable.'

Lucas held out a hand to stop him. 'Henry. I've seen all I need and trust you with my Lib-Lob. The two of you can iron out the boring stuff. I've got to get back to my studio.' He necked his double espresso. 'I'm an artist, repped by the Balbis gallery.' He frowned at Henry as if sizing him up. 'You're a man of good taste, right? Your father collects art?' Lucas didn't wait for a reply. 'You should come by my studio sometime.' He dug a card out of his pocket and handed it to him. 'I'm currently exploring the nature of creation and the divine feminine. My pieces would really compliment the Holbeins you've got at the Manor.' He nudged Libby. 'Let me out, love.'

She shuffled off the banquette seat, half desperate he would leave and half panicked about being left alone with Henry.

Henry exited his side of the booth and held out his hand. 'Thank you for meeting me, Lucas.'

Lucas took it and shook firmly. 'You know, you really

should come to the opening of my show next week. Super exclusive, but I can get your name on the door. It's Monday night at seven at Balbis. Invite the family. I think they'd like what they see.'

'Thank you,' Henry replied. 'I'll see if I can make it.'

Lucas dropped his hand and turned to Libby. He grabbed her, smashing his lips to hers and dipping her backwards. The space was small, and the back of her head connected with the side of the booth with an audible thud. Lucas didn't seem to notice as he righted her and removed his face from hers.

'Laters, Lib-Lob.' He grabbed the remains of his cronut and the bag with Libby's sourdough, gave Henry a chin-lift and strode out.

'Are you okay?' Henry asked, as Libby rubbed the back of her head.

She couldn't meet his gaze. She wanted the ground to swallow her up. That kiss was the second she'd received from Lucas, and nothing about it had been pleasant. Her dream man had given her a dream kiss, but she was left with a sour taste in her mouth.

'Sorry,' she mumbled, sitting back at the table. 'True love, eh?'

'Good lord, Libby, don't apologise for expressing the, er, passions of your relationship,' he replied, taking his seat.

She was going to be sick. She had to tell him Lucas wasn't her boyfriend. 'Henry...'

He placed the contract he'd prepared in front of her.

'Please look this over, Libby. I know you haven't made up your mind yet, but I want you to be able to make an informed decision.'

She thumbed through the sheaf of papers. 'How many pages are there?'

'A few. I tried to cover all bases.'

'Did you use a template?'

He cleared his throat. 'I'm afraid a web search for "fake relationship contracts" didn't supply the results I was hoping for, so I wrote it from scratch.'

She finally brought her eyes to meet his and smiled. She may not have known Henry Foxbrooke for long, but she knew in her bones he was a good person.

'Henry, this looks longer than my final year dissertation. How long did it take to write?'

He pulled an embarrassed face. 'A while. But it had to be right.'

She drew her shoulders back. 'Okay, wish me luck. I'm going in.'

'Would you like another coffee? Anything to eat?'

She instinctively put her hand on her tummy as it growled. 'Do you mind? I was so nervous I couldn't eat breakfast this morning.'

He frowned. 'I'm so sorry to cause you distress.'

'I'm fine. Honestly. Nothing a sandwich won't solve.' She reached into her bag for her purse. Hopefully she had enough money in her account to cover it.

'I'll get this, Libby. Please?'

She nodded with relief. 'Thank you. Anything will be fine.'

As he went to the counter, she read the front of the document.

'Contract between Henry Foxbrooke and Libby Fletcher for the details of their fictitious relationship.'

There was room for their addresses, signatures and the date. She opened the first page to reveal a note of the document's contents.

'Key players, Logistics, Timetable & Events, Backstory, Personal Requirements, Intimacy, Remuneration, Termination clauses, Non-disclosure agreement, Addendum.'

Holy shit.

She turned the page to the list of key players. Here was every member of Henry's family, plus friends and staff at Foxbrooke Manor as well as family pets. Most people had a photo, and everyone had a bio, listing their age, physical description, jobs, likes and dislikes. It went on for pages. At the end of the section was a family tree and four blank pages for her to add in the details of her own family and friends.

Henry placed a coffee and a plate of sandwiches and pastries in front of her.

'Are you sure you've listed everyone in Somerset?' she asked. 'I can't see any mention of a postal worker. You don't want them to feel left out?'

'You don't have to remember any of it. It's just a reference document, really. I have a fairly large family and they're all going to be there. I find them overwhelming at the best of times, so I wanted you to be prepared. If you take the job, of course.'

She flicked through to 'logistics'. This section contained details of how they would travel up and back to London (in Henry's car) as well as a description and scale drawing of his bedroom.

'I need you to understand how we will be in separate beds,' he explained. 'This is my room, here, and off it there is another room with a daybed. I used it as a playroom when I was growing up. Now it's mostly filled with junk. I'll be sleeping in there and you'll be in the main room.'

'Henry, I can't kick you out of your own bed!'

'It's not my bed, and I insist. Unfortunately, there isn't an ensuite, but there is a bathroom next door. You'll have sole access to this, and I'll use another one further along the corridor.'

'But—'

'I need you to feel safe and have your privacy. If another room becomes available then I'll move into it, and say that it's to save you from my snoring.'

'*Do* you snore?'

His cheeks went darker, and he cleared his throat. 'I don't think so. But if I disturb you from the other room, you must say, and I'll sleep on one of the sofas downstairs.'

'I'm sure that won't be necessary.'

'Well, let's see.'

She turned to 'Timetable and Events'. Most of the days were blank.

'I haven't been very involved in any of the planning,' he explained. 'But, when, *if*, we get there and there's any activity you don't like, you don't have to do it.'

'What kind of things might I not like? Surely, it's mainly centred around meals?'

'Sardines. That might not be your thing.'

'Tinned or fresh?'

He smiled. 'It's a Victorian parlour game. Like hide and seek in reverse. We used to love it as kids but haven't played for years. Summer, my youngest sister, is insisting we resurrect it.'

'Okay, I think I can cope with that.'

She turned the page to 'Backstory'. It was empty.

'I didn't know what we should say about how we met,' he said. 'I thought you might have some ideas? Maybe some kind of party?'

Her stomach knotted as she remembered a garden party four years ago at India's parents' house where she'd met Giles, her ex. He was just like Henry: well-dressed, well-mannered and upper-class. But no matter how much she tried to mesh their two completely different lives into one, putting a working-class girl with a toff was like trying to mix oil and water.

'What kind of events do you normally go to?' she asked.

'I'm mainly wining and dining clients, but I get invited to all kinds of things. Private views, opening nights, premieres, book launches.' He stared at the table, seeming embarrassed. 'I only get invitations because of my name.'

Libby knew exactly what kind of women went to these events. She'd seen their photographs in India's posh magazines. They were rich, well-connected and glossy. The polar opposite of her. But she still needed to hear from Henry just what sort of woman she had to pretend to be.

'What kind of women do you normally, er, date?'

He glanced at her, his forehead furrowed. 'Does it matter?'

She nodded.

He ran his hand over his head. 'I don't know if I have a type.'

'The woman you were meant to have a date with, what was she like?'

'Elizabeth?' He shrugged. 'She's nice. Er, a lawyer, tall...'

'Do you have a photo of her?'

'A photo?'

'Yes, to help me get into character.'

'I don't want you to be like her,' he said, looking increasingly uncomfortable. 'I just need you to be you.'

She bit the inside of her cheek. Being herself hadn't been good enough for Giles, and it certainly wouldn't be good enough for Henry.

'Show me, please?'

He pulled out his phone and tapped the screen before handing it to her. She scrolled through the photos. Elizabeth skiing. Elizabeth paddleboarding on azure blue water. Elizabeth in a slinky cocktail dress accepting an award. Elizabeth looking like she could advertise everything from toothpaste to management consultant courses.

Ugh. Libby wanted to tear the clip in her hair out. What had she been thinking? The red bow suddenly felt childish.

The photos of Elizabeth were on Henry's dating app, and she noticed it was still live. There were several messages waiting to be read. She handed the phone back to him.

'What about the women messaging you here? What about asking one of them?'

He shook his head. 'I've never met them before and they don't have your skillset.'

She turned her attention back to the contract and sucked on her lip. How could she measure up to what was needed for this role? Her mind jumped to Lucas, where it always went when she was down. But thinking of him now was like listening to the off-key organ music droning in Coffine House. Was she crazy to have hoped for so long that their relationship was ever going to be more than friends?

'Libby, you're perfect for this.'

She summoned a smile. 'Am I perfect because I exist?'

'That is a bonus,' he admitted. 'Look, you need to take your time going through the contract, but if you agree to this, I'll advance you half the money now so you can get anything you think you might need.'

Like the removal of my overdraft...

She turned the page to find a list of all their supposed previous dates, her heart skipping a beat.

'You took me boating on the river? We climbed the O2 arena? We took a spin on the London Eye? Bloody hell, Henry, we've been busy.'

'Feel free to delete any you don't like and add in any others.'

'We swam with sharks at the Sea Life Centre? Seriously?'

'I googled date ideas in London and put in a selection.'

Dear god. She caught his eye and raised her eyebrows. 'How about we stayed in and watched telly?'

He took the contract from her and scribbled notes in the margins.

'Or I introduced you to Serafina, and the joys of sourdough?'

'Serafina?'

'She's my starter. I've had her since I was a teenager. It's the longest co-dependent relationship I've ever had.'

'Starter?'

'A starter is a mix of flour, water and live yeasts. I keep feeding it, sorry, *her*, and she gives me bread.'

'Will she be coming with you to Foxbrooke?'

Libby nodded. 'You can put starters in hibernation, but I like to keep her close. Serafina is very well-travelled.'

Henry wrote more notes on the contract, then handed it back to her to read.

Next up was 'Personal Requirements', which was also left blank.

'What's this for? My rider?' she asked.

'Kind of, I suppose. It's things like dietary specifications, ideal room temperature, exercise equipment needs, whether you need to watch or listen to certain programmes at a particular time. That kind of thing.'

'Woah. Okay. I think I'm pretty easy.' *Said the actress to the bishop...*

She turned the page to 'Intimacy', her eyes widening as she read.

'"I, Henry Foxbrooke will remain at least eight inches away from Libby Fletcher at all times, in accordance with paragraph four, clause nine, and appendix one."' She glanced up. 'Henry...'

'Yes?' He looked nervous.

'How are you going to keep to eight inches? Are you going to carry around a ruler?'

'Um—'

'And why eight inches?'

'I thought that number would allow us to be seated next to each other at dinner.'

She scanned down to paragraph four. '"Any acts that involve bodily contact will be initiated solely by Libby Fletcher."' She paused. 'Henry, why is this here?'

He seemed confused. 'Because I don't want you to worry that I might touch you.'

'But what about the other way around? What is there to protect *you*?'

'Protect *me*? From what?'

'Me, of course. What if I have one too many of your granny's sherries and force myself on you?'

He looked so shocked that she laughed.

'It never crossed my mind that you would,' he replied.

'Okay.' She grinned. 'Moving on. "Clause nine. If Libby Fletcher is in physical danger, then Henry Foxbrooke may break paragraph one to assure her safety." How dangerous *is* Somerset?'

'Not particularly, but there might be an out-of-control car? Um, a wayward bee? Some food might go down the wrong way? Er, you might fall in the lake or the river?'

She slapped her hand over her mouth, but the laughter spilled out. 'Do you think I'm a total klutz, or do you moonlight as a Health and Safety Officer? That's hilarious!'

He looked surprised. 'It is?'

She reached across the table before thinking and squeezed his hand. 'You're naturally funny.'

Henry gazed down at their hands and she removed hers. 'It's alright. Paragraph four, remember?' She brought her attention back to the document and took a deep breath. 'Okay, let's see what Appendix one has to offer... "Hard and soft limits and safe words"?' she squeaked.

'It's not what you might think,' he said quickly.

She read out loud. '"If, at any point, Libby Fletcher rescinds in writing paragraph four, then the following points detail her hard and soft limits regarding physical intimacy." Okay, I'm reading.'

Below the opening statement was a list and next to each item were three boxes. The first was marked 'Yes (at any time)', the second was marked 'Soft Limit (maybe – consent must be requested again)' and the third was marked 'Hard Limit (no, under all circumstances)'.

Her heart racing, she scanned down the list.

Hand holding

Arm placed around the shoulder

Hand placed on the small of the back

Hand placed on thigh as long as in public and both parties are fully clothed

Face-to-face hug

Hug from behind

Kiss blown from a distance

Light, closed-lipped kiss on the top of the head

Light, closed lipped kiss on the cheek (facial cheek, not buttock cheek)

She snorted.

'What is it?'

'You've actually specified face cheek as opposed to arse cheek.'

'I didn't want you to worry.'

She held her sides, trying to hold the laughter in. 'Henry, I don't think anyone's ever kissed my bum.'

'Ah, okay. Are the items acceptable so far?'

'Let me reserve judgement until I've got to the end.'

She continued reading.

Light, closed lipped kiss on the back of the hand
Light, closed lipped kiss on the palm of the hand
Slow dancing
Loving glances
Declarations of love

'Declarations of love? *Loving glances?* They're not physical.'

'I know, but they are pretty intimate, so I thought I'd add them to the end. If you want to add anything else, be my guest.'

'A little light bondage... Orgasm denial...' She shrieked with laughter at the look on his face. 'I'm joking!' She read further. '"Safe words. Libby Fletcher is to supply Henry Foxbrooke with two safe words. The first should be considered a warning, and the second a hard no for him to cease whichever activity he is performing."' She looked up. 'Are you expecting me to start shouting "red" if you throw too many loving glances my way?'

'I just want you to feel safe.'

Her heart melted.

She reached across the table again and squeezed his hand. 'I do. I think you might be the sweetest man I've ever met.'

She held his gaze and smiled. His blush was evident, so she let his hand go and picked up the papers again.

'Right. Which chapters do we have left? Mark, Luke or John? Ah no, "Remuneration".' She read the page then fixed him with what she hoped was a stern look. 'Henry, *if* I take this job then this contract means I could scarper after a day and you'd still pay me five grand?'

He nodded.

'That hardly seems fair. To you.'

'Those are my terms.'

'If you say so, hot shot. Remind me not to make you my financial advisor. Okay, what's left? "Termination Clauses". Yep, yep, yep, once again weighted entirely in my favour. "Non-Disclosure Agreement". Fair enough. "Addendum".' She looked up. 'My name is now *Elizabeth*?'

'Er, yes. I was put on the spot by my mother and because I was about to go on a date with Elizabeth, I said her name. Everyone will still call you Libby. We can say it's what you prefer Elizabeth to be shortened to.'

Her throat tightened. The laughter that had so easily spilled out had now gone, revealing the wretched chasm of her own inferiority when next to someone as all-together as Henry.

He cleared his throat. 'So, when do you think you can give me an answer?'

$\mathcal{R}$ 7 $\mathcal{R}$

Henry's feet moved on autopilot, carrying him to the Central Line, while his mind churned over his meeting with Libby and Lucas. He thought he had a handle on Libby, a sense of what she was like. However, meeting her boyfriend had thrown these ideas into disarray. Understandably, Lucas was looking out for his girlfriend, but that hadn't translated into his actions. Henry stared at his frowning face in the window of the tube as it rattled through the tunnels. Why did he dislike Lucas so much? Had he turned into such a miserable bastard that he disliked almost everyone?

No. Just a lot of men. He leant forward, resting his elbows on his knees and pinching the bridge of his nose. He hadn't seen or spoken to his two best friends, Jack and Finn, for far too long. Jack had a flat in London but lived in the south of France, doing some kind of party-planning for the uber-rich. Finn was back in Foxbrooke, working as a carpenter and builder. Henry imagined ringing them up out of the blue. *Hey, I know we haven't talked in forever, but I just had to ask. Am I a misanthropic git?* A smile tugged at the corner of his mouth. Finn would reply, *not as much as me,* and Jack would laugh and tell Henry he needed to try harder.

The tube reached Bank station and Henry stepped off, striding towards the Conqueror offices. He'd spent so much time over the last couple of days creating the contract for Libby that he was behind with his work. He'd have to work the weekend as well as take his clients out on Saturday night.

A text pinged in.

> Summer: I was thinking of coming up to town this weekend. Want to meet up?

> Henry: Sorry, just about to sign a big deal so have to work both days. I'll see you back in Foxbrooke for the party?

By the time he'd reached work, he was still waiting for a reply. He messaged again.

> Henry: You okay?

He was pretty certain now that Summer wanted more money.

'Foxy! Where you been?' Carl was exiting the glass doors, an unlit cigarette between his lips.

Henry pocketed his phone. 'I was checking out a possible place to take clients.'

Carl lit the cigarette and took a long drag, exhaling the smoke into the street. 'Henry...'

'Yeah?'

Carl looked down, scuffing at the pavement with the tip of a shiny shoe.

Henry wasn't quite sure what to do. 'You alright?' he asked.

Carl barked out a laugh and raised his head. 'I'm golden,

mate.' He took another drag. 'Look, just keep an eye on Jamesy-boy, okay? I think he's up to something.'

'Isn't he always?'

'True. I just—' He flicked ash to the ground. 'I dunno, something just doesn't feel right.'

'Something doesn't *feel* right?'

Carl shrugged and grinned at him. 'I think it was that workshop. It's changed me. I've now got feelings and everything.'

Henry smiled. 'Thanks, Carl. I'll keep my eye on him. He won't get anything past me.'

IT WAS FIVE P.M. ON SATURDAY, AND HENRY'S CLIENTS weren't returning his calls. Keeping clients happy was a big deal in brokering. A few decades ago this would have involved a swanky dinner or the best drugs and women London had to offer. Times had changed, but the principle remained. After missing his table at Imperium earlier in the week, Henry had to wait before trying to cadge a favour there again. Now he'd secured entry to another restaurant with a nightclub, but by eight, he knew he'd been professionally ghosted. He sent a text to Summer.

> Henry: I know it's last minute, but I'm free now if you are? Client cancelled on me.

There was no reply from her either.

WHILST HENRY WAS SITTING ALONE IN HIS OFFICE, LIBBY was in her flat, pummelling Serafina into submission. India was out, Claire was too exhausted to receive visitors, and Lucas had just stood her up. She knew he was on a deadline with his show being on Monday night, but she needed to see him. She wanted to make sure things were okay between them and, more importantly, try and unpick her feelings towards him.

The meeting with Henry had not gone how she'd imagined. Henry had been so earnest and sweet, and Lucas had been... She didn't want to put words to how he'd been, but seeing the two men together had highlighted how very different they were. She'd been in love with Lucas for so long that nothing could taint the pretty picture she'd painted. However, Henry had accidentally brushed against it, knocking it to the ground and revealing the mouldy wall behind.

I love Lucas, she repeated in her mind. Once his show was out of the way, things would be better. He'd have the money to pay her back and she wouldn't have to contemplate Henry's job offer. She was at the limit of her overdraft and a month behind on her rent. Fortunately she'd found someone to do the improv night with her on Tuesday, but they didn't have time to rehearse so the two of them would be flying by the seat of their pants and hoping the other was carrying a spare parachute. And anyway, the small cash injection from the gig wouldn't solve her financial problems.

'Fuck!' She pounded the dough with her fists. She hadn't said anything to Lucas about him inviting Henry and his family to the show, but the anger was eating at her stomach like an ulcer. Maybe it was simply because Henry's family were rich and well connected, whereas hers... Whatever way she looked at it, she couldn't let it go.

LATER, ASLEEP IN BED, LIBBY'S SUBCONSCIOUS CONTINUED TO taunt her. She was at Lucas's opening night, handing out drinks to women who all looked like Elizabeth—taller, thinner, richer, and more beautiful than she was. Lucas was the centre of their world, shining brighter than the sun, and she couldn't get past the wall of Prada and perfume to reach him. One of the women gesticulated with her glass and champagne splattered over Libby's dress. She staggered backwards into another woman, who spilled her glass onto her face.

Libby wiped her eyes but the liquid kept splashing. Tossing in bed, she dragged herself awake. Fumbling for the light, she turned it on and sat up in bed, blinking as her eyes adjusted.

What the fuck?

Water was dripping from the ceiling in multiple places. She leapt out of bed and ran to India's room.

'India, wake up! There's water pouring through the ceiling.'

'What?'

India stumbled out of bed and followed Libby to her room.

'Jesus!'

The two women stared at the ceiling in horror.

'I'll go upstairs,' said India. 'You clear your stuff and put down pans to catch the drips.'

India dashed out and Libby ran for the kitchen. She flicked on the light to reveal a room with water pouring through a hole in the ceiling, and broken and damp pieces of plasterboard littering the table and floor.

There was a loud bang, then everything went dark.

A FEW HOURS LATER, LIBBY BUZZED LUCAS'S STUDIO, a rucksack on her back, her hands trembling. She was desperately trying not to cry. The upstairs neighbour had been drunk, set a bath running, then passed out in front of the television, at least six hours before Libby woke up. The building that housed the flats was old and the water had turned the ceilings to mushy cardboard. Most of her belongings were ruined and their home was now uninhabitable. Worst of all, a chunk of plaster, wood, and god-knows-what-else had landed in her starter. Serafina was dead.

'Fuck off.' Lucas's voice was a pissed off growl.

'Lucas! It's me.'

'Lib-Lob? Why are you here?'

'The flat's trashed. The idiot upstairs got drunk, ran a bath and forgot about it. I've got nowhere to stay.'

There was a pause. 'Hang on, I'm coming down.'

Five minutes later, Lucas stepped out into the street, shut the door behind him and drew her into his arms. The kind gesture was enough for the dam to break and tears spill out.

'Shhh. It's okay, Lib-Lob. It's okay.'

'I'm sorry, Lucas,' she sobbed. 'It's just been so awful.'

He stroked her back until she stopped crying. She disengaged and pulled out a wad of tissues, blowing her nose.

'Thank you,' she said shyly. 'I knew I could count on you.'

He held his hands out. 'What can I say? I've got that Butler magic.'

She giggled. 'You have.' She yawned. 'I really appreciate this, Lucas. And I promise you won't know I'm here. Right now, I just need to sleep.'

His smile turned into a look of confusion. 'What, here?'

She nodded. 'I've got nowhere else to go.'

He pulled at his hair and frowned. 'Lib-Lob, I'm sorry, but that's not going to work.'

'I, I don't have to share your bed,' she stammered. 'I can sleep on the floor.'

He sighed. 'The show's on Monday. My work is everywhere. There's just no room.'

Her throat tightened. 'Lucas.' Her voice cracked. 'I've got no money left.'

He nodded. 'Tell me about it. Look. Go stay at Claire's, and we can talk after the show.' He kissed her forehead. 'You've got this, Lib-Lob.'

'HE SAID *WHAT*?' CLAIRE PACED HER LIVING ROOM, CARRYING Harper over her shoulder and patting her back.

'He was being sweet,' Libby replied. 'Boosting my confidence. He believes in me.'

Harper let out an enormous burp.

'Good girl, good girl,' Claire cooed before turning her fiery gaze back to Libby. 'See? Even Harper knows he's a complete tool, and she's less than a week old.'

Libby wrung her hands in her lap. 'He's under so much stress. His big show is on Monday and I should have thought before asking if I could stay. It's just I didn't want to intrude on you.'

Claire sat, Harper's eyes now closing as she drifted off to sleep. 'Libby. Listen to me. You can always stay here. Harper's in with us at the moment anyway so you can have the nursery on the floor or the couch in here. But you do need another solution. What's India going to do?'

'Well, she's off soon for that shoot in Morocco, so she's going to stay with her parents in Surrey until then. The insurance claim could take months to go through, and the whole house might need to be gutted.'

'So, you're homeless.'

She bit her lip and nodded.

'What about work? We haven't talked about this since Harper arrived, but I could still do the odd gig—'

'Please don't,' said Ritchie poking his head around the door. 'You're still bleeding heavily, your hormones and emotions are all over the place, and in a few days Harper won't be sleeping like she is now. Just give it a few weeks before you go back. Please, love?'

As if to confirm her husband's words, Claire burst into tears. Ritchie came into the room and put his arm around her. 'It's okay, sweetheart. Let me take her for a bit and make you a cup of tea, eh?' Claire nodded and Ritchie lifted Harper into his arms. He kissed his wife on the top of her head. 'Don't worry, love. I've got this.'

'I shouldn't be here,' Libby whispered. 'You need your space.'

'Not as much as you need it, Lib.' Claire blew her nose. 'And I'm really worried about you. You promised you'd get work put in the diary, but it looks like you've done nothing.'

Libby's mouth opened, but she couldn't find the excuse to fill it. 'I'm afraid I was happily paddling up my favourite river.'

'De-Nile?'

She nodded, then started singing a hoe down in a soft and sad voice.

'I'm perky, I'm chirpy, my name is Libby-Lou.

My neighbour's made me homeless and I don't know what to do.

I'm in the red, my starter's dead, my life is in a mess.

The only thing I've salvaged is my gorgeous yellow dress.'

'Really?' Claire asked.

'You're the engine of this team,' Libby replied. 'I'm no good without you. I just turn up and pull funny faces.'

'Bollocks. I just think you're scared of change so you're avoiding it, and I haven't helped by doing all the admin. Look. It's easy to be comfortable in an uncomfortable life.'

Libby was too tired to understand her friend's words. 'What?'

'We do our shows, we do workshops, hell, we might occasionally go on tour. But we can do it with our eyes shut. It's always a challenge, but neither of us has the same wide-eyed panic we did at the start, do we?'

She lifted a shoulder in a half shrug, but Claire was right.

'It's easy,' said Claire. 'Well, it was, living with India. And it's safe to be in love with Lucas, because in your heart of hearts, you know nothing is ever going to happen. I mean, seriously, what would you actually do if he kissed you?'

Libby's cheeks were burning.

'I'm as much to blame,' Claire continued. 'I honestly thought I could pop Harper out, strap her to my chest and carry on as if nothing had changed. We've both been skirting around these issues and avoiding having a proper conversation about them. Change is inevitable, Lib. It's just up to you whether you take the initiative or have it forced upon you.'

Libby bit her bottom lip. She was beginning to wonder if her relationship with Lucas would ever be different. And what should she do about Henry's offer? She'd promised him an answer by Tuesday after Lucas's show. It didn't matter that it was fake with Henry, or that they'd never even have to touch. If she had even the slightest chance with Lucas, then she'd never take the job.

Claire started singing.

'You're clever, you're funny, your name is not Lib-Lob.

Your luck will change, I promise you. You'll get another job.

I know that you can do this, some faith is what you need.

So don't be scared, go take a risk, who knows where it might lead?'

＊ 8 ＊

Henry sat opposite Lorna Ferguson, Conqueror's HR Manager, his foot tapping impatiently. He had better things to do with his time than have a meeting at nine a.m. to discuss why he hadn't taken any annual leave in the past ten months.

'Biscuit?'

No, I don't want a sodding biscuit. He shook his head. He wanted to get back to his desk and work out why his clients had gone radio silent when the deal was nearly complete.

'Henry, I know that a culture of long hours exists within City firms, but here, at Conqueror we do care about our employees. No-one in the brokerage team works longer hours than you. It's unsustainable.'

'I'm fine. I'm happy.'

'Well, to be frank, Henry, I'm not. I don't want you to burn out, be signed off for six months, then permanently bugger off to an Ashram to be a yogi.'

He raised his eyebrows.

Lorna waved her hand in a dismissive gesture. 'It was a

while ago. The point is, Henry, you're not a machine. Everyone needs time away from work to rest and recuperate. You don't have to lie on a beach and do nothing, but you do need to take some of your leave or you'll be forced to take it.'

'What?'

She sighed. 'Conqueror will not be a company that allows its employees to work three hundred and sixty-five days a year.'

'I'm taking time off next week.'

'But will you? You told your line manager you'd be away for the weekend but hoped to be back by Tuesday lunchtime at the latest. How is that time off?'

'I'll take the week off.'

'Good. It's a start, but I need you to show a greater commitment to your mental health and well-being.'

He willed himself to relax. *Mental health and well-being? Fuck's sake.* He was absolutely fine. Apart from his family, everything in his life was just the way he wanted it.

Henry stood, his chair falling to the floor behind him with a crash.

'Where the fuck is Hunter-Savage?'

Heads popped up from behind screens. Everyone looked surprised except for Carl. He gave Henry a sympathetic look and shook his head.

Henry stalked out of the office, slamming the door behind him. He jabbed at the lift button as if it were James's eye. *Fucker.* They were meant to be on the same team. It wasn't uncommon for clients to be poached, but on a deal this big? That he'd been working on for so long? Especially when he needed the money so badly to keep bankrolling his youngest sister's education.

He left the building and strode onto the street. He didn't

know where he was going, but he needed to get out. To think. And to stop himself from murdering James. What options did he have? None. Once the clients jumped ship, there was nothing he could do. Conqueror still got the deal. As long as they got their cut and the prestige, they didn't give a shit which of their minions engineered it.

A flash of yellow caught his eye and he stopped outside an artisan bakery. The golden pastries and heat-browned loaves sat in wicker baskets lined with yellow gingham fabric. A sign for San Francisco Sourdough caught his eye and he thought of Libby. Would he ever get to taste Serafina? A smile tugged at his mouth at the innocent thought that also sounded so inappropriate. He bit back a sigh. Would she agree to his crazy plan? And did he *want* to inflict his family on her? Wouldn't it be easier to say that 'Elizabeth' was ill and couldn't come?

He rubbed his face with both hands. This was such a mess. Perhaps Lorna was right. Maybe he did need some time away from work. He could spend a few weeks in France with Jack? A break that long should sort his head out. James was a massive wanker and had screwed him over, but it was only work. Feeling calmer, he turned around.

As Henry approached the glass-fronted Conqueror offices from the other side of the street, he saw a head of blonde curly hair he'd known almost as long as he could remember. His youngest sister was standing by one of the huge plants in the lobby and cracking up as if she'd just been informed that Henry had won 'funniest employee' of the month award. Whoever she was talking to was entirely obscured by the greenery.

A sharp shock of dread shot up his spine. *Please, god, no.*

Summer's hand reached out to touch the hidden figure. She threw her head back and laughed so loudly he could hear it from the street.

His pace quickened.

He threw open the door as his sister stepped backwards, giggling. A man followed her.

'Motherfucker!' Henry yelled, as he launched himself at James, pushing him away from his sister.

'Henry!' she cried.

But the red mist had descended, plunging him into a lava pit of rage. He punched James's face.

James staggered back, raising his own fists.

'Can't accept defeat, Foxy?' he taunted.

Henry didn't bother trying to land another blow, rugby-tackling James to the floor.

'Henry, stop!' Summer screamed.

Sitting astride James, Henry punched him again. 'That's for stealing my clients.' He landed another punch. 'That's for Elizabeth.' He drew his arm back. 'And this one is for even *looking* at my sister.'

But before his fist could descend, he was pulled back and lifted off James, his arms pinned in place by the office security guards.

James staggered to his feet, holding a bloody nose.

'Henry!'

He spun around to see Lorna Ferguson looking at him, her face white.

'My office. Now.'

❧

During a British summer, rain was more likely than sun. Good for plants, but not good for Libby as she walked the five miles from Claire's home in St. John's Wood to Shoreditch, for Lucas's show.

Lucas had told her to wear black and white, but half of her

clothes had been ruined. She would have washed and dried them, but the building inspectors said they could be contaminated and dangerous, so she threw them out. Now, her lucky dress was being splashed by buses she couldn't afford to take and she was running late.

Out of breath, she finally reached Balbis and pushed the large black door open. On the other side, a woman stood with a clipboard.

'Hi, I'm Libby Fletcher.'

The woman looked down her list, then to Libby's clothes. 'You're down as waiting staff.'

She drew herself up. 'I'm Lucas's friend.'

'Are you one of his models?'

Models? 'No, I'm here to support him. He asked me to help serve drinks.'

The woman sniffed. 'It won't be appropriate dressed like that. Just go on in. You can leave your coat and umbrella over there.'

Libby hung her coat on a rail, put her brolly in a bucket, smoothed her hair and straightened her shoulders. This was it!

The gallery was situated in an old warehouse with a high ceiling and brick walls painted white. The place was packed. Just as in her dream, most of the people were women, thoroughbreds compared to her. She couldn't see Lucas.

Her focus shifted to the paintings. Each one was about a foot square. They were mounted at the same height, running at eye level around the space. In the middle of the room was a temporary square structure, accommodating more of his art.

Libby blinked.

Every painting was of a vagina.

Two women holding champagne glasses stood in front of her. 'Have you found yours yet?' one asked.

The other woman smirked. 'I have. He's done an amazing

job. Marcus is going to buy it and hang it in the downstairs loo.'

'Brilliant idea.' The two women chinked their glasses.

'He's such a find,' the second woman continued. 'And sexy, if you're into that kind of thing.'

'Well, Saphy certainly is. Why do you think she's gone to all this trouble?'

'No, really? I thought he was seeing Clara? She said he was very hands-on during their sessions.'

'Who knows. Saphy has to keep it quiet because of hubby.'

'Is he here tonight?'

'No, Dubai.'

The women wandered off, and Libby struggled to breathe. This had to be a mistake. She had to be at the wrong gallery. The wrong day. The wrong everything. They couldn't be talking about Lucas. *Her* Lucas.

But there he was, over to one side, chatting to a beautiful woman, his hand on the small of her back. She placed her head by his ear as if to whisper something to him, then nipped his earlobe. Lucas's hand moved down to her bum and he squeezed. The woman disengaged from him to greet more people and, as if drawn against her will, Libby moved forwards. Lucas noticed her as she approached and raised his glass.

'Lib-Lob!'

He drew her in for a quick hug. The smell of white spirit and body odour wasn't as alluring as it had been before.

He looked at her dress, frowning. 'Why aren't you in black and white?'

'The flood, remember?'

'That was days ago. You could have bought something.'

'I don't have any money, Lucas.'

'Charity shop? Come on, Lib-Lob. Improvise!' He chuckled at his own joke.

'Lucas.' She tried to keep her voice steady. 'Is this your entire exhibition?'

'Yeah. I know. I've worked my arse off.'

'Vaginas?'

He cocked his head to one side. 'Vulvas, Lib-Lob. They're vulvas. You should know the vagina is the internal part.'

'So...' Her voice shook. 'I've been paying your studio rent for the last six months so you can paint women's... vulvas?'

'And I appreciate it, Lib-Lob, don't get me wrong. It's been the best gift—'

'Gift?' she squeaked. 'Lucas, I need that money back. It's not a gift. It's *never* been a gift.'

'Look, we'll talk later. Now's my moment. Don't spoil it, okay?' He patted the side of her arm and glanced over her shoulder. 'Belinda, Scheherazade! You made it!' He pushed past her.

Libby stumbled out of the room, grabbed her coat and brolly and ran. The betrayal felt like coming home to find your saintly husband shagging your best friend and every female member of your family.

Not your husband, Libby. Not even your boyfriend.

Outside, the rain had passed and the air was cool on her flushed cheeks. She sucked in a shuddering breath. *What have you done?* The chances of Lucas paying her back were almost zero. She couldn't stay with Claire any longer, and going home to Birmingham to share a room with two of her sisters was a total non-starter. She needed money now. Enough to buy her breathing space so she could work out what the fuck to do with her life.

She rang Henry.

'Libby! Hi, how are you doing?'

'Oh, just tickety-boo.'

'I'm sorry I haven't made it to Lucas's show tonight. Things have been a bit, er, crazy at work. How is it?'

She stifled her scream. 'Fine. Look, I know I should have given you my answer sooner, and I apologise for messing you around—'

'Libby, you haven't messed—'

'Is it still on?'

'What?'

'The job offer.'

'Yes.'

'Okay.'

'Okay?'

'I'll do it. I'll be your fake girlfriend.'

$$\text{❧ } 9 \text{ ❧}$$

Libby sat in the passenger seat of Henry's car, knees together, hands resting demurely on her lap as he drove them out of London.

'So, who are you again?' he asked.

'I'm Elizabeth "Libby" Bennet,' she replied, the words feeling strange in her mouth.

Despite supposed social mobility, class consciousness still pervaded every strata of British society, and one's name and occupation were some of the quickest ways to be pigeonholed and judged. 'Fletcher' was resoundingly lower-class, and 'Liberty' not only shared that status, but—according to Giles's sister—was what a third-rate reality TV star might be called.

'And you're not an actress, you work in publishing?'

'Yes, like India's sister, Savannah. She's my avatar.'

'Er... she's blue?'

Libby clapped her hand over her mouth as she snort-laughed. 'Oh my god, that's hilarious!'

The corner of Henry's mouth twitched. 'So, I'm guessing she doesn't live on Pandora?'

'Not when I last checked... Savannah is who I'm basing Elizabeth Bennet on. She's the perfect type, went to Godolphin girls' school, then Oxford to read English. Her godfather owns Winterblossom Press, so he gave her a job there.'

Publishing houses were, for the most part, owned and run by the upper-middle and upper classes. If you loved books and were named Saskia, it was highly likely you'd find yourself working at a literary agency, *Tatler* magazine, or Winterblossom Press before you left to marry someone called Tarquin.

India's parents were lovely and indulged their daughter's passion for acting even though they didn't understand it. However, in their social circles, there was always a slight bias that set publishing above acting, as if somehow the stage were still synonymous with lower-class living and prostitution. It didn't make a difference to Libby that Henry's mother was a model and actress. His mom was also a Duchess, so could do what she liked. And anyway, Libby wanted to be the kind of fake girlfriend that Henry wanted to be with, someone like his last date, Elizabeth.

'And we met at a book launch for... hang on. Polly Hart?' Henry asked.

'Yes, for her latest release, *Springtime Kisses and Daffodil Wishes at the Little Cornish Cupcake Café on Mermaid's Cove.*'

'Jesus,' he exhaled. 'I'm never going to remember all that.'

'Don't worry, you don't have to. That's all part of your charm. You accidentally congratulated Polly for writing *Summer Wishes and Dandelion Kisses at the Little Cornish Cottage.* Which, incidentally, is almost the same title as a book she brought out last year.'

'And you stepped in and recommended I check it out?'

'Yes. Then we got chatting about books in general and *Pride and Prejudice* in particular.'

Henry rubbed the back of his neck. 'Because the female lead is called Elizabeth Bennet.'

'Yes, and can I just say again that I can't believe you haven't read it.'

'Is that important?'

'Kind of. I have, I mean *Elizabeth* has a Jane Austen obsession and thinks you're her Mr Darcy.'

'He's the hero?'

'Mostly.'

'What do you mean, mostly?'

'Just read the book. It'll all become clear.'

'Can I watch the film instead?'

Libby glanced across at Henry. Everything about his face was taut with tension. Her stomach may have been in knots, but at least she could hide it.

'Yes, but the 1995 TV series is the best adaptation. Honestly, Henry, it's all fine. *Elizabeth* just fantasises that you're like Mr Darcy. A bit aloof and standoffish.'

'I can do that alright.'

'But inside you're soft and gooey. You're a cinnamon roll.'

'I'm a *what* now?'

'You're a hero who is sweet inside even though you might have a gruff exterior.'

'Sounds like my friend, Finn. He spends his whole life acting like a bear with a sore head.'

'But his insides are honey?'

The corner of his mouth turned up. 'If we get a chance to meet him you've got to tell him that.'

'Will he growl if I do? Bite a piece of furniture?'

'Probably. If he does, just remember he's harmless.'

'When did you last see him?'

'Last year. We managed one evening in the pub.' Henry shook his head. 'I can't believe it's been that long.'

'What about Jack, your other best friend?'

The smile disappeared and the frown retook residence on his face. 'We keep in touch sporadically by phone, but I haven't seen him in years. He's got a flat in London but spends most of his time abroad in France. He never comes back to Foxbrooke.'

They settled into silence as the busy road turned into a busier motorway. Last night, Libby had told Claire about the job. Her friend responded as if she'd won the lottery. 'It's just an improv gig,' she'd replied. Claire, however, had acted as if they'd just discovered Libby was the heir to a small European principality.

And now she was here, trying to imagine being Henry's real girlfriend. But each time she pictured the two of them together, a stone wall appeared between them, and a sign appeared on her side informing her that peasants would be shot on sight if caught trespassing. It felt like being back with Giles.

Henry's car was a perfect example of how different his life was from hers. He drove a smart, navy BMW. The seats were leather and the interior was immaculate. Every one of her friends' cars had dust over the dash, dirt and grit in the footwells and rubbish stashed in the door recesses. Henry's car was like its owner—far too nice to touch.

'I'm sorry,' he began. 'I haven't asked you more about Lucas's opening night.'

'Oh, yes.'

The memory of his show sat in Libby's guts like a bad meal that reminded you of its presence days later. Her emotions had been bouncing between anger, embarrassment and grief. Why had she been so stupid?

'Was it a success? Did he get many sales?'

'I don't know.'

'Oh.'

Silence.

Henry tried again. 'Was his work abstract? Figurative? Conceptual? He said it was about creation and the divine feminine?'

Libby swallowed to keep her nausea down. 'Er, yes. It was, erm, divinely feminine.'

'That sounds lovely,' he said with enthusiasm. 'Were they religious paintings? Portraits?'

Images flashed across her mind, like a perverted slide show. How on earth could she tell him?

'Landscapes?' he continued, sounding unsure in the face of her silence. 'Still life—'

'Vag—vulvas. He painted vulvas. Each piece was a different woman's vulva.' *Stop saying vulva!*

'Oh. Um, er—'

'None of them was mine.'

Henry focused back on the road. 'Were you, er, aware of the content of his exhibition?'

'No.'

More silence.

He cleared his throat. 'Oh, I forgot to ask,' he said with the kind of fake jollity she was used to hearing at improv workshops from panicked participants. 'Did you pack your best friend?'

What, Claire? Confused, she glanced at him. His smile looked forced.

'Serafina. I can't wait to meet her.'

She scrunched her hands into fists. *Do not cry!*

'Libby?'

She nodded as if that would negate the need for speech.

'Is everything okay?'

Her lower lip was trembling as she took a shaky breath. 'She's d—dead,' she whispered.

From Henry's reaction it was as if she'd lost a close family member. 'Oh god, Libby. I'm so sorry! What happened?'

'Our upstairs neighbour, got, got a bit drunk,' she hiccupped, trying to tell him the story, but being waylaid by gulping sobs as the emotion and exhaustion of the last week came tumbling out.

'Hang on, there's a services up ahead. I'm pulling in.'

As Henry indicated and moved into the left lane, Libby recounted what had happened. By the time the car eased to a halt she was in full sob mode, letting the pain of Serafina's demise engulf her.

He pulled a handkerchief out of his jacket pocket and gave it to her.

'I'm so sorry,' he said.

She blew her nose and nodded. She didn't know what to say next, and embarrassment was starting to replace some of the grief.

'So where are you and India going to live now?'

'India's staying with her parents until her shoot in Morocco. I'll find somewhere else soon.'

'So, you're homeless, most of your belongings have been trashed and Serafina is no more?'

She nodded again.

His left knee was bobbing up and down. He splayed his fingers and pressed his hand onto his thigh to stop the movement.

'Would you like a coffee?' he asked.

She reached for her bag and he brought his hand towards hers, stopping abruptly before he touched her.

'Libby. As per our agreement, all expenses for this trip are to be carried by me.'

'Are you sure?' Her voice sounded weak and uncertain.

'Absolutely. I take this contract extremely seriously. My word is my bond.'

She glanced at him. He looked so earnest and serious she wasn't sure whether she wanted to cry at his sweetness or laugh.

'Henry.'

The worry lines in his forehead deepened. 'Yes?'

She wiggled her eyebrows. 'Just now, you nearly touched me. I don't have my regulation ruler to hand... but that was definitely less than eight inches.'

He shifted his whole body closer to the driver door. 'I'm so sorry, Libby. It won't happen again.'

She reached across to squeeze his hand and smiled.

He stared at it.

'Henry, I was joking. It's all good. I promise. Now, let's go and get some caffeine.'

An hour and a half later, they'd left the motorway behind and were whizzing along the A303 through Salisbury Plain. The undulating fields stretched away on either side of the road, the golden heads of sun-ripened wheat swirling as the breeze brushed past them in waves. Libby couldn't help but stare. After a life spent in cities with the view shortened by buildings, here her gaze could travel to the horizon.

'It's so beautiful,' she murmured. 'I haven't spent much time in the countryside.'

'Where was the last rural place you visited?' Henry asked.

She thought. 'Does a walk around Cobham in Surrey with India count?'

'Did you encounter any mud? Any dung?'

'No.'

He grinned. 'Not really the countryside, then.'

Libby shuddered. She knew she liked the *idea* of the countryside. However, this was always through the lens of whichever Austen adaptation she was watching at the time. It was easy to indulge a bucolic fantasy when snuggled up under a blanket with a takeaway pizza and bottle of wine from the off-licence around the corner.

'You look worried,' Henry said.

'I'm not sure if the countryside and I will really get along.'

'It's only for a few days and you don't have to leave the Manor if you don't feel like it.'

She stared past him out of the window. 'Oh my god, is that Stonehenge?'

He glanced to the right. 'Sorry, I forgot to mention we were going to pass it.'

'Wow. It's real.'

He laughed. 'It is.'

'Can we visit on the way home? If there's time?'

Henry looked happy. 'Yes, of course.'

Libby smiled back. Leaving London behind she was beginning to feel more like herself. This job may be slightly terrifying, but it was also exciting. Everything was going to be fine.

Until it wasn't.

The nerves started to bite as soon as they turned off the A36 and the roads became narrower.

Within ten minutes they'd crawled to a stop behind a slow-moving wall of Friesian heifers. As the first waves of *Eau de Countryside* assaulted her olfactory nerves, Libby grabbed Henry's handkerchief and held it to her nose.

'Er, sorry, hang on,' he said, tapping the aircon's recirculate button on the dashboard.

The action didn't seem to make any difference to the overwhelming stench.

One of the farmers, dressed in dirty blue overalls and shit-stained wellington boots did a double-take when he saw them and strode forward. Henry wound the window down.

'Henry! How be on, young 'un?'

The man appeared to be in his sixties, with ruddy cheeks and grey hair sticking straight up. Under his overalls he wore a red t-shirt consisting of more holes than fabric.

He leant down and shook Henry's hand, then peered in at Libby. She brought the handkerchief away from her face. The smell was unreal.

'Eh up, and who's this lovely young lady then?'

Henry cleared his throat. 'This is my girlfriend, Libby,' he said confidently. 'Libby, meet Richard Rogers, one of the farmers in the area.'

She smiled and waved, trying to breathe as little air as possible.

'Well, well, well, three holes in the ground.' Richard shook his head. 'You staying long?'

'Until Tuesday,' Henry replied.

Up ahead, the cows were squelching their way into a field.

'Right you are then.' Richard glanced across at her. 'First time meeting the family?'

She nodded.

He let out a bellow of laughter. 'Good luck.' He patted the side of their car then jogged down the road after the cows, giving Henry and Libby a wave as they drove slowly past.

Henry pulled the collar of his shirt away from his neck. 'They're not that bad, I promise.'

'The cows or your family?' she joked weakly.

He shrugged in response.

There was nothing he could do or say now to calm the butterflies in Libby's stomach. The flapping of their wings increased to a frantic thrum when they drove through the centre of Foxbrooke. The high street was old and chocolate-box quaint, built from Cotswold stone. There were no chain shops or coffee houses. It was so different from London.

'We have a Costa Coffee in the Precinct centre, which is behind the high street,' Henry said, as if reading her mind. 'And a small Co-Op. But if you want a larger supermarket, you have to head to Bath or south towards Midsomer Norton and Paulton.'

He turned right down a narrow street lined with small cottages on either side.

'They're so pretty,' she said, her voice breathy.

Henry stopped the car and pointed to a tall and crumbling ruin behind the row of houses on the left.

'That's a folly, built by my great, great, great grandfather so he didn't have to look at any of the poor people who lived here. He didn't think the houses were particularly pretty.'

'Bloody hell.'

'Welcome to the aristocracy,' he replied with a roll of his eyes. 'Okay, so we're nearly there. You ready?'

Libby nodded.

Henry eased the car forward into a large open space, half filled with cars facing a church.

'That's Saint Saviour's. Believe it or not, my family are heavily involved in the church. Well, mainly my grandmother. Although she seems to be at war with the new vicar.'

'Oh dear, is he too radical?'

'*She*, and yes, a bit. My twin, Estelle, is good friends with her. Explains a lot as far as I'm concerned.'

He swung the car left between massive stone pillars that flanked the entrance to a long drive.

'And this is Foxbrooke Manor.'

$$\mathbf{10}$$

'*This* is your home?' Libby croaked.

No amount of googling could have prepared her for the size and drama of the place. Nor how small she suddenly felt.

'No,' Henry replied. 'My home is in London.'

Built in fifteen eighty-two on the site of the King of Wessex's summer palace, Foxbrooke Manor was a three storey, double-fronted building with two large wings projecting from the front. The roof was gabled, and extensive modernisation had been undertaken since the eighteen hundreds by Capability Brown and John Nash. How did someone as ordinary as her fit in here? Even for a few days?

Come on, Libby! You've performed for Prince William before. If you can handle the future king of England, you can cope with a long weekend at Foxbrooke.

Henry was glancing around. 'At least no-one's here to greet us. I'll take you to your room and give you a tour, then we'll see who's about.'

She bit her lip. 'Okay. We can do this.'

He parked around the side of the Manor and they got out. Used to her boots and the solidity of London pavements, Libby found the hard, sandy surface strange under her ballet pumps. She'd decided that her alter ego had a boho chic dress sense and so spent some of Henry's advance on a wardrobe from upmarket charity shops. Her Doctor Martens had been left behind at Claire's. Footwear like that belonged at Foxbrooke even less than she did.

Henry opened the boot and lifted their bags. 'The quickest way to your room is through the front door, so we'll go that way.' Libby went to take hers from him, but he shook his head. 'I'll carry the bags and you carry me.'

'Figuratively?'

'Most definitely. You could always try and pick me up, but I'm quite heavy.'

'And don't forget, lifting wasn't in the contract, either.'

He frowned, as if considering this an omission that needed to be rectified.

'Henry...'

They grinned at each other and her heart fluttered. India and Claire were right. Henry was ridiculously good-looking when grumpy, but when he smiled, he was so beautiful she didn't want to take her eyes off him.

Behind her she heard loud barking.

Henry dropped the bags and lunged forward.

'Caligula! Borgia! No!' a man shouted. Libby turned to see two hounds of hell leaping towards her, their tongues flapping out of their mouths like scarves caught in the door of a moving car, and spittle flying from their glistening teeth.

'Get back here! Heel!'

She caught a glimpse of a man running after them just before Henry pushed her out of the way, holding his arms wide.

The dogs launched themselves forward, hitting him square in the chest and knocking him to the ground.

He didn't move.

They continued barking and drooling. One of them now had Henry's head in its massive jaws.

Libby screamed.

'It's okay! They're only playing.' The man leaned over Henry, tugging on the dog's collars. 'Come on, you daft buggers, get off him.'

She ran to Henry's side as the hounds were pulled away. He looked like he was trying to speak, but only wheezing sounds were coming out of his mouth.

'Henry! Oh my god, are you okay?' She helped him sit. 'Have you punctured a lung?'

He shook his head. 'Winded,' he whispered.

'Ha! See, right as rain.' The man turned back to the dogs. 'Who's good doggies? Who's a little over-excited to see our Henry? Yes, you are. Oh yes, you are!'

Henry got to his feet, wiping drool off his face and brushing the dirt off his navy suit. He looked like a model who'd been attacked by a water blaster, then pushed into a sandpit.

'Libby.' He straightened his spine. 'I'd like to present my father, Arthur.'

'Henry! Henry, my darling!'

A woman was running towards them, arms outstretched. Libby blinked. What *was* she wearing? She reached them and grabbed Henry's head, kissing him full on the lips.

'You're home!' she cried.

'And my mammy,' Henry continued, his face tense. 'Dervla.'

'You must be Libby!' Dervla pushed her messy blonde hair out of her eyes. 'Oh, aren't you a beauty!' She clasped her hands to her chest and glanced at Arthur. 'Isn't she a beauty, darling?'

She didn't wait for an answer, drawing Libby in for a hug. 'Come to Mammy.'

Libby was engulfed in a large bosom and the smell of patchouli. The fear of asphyxiation heightened as another set of arms clasped her tightly.

'Welcome to the family, my dear,' barked Arthur.

'Dad! Mammy! Get off her! Please!'

Libby gulped in a breath as she was released.

Dervla's brow furrowed. 'Are you faint? Do you want something to drink? The loo?'

'I think maybe we should just go straight to our room,' Henry said.

'Nonsense!' replied his father. 'Estelle's on her way, and Summer's around somewhere. Libby needs to meet the family.'

Libby stood in silence as Henry argued with two thirds of his parents. Despite the dirt on his clothes, he was dressed immaculately. Arthur and Dervla looked like they'd raided the dressing-up box at a hippy commune.

From the waist down, Arthur could have passed for a member of the upper-class, with his faded coral-red chinos and battered leather deck shoes. However, from the waist up it was a different matter. Both his ears were pierced, his neck was adorned with an array of necklaces and prayer beads, and his sun-browned chest was bare. The only piece of clothing on his top half was a waistcoat made from patches of brightly coloured fabric and small mirrors.

His wife's ensemble appeared demure at first glance, however the illusion was broken when Libby realised that she could see Dervla's leopard-print thong and breasts swaying underneath her clothing, which seemed to consist solely of translucent tie-dyed scarves.

Henry was looking increasingly irate, gesticulating with one hand, the other alternating between rubbing the back of his neck and pinching the bridge of his nose.

'Arthur, Dervla,' Libby said loudly.

Everyone stopped talking.

She smiled. 'It has been a long drive, and I would dearly love to freshen up. Might I do that before we meet the rest of the family?'

'Yes! Yes, of course, darling.' Dervla took her hand. 'But please, you must call me Mammy. I don't think anyone calls me Dervla except for Arthur's mother and the vicar.'

'And excuse us jabbering on,' added Arthur. 'It's just so wonderful to have Henry back and to meet you.'

They led Libby through the front door into a hallway big enough to contain the whole of India's destroyed flat. It was panelled in dark wood up to the high ceiling, and an ornate staircase started on the far right hand side and looped up to the first floor. Libby wanted to stop and gape, but Henry strode ahead up the stairs with their bags. Arthur glanced at Dervla, winked and gestured with his head towards him.

'Someone's keen to get to the bedchamber,' he whispered loudly.

Henry stiffened but didn't slow his pace. Libby caught him up and followed him along corridors until they came to an old wooden door. His shoulders relaxed as he touched the handle.

'Dad, Mammy, thank you. We'll come and find you in a bit.'

'Oh no!' Dervla cried. 'We want to show you your room.'

He tensed. 'Not necessary, we'll be fine.'

'Nonsense, son,' Arthur replied. 'We've got a surprise for you both!'

'You haven't removed the lock again, have you?'

His father waved his fingers as if to dismiss the concern. 'This is a family home, not a bloody hotel. No locks are necessary. If you want privacy, you know the drill.'

Henry bowed his head.

'Sock on the door handle,' Arthur said out of the corner of his mouth to Libby. 'Tea or coffee in the morning?'

'Er, tea?'

'Dad! No!'

Huh?

Arthur raised his hands. 'Okay, okay.'

Libby glanced at Henry and raised her eyebrows in question. He gave a tiny shake of his head.

'Okay, you two lovebirds,' said Dervla. 'In you go.'

Henry put their bags down and opened the door for her.

'You aren't going to carry her over the threshold?' Arthur asked.

'I, er, wasn't planning to.'

'My god! What's wrong with you, boy?'

'I am a bit heavy,' Libby said, hoping to deflect his father's attention.

Arthur looked her up and down, his forehead furrowing. 'Rot! You're a slip of a thing.'

Henry was looking longingly at the open door, as if sanctuary was only a small step away.

Libby tentatively touched his arm. 'I don't mind if you carry me in. Only if you want to, of course.'

He closed his eyes briefly and exhaled, then lifted her into his arms. She reflexively held around the back of his neck.

Their eyes met.

Libby was suddenly aware of just how close they were. How much of him was currently touching her. Henry's eyes were dark and she couldn't see anything but them. He blinked and the sweep of his long lashes sent a tremor through her.

Loud clapping from Arthur and Dervla broke the moment.

Henry blinked again and readjusted his features to those of a man one step away from disowning his parents.

He carried her into the room then stopped, his mouth hanging open.

In the centre of the room was an enormous four poster bed. It was modern, created from strips of pale, cream-coloured wood that had been steamed and shaped into sinuous, sensuous curves. The four posts were interwoven spirals, reaching up like spires to touch the ceiling. Each point supported a gauzy white canopy that draped over the bed. Each side was separated in half, the sections tied to the posts with white silk ribbons. A white coverlet embroidered with cream thread lay on top. It was strewn with hundreds of rose petals.

Libby gasped. 'That's the most beautiful thing I've ever seen.'

'That's not my bed,' said Henry.

Dervla stepped forward and untied a thick ribbon from one of the posts. She wrapped it around both of her hands and tugged, demonstrating how strong it was.

'Dual purpose,' she said with a wink.

Henry ignored her and gently let Libby to the floor. Her legs wobbled and her hand shot out to steady herself.

'Thank you,' he said stiffly. 'It is very lovely. And I look forward to, er, sleeping in it.'

Dervla retied the ribbon. 'Or not...'

Henry took one of his bags from his father and placed it on a wooden dresser, then cleared his throat. 'Okay. Thank you both very much. We're going to unpack now.' He unzipped his bag with a flourish.

'But you haven't seen the bathroom!' said Dervla.

'What bathroom?'

'This bathroom!' said his father, triumphantly, pushing open a door. 'We've re-modelled that ghastly old playroom of yours and turned it into a place to bathe, pamper and play.

Come take a look!'

Libby's feet were lead as she followed Henry into the adjoining room.

'His and hers sinks,' said Dervla. 'A party-sized rainforest shower with extra detachable heads—'

'Very powerful,' said Arthur. 'Got your mom off within five minutes.'

'And a two-person jacuzzi with ten speeds,' Dervla continued.

'Got your mammy off within—'

'My old daybed? Where is it?' Henry asked, as if refusing to believe what was in front of his eyes.

'Eh? Whatcha worried about that old thing for?' replied his father. 'We chucked it. Sodding squirrel got in the window anyway and tore it to bloody pieces over the winter.'

Henry bent over one of the sinks, his hands gripping the edge of the basin.

'Come on, Arthur. Let's leave these two to enjoy themselves.' Dervla took his hand and led him out of the room.

'Don't do anything we wouldn't do,' his father called out before Libby heard the bedroom door close.

Henry sat on the edge of the jacuzzi, his head in his hands.

'I'm so sorry, Libby.'

They'd been at the Manor less than ten minutes and he already looked broken. Libby touched his shoulder.

'Bloody squirrels,' she said. 'That's another black mark against them. I'll have to add "daybed destroyer" to the song.'

He stood, a muscle twitching in his jaw. 'I'll find another room tonight. From tomorrow I'll sort somewhere else. I can sleep in the car, find a sofa, sleep outside maybe? It's warm enough.'

'Henry—'

'And I need to amend the contract.' He strode out of the bathroom.

Libby followed.

Grabbing the contract and a pen from his bag, Henry swept the rose petals off the bed and sat with a thump.

'If only I could have a contract for my parents,' he

muttered, flipping through the pages. 'They *promised* they would dress appropriately and act normal. The bloody dogs are more obedient than they are.'

'They *were* wearing clothes.'

'Barely.'

'And they're just excited you're here and have a, er...'

'Fake girlfriend?'

She nodded. The bedroom situation was the least of their worries. She was more concerned with Henry's state of mind. She was beginning to understand why he'd been so reluctant to bring a girlfriend home before.

'Thank god this *is* all an act,' he grumbled. 'If you were real, you'd already be out of the door.' He scribbled notes on the contract. 'I'm adding "lifting".' He flipped back, turned the pages ninety degrees and began a drawing of the new bedroom and bathroom in the margins.

'Henry, you really don't have to do this.'

He looked at her, his face tight with tension. 'I do, Libby. Right now, this is the only thing I have control over and I'm not breaking my word. Why don't you unpack whilst I finish this?'

She glanced around the room. 'Which wardrobe should I use?'

He waved his hand. 'Any of them. I'll fit around you.'

Which one should she pick? The furniture was older than the average London flat, and the room had a footprint twice the size. Henry put the papers down, went to the nearest wardrobe and opened the door with a creak.

'I haven't used any of them for years.' He pushed a few coats to one end. 'Plenty of room here.' He moved to a chest of drawers, pulling socks and boxer shorts from the top two drawers to stuff in the bottom one. 'Is that enough space?'

Libby nodded, her cheeks heating at the sight of his underwear.

He cleared his throat. 'Sorry. I'm being insensitive. I'll give you five minutes.'

He bolted out the door, closing it behind him before she could reply.

Libby let out a breath. Henry was clearly stressed to the point of snapping. She'd spent plenty of her adult life around crazy creative types and was used to nudity. But the fact that Henry was so straight-laced and his parents so bohemian made the contrast between them that much starker.

She quickly unpacked, then opened the door. Henry was standing at the end of the corridor in front of a large window that looked out onto parkland, his arm raised as if waving to someone outside.

'Henry?'

He turned. 'All done?'

She nodded. 'What should we do now?'

'Are you hungry?'

'Not really.' She scrunched up her nose. 'I'm too nervous. Do you want to get something to eat?'

He shook his head. 'I'll wait till dinner. Do you want to meet my twin sister?'

'Estelle?'

'She's just arrived. You're going to have to meet so many people over the next few days, you might as well get this one out of the way.'

Libby swallowed.

'Oh no, don't worry, she's lovely,' Henry said in a rush. 'My siblings are not like my parents, I promise.'

She let out a breath and forced a smile. 'Okay.'

. . .

HENRY LED THE WAY DOWNSTAIRS. THE MANOR WAS SO BIG Libby felt like she needed to leave a trail of breadcrumbs in order to find her way back to their room.

'Estelle runs a livery stable on the other side of the park and helps manage the estate,' he said, as they went down yet another corridor lined with oil paintings. 'She rides here and back. She says it's quicker and better for the environment than using her Land Rover.'

Libby nodded, trying to stay cool and hoping they'd steer well clear of any horses. She'd only ever seen one in person once and had been petrified at the size and power of it.

They exited the side of the Manor into a cobbled courtyard surrounded by double-height buildings.

'This is the old stables and the carriage house,' Henry said. 'But Estelle still uses them.'

A horse whinnied loudly and Libby's hand shot out and grabbed his. 'Hell no to the neigh,' she muttered.

Henry froze, then folded his larger hand around her smaller one as if to reassure her.

'It's okay. You don't have to go near him.'

Inside the stables a horse's backside poked out from behind a stall. Its tail lifted and it deposited a steaming pile of manure onto the stone floor. An English Setter was lying nearby and a small, fluffy black dog was sniffing around.

'Duke, seriously?' came a voice from behind the wooden partition.

The horse whinnied in response and Libby clutched Henry's hand a little tighter.

A shovel appeared, followed by a woman. She scooped up the poo, then turned to face them. So, this was Henry's sister.

Estelle was as beautiful as Henry was gorgeous, with the same high cheekbones, amber brown eyes and dark skin as her twin. But where his hair was cropped short, hers was long, the black curls tied back in a loose ponytail. She was nearly as tall as her brother, with a figure that seemed to be designed to bring men to their knees. Tight fawn jodhpurs clung to her curves and knee-high black riding boots gave the illusion of never-ending legs. A crisp white shirt caressed her upper half, the top buttons undone to allow for her cleavage. She looked like a centrefold model from *Country Life* Magazine. Libby tried hard not to stare.

'Oh.' Estelle's gaze moved from their faces to their clasped hands. Henry let go.

'Hi,' said Libby. 'I'm—'

'Hang on.' Estelle jogged past them. 'This was not the first impression I was hoping for.' A ball of dung fell off the shovel. She kicked it forward like a football without breaking stride, then disappeared around the corner, followed by the fluffy dog.

Libby glanced at Henry. 'There's a lot of poo in the countryside.'

'I fear you have witnessed a disproportionate amount this afternoon.'

She smiled. 'Do you ride as well?'

'Yes, although I haven't for a long time.'

Her heart beat faster at the idea of Henry on a horse, dressed like Mr Darcy. 'Do you wear boots like Estelle's?'

He nodded, and her heart sped up to a gallop.

'Do you ride?' he asked.

She shook her head.

'I can take you if you fancy it?'

Ohmygod, ohmygod, ohmygod.

He frowned. 'Are you too hot? Would you like a glass of cold water?'

Cold water? Right now, she needed a cold shower.

'Right! All sorted.' Estelle strode towards them, wiping her hands on her jodhpurs. She extended her hand towards Libby. 'It's clean, I promise. I just washed them under the outside tap.' She gave Libby's hand a bone-crunching shake. 'I'm Estelle. But it doesn't take a genius to work that out.' She pointed at the English Setter. 'That's Joy, and—' She looked around and whistled.

The black fluffy dog re-appeared, a massive and very dead rat in its mouth.

'This is Chester.' Estelle knelt. 'Who's a good boy? Yes, you's a good boy! Well done, Chester-Chops! You going to eat that now?'

Chester dropped the rat at her feet.

'Fair enough, can't really blame you.' She stood and booted the rat to the wall, then turned her attention back to Libby. 'Don't worry, I'll deal with it later.' Estelle put her hands on her hips. 'Look, I need to make a few things clear from the get-go. Our parents are fucking mental, but we love them. We can slag them off to Bath and back, but you can't say a word against any of them. Ever. Okay?'

Libby shut her mouth and nodded in quick succession as Henry cried, 'Estelle!'

She ignored her brother. 'And that goes for the rest of us too. If you don't like us, keep it to yourself or fuck off.'

Bloody hell. Henry's sister wasn't taking any prisoners.

'Estelle! Shut up!'

'But you can say what you like about Cousin Rupert,' she continued, 'he's a right twat. Oh, and Julian, Cousin Catherine's husband, too. Don't go anywhere near him after he's had a few. Bloody perve.'

'Estelle! Fuck's sake—'

She held up her hands. 'Okay, okay, I'll back off, little bro.' Her frown turned into a beaming smile, and she pulled

Libby into a hug. 'Welcome to the family.' She disengaged, grabbed Libby's arm and dragged her out of the stables. 'You can meet Duke later if you're interested in horses. All the best people are. Well, apart from Rupert and Julian. Do you ride?'

Libby shook her head and glanced over her shoulder at Henry as he followed with the two dogs. He mouthed '*sorry*'.

'I'll fix that,' Estelle continued. 'I run a stable. Anyway, I wanted to meet you before everyone else so I could break you in gently.'

Gently? 'Er—'

'Have you met any of the family yet?'

'Your dad and mammy,' she replied as she was frogmarched across the courtyard, her feet doing two steps for every one of Estelle's.

'Were they wearing clothes?'

'Mostly.'

Estelle nodded. 'Well, that's progress. Anyway, my mom can be a little overbearing, and Gram-Gram is a veritable dragon. Kind of like Voldemort in a dress. But underneath the snark, there's a heart of gold. Connor, Leo and Willow are relatively normal. Summer is so full of herself she might explode, and Henry is less flexible than a straight-jacket. But you knew that already.'

She stopped abruptly and faced Libby, gripping her upper arms.

'You're the first outsider any of us have ever brought home, and you need to know we're very protective of each other. But thank you for being here and for putting up with my brother. Do you like Chelsea buns?'

'What?'

'Chelsea buns. They're like cinnamon rolls but glazed and made with dried fruit and mixed spice. Perry, our cook, makes the best ones ever and brought some out of the oven twenty minutes ago.'

Libby caught Henry's eye and the corner of her mouth turned up.

'What?' Estelle asked.

Henry cleared his throat. 'Apparently Libby thinks I'm like a cinnamon roll.'

His sister blinked, then burst out laughing. 'Overly sweet, a bit doughy in the middle and lacking spice? Yep, that sounds about right.'

Libby's cheeks flushed. Estelle may have said that she was allowed to slag her family off, but Libby wasn't putting up with any criticism of Henry, fake boyfriend or not.

She squared up to Estelle. 'I'll have you know that Henry is hotter than a Habanero and spicier than a street market in Marrakesh.' She lifted her chin. 'And there's nothing wrong with being sweet. I'll take sweet over sour any day of the week.' She planted her hands on her hips. 'And whilst I'm at it, I won't hear a word said against Henry. Ever. Okay?'

There was a stunned silence and her eyes darted between the Foxbrooke twins. They were mirror images, with wide eyes and open mouths as they stared at her.

Estelle was the first to break, bursting into peals of laughter. She hugged Libby tightly, lifting her off the ground. 'Oh, you're just too adorable for words!' Her two dogs barked in agreement. She let Libby back down, but kept a tight grip on her shoulder as she propelled her towards the side of the house. 'Honestly, I don't know how he managed to bag someone as interesting as you—'

'What—'

'Oops. Sorry, force of habit. I'm sure you're simply perfect for each other. True love and all that bollocks.' Estelle pushed open a door. 'Right, Libby Bennet, it's time to follow your nose. And this time it's not dung you're smelling, but freshly baked buns.'

'Perry!' Estelle cried as she led the way into the kitchen. The room was large and ancient, with a big open fireplace that was used in the past to roast whole animals. Libby tried not to gawp. The kitchen appliances were modern, and light streamed in through the window onto the marble countertops.

In the centre of the room was an enormous prep area with a butcher's block at one end and a stainless-steel table at the other. Sitting on the top was a plate containing two marrow bones and another containing a pile of Chelsea buns. Estelle tossed the bones into the old fireplace for Chester and Joy, then bit into a bun.

'Perry,' she groaned. 'You're the best.'

A woman in her late fifties, her dyed blonde hair tied back in a ponytail, was untying an apron. It had the words 'cook knows best' printed on the front. She took it off and held her arms out to Henry.

'Come here, love.'

He leaned down to hug her. 'Hello, Perry. It's good to see you.'

She grabbed his cheeks. 'Not as good as it is to see you, young man.' She looked past him at Libby and smiled. 'And you must be Libby Bennet.'

Libby smiled in return, but her stomach was knotted with anxiety. Every time someone referred to her as Libby Bennet, it reminded her of all the lies she was telling.

Henry drew his shoulders back. 'Yes, this is my g-girlfriend, Libby. Libby, this is Jan Perry, who has been the cook here for as long as I can remember.'

'G-girlfriend?' said Estelle. 'It sounds like you c-can't b-believe it.'

Jan tutted. 'Less of that, young lady. You're just jealous that Henry has finally found love.'

'Barf,' Estelle replied. 'Don't put me off my b-buns.'

Jan ignored her and hugged Libby. 'You can call me Jan or Perry, like everyone else. Sit down and help yourself.'

Henry pulled out a chair for her and she sat as Perry placed a bun on a plate. 'Tuck in while they're warm. Cup of tea?'

Libby nodded. 'Thank you.'

She peeled back a strip of bun, tore it off and placed it in her mouth. The spice and fruit zinged on her tongue and her stomach decided that lying to nice people was okay as long as freshly baked Chelsea buns were consumed at the same time.

Henry took a seat and held his bun up to hers as if making a toast.

'Congratulations,' he said. 'Not counting animals, that's four family members down and you're still alive.'

She tapped her bun against his and smiled.

'How are they?' Perry asked her. 'Up to London standards?'

'You must know they're a million times better,' Libby replied. 'I've only tried to make them once with my sourdough starter, but they didn't work very well.'

'Ah, they do take a fair amount of yeast. Did you prove them long enough?'

'Three hours?'

Perry shook her head, her face scrunched as if biting into a lemon. 'Not long enough, love. Weather dependent, I'd give them twice that. Have another go and let me know how you get on. I don't have a starter myself or we could have tried it.'

Libby swallowed the lump in her throat. Out of everything that had recently happened to her, the loss of Serafina was hardest to come to terms with. As silly as she knew it was, it felt like she'd lost a friend.

Henry was watching her, concern in his eyes. He reached across the table towards her, then stopped, his hand approximately eight inches away.

His sister rolled her eyes. 'Don't stop your PDA on my account. This place is hardly a convent.'

'A convent? Now that *would* be fun,' came an American accent as Henry and Estelle's mother swept into the room.

Libby stood, trying not to choke, as the face she'd admired advertising Chanel in Vogue and starring in Hollywood films directed its focus on her. Unlike most actors, Vivienne was taller and more stunning in real life. She was dressed in a red playsuit, the front of the top split from navel to neck.

Henry pushed back his chair to stand by Libby's side. 'Mom—'

'You must be Elizabeth.' Vivienne's eyes flicked over Libby as she extended a manicured hand.

Libby fought her legs as they demanded she curtsey. 'Please, call me Libby,' she managed to reply.

Vivienne drew her in, kissing her on both cheeks. 'I'm so glad to find you're real. Please, sit. Don't let me stop you.'

'Can I get you a plate, Vivienne?' Perry asked.

She passed a hand over her flat stomach. 'No, thank you, Perry. I'll wait until dinner.'

Vivienne's gaze drifted to her daughter. Estelle took another Chelsea bun and crammed as much as she could into her mouth.

Vivienne turned her attention back to Libby. 'I'm so looking forward to getting to know you better over dinner. And finding out everything about the publishing world. Arthur will tell you all about his autobiography as soon as he gets the chance. It's illustrated.' She looked at Henry. 'Did you like your new bathroom, honey? And the bed?'

Estelle rolled her eyes as Henry swallowed. 'Thanks, Mom. It's, er, very nice.'

'Well...' His mother lowered her voice. 'I'm sure you're gonna enjoy christening it later.' She winked at Libby, then turned on her heels. 'Have fun, kids. See you at dinner,' she said, sashaying out of the room.

❧ 12 ❧

Libby stared at her reflection in the mirror as the sound of a gong reverberated along the corridor. A few seconds later there was a tentative knock on the door from outside.

'Two secs,' she called out.

This was it. Game face on. Time for Elizabeth Bennet to meet the family.

She was wearing her favourite yellow dress, paired with the annoyingly insubstantial ballet pumps. Her make-up was light and the only jewellery was a bright necklace made from cloth beads, which Claire had given her. Libby hoped it wasn't too wacky for an upper-class girl who worked for a publishing company.

After the double whammy of Estelle and Vivienne, she'd escaped to Henry's room and he'd left her in peace and quiet for a few hours. She was exhausted but still had to face the rest of his siblings and his grandmother. When she opened the door, Henry retreated to the far wall of the corridor.

'Do you want to use the room?' she asked.

'If you don't mind? I won't be long.'

As he came forward, she stepped back, maintaining the distance between them.

He cleared his throat. 'Libby,' he began, then paused.

'Yes?' *Oh shit.* Was something wrong?

'I hope you don't take offence, as that is not my intention...'

Bloody hell. She knew the necklace was a step too far.

'And I never want to make you feel uncomfortable—'

Her hand moved to her throat. 'Sorry, I'll take it off.'

'What?'

'The necklace.'

He raised his hand. 'What? No, please. It's fine. That's not—'

'What should I change? I'm sorry, I thought I'd pitched it right.'

'Don't change anything.'

'Then what's wrong?'

Henry gazed at her in confusion. 'Nothing.'

'Then why would you be about say something that would make me feel uncomfortable?'

He let out a breath, looking as agitated as she felt.

'Libby, you look lovely.'

'Oh.' Relief flooded her veins. 'Was that what you thought would offend me?'

'I take the contract between us extremely seriously.'

God, that *bloody* contract. She wanted to rip it to shreds.

'And my intentions remain, as ever, honourable.'

Of course they do.

'I just wanted to try and put you at ease, and reassure you politely, that—'

'Henry,' she interrupted.

'Yes?'

'Go and change.'

He nodded and entered the bedroom.

Libby let out a sigh and went to the end of the corridor. The Manor was on the very edge of Foxbrooke village, with the parkland extending on the other side. It was a bucolic dream, with gently sloping hills, stands of ancient oak trees and a lake glinting in the distance. This was a world for Elizabeth Bennet, not Libby Fletcher. Luckily, she knew how to talk to people... and more importantly, how to listen. She would draw conversation out of everyone she met and deflect attention from herself.

The door to their room opened and Henry stepped out.

Libby bit the inside of her cheek to stop herself drooling, wishing she could be biting into something taut, delectable and dressed in an impeccably tailored suit.

She strolled towards him, a frown on her face. 'Henry...'

'Yes?' He looked panicked, and she tried not to grin.

'I hope you don't take offence, as that is not my intention...'

His frown turned into a relieved smile and he held his arms out. 'Is this good enough for you?'

'It'll do. Where did you get it? Primani?'

'Er.'

She rolled her eyes. 'Of course, it's Armani.'

'Um, actually, this one's Gucci.'

Libby swished the skirts of her dress. 'Well, I'll have you know this little number is from Oxfam, so try and up your game next time, okay?'

Henry grinned. 'I will.' He inclined his head. 'Shall we?'

She nodded. 'Please don't leave my side tonight. I'm scared shitless about meeting the rest of your family.'

'I won't. I promise.'

'Can I hold your hand?'

He glanced down the empty corridor. 'What, now?'

'It would reassure me. As long as you don't mind?'

He shook his head and she took his hand. The warmth made her shiver.

'You okay?'

She nodded. 'Yep. Let's do this.'

ENTERING THE OPULENT DINING ROOM, LIBBY GRIPPED Henry's hand tighter. The room was full of beautiful people and their eyes were all on her. Estelle, now wearing a sleek black dress, rushed forward and bent slightly to whisper in her ear.

'Don't worry. I've told everyone you're gorgeous and perfect and to give you a break. I've also given Gram-Gram two sherries to soften her up.'

Estelle broke away, let out a loud chortle and slapped her thigh.

'Oh, Libby, you're the best!' she cried, then leant forward, whispering again. 'And the Oscar goes to—'

'Not you,' Henry muttered.

His sister stuck her tongue out at him then spun on her heels to address the room.

'Okay, Foxbrookes and friends. You know the rules. No gawking, no mauling, no propositions, and no inappropriate questions. No doubt Henry has drawn up a list of what he thinks *is* appropriate to talk about and will be passing it out shortly.'

Henry shook his head and led Libby over to a high-backed chair where an old lady was sitting, draped in jewels. Her back was ramrod straight, as if a poker was inbuilt into her genetic code, and her nose was large and aquiline. Despite her seated position, she still managed to look down it at Libby.

'Gram-Gram, I'd like you to meet Libby.'

'Humph.'

'Good evening, my lady,' Libby said. 'It's a pleasure to make your acquaintance. Henry has spoken many times about you.'

The tight wrinkles of her face relaxed slightly. '*Has* he indeed. And what has he said?'

'He said...' *Oh, shitsticks.*

Gram-Gram leaned forward. 'Yes...?'

'He said he reminded you of your firstborn son.'

There was an icy pause. 'In what way?'

'Your son, Henry, was thoughtful and polite, sensible and kind.' Libby glanced at Henry. 'Just like his nephew.'

The Dowager Duchess gazed with affection at her grandson. 'Yes. That is all true. My son was the finest of men, and Henry lives up to his name.'

Gram-Gram reached for his hand. 'Come here, darling boy.'

He kissed his grandmother, and her stern face softened into smiles.

'You will come and visit me outside of this circus?' she asked.

'Of course.'

'And bring Elizabeth with you.'

Henry looked confused. 'Elizab—'

Libby laughed. 'Are you so used to calling me Libby that you've forgotten what my real name is?'

'Oh yes. I have. Ha ha ha.'

Gram-gram stared at him askance. 'What *is* the matter with you, dear? You sound like your cousin, Rupert.' Her liquid blue eyes bore into Libby's. 'You'll meet my daughter's family tomorrow, and all the Americans.' She sniffed. 'I can't abide most of them. A bunch of braying half-wits on one side and the nouveau riche on the other flashing their wealth like it's some sort of competition.'

Libby's gaze drifted from the tiara on Gram-Gram's head, down past the necklaces, to the rocks on her fingers.

'Which of course, they could never hope to win,' she said, before thinking.

Henry's grip on her hand tightened.

Gram-Gram's eyes narrowed, then she barked out a laugh. 'Yes. Very true. There's no money like old money.' She looked past them and frowned. 'Marie?'

A woman in her forties, dressed in a plain suit, materialised by her side. 'Yes, ma'am.'

'To the table.'

As Marie helped Gram-Gram to her feet, Henry took her other arm.

She brushed him off. 'I'm not an invalid.' She eyeballed Libby. 'Make sure he brings you to the Dower House next week.'

LIBBY STAYED CLOSE TO HENRY'S SIDE AS HE INTRODUCED her to the rest of his brothers and sisters. He didn't hold her hand again and she didn't reach for his. Connor, the son Dervla had when she'd first met the Duke and Duchess, had black hair and piercing blue eyes, but his half-siblings from his mother were all fair. Leo was tall and blonde and had brought his best friend, Ella, to the dinner. Willow's hair was dyed blue, and Summer, the youngest of the family at twenty-one, had perfect blonde curls and the confidence to match her age, social status and beauty. She'd brought a friend with her, Jasmine, who tittered every time Henry said anything.

A loud rapping drew their attention. Gram-Gram was banging her cane on the floor.

'Come on. I haven't got all night.'

Henry led Libby to her setting, where the name 'Elizabeth

Bennet' was beautifully written on a piece of card. She sat between Henry and Connor. Opposite her was an empty space, then Estelle, who was sitting next to a stunning woman. She looked like Jessica Rabbit brought to life, with long deep red hair and a bright red dress. The woman waved to Libby across the ornate candlesticks and flowers that filled the centre of the table.

'Hi, you must be Libby. I'm Eveline. It's lovely to meet you.'

'Hi—'

'Guess what her job is,' Estelle interrupted.

Summer opened her mouth to speak, but Estelle turned to her across the empty setting between them.

'Shuddup, Summer. I hardly ever get a chance to play this game.'

Eveline smiled and shrugged as if reluctantly indulging Estelle.

Libby took her in. She was naturally stunning and voluptuous, and wasn't wearing much make-up. The red dress, though figure-hugging, did not show as much cleavage as Libby would have expected. Her nails were short and unpainted, and her only jewellery was a simple gold cross around her neck. Eveline was beautiful but didn't accentuate it, and by the excited glint in Estelle's eyes and the way everyone else had drawn forward, her job was unusual.

'Can I get three questions?' she asked.

Estelle huffed. 'Oh, go on then.'

'What's your job?' said Libby.

'Yes or no answers only!' half the table shouted.

She jumped in her seat. *Bloody hell.*

Someone to her right oinked like a pig.

'Leo! Shut-up!' Estelle huffed.

'Do you work with animals?

A collective 'ooh' ran around the table and Eveline put her head to one side.

'Part-time,' she replied.

'Yes, or no!' Estelle cried.

Okay, so probably not a farmer or a vet.

'Do you work in the village?'

'Yes.'

Libby looked at Estelle. 'Can I ask any more questions? This is impossible.'

'Yes,' said Eveline as Estelle said 'no'.

'Twenty?'

'Five more, and that's your lot,' Estelle replied.

Libby glanced at Henry. He mimed zipping his lips shut and she rolled her eyes.

'Okay. Is the "working with animals" bit a hobby?'

Eveline nodded.

'Are you a teacher?'

Her eyes widened a little as another 'ooh' went around the table.

'Some people might say that was an aspect of my job,' she replied. 'But I don't work in a school, college or university.'

'Yes, you do,' said Summer.

'Oh yes, sorry. I do teach at the local schools every week.'

'Three more questions!' said Estelle.

Libby looked around. Every face seemed like it was about to burst with excitement. Eveline's job must be super weird. Was she an extra wife of Henry's parents? No, he would have told her. The crucifix around her neck also implied she probably wouldn't be down with the idea of joining a three-way marriage with people a couple of decades older than her.

'How many people have the same job as you in the UK?'

'Hmmm. About eight thousand? Around two thousand of them are women.'

'Yes or no!' Estelle banged her knife on the table. 'Two questions left.'

'Is your job contentious?'

Eveline glanced across the table at Gram-Gram, who sniffed loudly and turned her head away.

'Sometimes.'

'One more!' Estelle cried.

Police officer? No. There would be way more than eight thousand in the UK. *Who else works in schools every week?*

She remembered Henry talking about Estelle's best friend and a light bulb went off in her head. 'Oh my god, are you the vicar?'

'Fuck's sake!' Estelle dropped her knife with a clatter. Everyone apart from Gram-Gram and Eveline cheered and clapped.

Eveline nodded. 'And part-time pig farmer.'

Holy shit. Libby was buzzing with questions. 'What's the most contentious part of your job?'

Eveline hesitated, looking across at Gram-Gram again.

'Where's the food? We're not waiting on that boy, are we?' Gram-Gram asked, loudly.

As if on cue, a man entered the room wearing a shirt that needed ironing.

'Sorry I'm late, everyone,' he said gruffly, taking the empty seat between Estelle and Summer, opposite Henry and Libby. He hugged Estelle. 'Happy almost-birthday, Stelle.'

Estelle ruffled his messy hair and poked his scruffy beard. 'Glad to see you made an effort.'

'It's a clean shirt.' He grinned, then leaned across the table to shake Henry's hand. 'Mate.' He smiled, 'it's been a while.' He turned his attention to Libby. 'Hi, you must be Libby? I'm Finn, Henry's first, and therefore the best, best friend.'

'Nice to meet you. Who's his second?'

'Jack,' Finn replied. 'He joined Foxbrooke Infants a week after us, so got second place.' He glanced at Henry. 'Is he coming this time?'

Henry shook his head.

'Finn.' Summer poked him in the ribs. 'Where's my hug?'

He turned towards her and hesitated, then patted her shoulder and smiled. 'Hey, Summer.'

She pouted. 'What's your costume for the party on Sunday?'

'I'm not going.'

'What? But you have to,' Summer whined. 'Everyone's going to be there. Don't be so fucking boring. You're as bad as Henry.'

'There's a costume party on Sunday night?' Libby asked.

'Yes,' replied Summer. 'Who are you going as?'

Libby glanced at Henry.

He shrugged. 'I didn't know. We don't have to dress up.'

'Ugh!' said Summer. 'Yes, you do.'

'Okay,' he replied. 'I'll go as a broker from the City.'

'No, you bloody won't,' said Estelle. 'You and Libby can come with me to the theatrical hire shop in Bath tomorrow and pick something out.'

Libby gazed at her place setting. *Elizabeth Bennet.* Could she go as the real Lizzie Bennet? Persuade Henry to dress as Mr Darcy?'

'Thank you,' she said, before Henry could protest. 'That would be lovely. I've always wanted to visit Bath.'

'Any particular bit?' Estelle asked, as waiters served their first course, a multi-layered terrine and salad.

'Anything Jane Austen related.'

'Oh, of course. Because of your name.'

'And she works in publishing,' Dervla added, from further

up the table. 'Libby, darling, you must speak to Arthur about his autobiography. It's illustrated.'

'But I can't get any of the buggers from the big five to take it on,' Arthur complained. 'No vision. It's a *Kama Sutra* for the modern age. Could be a bloody classic.'

'What about *your* publishing house?' Vivienne asked Libby. 'Can you speak to them about it?'

Gram-Gram cleared her throat. 'Ridiculous notion.'

'Could you?' Arthur asked.

'I'm not sure it would be a good fit,' she replied. 'Winterblossom Press publishes women's fiction, chick lit and romance novels only.'

'Plenty of romance in it, I can tell you,' said Arthur. 'With pictures.'

Libby felt Henry stiffen beside her.

'Dad,' he said. 'Your book is an autobiography. Winterblossom only publishes fiction.'

'I could change the name?' he suggested, a hopeful tone in his voice. 'How about *Sunny Spells and Snowdrops at Fluffy Bunny Farm?*'

Libby bit the inside of her cheek to stop a snort escaping. 'I don't think it would work. However, that is an excellent title for our target market.'

'That's how you met Henry, right?' Summer asked. 'At a book launch.'

'Yes, for *Springtime Kisses and Daffodil Wishes at the Little Cornish Cupcake Café on Mermaid's Cove*, by Polly Hart.'

'I love her books,' said Eveline. 'So romantic.'

Estelle pretended to gag on her terrine. 'Give me *Fifty Shades* any day of the week over that yawn-fest.'

'Have you even read any of her books?' Eveline asked.

Estelle shook her head. 'Don't need to. I'm judging them by their covers.'

'And when has that ever been a good idea?'

Estelle shrugged. 'Always works for me.' She turned back to Libby. 'Why are the titles of those books so long and sappy?'

'Our audience likes them.'

'But the covers are mainly words. If it's meant to be romance, then where are the people?'

'Our target market doesn't like figures on the front. We believe it's because they don't want anyone to know they're reading a romance novel.'

Estelle rolled her eyes.

'How do you come up with the titles?' Eveline asked.

'Oh, that's the fun part,' Libby replied. 'In the office we have a series of jars labelled with different categories. We've got one for seasons and holidays, one for greetings or physical contact, one for location, one for job, one for animals, one for dwelling, one for flowers, and so on. Whenever we need a new title, we just pick a word from each jar. It's easy.'

'What a lovely idea,' said Eveline.

Gram-Gram tutted. 'Preposterous.'

'So,' said Estelle, 'it would be something like *Summer Shagging at the Cockroach Café in Skegness?*'

Henry sighed. 'Estelle. Really?'

Libby couldn't help grinning. 'That's the general idea, but cockroaches have never taken off. Figuratively, of course. At the moment bees and beekeeping are very on-trend.'

'And squirrels?' Henry asked, a smile turning up the corners of his mouth.

She held his gaze. 'Squirrels are always popular.'

'Not here, they're not,' said Arthur. 'They're rats with fluffy tails.'

Henry's smile widened and her heart thumped faster in her chest.

'When are you going to shoot them?' Gram-Gram asked Estelle. 'They're causing untold damage to the arboretum.'

Estelle took a big glug of wine. 'I've been a bit busy recently,' she growled, then thumped her glass on the tablecloth.

Henry's smile faded, and he looked away.

❦ 13 ❦

Henry lay his cutlery down and ran his finger back and forth along the edge of the china plate. The food at Foxbrooke was always delicious, but sitting next to his fake girlfriend, and surrounded by his all-too-real family, he'd lost his appetite.

It wasn't just the fear of discovery that knotted his stomach. His sister's anger felt like a knife stabbing at his twisted gut. The bond he shared with his twin couldn't be broken, but over the last few years, when more responsibility for the estate had landed on her shoulders, it had become strained. Henry had spent his life distancing himself from Foxbrooke, from his parents and the expectations they had of him to run the estate. He loved his family but the scars from his upbringing ran deep. He wanted a life of order and calm, not chaos.

'You up for the pub on Tuesday?' Finn asked him as coffee and chocolates were served. 'It's quiz night.'

'I think we'll be back in London by then. Do you want us on your team?'

Finn pulled a face. 'Libby maybe, but not you. I'm in it to win it.'

'Jasmine and I will be on your team,' Summer said.

He shook his head, not meeting her eyes. 'No thanks.' He glanced across the table at Libby. 'What's your specialist subject?'

'I don't think I have one.'

'Books? Jane Austen?'

'Jane Austen, maybe. Are they likely to have any questions on her work?'

Finn rubbed his beard. 'Probably not.'

'We should play sardines,' said Summer. 'We've got the perfect amount of people.'

'Yes!' agreed Jasmine. 'Henry, you have to play.'

Libby's hand drifted towards his, as if she wanted to hold it, then stopped.

'I'm in,' said Leo. 'We haven't played in years. Ella, you up for getting far too close and personal with my family?'

His best friend laughed. 'As long as Estelle doesn't fart in the wardrobe again.'

'That was Dad's fault,' Estelle replied. 'His onion bhajis are the best.' She pointed her finger at Ella. 'Go on, pull it.'

Ella shook her head. 'No way.'

'God, Estelle, you are so gross!' shrieked Summer. 'Finn, are you playing?'

He shook his head.

'Oh, come on. Please?'

'Only if Estelle promises to let rip without warning.'

Estelle high-fived him. 'You're on.'

As people got up from the table, Henry turned to Libby.

'You don't have to play if you don't want to,' he murmured.

'I don't know my way around the house at all,' she whispered back.

'Elizabeth,' said Gram-Gram, 'if you do not wish to partake, then you may keep me company. I have questions for you.'

Libby swallowed. 'Thank you, but I feel the game may give me a chance to get to know the Manor better.'

'Humph. Very well. I shall speak with Eveline instead.'

Henry glanced at the vicar. She'd only been in Foxbrooke a couple of years and he hardly knew her. She didn't look excited about the prospect of being button-holed by Gram-Gram.

'Okay! Listen up,' said Summer. 'You can only hide in the main house—not the attics or cellars, and you have to choose a place that can hold at least eight people comfortably. Finn, you go first. We'll give you three minutes.'

'Are there any places that are off limits?' Libby asked as Finn left the room.

'Nothing's off limits at Foxbrooke,' laughed Vivienne.

'Except the chimney in the kitchen,' replied Estelle. 'Connor and Henry got stuck up there once.'

'We were eight!' they chorused in unison.

'Can I play the first round with you?' Libby whispered in Henry's ear.

He nodded, his heart rate rising. The warmth of her breath felt like a caress.

'Right, let's go!' Summer dashed out of the room.

Henry got to his feet, held out his hand for Libby without thinking, then dropped it again. She blushed. A loud throat-clearing snapped his focus from her pink cheeks. Gram-Gram was staring at them.

'Come on,' he said. 'Let's go find Finn.'

'THERE ARE TRADITIONAL SPOTS FOR SARDINES,' HENRY TOLD Libby as they started their search. 'Under my parent's bed because it's so big, in some of the wardrobes, behind the curtains in the middle corridor and inside the jam cupboard. There are also lots of small storage rooms that are perfect. The game can take hours if you don't know where to look.'

'So where are we going first?'

'The broom cupboard underneath the servant's stairs. Finn always chooses it.'

Sure enough, Finn was right at the back, looking as if he were trying to merge with the stone wall to get away from Summer, who was pressed against him.

'How come you were so quick?' she grumbled as they moved into the space and shut the door.

'Because Finn's entirely predictable,' Henry replied. 'That's why I'm still friends with him. I know what I'm getting.'

'Mister Grumpypants,' said Summer.

'A bear with a sore head,' he added, sneaking a look at Libby in the half light. 'But his insides are honey.'

'Eh?' said Finn. 'Fuck off.'

Libby giggled. 'I may have suggested to Henry that whatever gruff exterior you possess, you must be sweet inside.'

'Bollocks,' Finn muttered as the door opened.

'This early in the evening?' asked Leo as he crammed in. 'Testicles away please, gentlemen. I'm not interested.'

With each new person entering the broom cupboard, Henry found himself getting physically closer to Libby. He'd promised he wouldn't put himself within eight inches of her, and now he was pressed against her soft form, trying not to breathe in the scent from her hair. The only thing stopping his body from betraying him was the extremely close proximity of his siblings and best friend.

'Bloody hell, Henry, are you grinding your teeth?' Leo asked.

His jaw was so tight it took a moment to loosen it enough

to speak. 'No,' he lied.

'It's just the sound of the stick he's got clenched up his butt,' said Estelle, closest to the door. 'My backside, on the other hand, is so relaxed, that—'

'Get out!' Leo yelled as Finn laughed. 'Before it's too late!'

Everyone spilled into the hall.

'But we don't have everyone here yet,' Estelle complained.

'Doesn't matter,' Summer replied. 'Let's go again. This time Henry can go first.'

He glanced at Libby. 'You okay to go on your own?'

She nodded.

'Right, Henry, go!' Summer yelled.

HENRY EXITED INTO THE MAIN BODY OF THE MANOR AND tried to think of a place to hide. He considered behind the curtains in the middle corridor, but after a couple of minutes his feet brought him to his childhood room. He pushed open the door and entered.

It was so different now, sensuous and decadent, two words he never thought he'd associate with himself. He moved to the large wardrobe where Libby had hung her dresses, opened it and climbed in.

The darkness enveloped him. Over the familiar and comforting smell of old wood was the unfamiliar and intoxicating scent of *her*. He pinched the bridge of his nose.

Everything about this was wrong. Libby was the perfect fake girlfriend because she was a brilliant actress. But earlier, when he'd lifted her into his arms and carried her across the threshold of his bedroom, he'd had the sudden, mad urge to kiss her. And now, all he could think of was the feeling of her body against his.

She has a boyfriend!

Yes, but he's a twat.

Her twat, not yours.

She didn't exactly seem thrilled about his vulva paintings?

That doesn't mean you can try anything on.

She deserves better.

And that's you, is it?

Shut-up.

Self-loathing turned his stomach. He needed to get out of the wardrobe and find somewhere else to hide. Somewhere he couldn't associate with her. The door to the bedroom opened and he froze as someone entered.

They walked to the bed and... sat down?

He peeked through the tiny gap in the wardrobe door to see Libby sitting on the bed, her shoulders slumped as she stared at her phone. She stifled a massive yawn, then pressed the screen and held it to her ear.

'Hey Claire, it's me. I hope you're all asleep. I just wanted to let you know that I've arrived. It's—'

Henry opened the door.

Libby screamed and threw the phone at him.

'Sorry! I didn't want to listen to your private conversation.' He raised his hands to show he wasn't carrying an axe.

She started laughing, her hand pressed to her chest. 'Jesus, Henry, you scared the bloody life out of me.'

'Sorry.'

Libby retrieved her phone. 'I need to leave another message before Claire thinks I've just been murdered.' She put the phone back to her ear. 'I'm alive, I just got startled by Henry hiding in a wardrobe. There's a perfectly logical explanation, I promise. We were playing sardines. Google it or I'll explain tomorrow. Love you, and love to Harper.'

She smiled at him and his heart skipped a beat.

Footsteps sounded in the corridor and she ran towards the

wardrobe and climbed in, shutting the door behind her.

'Libby—'

'Shhh!'

Henry held his breath, but whoever it was walked on.

'I never knew sardines could be so exciting,' she whispered. 'I think they're now my favourite fish.'

He smiled. 'How are you doing? Today must have been a bit, er, intense.'

'Are they always like this?'

He hesitated. 'No, not really.'

'Phew.'

'Um...'

'Yes?'

Henry sighed. 'They're usually worse.'

Libby giggled and he felt her hand on his. She squeezed. 'I like everyone I've met so far.'

'Really?'

'Don't sound so sceptical. What matters most is their intentions, and everyone loves you.'

He didn't know how to reply. She was right.

'Especially Jasmine.'

'Well, I'm very glad you found me first and not her.'

She squeezed his hand again. 'You're a catch, Henry Foxbrooke. Own it.'

In the silence he could hear her breathing. It matched his own. Her thumb was making tiny circles on the back of his hand. The circles suddenly stopped but she didn't let go.

The door to the bedroom opened with a crash.

'If you're in here, you'd better not be shagging,' Estelle shouted.

'I need a new lock,' Henry whispered.

Libby giggled and Estelle threw open the wardrobe.

'There you are! Knew it. Right, budge up.'

Estelle clambered in, pushing Libby further up against him.

'This spot could only fit eight if we were playing with fifteenth-century-sized people,' she grumbled. 'Even Libby would be considered a giant in those days.'

'Are you okay?' Henry asked Libby as she was sandwiched between them.

'I can just about breathe,' she replied, her head muffled by Estelle's breasts.

His sister snorted. 'You're facing the wrong twin.' She turned Libby around so her front was now firmly pressed up against his. 'That's better.'

No, it's really not.

Henry squeezed his eyes shut and ran through the very long list of things and people he didn't like. James Hunter-Savage, mess, public toilets, his family's portrayal in the media. The list was long, but not long enough, and as Finn, Jasmine and Ella joined them in the wardrobe, the sense of Libby overwhelmed all other thoughts.

Rats. I hate rats. They're squirrels without the fluffy tails. They're cute, they're fluffy, yes, red squirrels are the best! Fuck!

'Are you okay?' Libby whispered to him. 'You're as stiff as a board.'

You have no idea. Henry kept both hands clamped over his dick so she wouldn't experience just how stiff he was. This was bad. Very, *very* bad. And he was the worst of the worst. He doubted even Hunter-Savage would have employed a fake girlfriend, then ended up wanting her more than anyone else. The thought shocked him. Did he *really* want Libby more than his last date? Or any of his previous girlfriends?

'There you are.' Leo opened the wardrobe door and pushed in. 'I should have known to look here first. 'Who else have we got?'

'Everyone except Willow and Summer,' Ella replied.

'Connor went home as he's got an early shift in the morning.'

Libby was now so close Henry could feel her heart beating. Or was it his own?

'Could you possibly move your hands?' she whispered. 'They're really digging into my tummy.'

Henry had never been a particularly religious person, but right now he was in fervent prayer that this round of the game would end immediately.

The sound of Estelle farting filled the tiny space.

Thank you, God.

Finn laughed as everyone else stampeded to get away with more speed and determination than shoppers at a Black Friday sale.

'Hold your breath,' Henry said to Libby. 'And don't breathe again till you're outside the room. I'll open all the windows.'

'Ah, c'mon,' Estelle protested. 'It's not that bad.'

Leo pinched his nose. 'Don't take any risks, people. Run for your lives.'

After throwing open the windows, Henry joined the others in the corridor. Libby was giggling and shaking her head as Estelle held her finger out, trying to persuade her to pull it.

'You're no fun,' Estelle told her. 'Anyone else?'

Everyone backed away.

'That's enough of your insides for one night,' Finn said. He looked at his watch. 'I'm going to head home. I'll see you all tomorrow.'

'Another game?' asked Leo. 'Or billiards and more booze?'

Henry glanced at Libby. She was still smiling, but he remembered her sunken shoulders and yawn from earlier. She must be exhausted.

'I think maybe Libby and I will turn in for the evening,' he said.

'Turn in?' Estelle scoffed. 'Have you got your striped

pyjamas and teddy bear ready?' She smirked at Libby. 'You'd better grab a hot water bottle. It'll be the hottest thing you ever experience in that bed.'

Libby drew herself up and put her hands on her hips.

'It was a joke! Yes, I know. You think my brother's spicier than a Vindaloo and keeps you up all night...' Estelle gazed at Finn, her eyes dancing.

'On the toilet?' he supplied.

She whooped and high-fived him. 'Didn't let me down, Finley. I'm proud of you.'

'There you all are.' Summer was striding down the corridor towards them. 'We're playing again?'

Leo shook his head. 'Don't think so. Finn's off home, Henry and Libby are going to "bed", and Ella's going to bust my balls in the billiards room.'

'Boring,' Summer grumbled at Finn, then turned to Jasmine. 'Let's find Willow and get another drink.'

As everyone wandered off, Henry stood with Libby, waving like long-suffering hosts making sure their guests actually left.

'Thank you,' she said as the last one disappeared around the corner. 'It's been a bit of a day.'

'No, thank *you*. You've been amazing.'

'You think they bought it?'

'Which bit?'

She shrugged and her eyes darted down. 'I don't know. Me being posh and working in publishing. Us being a real couple...'

'You don't need to be posh to work in publishing.'

'So why does India's sister, Savannah, only work with people called Saffy and Jocasta?' She scuffed the thick pile carpet with the tip of her shoe. 'I don't fit in here, Henry.'

He kept his arms by his sides, resisting the urge to take her hand.

'Do you think any member of our family, apart from maybe

Summer, Leo and Gram-Gram, fit into the British upper-classes?' he asked.

Libby looked at him. 'Of course, they do, it's a confidence thing. Look at Estelle. She rides horses, shoots stuff and could probably run a fox to ground all by herself.'

He smiled. 'But you have confidence. I could never in a million years get up in front of strangers, think up clever things to say on the fly and make them laugh like you do. You're incredible, Libby. And Estelle isn't as confident as she makes out. Here, at Foxbrooke, she can be. But outside?'

'Don't judge a book by its cover?'

He nodded.

'So, Estelle's *Red Storm Breaking at the Edge of the Event Horizon*, but also *Christmas wishes and Mince Pie dishes at the Prancing Pony Stables?*'

He grinned. 'Absolutely. But don't ever say that to her or she'll go full mediaeval on you.'

'And Henry, you're *An English Gentleman's Guide to Etiquette, Contract Negotiations and the Eight Inch Rule*, but also...?'

'*An English Gentleman's Guide to Etiquette, Contract Negotiations and the Eight Inch Rule, Second Edition*,' he replied. 'I know I'm extremely boring, but it's fine. That's the way I want my life to be.'

'Henry! You're not boring!'

'Yes, I am. I'm a City broker who never takes holidays and looks at market figures and spreadsheets for fun. I'm having to pay you to pretend to like me because I can't find anyone who wants to be with me. Trust me, I know I'm boring.'

Libby's eyes filled with tears. 'No, you're n—'

'Yes, I am.' Irritation scratched at his soul. The last thing he wanted was a vivacious, beautiful, talented woman feeling sorry for him. Libby's boyfriend didn't seem to realise how lucky he was to have her.

'But—'

He started for the bathroom, desperate to get away. 'I'm going to find another room for the night and leave you in peace. I'm sure you need to catch up with Lucas? Let him know you're okay?' He didn't wait for a reply. Instead, grabbing his wash bag, he headed for the corridor. 'Thank you for today,' he said, pausing at the door. 'I really appreciate it. I hope you sleep well.'

'Henry—'

He strode out.

HENRY JOGGED ALONG THE CORRIDOR AND UP A FLIGHT OF stairs to the attic rooms, all prepared for the extended family who were arriving the next day. He chose one at random, entered and flicked on the light. He went to the window and stared out into the blackness.

In the near distance, the lights of the Dower House twinkled. Gram-Gram was back home. She was fiercely protective of him and the one member of the family most reluctant to embrace Libby with open arms. His stomach knotted. Gram-Gram missed nothing. They would have to be extra careful around her.

He rested his forehead against the cool glass. Where would he sleep tomorrow? One thing was certain, he could never share a room, let alone a bed, with Libby.

He washed, cleaned his teeth, then lay on top of the pristine counterpane, staring up at the ceiling. Day one was over. *Just keep it together until Tuesday morning, then life can go back to normal.* He turned off the light, but his eyes wouldn't close. Each time he forced them shut, images of Libby danced before him. He rolled over to face the wall. He'd fall asleep eventually. He just had to wait.

❧ 14 ❧

'Happy birthday!'

Libby woke with a start from a deep sleep, cocooned in the comfiest bed she'd ever lain in. Where was she? Her discombobulated dream was fading, leaving her facing the nightmare of an older man who hadn't done his dressing gown up enough to hide his genitals.

'Happy birthday to you, happy—'

Libby's subconscious took care of the situation by making her scream.

The man took a step back. 'It's only me! Where's Henry?'

Reality crashed through her in fractured waves and her scream cut off. She was at Foxbrooke Manor. In her nightie. Facing Henry's father who was carrying a tray with two mugs on it and a cupcake with a dribbling candle stuck in the top.

'Gone for a run—'

The door banged open and Henry entered, wearing the clothes he'd been wearing the previous night.

'Libby—' He stopped dead.

'Happy birthday, m'boy!'

Henry's gaze dropped to his father's crotch. 'Dad! Fuck's sake! Do your dressing gown up properly!'

Arthur glanced down. 'Oopsies.' He passed the tray to Henry. 'Here, take this.'

He took it. 'Dad, what are you doing here?'

His father looked confused. 'Bringing you both a cup of tea and wishing you happy birthday. Isn't that pretty clear? Go on, blow it out. Make a wish.'

Henry blew the candle out. By the thunderous look on his face, Libby guessed he was wishing his father would disappear as easily as the flame.

'But, Dad. What if we had been, erm...'

'Shagging?' His father frowned. 'But you weren't.'

'How on earth would you know that?'

Arthur shrugged. 'Sock wasn't on the doorknob. Ergo, open for visitors.' He gazed out into the middle distance. 'Thirty, eh. By the time I was your age, I had two wives and six kids.' He winked at Henry. 'Chop, chop.' He inclined his head towards Libby. 'I want grandchildren and you two are my best bet.'

'Dad!'

Arthur grinned and went to a chest of drawers, opening it and rummaging around.

'Aha!' He pulled out a sock. 'No excuses now. I'll put it on the handle outside for you.'

Henry pushed his father towards the door.

'Ooh, do you think you might have twins, Libby?' Arthur called over his shoulder. 'They run in our family. Any on your side?'

She sunk her head into her hands as Henry slammed the door.

'Sock's on!' Arthur yelled from the corridor. 'Condoms off!'

The slap slap of his carpet slippers faded as he walked away.

Libby looked up. Henry's eyes were pinched shut.

He opened them. 'Libby, I am so fucking sorry.'

She let out a breath. 'Well, that's one way to wake up.'

He put the tray by her side of the bed. 'I'm buying a lock for the door today. There's no way you're going through that again.'

'Does he usually wake you up with a cup of tea?'

Henry nodded. 'It's one of the things he likes to do. That, and making curries, naturism, and running wild sex parties.'

'Curries?'

'Yeah, he spent a few years in India on the hippy trail and fell in love with the food.'

'I love making curries, too.'

'I remember you said that at the workshop. Have you been to India?'

She shook her head. 'But I was brought up in Birmingham, remember. It's the home of the Balti. My father said curry was part of Brummie culture and cured all ills.'

The door banged open and Estelle bounced into the room.

'Morning! And happy bloody birthday, younger brother.'

'There was a sock on the door!' Henry cried.

Estelle sat on the bed, took the cupcake from the tray and bit into it.

'Yeff,' she replied. 'Ut I urd oo alking.' She swallowed. 'So, I knew it was safe to enter.'

'Fuck's sake!' Henry rubbed his forehead. 'And happy birthday, *older* sister.'

Estelle grinned at Libby. 'Twenty minutes, and I'll never let him forget it.' She glanced at her watch. 'And that's how much time you've got before we go into Bath.'

'Estelle,' Henry said. 'We're not on your deadline here.'

'Oh, I don't care if you come or not. But if Libby wants to do the Jane Austen centre, the Circus and Royal Crescent, the Fashion Museum, the Roman Baths, and the theatrical hire shop to get a costume for tomorrow night, then we need to get a move on.' She looked at Libby and raised an eyebrow. 'What does Elizabeth Bennet want to do?'

'I can be ready in fifteen,' she replied.

ESTELLE DROVE A BATTERED OLD LAND ROVER DEFENDER. The outside was splattered with mud and the inside was grimy with dirt, straw and dog hair.

'No,' Henry said to his sister. 'You can come in my car, but I'm not getting in the Defender without overalls on.'

Estelle turned to Libby. 'Want to ride shotgun with me?'

Libby tried to stop her nose wrinkling. The vehicle was the personification of the dirtiest side of the countryside and she didn't want to go anywhere near it.

'If you don't mind, I'd like to ride with Henry.'

Estelle rolled her eyes. 'Okay, love's young dream. I'm parking in Southgate. I'll see you there.'

She hopped in and set off down the long drive, the exhaust belching black diesel smoke.

Henry opened the passenger door of his car. 'Shall we?'

DRIVING DOWN THE COUNTRY LANES, LIBBY'S STOMACH turned over. It wasn't the twists and turns that were making her feel sick, but the thought of Lucas, her other fake boyfriend. Pretending to be Henry's upper-class girlfriend with a super important job in publishing was bad enough, but continuing to deceive Henry about her relationship with Lucas was something else. If she didn't tell him and he found out later, he might be angry at her deliberate deception. But right now she was mortified at how stupid she'd been and didn't want Henry thinking she was a total fool.

Until Henry had mentioned Lucas's name the previous night, thoughts of him hadn't crossed her mind for nearly a day. Was Lucas even her friend anymore? She'd considered him one of her best friends, but to what extent had he taken advantage of her? Anger fought with embarrassment. Would she ever be able to get her money back?

Libby gazed out of the window into a little valley. A tiny farmhouse rested in the dip. Cream-coloured cows clustered under a tree in a next-door field, swishing their tails. Foxbrooke was a beautiful bubble. Soon it would burst and she'd have to find somewhere to live and a job that didn't involve Claire.

The previous Tuesday she'd performed their comedy night above the pub with an acquaintance taking her friend's role. But the performance didn't have the same zing. Working with Claire was almost telepathic. How could she create the same chemistry with anyone else?

And as for her bank balance... The money Henry was paying her for this weekend wouldn't last long. Most of it was already gone on servicing her debts. Debts she'd accrued because she was busy funding Lucas's vulva paintings.

'You okay?'

She glanced at Henry, full of shame about Lucas, and too cowardly to tell him the truth.

'I haven't got you a birthday present. Or Estelle.'

'I don't want or need anything. And I know my sister won't be expecting anything either.' He yawned and tried to cover it with his hand. 'Sorry.'

'How did you sleep last night?'

'As well as could be expected. There's a Travelodge outside Frome that I'm going to book for tonight. I can't use any of the local B&Bs as it'll get back to the family. I need somewhere anonymous.'

'You don't have to do that. People might notice your car is gone. We can find a way to make it work.'

Henry shook his head. 'You need a quiet space for yourself. You've been through enough already.' He sighed. 'Christ, I'm so sorry about my dad this morning. I'm going to buy a lock and a deadbolt so that won't happen again.'

'Don't worry, it's just comedy material.'

His head snapped around, his eyes wide. 'Libby—'

'I was joking! Sorry. I didn't mean it like that. I'd never betray your family's confidence.'

He nodded, but she could see the stress on his face, his fingers tight around the steering wheel.

They drove the rest of the way to Bath in silence.

'THEATRICAL HIRE PLACE FIRST?' ASKED ESTELLE AS THEY exited the lift from the underground car park into the middle of Southgate shopping centre.

Henry shook his head. 'I don't want a costume. You two go and I'll meet you later. I'm off to buy some locks.'

'Aw, c'mon,' Estelle moaned. 'Libby. Back me up here.'

He looked at Libby and raised an eyebrow.

Butterflies took off in her tummy. 'It might be fun?'

He raised his other eyebrow. 'Fun?' he said, as if the suggestion were last on his list of enjoyable things to do.

She nodded. 'How about we get you a couple of costumes and you can pick one of them?'

Estelle's face lit up and Henry frowned at her.

'No costumes for women.'

His sister's face fell. 'Fuck's sake,' she muttered.

'Nothing that reveals more than five per cent of my body,' he continued, 'and nothing that our parents would approve of.'

Estelle threw her hands in the air. 'I might as well cut two holes in a sheet and chuck it over your head so you can go as a ghost.'

'I'm happy with that suggestion.' He glanced at Libby. 'And Libby decides what I'm going to wear.'

'Ugh,' Estelle grunted. 'We'll have to see if they have any "fun police" outfits.'

'You okay to choose for me?' he asked Libby.

She tried to hide her excitement. She knew exactly what she was going to get.

AN HOUR LATER, LIBBY AND ESTELLE HAD LOADED FOUR garment bags into the back of Estelle's Land Rover, then returned to the centre of Bath. The pale stone buildings reflected the Saturday morning heat and radiated even more.

Estelle pushed her way through the crowds like a battering ram. 'Bloody tourists, clogging the place up.'

'I'm a tourist.'

'You're different.'

'How?'

'You're with me.' Estelle stopped and twisted her ponytail into a bun. 'It's so fucking hot. I want to go home and jump in the river.'

'The one near the Manor?'

'Yeah. The Foxbrooke. It joins the Avon near Freshford.'

Libby's phone pinged with a message and she pulled it from her bag.

'Is it Henry?' Estelle asked. 'Has he finished buying a portcullis for your bedroom door?'

Libby's stomach turned as she read the message.

Lucas: How's it going with the nobs?

She shook her head. 'Just a friend. Should I ring Henry? Do you need to get back?'

Her phone pinged again.

Lucas: Ring me, babe x

Babe?

'You alright?' Estelle asked. 'You look how I feel ninety-nine per cent of the time.'

'It's fine. I'll deal with it later.'

Ping.

Lucas: Miss you, Lib-Lob. As does my stomach!

Fuck off!

Her phone rang. *Henry*.

'Oh, thank goodness it's you. I thought it might—er, um... We've finished at the hire shop, and you'll love what I've chosen for you. But it's a secret. You can't see it until tomorrow night. Have you finished? Did you get everything you needed? Estelle said you were trying to buy a portcullis. Where are you now? Can we meet you?' *Shut up!*

'Do you need a wet wipe for your verbal diarrhoea?' Estelle asked.

There was silence on the other end of the line.

'Henry?'

'I'm still here,' he replied. 'They were out of portcullises in the shop so I bought a drawbridge and moat. They've got boiling pitch and a dragon on back order for me. That ought to keep my family at bay.'

She giggled. 'I think you need more than that to keep your twin sister out.'

'Eh? What's he saying?' Estelle demanded. 'Where the arse is he?'

'Here,' Henry replied from behind them.

Libby turned and met his smile with her own. Her heart leapt and she launched herself forward to hug him before realising what she was doing. Eight inches away and closing, she wondered if he would rather not have physical contact, and attempted to abort the manoeuvre. This resulted in an ungainly fall sideways, her arms locked beside her body. Henry reached for her, accidentally grabbing her breast, then froze and let go as if he'd touched a live wire. Libby stumbled into Estelle, who caught her before she hit the ground.

'Jesus Christ, what the hell is wrong with the two of you?' Estelle asked as she returned Libby to a vertical position. 'How do you even manage to have sex? It must be like a couple of Morris dancers on a fucking trampoline.' She did a demonstration, her legs and arms flailing, her mouth contorted as if in a wind tunnel.

Libby snorted and even Henry grinned.

Estelle stared at her brother. 'Honestly, I know you don't want to be like our parents. But if you're that cack-handed you're going to need to read Dad's autobiography, or at least look at the pictures.'

Libby put her hands on her hips. 'Estelle...'

'Oops, oh yes, soz. I forgot no trash talk is allowed where my little brother is concerned. Right then, Casanova. Can I leave Libby with you? I have to get home and sort some shit out before tonight.'

'Horse shit?' Libby asked.

Estelle sighed. 'Every one of my jobs is horse shit.'

'On your birthday?'

She shrugged, suddenly seeming smaller, as if her balloon of energy had deflated. A brittle smile appeared. 'No rest for the wicked. I'll see you two lovebirds later.'

She sauntered off with a wave.

Libby glanced at Henry. He was watching Estelle, a frown on his face.

'Is she alright?'

He rubbed his hand over his short hair. 'I need to talk to her.'

'Is everything okay?'

He shook his head. 'Probably not.'

'Do you want to go after her now?'

'No, it can wait for a quieter day. I want to show you Bath.'

'Are you sure? It's your birthday, so you need to do something that *you* want to do.'

'I want to go to all the places you want to visit. Apart from the Roman Baths, I've never been to any of them.'

Libby bounced on the balls of her feet and clapped her hands in excitement.

Henry's smile lit up his face. 'Jane Austen centre first?'

Being with Estelle was like trying to keep up with a hurricane. Libby had wanted to stop every few feet and take pictures, but Estelle didn't even pause to breathe. Being with Henry was a completely different experience. He let her set the pace and at no time seemed anxious to move on. Whenever she looked for him, he was there, his focus dedicated exclusively to her.

Her mind flicked back to when she'd once accompanied

Lucas to an art exhibition. Libby had wanted to take her time looking at the paintings, but Lucas had been in a mood. He'd criticised the artist loudly then marched off, leaving her behind. The enjoyment sucked from her, she'd finally located him at the exit, smoking and scrolling through his phone.

And before Lucas, when things had started to go horribly wrong with Giles, his dissatisfaction with her had pressed so tightly on her chest, she'd felt like she couldn't breathe.

Growing up in a large family and having a job that required acute attunement to the emotions of others, Libby couldn't relax around stressed and unhappy people. She knew she was a people pleaser, but she hadn't fully appreciated how much she put her own desires second until now.

'Are you sure you don't mind doing this with me?' she asked again as they stopped for more photos in Queen Square.

'I honestly can't remember the last time I felt so relaxed,' Henry replied. His entire demeanour seemed lighter than when they'd been at Foxbrooke. 'Bath looks completely different through your eyes. And you're just so easy.'

Er?

His hand flew to his face at the change in her expression. 'Easy going! Easy to hang out with! That's what I meant!'

Henry looked so horrified she burst out laughing. 'You will tell me though if we need to go, or you get bored?'

'I will. Although I can't see that happening. I'd rather be with you than anyone else in the world right now.'

He blinked and his cheeks darkened. He turned his back on her, staring up at the trees.

Libby shook her head. *Get a grip. It's only because he doesn't want to go home and face his family.* 'Is the Jane Austen Centre close?'

He nodded. 'It's just the other side of the square.'

Outside the building an older man in Regency dress and

sporting a bushy white pork-chop moustache bowed deeply. Libby tried to contain her excitement.

'Good morning, my lady, sir,' he said. 'Allow me to introduce myself. I am Mr Bennet. Are you calling on us today?'

Libby curtsied. 'Indeed sir, we are. My name is Miss Elinor Dashwood, and my companion is Mr George Knightley.'

Mr Bennet doffed his hat. ''Tis a pleasure to make your acquaintance. If you would like to make your way inside, you will be attended to by Mr Wickham.'

'He's here?' she squeaked. 'Wickham?'

The man nodded and stroked his beard. 'Indeed.' He gazed at Henry and lowered his voice. 'Mr Wickham is very popular with the young ladies of the ton. Be on your guard, sir!'

'I thought Mr Darcy was your favourite?' Henry asked her as they entered the building.

'Oh, most definitely,' she replied. 'But everyone loves a Regency bad-boy.'

LIBBY BEAMED HER WAY THROUGH THE TOUR OF REGENCY society. The actor playing Wickham was over the moon that she interacted with him in character, and Henry couldn't stop smiling, which delighted her even more. It reminded her of the day they met at the workshop. His genuine happiness filled her heart.

After the Jane Austen centre, they carried on to the Roman Baths. She was in heaven as they met more actors, this time dressed as citizens and slaves.

'Honestly, Henry, this would be my perfect job,' she whispered.

'Doing this?'

'Yes. Being a living history performer. You get to spend all day in an incredible place, bringing the past to life and telling kids that the Romans used Portuguese pee as mouthwash.'

He looked horrified. 'They did?'

'Yup. And you'll never guess what they used to clean their backsides...'

Bath was undeniably a beautiful city, but seeing it through Libby's eyes awakened a deeper sense of appreciation in Henry.

She has a boyfriend. She has a boyfriend. She has a boyfriend.

He repeated this mantra over and over, trying to squash the growing attraction burning in his chest. He didn't like Lucas, but he would like himself even less if he told Libby his feelings towards her were not entirely honourable.

Despite her protestations that a sandwich would suffice, he took her to the Pump Rooms for lunch and they dined under the chandeliers whilst a man in black tie played a grand piano on the low stage. If Henry could just hang out with Libby until they returned to London, everything would be perfect. He had no desire to return to the Manor and greet his extended family.

Libby sipped her tea. 'Are all of your mother's relatives coming to the party?'

'Not all of them. My grandparents are in their eighties and it's too far for them to travel. Mom's elder sister, Simone, is coming. She's fine—' *unless she's trying to persuade me to model for her* '—and her French husband and kids are cool. Mom's brother, Louis, is a TV chef.'

'I've seen one of his shows from the States. He's a bit, um…'

Henry smiled. 'Yes, he does come over a bit full of himself. But ten minutes with his sisters soon squashes it out of him, and then he's actually fun to be around.'

'They sound great.'

He nodded. They were. It was his father's side of the family that caused him most of the headaches. His aunt's party of fifteen were arriving that afternoon and he wanted to defer meeting them for as long as possible.

'So, I've tried to memorise the family tree from the—' Libby's cheeks pinked as she hesitated '—*contract*. Your father's older sister is Charlotte?'

'Yes. Be warned. She'll tell you she should have been born a man so she would have inherited the Manor and title instead of her "feckless embarrassment of a younger brother".' He rolled his eyes. 'She has a point, but the way she goes on about it is tedious.'

'And she's married to a Tory MP?'

Henry raised his cup, his pinkie finger deliberately extended. 'Sir Humphrey Hatton-Blythe. They have three children, who have also married appropriately and produced the requisite heirs.'

'They sound extremely…' Libby furrowed her brow as if trying to find the right word.

'Posh?'

She nodded.

He sighed. 'Yes, they are.' He didn't want to talk about them anymore. 'Want to go to the Fashion Museum next?'

Her eyes lit up and her head bobbed.

Henry couldn't stop the smile spreading across his face. Libby was happy and they were miles away from Foxbrooke.

'Are you sure we shouldn't go back?' Libby asked as they exited the Museum an hour later.

'Drinks aren't until six,' Henry replied. 'I'm viewing the next few days as an endurance marathon that I want to delay.'

'And here I was, thinking you loved Regency fashion.'

'It's quite smart. I just can't get over how small people were.'

She stood on her tiptoes, her eyeline nearly reaching his. 'I would have been considered tall in those days.'

Her lips were so close. So pink and utterly kissable. *She has a boyfriend, she has a boyfriend, she has a boyfriend.*

'You would have been the most sought-after debutante of the season,' he said before thinking.

Her heels clicked back to the ground and she frowned. 'Hardly. I would have been the chambermaid, if I was lucky. You, however, would have been mobbed by all the ambitious mothers on behalf of their daughters.'

He raised an eyebrow. 'Really?'

She nodded. 'And you'd get bonus points for not being a venereal-disease-riddled rake.'

'That is true.' He rubbed his chin, thinking of his colleagues back at Conqueror. 'I don't know about the disease part, but I work with lots of men who Austen would have considered rakes.'

'I know.'

'You do?' *Did James try it on?*

'Working with big City firms, you get to know the type. And the faster they try to get your number, the faster you know to run in the opposite direction.'

'Did anyone at Conqueror...?'

Libby shook her head.

Everything inside him sighed with relief. 'Not even James?'

'The tall guy who left early?'

'That's him.'

'No. And even if he did, I wouldn't touch him with a ten-foot pole. He's far too dangerous.'

'Dangerous?' Now Henry was wishing he'd punched him harder.

'Not physically dangerous,' she said in a hurry. 'He's just very insecure.'

'Insecure? James Hunter-Savage?'

'Yes. That's why he acted like an idiot. He felt too vulnerable and exposed, too scared to open up.'

'Really?'

'He's not that different to anyone else. I'm insecure just like he is.' Libby shrugged. 'But I try and fight my fears.'

'Feel the fear and do it anyway?'

She smiled. 'Something like that.'

'I think my approach is "feel the fear and run away in the opposite direction as fast as I can".'

Libby grinned. 'Or, feel the fear and enter another museum?'

'Definitely. We've got time to visit the Holborn and or Number 1 Royal Crescent if we walk fast enough.'

'You really don't want to go back to the Manor.'

'No, I don't. I don't want to face Cousin Rupert braying about politics, or Cousin Catherine's husband, Julian, giving Willow and Summer the eye. I can't fucking stand them.'

'You could remind them who's going to become Duke of Somerset one day? They can't top that.'

His heart sank. The last thing he wanted was his father's title and the responsibilities that came with it.

'Oh god, Henry. I'm so sorry. That was insensitive of me.'

'It's fine.' He forced a smile. 'I'd just rather be plain old Henry.'

'You're not old and you'll never be plain, but if it makes you feel any better, I can't remember your titles and full name so you're just Henry to me.'

'I can cope with Henry Arthur Fitzwilliam Foxbrooke. It's the Lord and Viscount bit I don't want.'

Libby's face lit up. 'Fitzwilliam? Oh yes! I'd totally forgotten.'

'What?'

'That's Mr Darcy's first name. I need to tell India.'

'Your flatmate?'

She frowned, and Henry remembered that she didn't have a home to go to when they got back to London.

'Yes. We used to try and put men into Austen categories. Most of the men I met at workshops in the City were either Darcy or Wickham.'

'And who am I?'

'You're a cross between Darcy and Bingley.'

'I am? Is that a good or a bad thing?'

'It's a perfect thing. You've got the best bits of both.'

'And Hunter-Savage would be Wickham?'

'Most definitely.'

'And who would Lucas be?'

Libby's face clouded, all the light and sunshine disappearing.

'I, I don't know,' she replied, her eyes flicking away.

See? Even she's starting to think he's a twat!

Mind-reader are we? You can't know that.

Then why does she seem so unhappy?

Maybe because you've said something wrong?

Well hurry up and say something right, then!

Shut-up! I'm trying to think!

'Actually, Henry, do you mind if we head back?'

'No, not at all.'

'And can we stop off at a bookshop?'

He nodded. 'There's one on the way.'

WHILST LIBBY WAS SHOPPING, HENRY DASHED BACK through the pedestrian streets, past the Abbey to a bakery he'd spotted earlier. He bought a sourdough loaf then ran back to meet her outside the bookshop.

'This is for you,' he said, giving it to her.

She peeked inside the paper bag. 'Henry!'

'I know it won't be as good as yours...'

'How do you know?'

'Because you're brilliant at whatever you do.'

She pulled a face. 'I'm really not. And it's your birthday, not mine. You should be getting the presents.' She sniffed the loaf and smiled. 'Thank you. I love it.'

His heart lifted. Her happiness was the ultimate gift.

'Close your eyes,' she said.

'Huh?'

'And hold out your hands.'

He did, feeling something light land on his palms.

'Happy birthday, Henry. It's not wrapped, I'm afraid.'

He opened his eyes to see a paperback of *Pride and Prejudice*.

'Thank you, Libby. This is perfect.'

'If you really don't get on with it, I'll get you the TV version.'

He flicked through the pages. 'I'm sure I'll be fine. It's about a fifth of the size of *War and Peace* and I managed that when I was fourteen.'

She grinned. 'Well, I expect a full report by the end of the week.'

THE DRIVE AT FOXBROOKE MANOR WAS FILLED WITH TESLAS, Audis and Aston Martins. Henry suppressed a sigh as he pulled into a space. A Range Rover twice the size of Estelle's and twenty times the price screeched to a halt behind them in a shower of gravel, blocking them in. It was his cousin, Rupert Hatton-Blythe, four years his senior and a hedge fund manager in the City.

'Foxy, you bastard!' Rupert roared as he climbed out of his car. 'Happy bloody birthday!'

Henry got out of the BMW and went to open the door for Libby.

'Hi, Rupert,' he replied. 'Can you move? I need to get out later.'

'What the devil for?' Rupert stood with his hands on his hips as his wife, Cecily, helped their children out. 'Tonight's the night to partaaaay!' His gaze slid to Libby.

'This is my girlfriend, Libby,' Henry said. 'Libby, my cousin, Rupert and his wife, Cecily. And their children, Araminta and Montgomery.'

'Hi, nice to meet you,' Libby said.

Rupert frowned. 'You work in the City?'

She shook her head.

'You sure? You look bally familiar.'

Libby's smile looked forced. 'No, I work in publishing.'

He sniffed. 'Oh well, you remind me of someone. No idea who.' He turned his head. 'Minty! Monty! Come say happy birthday to Uncle Henry.'

Henry went to the boot of Rupert's car to help Cecily lift their suitcases.

'Leave them, Cec,' Rupert barked. 'Staff'll sort 'em out.'

'There's no-one around to help right now,' Henry said as Libby came to assist. He brought his mouth as close to her ear as he dared. 'Run,' he whispered. 'While you have the chance. I'll meet you in the room in a bit.'

'What about Perry, or whatever her name is?' Rupert asked.

'Perry's in charge of food and will be up to her eyeballs right now.' Henry replied, lifting two enormous Louis Vuitton suitcases out of the boot. 'Bridget is the housekeeper but, again, is a bit tied up.'

Rupert guffawed. 'Into Uncle Arthur's kinky sex games is she, eh?'

'Roo-Roo, shush!' Cecily hissed as Minty and Monty giggled.

'You sure you don't want me to stay?' Libby whispered to Henry.

He shook his head. 'Have a bit of peace and quiet before it all kicks off.'

She smiled at him, made her excuses to Rupert and Cecily, and left.

'Pretty young thing,' Rupert said to Henry as Libby entered the Manor. 'Where did you pick her up?'

'We met at a book launch.'

'What was the book?' Cecily asked.

'Er... *Summertime kisses and,* er, *cake at the Dandelion café in Cornwall.' Fuck!* He couldn't even remember the bastardised version of the title.

'Do you mean *Springtime Kisses and Daffodil Wishes at the Little Cornish Cupcake Café on Mermaid's Cove?*'

'Yes, that's the one,' Henry replied.

'What'cha reading that toss for?' asked Rupert.

'I love Polly Hart,' Cecily said. 'I'm in a book group called "Hart's Hearts". I think Genevieve was at the launch? She didn't mention seeing you there.'

'Ha!' Rupert replied. 'That's because he was probably behind a bookshelf with his hand up Libby's skirt.'

'Yes,' Henry said, hating every word that came out his mouth. 'That's about right.'

Rupert clapped him on the back. 'Just like your dad, eh? Apple doesn't fall far from the tree and all that.' He winked. 'Bet you're in a tasty threesome by Christmas.'

By the time he'd seen his cousin and family to their rooms, Henry was ready to bolt straight back out the front door, start running, and never stop. He took the main stairs two at a time, hurrying to get back to Libby and tell her Cecily's friend had been at Polly Hart's book launch.

'Henry! Wait up!'

He stopped. Summer was jogging up the stairs behind him, her blonde curls bouncing.

'Where have you *been* all day?' She pouted. 'I've been trying to find you.'

'I was in Bath with Libby.'

'Oh. Yes.'

In the silence that followed, he realised the strangeness of a Foxbrooke sibling having a partner. He wasn't used to it and neither was the rest of the family.

'Henry, can I talk to you?'

'Sure.'

They went to a window seat at the end of the corridor. It may have been a public space, but privacy was guaranteed as they had a clear sight line of anyone approaching.

'What happened to that guy?' Summer whispered as they sat.

Henry didn't answer. After he'd launched himself at James, he'd been hauled off by HR. Summer had left the Conqueror offices by the time they'd finished dealing with him.

'The man you attacked.'

'He's fine.'

'What did he do to Libby?'

'What?'

'After you punched him, you said something like "that's for Elizabeth".'

'Um...' *Think!* 'Er, he'd asked for her number after the work —at work.'

'Libby works with you?'

'No, she came in to visit me.'

'And you punched him because he asked for her number?' Summer didn't sound convinced.

'That was the last straw.'

'Oh. And what about you? Did you get the sack?'

Henry winced. Officially he'd been suspended and put on gardening leave, but he was increasingly concerned it might be extended indefinitely.

He cleared his throat. 'No. I'm just taking my accrued holiday.'

'Ah. Okay.'

Summer was silent, the fingers of one hand drumming on her leg.

'Is everything alright?' he asked. 'With your new course?'

'It's really boring.'

He held his breath.

'I don't think I'm going back in September.'

Again? 'I thought this was it? You'd found something you liked?'

'I just don't see the point.'

'Better job prospects?'

Summer picked at the hem of her dress. 'Most graduates can't find a job when they leave. I'd be better off in the real world, gaining experience.'

'At what?'

'I can't be a catwalk model as I'm not tall enough. So, I've decided to be an influencer.'

Henry tried to keep his tone even. 'Influencing whom?'

'People. Women.'

'To do what?'

'Buy stuff.'

'And who is going to pay you to do this?'

'Duh! Companies, of course.'

'And why are they going to choose you?'

She re-crossed her legs and struck a pose. 'Because I'm Summer Foxbrooke. I've been building my brand and already have thirty-four thousand followers on Insta.'

'Can't you do that *and* get a qualification? Have something to fall back on?'

'I won't need to. If it all goes wrong, I'll just come back and live here.'

It was pointless arguing with her. Once his youngest sister had made up her mind, that was that. At least he wouldn't have to pay her university costs anymore.

'You're sure about this? You're not going back to Uni in September?'

'Yep. I'm going to base myself in London.'

'Where?'

'Jasmine and I are going to get a flat.'

'How are you going to afford it?' he asked, now knowing exactly where this conversation was going.

'I was, er, hoping you could keep helping me out?'

'It's not university.'

'It's the university of life?'

Henry rubbed his hand over his head and held her gaze.

'Summer, I've spent the last eight years funding your education. It's cost me hundreds of thousands of pounds, and I'm almost broke. I can't keep going indefinitely.'

She glanced away and bit her lip. 'But you've got loads of money.'

'Do I? I've had the same car for five years, the same tiny flat for eight, and I never go on holiday. I only have nice clothes because Aunt Simone gives them to me in her attempts to bribe me to model for her.'

'You should do it. If I was you, I would.'

He shook his head. 'There's more to life than looking pretty.'

She shrugged, clearly believing the opposite.

'I'm sorry, Summer. You'll have to ask Dad.'

She stood. 'Fine,' she huffed and flounced away without a second glance.

Henry took in her designer outfit as she left. He didn't regret the money he'd spent, he just wished Summer hadn't grown up so entitled.

❧   16   ☙

Libby bounded off the bed at the knock on the bedroom door and flung it open.

'Henry!' She pulled him inside. 'Oh my god, I know Rupert. We did a workshop for his company a couple of years ago. He recognised me.'

'I don't think he remembers you enough to remember the context.'

'But what if he does?'

'Say you now work in publishing?'

Libby slumped on the bed and put her head in her hands. 'This is never going to work.'

He sat next to her, three feet away. 'They're probably only staying till Monday. And there's enough people and alcohol to distract him.'

She looked up. 'At least it's only him we need to be worried about.'

'Ah...'

'Oh god.' She groaned. 'What now?'

'Cecily is a Polly Hart fan. Apparently, her friend Genevieve was at the launch and "didn't mention" seeing me there.'

'How on earth are we going to explain that away?'

He gazed at his clasped hands, then brought one up to rub the back of his neck.

'Henry?'

'Cousin Rupert surmised the reason Genevieve didn't see us was that, er...'

'What? We were wearing an invisibility cloak?'

He seemed deeply embarrassed. 'We were behind a bookshelf and I had my hand—' He cleared his throat. 'Um, my hand was inside your, er, skirt,' he finished, staring intently at the floor.

'And what did you say?' Libby asked, suddenly so hot she thought she might faint.

'I said "that's about right".'

There was a pause.

'I'm so sorry, Libby. I didn't know what to do.'

Her laugh was as breathless as she felt. 'You did fine, Henry. Honestly, that sounds absolutely perfect.'

He glanced up.

'I mean your response!' she squeaked. 'To Rupert.'

He stood. 'I bought locks for the door today,' he said, addressing the wardrobe. 'We've got about an hour before we have to be downstairs. Do you mind if I try and fit them?'

'That's fine,' she replied staring at the bedside table. 'I'll get ready in the bathroom.'

LIBBY GAZED AT HER REFLECTION IN THE MIRROR. SHE didn't need any blusher. Her cheeks were bright pink. There was no point in pretending any more. She had a massive crush on Henry Foxbrooke. But was it real? Up until a few days ago she'd believed herself utterly in love with Lucas. Her mind was confused by the mess of thoughts and feelings it was trying to unravel, but it seemed her body knew exactly who it wanted, and that was Henry.

'Is it safe to come out?' she called through the bathroom door.

'Yes.'

Libby entered the bedroom and bit back a moan. Henry looked like he'd stepped off a catwalk. His dark suit was impeccably styled to frame his physique and he had a jaw that could cut glass.

He glanced at her and swallowed. 'I don't want to speak inappropriately…'

Please do!

'But you look altogether lovely, Libby.' He stepped back, as if to make sure there was enough distance between them. 'I'm honoured you're my fake girlfriend.'

Her heart squeezed. How was he still single? It was utterly incomprehensible to her.

'Henry. You're the best and most wonderful fake boyfriend I've ever had.'

Silence filled the room as he gazed at her. It was like being in his arms again. Everything else apart from him disappeared.

'Lucas is a very, very lucky man,' he said, softly.

The mention of Lucas's name slashed the moment to shreds. The sick feeling in the pit of her stomach was back. She *had* to tell him.

'Henry—'

The gong sounded from downstairs and he checked his watch. 'We've already missed the first one. We really should go. You ready?'

She nodded. Lucas would have to wait.

. . .

HENRY LED LIBBY INTO ONE OF THE OPULENT DRAWING rooms in the Manor. She hadn't been in this one and couldn't take in much of the interior as the room was filled with people. They went to where Estelle was standing, chatting with Eveline and Finn.

'Can I get you a drink?' Henry asked Libby.

'Yes please,' she replied.

'Champagne?'

'Do it,' said Estelle. 'It's proper stuff. Aunt Simone brought it from France with her.'

Libby nodded to him. 'Thank you.'

Henry walked off through the crowds and Libby moved closer to Estelle.

'Don't worry,' Estelle said. 'We've got you covered. I've got a shotgun, Finn's got a nail gun and Eveline's got the almighty on speed dial in case you need an emergency smiting.'

Finn rolled his eyes, and Eveline grinned and shook her head.

Estelle put her hand on Libby's arm. 'Seriously, you don't have to be left alone with any of them if you don't want to.'

'I met your cousin, Rupert earlier,' she replied.

Estelle's eyes widened. 'On a scale of one to ten, how much of an arse was he?'

'Estelle,' said Eveline. 'Shush. He's only over there.'

'And he's looking at Libby,' added Finn.

'Quick! Eveline!' Estelle whispered as Libby froze. 'Smite him! Smite him! And whilst you're at it, get Julian as well.'

Finn snorted and Eveline covered her mouth to hide a grin.

Libby took a wrapped parcel out of her bag and gave it to Estelle. 'Happy Birthday.'

She frowned. 'This is for me?'

Libby nodded. 'Apparently it's customary on someone's birthday to get them a present.'

'You really didn't have to.' Estelle felt it. 'A book?

'Maybe...'

'Have you got me Pride and bloody Prejudice?'

She smirked. 'That's what I got Henry. I've actually got you two books.'

'Ooh! Because I'm twice as important as he is?'

'Come on, Stelle,' said Finn. 'Rip it!'

Estelle tore the paper and stared at the books. One had a photo of a naked man's torso on the front and was titled *Banging the Billionaire Daddy Dom*. The other was *Springtime Kisses and Daffodil Wishes at the Little Cornish Cupcake Café on Mermaid's Cove*.

Estelle threw back her head and roared with laughter. She held up the Polly Hart book. 'I won't be seen dead reading this.'

'I know,' Libby replied. 'That's why I've swapped the covers. People will think you're reading *Banging the Billionaire Daddy Dom*, but in fact you're reading about daffodils and cupcakes.'

'Oh my god, that's amazing. How did you do it?'

'A very sharp knife borrowed from Perry, a glue stick, and a fair amount of swearing.'

'Sounds like my day-to-day life. Well, minus the glue stick.' Estelle winked at Eveline. 'You can borrow this one if you like? People will think you're reading fluffy twaddle but actually you're reading a filthy hot billionaire bang-fest.'

Eveline blushed as red as her hair. 'Estelle,' she murmured.

'What? No-one apart from us will ever know. You can trust me and Finn. And if Libby rats you out, you can smite her.'

Eveline shook her head but couldn't keep the smile off her face.

Estelle turned to Libby. 'These are awesome presents. Thank you. But honestly, just seeing how happy you've made Henry is the best present I could ever wish for.'

'I have?'

Estelle stared at her as if she was mad. 'Course you bloody have. Look at him. He never smiles.'

Libby turned to see Henry weaving through the crowds holding two glasses of champagne, his face bright and happy.

'Oh,' was all she could think to say.

Henry handed her a glass and chinked the side of it with his.

'Happy birthday,' Libby said. 'And happy birthday, Estelle.'

'Cheers.' Estelle took Henry's glass from him and downed it. 'Did you see what Libby got me?' She showed him the books. 'I got more presents from your girlfriend than you did.'

'That's what you think,' came a voice behind Libby. 'But you're not getting a birthday blow-job later.'

'Ah, Julian.' Henry's face was set tight. 'Please apologise, then go away.'

Libby turned to see a man in his early thirties, dressed in black tie. He had sandy blond hair, a bright red face, and judging by the fumes emanating from him, had already been drinking a while.

His eyes slid over her like an oily caress. 'Well, hel-lo. Julian Mountjoy at your service. You must be Libby. Rupert's told me *all* about you.'

'Smite him! Smite him!' Estelle hissed at Eveline.

Henry glanced at Finn and the two of them moved as one, standing either side of Julian, lifting an arm each and propelling him away.

Libby's hand fluttered to her chest as if to keep her heart from leaping out and following them.

'Are you about to swoon?' Estelle asked.

She nodded. 'I think so.'

Eveline laughed. 'Henry and Finn are good men.'

Estelle sighed and looked at her friend. 'Shame you won't shag him.'

'What?' said Libby.

'Not Henry, doofus, *Finn*. Eveline wants a husband so I've been trying to set her up.'

'Estelle! Shush!'

'Oops. Soz. But Libby is in the circle of trust. Anyway...' Estelle turned back to Libby. 'She doesn't fancy Finn, or Connor or Leo, and all her acolytes—'

'Parishioners,' said Eveline, firmly.

'*Parishioners*... Have one foot in the grave. The only eligible man left in the village is Isaac, but I've bagsied him.'

'Isaac is my friend,' Eveline said.

'He's a yoga teacher,' Estelle said to Libby. 'Have you ever done hot yoga before?'

'No,' she replied. 'Is that what he teaches?'

'No, he teaches Devanandara yoga, but he's hot as fuck. I invited him tonight but I don't think he'll come. He's playing hard to get.'

It was half past seven by the time they were ushered into the dining room. Libby was buzzed after two glasses of champagne, and her hand kept drifting towards Henry's only for her to wrestle control of it and clamp it back to her side. She was used to meeting new people through her work, but it was exhausting playing a part and the stakes were so much higher for Henry. She couldn't let him down.

His aunt, Simone, and her family were ridiculously glamorous and she was painfully aware how their gazes flicked over her outfit as if assessing it from all angles.

Henry and Estelle had made some last-minute adjustments to the place settings to ensure Libby was buffered by them, their friends and siblings. Libby smiled and chatted, but the meal went on for hours, with seven courses, speeches and endless alcohol. By eleven, she was exhausted.

'You don't have to stay,' Henry murmured in her ear. 'It's going to go on all night.'

Goosebumps rippled over her skin at his closeness. She turned her head, allowing her cheek to touch his.

'Are you sure?' she whispered.

He nodded. 'I reached my limit a couple of hours ago. To be honest, you're the perfect excuse for me to leave as well.'

Her heart sprinted off the blocks. 'You're coming with me?'

'The Travelodge was full, but I found a bunkhouse for cavers in the Mendips that had a bed free. I just need to get Rupert's car keys, so I can move his Range Rover and get out. Then I'll head off.'

Oh. 'A bunkhouse? What's that?'

'It's a bit like a youth hostel but more basic. There's a large room with a load of beds in it, and a kitchen and bathroom. There's an honesty box outside for payment, so I can use cash and no-one will know I was there.'

Libby glanced around the opulent dining room, trying to imagine Henry on a bunk bed in a room full of snoring cavers.

'Do they even have bedding?'

He paused.

'Henry!'

'What are you two whispering about?' Estelle asked.

Henry looked like a deer caught in headlights.

'We're tired actually,' Libby replied. 'So, we're probably going to turn in.'

'Already?' Estelle looked horrified at the prospect.

'Estelle,' Eveline said gently. 'It *is* Henry's birthday. Gram-Gram's already left, and I'm going to head off now, too.'

'But she's eighty, and you're a vicar!' Estelle protested. 'Going to bed early is in your job description.'

'Stelle,' Finn said. 'Let Henry and Libby spend some time together.'

'But—'

'Alone,' Finn continued.

Estelle puffed out her cheeks and sighed. 'I'm not going to be this boring when I cop off with Isaac.'

Henry pushed out his chair and whispered to Libby. 'I'm just going to speak to Rupert and get his keys.'

'How's the grand seduction of Isaac going?' Finn asked Estelle.

She wrinkled her nose. 'It's not. I think he's taken a vow of chastity or something.' She turned to Eveline. 'Has he? You spend loads of time together. You must know.'

'Estelle, I am not breaking his confidence by telling you anything about him.'

'Oh, come on!'

Libby glanced along the table. Henry was arguing with Rupert.

Estelle followed her gaze. 'What's he talking to that pillock for?'

'You're not shagging in my bally car!' Rupert yelled.

The table fell silent.

'Please tell me he's joking?' hissed Estelle.

'We're not doing anything in his car,' Libby whispered back. 'He's blocked Henry in, that's all.'

'Can't you sort it out in the morning?'

She shook her head and stood as Henry approached, a thunderous look on his face.

'You can shag in my car,' Julian yelled. 'But only if I can watch.'

Rupert brayed with laughter as his wife loudly shushed him.

Libby took Henry's hand, murmured goodnight to those around her and pulled him out of the room to a chorus of whistles and cheers.

'Fuck's sake,' he said as they exited into the quiet of the corridor. 'They're like a bunch of bloody animals.' He took out his phone. 'I'm going to call a taxi.'

A member of the waiting staff passed them carrying a tray loaded with dishes.

'Call them from the room,' Libby said. 'You don't want anyone to hear.'

TWENTY MINUTES LATER, IT WAS CLEAR THAT HENRY WASN'T going anywhere fast. Libby had doubted the availability of taxis in rural Somerset at half eleven on a Saturday night, and by the time Henry had been laughed at for the fourth time, she knew he wasn't leaving Foxbrooke that evening.

'I'll... Sleep in the car?'

'Henry, please. You don't have to do that.'

He grabbed the contract from his bag and waved it in the air with the confidence of Neville Chamberlain in nineteen thirty-eight holding a piece of paper signed by Hitler promising peace.

'Yes, Libby, I should. I've taken advantage of you enough.'

No, you really haven't.

She cleared her throat. 'Henry, think about this. People are going to be coming and going all night. Someone is bound to spot you in your car, and if they don't, one of the dogs will sniff you out and cause a scene. Look. This bed is huge. If it makes you feel any better, how about we put a wall of pillows down the middle?'

His shoulders slumped. 'I can sleep on the floor of the bathroom?'

'No. Sleep on the bed.'

He hesitated. 'On top of the covers? Fully clothed?'

'If that would make you feel more comfortable?'

'It's not about me. What would make *you* feel more comfortable?'

'For you to stop acting like it's the end of the world and come to bed.' She froze as soon as the words were out of her mouth.

He abruptly turned his back and picked up a pen, then sat on the floor and started adding notes to the contract.

'Are you specifying the height of the pillow wall?' she asked, trying to make a joke.

He glanced up. 'Do you have a ruler?'

She rolled her eyes. 'I don't normally pack one when I go for a long weekend in the country.' She hopped off the bed. 'I'm going to clean my teeth and get changed.'

Ten minutes later, Libby re-entered the bedroom to see a line of pillows down the centre of the bed.

Henry was nowhere to be seen.

Getting under the covers, she picked up her phone to send Claire a text.

> Libby: Survived the night. Lots to talk about but it can wait. Love you xxx

There was a tentative knock on the door.

'Yes?'

Henry entered, carrying a washbag. 'I used the bathroom down the hall.' He pushed the newly-installed deadbolt across the door. 'This should be enough, and I want to make it easy for you to leave in a hurry if you need to.'

'If your killer snoring becomes too much?' she joked.

He didn't smile back.

'Henry! Honestly! It's okay! Just get onto the bed and try to go to sleep.'

He took off his shoes and lay stiffly on top of the covers.

Her phone pinged. *Claire?*

> Lucas: Looks like you're living the high life with your new friends…

> Lucas: [Screenshot from Summer's Instagram account, with a picture of Libby, Summer, Estelle and Willow.]

'Is that Lucas?'

'Yes.'

'Should I speak to him to explain what's happened?'

> Lucas: Don't forget all of us on the other side of the fence.

> Lucas: Ring me when you get this x

Libby turned off her phone and took a deep breath, fighting to keep her nausea at bay.

'Henry, I need to tell you something.'

His head appeared over the top of the pillow wall. 'Are you okay?'

She turned on her side, hugging her knees into her chest as she gazed up at him. He looked worried.

'Lucas isn't my boyfriend.'

He frowned. 'But—'

She sat up. 'I'm sorry. You assumed I had a boyfriend and I panicked and didn't correct you.'

'But, when we met, he kiss—'

'I know. It wasn't real. I told him about your, erm, proposal and that you thought I had a boyfriend. He said he would pretend to be one and check you out.'

Silence.

'I'm so sorry. I didn't know how to tell you.'

Henry sat up. 'So, who is he?'

'He's just a... a friend.'

She could feel his eyes on her. 'Are you in... do you like him?'

Libby's face was suddenly far too hot. She nodded, her focus on the bedcovers. 'I did. For a long time.'

More silence.

'Did?'

She nodded again. 'A lot of things have changed,' she said quietly. 'I don't think I even like him as a friend anymore.'

'So, that kiss...'

'The one with a bonus injury?'

He huffed out a short laugh. 'Yes, that one. It wasn't real?'

'Oh, it was real, alright.' She rubbed the back of her head. 'I think I've still got the bruise.'

He laughed again and she risked glancing up.

'I'm sorry I didn't tell you sooner.'

Henry grinned. 'Frankly, I'm shocked and appalled you didn't inform your fake boyfriend about your other fake boyfriend.'

Libby's heart lifted. 'Thank you for being so cool about it.'

He shrugged. 'That's me. Cool as a cucumber.'

The light dimmed from his smile slightly and he stared intently at her.

Oh no. What now?

'Libby.'

'Ye-es?'

'I'm really glad Lucas isn't your boyfriend. You deserve someone so much better.' He broke her gaze, lying down and facing away. 'Goodnight, Libby.'

She lay down and turned off the light, her eyes wide open in the darkness. 'Goodnight, Henry,' she replied.

❧ 17 ❧

Libby wasn't sure exactly where she was in her dream, but she was feeling warm, comfortable and very sexy. She rolled onto her back and stretched like a cat in the sun. She needed to be stroked.

Mmm... I'll purr for belly rubs.

'Libby?'

'Touch me,' she murmured.

A loud knocking interrupted the softness of her dream.

'Purr—'

'Hang on! It's locked,' Henry's voice called out.

There was a loud crash.

'Dad! Fuck's sake! Now look what you've done!'

She sat up with a start. Henry was striding towards the bedroom door, fully dressed. The door was open, half of the dead bolt hanging off. His father was in the corridor in front of him, picking a tea tray from the floor, his dressing gown still not tied sufficiently to cover what was underneath.

'You didn't have a sock on the handle,' Arthur replied. 'I

thought it was jammed.' He glanced at Libby. 'Morning Libby! Sleep well?'

Henry stared from the splintered door frame to his father and took the tray from him. 'Do your bloody dressing gown up. Nobody wants to see that.'

'Nonsense!' Arthur replied. 'Couldn't disagree more. In the past I had people queueing for a ride.'

Henry brought the tray over and placed it on the table beside her.

'I'm so sorry,' he murmured. 'Again.'

'Bloody woodworm. That or dry rot.' His father picked at where the lock had given way. 'Lasted nearly five hundred years though. Can't say fairer than that.' He glanced up. 'Maybe Finn could fix it. Is he coming over today for the picnic? The party later?'

Libby's heart hadn't slowed since she'd woken up. It was all too much to take in. Had she been purring? Her dreams were disappearing like smoke from a snuffed candle.

'I don't know. I think so,' Henry replied. 'But you can't ask him to fix it.'

'Why not? He's a carpenter.'

'It's his day off.'

'Is it?'

'Yes. It's the weekend.'

Arthur winked at Libby. 'I do my most important work on the weekend. No rest for the wicked and all that.'

Henry pointed at the door. 'Out!'

'Okay, okay.' He backed away, holding up his hands. 'Got to get dressed for church, anyway.'

Libby closed her eyes.

'And do your bloody dressing gown up properly!' Henry yelled.

His father waved and shut the door behind him.

However, now the door was damaged, it drifted back open, revealing Arthur holding both sides of his dressing gown apart, the Foxbrooke jewels on full display.

'I was doing it up!' he cried.

Henry dashed to the door and slammed it shut in his father's face.

It fell open again.

'Well, that won't work,' Arthur said, mildly. 'The frame's gone. I'd call Finn if I were you.' He looked around Henry's shoulder and gave Libby a wave. 'Church in forty minutes, picnic in a couple of hours. Toodle pip!'

He turned on his heel and walked away, whistling, the slap-slap of his ancient carpet slippers echoing down the corridor.

Henry pushed a chair against the door, then glanced at her. He seemed one straw away from breaking.

Libby burst out laughing and raised her hands in resignation.

His shoulders sagged and he came and sat on the edge of the bed.

'Church?' she managed, before giggling again.

The corners of his mouth lifted. 'Yes. All three of my parents are regulars at Saint Saviour's even though Mom was raised a Baptist and Mammy a Catholic. They say God is everywhere and loves everyone. Plus, Dad and Dervla are in the church choir.'

'Seriously? Do they wear clothes?'

'Yes and yes. They're quite well-behaved in church, and choir members have robes anyway.'

'What do the locals think? Eveline?'

'Pissing off the locals is one of Dad's favourite hobbies, but most of them have accepted he's here to stay. And of course, no-one wants to get on the wrong side of Gram-Gram. The previous vicar hated my dad. He was really High Church, all smells and bells, fire and brimstone, which Mammy loved. Eveline's far more laid-back and progressive.'

Libby remembered the first night's meal and the tension between Eveline and Gram-Gram.

'And what does Gram-Gram think of her?'

Henry raised his eyebrows. 'I'm sure she thinks women shouldn't be allowed to be priests in the first place. Estelle says Eveline is trying to bring Saint Saviour's into the twenty-first century, and Gram-Gram's trying to boot it back to the dark ages.'

Libby took a sip of tea. 'I could get used to this.'

'Tea in bed?'

'Yes, just without the near-naked room service.'

'And complete lack of boundaries?'

'Well, his heart seems to be in the right place...'

Henry rolled his eyes. 'His one saving grace.'

'And his bollocks definitely are.'

He dropped his head with a sigh and she snorted with laughter.

'So then Henry, what are we doing today? The costume party is tonight?'

Looking up, he nodded. 'When are you going to show me what my dress options are?'

'Ten minutes before the first gong.'

His eyebrows raised, and she took a sip of her scalding tea. Henry was way hotter.

He cleared his throat. 'There's a picnic planned for most of the day by the lake. The weather's fine, so we might get the rowboats out. If you want to skip it, we can.'

'No, it all sounds lovely.'

'And I thought this morning you might want to go for a walk around the estate?'

'How much mud and dung will there be?'

He grimaced. 'Your first impression has not been an entirely accurate representation of Somerset.'

'It smelled pretty accurate to me.'

'It hasn't rained for days, and it's the height of summer. I promise it'll be better than you expect.'

AFTER BREAKFAST, LIBBY LEFT THE MANOR WITH HENRY. To one side of the building, at the edge of the formal gardens, lay a high stone wall with a tall wooden gate set into it. He opened it for her and she passed through the gap into a small copse on the edge of the parkland. A path lay in front of them leading through the trees. Dappled sunlight moved gently across the ground as if dancing to the sounds of the leaves rustling overhead. Libby stopped, taking it all in.

'Is everything okay?' Henry asked.

She nodded. 'It's so quiet.'

Birds trilled around her and a dog barked in the distance.

'I mean, there's no...' She tried to think of all the sounds that made up the white noise of her daily life. All the beeps of horns, squeals of brakes and revving of engines. The constant cacophony of people living cheek by jowl. In London she lived with man-made noise, twenty-four-seven. Only in its absence did she realise how deafening it truly was.

Even over the last couple of days at the Manor, there were the odd traffic noises from the village, people talking and laughing, and the creaks and groans as the ancient house grumbled. But here, behind the high wall, there was nothing except the birds and the whispers of the wind as it rustled through the trees.

A wave of emotion moved through her. She gazed at Henry and the sensations grew stronger. Why was he affecting her this way? She felt ungrounded, as if she might float away.

'Henry, do you mind if I hold your hand?'

He swallowed, then extended his arm towards her.

She interlaced her fingers with his, the warmth from his touch shimmering across her skin.

'Thank you.'

He held her gaze and her mouth ran dry.

'I, I didn't know it would be like this,' she said.

His eyes widened.

'The countryside,' she added.

'Yes, yes of course.' Henry paused. 'But we, er, haven't gone very far.'

She glanced at the wall behind them. 'You're right. I think it's just how it sounds that surprised me.'

He was silent, his head cocked slightly as he listened.

'You're right. Living in a city you forget what it's like.'

'It's weird. It's like I can hear myself breathing, but not just my lungs... my whole body.' She frowned. 'I hope that doesn't make me sound like a nutter. Did your dad slip something into my tea this morning?'

He shook his head and smiled. 'Even though dad might look like a crazy cult leader, he would *never* do that. And you're not a nutter.'

'I feel as if I might float away if I didn't hold onto something.'

Henry squeezed her hand. 'I'll keep your feet on the ground. I'm sensible, dependable and most importantly, heavy.'

Libby laughed and threw her arms around him, hugging him tightly, then immediately let go.

'Sorry...'

He opened his arms. 'Any time. Remember our contract states you can initiate any act that involves bodily contact.'

Oh god. Now, she was thinking about acts that involved *intimate* bodily contact.

She tilted her head to one side. 'Are you a hugger, Henry?'

He looked away, his cheeks colouring. 'Under the right circumstances.'

Had she pushed him too far? *Fuck*. She'd been flirting with someone who, for these few days at least, she should be in a business relationship with.

'Okay,' she said brightly. 'So far, I've almost been completely overwhelmed by some trees. Want to tip me over the edge by showing me a field?'

He grinned. 'And if that doesn't do it, I can throw in some spectacular hedges.'

LIBBY'S EXPERIENCE OF THE ENGLISH COUNTRYSIDE WAS entirely informed by film and television. She may have walked for miles in the rain with Lizzie Bennet to visit Jane at Netherfield Park, or picnicked with Emma on Box Hill more times than she could remember, but each trip was undertaken from the comfort of a sofa or a cinema seat. Now she was strolling through open parkland on a perfect summer's day, with the quintessential English gentleman by her side.

'I'm going to show you the highlights,' Henry said as they strolled through the short grass. 'The estate is pretty large, so we're going to do the arboretum, Dad's biodynamic fields, and finish at the lake.'

She could already see it in the distance, people setting up marquees by the edge of the water.

'Can I hear pigs?'

'Yep, they're Eveline's,' he replied, pointing to a large house and garden that lay between the Manor and the church behind them. 'Gram-Gram pitched a fit when she turned part of the rectory garden over to them. I don't know why, it was a jungle of brambles before that.'

'Eveline said she's a part-time pig farmer?'

'From what Estelle says, Eveline isn't a part time anything. Apparently, she works longer hours than I do, which is saying something.'

'What does she do with the pigs when they're grown?'

'Everything from sausages to bacon to charcuterie. I've tasted some of it and it's out of this world.'

'Does she sell it?'

Henry shook his head. 'She's not allowed to, but I think she'd just give it away anyway. Gram-Gram told Estelle that Eveline was using it to bribe people to like her.'

'That's a bit harsh!'

He grinned. 'She's only jealous. She tried to make some kind of point a while back by refusing a side of bacon, and now regrets that decision.'

Henry stopped and pointed at the landscape before them.

'So, Foxbrooke village is behind us, and the Manor, church and rectory are all on the edge. Over there we've got the lake and the Dower House where Gram-Gram lives. Beyond the wood in the distance is the river Foxbrooke. It marks the border between our land and another estate which is currently up for sale. And to the left, up the hill, is the arboretum that my great, great, great grandfather planted. It's not far.'

As they walked, Libby thought about what her great, great, great grandfather might have planted. A potato? Henry's world was so far removed from hers, the only overlap she could comprehend was the present moment.

To an outsider, they might look like a couple on a walk. But he was travelling through life first class, and she belonged in steerage. The thought of them having any kind of relationship outside a weekend of fake dating was like Rose and Jack on the Titanic; doomed from the outset.

However, fantasising about a life in the countryside wasn't

off limits. The sun was warm on her skin, the sky a brilliant blue, and surrounding them were thousands of shades of green. Despite her inherent fears about dirt, everything smelled fresh and clean.

The arboretum was large, with plenty of space between the tallest trees and the smaller ones planted between them. Henry pulled down a low-hanging pine and crushed some of the needles between his fingers and thumb. He brought them to his nose and breathed deeply.

'I love this smell.' He offered the crushed needles to her.

She couldn't resist taking his hand and smelling his skin.

'I can't wait to tell India she was right.'

Henry raised an eyebrow. 'About what?'

'She said all the best men smell like they've rolled around in pine needles.'

'Huh?'

'All those "woodsy" notes in aftershave?'

'Ah.' He stared at the ground. 'No wonder I haven't been able to find a girlfriend. I haven't been rolling around under trees enough.'

Libby bit her lip. She was desperate to tell him how amazing she thought he was, how any woman would be beyond lucky if Henry Foxbrooke wanted to be with them. But she kept quiet. She'd already stepped out of her box by flirting with him and grabbing him at any opportunity. Around Henry, she felt like she had less control than one of his dad's dogs.

So she kept her mouth shut and let him talk to her about the different trees as they strolled, her senses drawing everything in, like a plant desperate for water.

They left the arboretum and started down a track between hedges bursting with life. Was she just caught up in the romance of Jane Austen, or was this revelation about the countryside real? Would she feel the same if it was pissing down with rain in the depths of winter and Henry wasn't by her side? This was a fantasy. Take the weather and him away, and all that was left was cold, wet mud.

But then Henry led her through a gate into a field and she nearly wept.

'Do you like it?' His forehead was furrowed as if uncertain.

'Is this for real?'

He nodded. 'Dad is really into biodynamic farming and regenerative agriculture. Wildflowers are part of that.'

The field was on a slope, leading up to a giant oak tree and was thigh-deep in colour.

'I don't want to walk through and ruin it,' she whispered.

'You should see what happens when the cows come through. It's all part of the process.'

He held his hand out to her, then brought it back to his side.

Fuck it. She was going to live out her fantasy for a few more moments. She took his hand and led him forwards up the slope, the flowers stroking her legs.

At the top, the base of the tree spread out, creating natural seats. Libby sat, feeling the smoothness of the bark as if someone else had run their hand over it many times before.

'Estelle, Connor, Finn, Jack, and I used to come here when we were kids,' Henry said. 'That was Estelle's seat.' He sat next to her, and they looked out over the field of flowers, the lines of hedges and fields and the glinting sunlight on the surface of the lake in the distance.

She sighed. 'It must have been an idyllic childhood.'

He huffed. 'Apart from being dragged away from our parents by the police and put in emergency care, then the savage bullying at school, yeah, it was dandy.'

18

Libby shifted to face him. 'Oh my god!'

Henry's face was taut. 'Sorry.'

'Don't apologise.'

He shrugged. 'It's first-world problems. A poor little rich boy complaining about life when one day he's going to get all of this.' He gestured at the countryside in front of them.

'Henry. Bullying is bullying. Having money doesn't make it any easier. And being taken from your parents? How old were you?'

'Estelle, Connor and I were six. Leo was two and Willow was a baby.'

'Jesus Christ. What happened?'

He rubbed his forehead. 'Dad was running his sex parties, but they were wild and there were loads of drugs.'

Her mouth dropped open, and he raised his hands.

'We were in a separate section of the house with Mammy and never saw any of it. But that didn't matter. One of the newspapers organised a campaign against him. After about a month of the letters arriving, our parents took us into the town centre one Saturday afternoon and burnt them all. Apparently the police had already started an investigation, so when they were called out, they arrested Mom, Dad and Mammy and took us into emergency care.'

She pressed her hand against her chest, her heart thudding. 'That must have been terrifying.'

He nodded. 'My whole life, I've never been as scared as I was then. It was like the worst possible night terror, only it was real. Willow was only a few weeks old and screaming like she was being attacked. Leo was howling and wet himself with fear. Connor and Estelle followed the lead of our parents and fought like animals. I just stood there, frozen, as everything I loved was ripped apart.'

'How long were you...'

'A week.'

Libby reached across the low tree root and squeezed Henry's hand. 'I'm so sorry.'

He nodded. 'Me too. Don't get me wrong, my parents drive me insane, but we were never at risk. We didn't even know about the parties until we were taken away.'

'What happened then?'

'They carried on, but with risk assessments, better security, a no drugs policy, and us shipped off to Gram-Gram's.'

He stroked the back of her hand as he looked down the hill again.

'That's when school became an issue. Dad believes in equality, so sent us to the local primary. Other kids gave us shit because of what their parents had told them. We could handle it because the school only had one class for each year, so Estelle, Connor and I were together with Finn and Jack. It changed though when we got to secondary.'

He paused, the silence filled with the trills of birdsong. She waited, her heart breaking for him.

'Foxbrooke is small, but the secondary school is huge. It takes kids from all villages in the area and has an eight-form entry each year. Our parents asked for us to be put together, but they split us up anyway. Connor and Estelle were fighters and fitted in better than I did, and Finn and Jack could distance themselves from us during school hours. I just shut down.'

'What happened?'

'Dad was adamant we needed to be state educated so we didn't end up like his sister and her family, so I begged Mom to pay for me to go to private school.'

'Was it any better there?'

He shrugged. 'A little, but difficult in other ways.'

'Did Estelle and Connor stay at the local school?'

Henry nodded. 'Estelle didn't ask to leave, and I don't think Connor felt like he could ask Mom for the money because she wasn't his biological parent.'

'Did you ever talk to them about it?'

He shook his head. 'Sometimes, in families, you can't talk about the biggest things of all.'

'What about Leo, Willow, Summer?'

Henry let out a breath. 'Like Connor, they're not biologically Mom's kids, and Mammy doesn't earn any money of her own so couldn't pay for them even if she wanted to. As far as I know, Leo and Willow never asked to move.'

'And Summer?'

'I paid for her to go to private school.'

'How?'

'I'm nearly ten years older. I made sure I got into the right university, studied the right subject, got the right job. I wanted to help all of them but could only afford one set of fees. Leo had almost finished school, and Willow seemed settled, so I paid for Summer.'

Bloody hell. 'That must have set you back a bit.'

'I don't regret a penny. I just wish she'd completed a degree.'

'You paid for her to go to uni as well?'

He nodded.

Libby thought about how much debt she'd accrued to go to university. It was a huge amount and she expected to spend most of her life repaying the loans.

Henry squeezed her hand. 'I never meant to tell you this. You're just such a good listener, it all came out.'

'Have you ever talked to anyone else about it?'

He shook his head. 'Everyone knows. But like I said, it's a subject we never discuss.'

'Is this why you don't want to come back here?'

He hesitated, then nodded. 'I can't control anything here, but I can in London. I want to feel normal. I want to fit in. Like you.'

'Me? Fit in?'

His expression was earnest. 'Yes. You fit into any situation you're placed in, perfectly.'

'God, Henry, that's just acting and false confidence. Most of the time I don't feel like I fit in at all.'

He looked at her as if she'd just announced she was a shapeshifter from the planet Xarg.

'Henry, when did you last look at yourself in a mirror? Seriously, you've got a great job and are adored by your family—'

'I wouldn't go that far—'

'You're sweet, kind, clever, funny, and better looking than a model. Jesus, Henry, you've got it all.'

He frowned. 'It doesn't feel like that.'

She understood. Just because she thought he was amazing and had all his ducks in a row, didn't mean he agreed.

'Libby?'

Oh god, please just kiss me! 'Ye-es?'

'I feel normal when I'm with you. Most of the time.'

'Most of the time?'

Henry let go of her hand, his cheeks colouring. 'Sharing a bed with you doesn't, er, feel particularly normal.'

He leapt to his feet, shading his eyes as he looked towards the lake. 'They're setting up for the picnic. Do you want to wander that way now?'

No! I want to stay here with you! Libby stared at the field. 'Are we allowed to pick the flowers?'

'Sure. Do you want them for the room?'

She shook her head. 'I want to be a flower fairy for the day.'

❦

HENRY STOLE GLANCES AT LIBBY AS THEY MADE THEIR WAY to the lake. When he'd first met her in London, he thought she was a pixie who'd floated in through the window on a sunbeam. Now, with a garland of wildflowers around her head, she was a fairy queen. She was effortlessly beautiful and effortlessly herself. He wanted to be close to her always, to allow her light to banish his shadows. As the path narrowed, he indicated for her to go ahead. Strolling behind, he admired her beauty and the countryside.

Henry had deliberately built his life in London. The urban environment was full of straight lines and monochrome shades. It was the subjugation of nature into something more ordered and controllable. But with Libby he saw his home through new eyes. The hedges either side of the footpath were overgrown and chaotic, but within the chaos was an abundance of life. His father had once said you could tell how old a hedge was by how many species of tree were in it. These hedges might be as ancient as the Manor.

Libby ran her fingers over the foliage, her smiling face taking everything in. He ached for her. Could things be different between them now he knew she didn't have a boyfriend? He shook his head. He was as arrogant as Hunter-Savage to presume that just because he wanted her, she would want him in return. If she was attracted to arty types like Lucas, what chance did a boring City suit like him have? And anyway, he couldn't break the contract between them and destroy her trust.

'Oh my god!'

Libby had stopped at the juncture between where the foot-path met a lane and was staring at a cottage set back from the small road.

'Everything okay?'

'Look at it!'

The building appeared as though it hadn't had tenants in years. The windows were grimy and the thatched roof was blackened with age.

He wrinkled his nose. 'Yeah, it is pretty knackered. No wonder no-one wants to rent it.'

'Henry, are you insane? It's beautiful!'

'Er. It is?' It looked like it needed to be accidentally-on-purpose run over by a tractor.

She clasped her hands to her chest and sighed. 'Look at the climbing roses! It's perfect.'

'I doubt it's even on mains sewerage.' He glanced around. 'And I can't see a phone line or electricity.'

She clutched his arm. 'Look! There's a chimney! Imagine sitting in front of an open fire in the middle of winter.'

Henry gazed at her animated face, imagining the two of

them doing far more than just sitting in front of the fire. God, he wanted to kiss her so much it hurt.

Clearing his throat, he stepped back. 'Lighting a fire in there would be extremely dangerous. I expect the only reason the cottage hasn't been demolished already is that there's some kind of preservation order on it.' *Fuck me, I sound like a nob.*

Libby's face fell and she nodded. 'You're right. I'm just getting carried away.' She raised her hand to the flower garland as if to remove it.

'Please keep it on.'

She frowned. 'Why? It's silly.'

He shook his head. 'It's beautiful. It suits you.'

Her expression was uncertain as she lowered her hand. 'Really?'

Yes! You're so fucking beautiful!

Henry nodded. 'Come on, we should go.'

He turned to continue down the road, feeling like he'd just trampled on her dreams.

WITH EVERY STEP, HENRY FELT MORE AWKWARD. APART from his father's parties, the Winter Ball and a few other public events, his family wasn't particularly ostentatious. However, this week they'd gone all-in. The lakeside looked as if the Royal enclosure at Ascot had decamped there for the day, with luxury gazebos, rattan furniture, and waiting staff carrying drinks and arranging food on long tables out of the sun.

Libby's family was at the opposite end of the socio-economic scale. Did she feel uncomfortable at this display of wealth? He stole glances at her. What was she thinking? His extended family was already by the lake, either sitting and chatting, or playing croquet. *Fucking croquet.* Could they have *been* any more upper class?

'Oh my god,' Libby exclaimed. 'Is that Estelle?'

Ah yes. His sister was raising the upper-class bar even higher by arriving at the event on horseback, with Joy, her English Setter, running by Duke's side.

'She's so badass.'

'If you tell her that we'll never hear the end of it. Can I guess what her costume choice was for this evening? Lara Croft from Tomb Raider?'

Libby's eyes widened. 'How did you know?'

Henry shrugged. 'It's either that or Amelia Earhart. She likes kickass women who wear trousers. She's never going to come dressed as a princess.'

His sister galloped past everyone at the lakeside towards them. Libby ducked behind him as Duke reared to a halt and his sister dismounted.

'It's okay,' Estelle said to her, shucking a pack off her back with a fluffy head sticking out the top. 'Duke may be huge but he's good as gold.' She unzipped the pack and Chester bounded out. 'He can't run as fast as the others, so he gets to ride with me.'

Libby crouched down to pet him. 'I think you're the coolest person I've ever met,' she said to Estelle.

A brief expression of shock crossed his sister's face before her smile almost split it in two.

She punched Henry on the arm. 'Hear that? Although it's not hard to be cooler than you, let's face it.' She turned to Libby. 'And you look like a summer goddess. Fancy a ride on Duke?'

Libby stood, shaking her head so fast a few petals fell off her garland.

'Can Henry ride him?' she asked.

'Yes, of course.' Estelle narrowed her eyes. 'Hang on, is this some kind of Regency role play fantasy thing for you, Elizabeth Bennet?'

'No, not at all.' She blushed. 'Erm, I just didn't, er, believe that Henry could really ride. That's all.'

Did Libby have a thing for men on horseback? Henry didn't hesitate, swinging himself onto the saddle.

'Did you just squeak like a mouse having an orgasm?' Estelle asked, incredulously. Henry couldn't see Libby's face as she stared down at the grass.

'That was Chester,' she mumbled.

Estelle snorted. 'Yeah, right. Your costume choices are now making a whole lot of sexy sense.' She looked at Henry with a smirk. 'Brother, you are getting it tonight.'

The thought that Libby might like a man who could ride spurred Henry on. He nudged Duke and the horse took off. He laughed out loud at the thrill. It had been years since he'd ridden and he'd forgotten how joyous it was. They galloped across the park then wheeled around and cantered back to Estelle and Libby, slowing to a walk as they approached so as not to scare her.

Libby's cheeks were pink, her mouth open, her nostrils flared. Henry's heart thumped faster in his chest. Did she like *him*? Or just the fantasy? Right now, he didn't care either way. Her attention was so entirely on him, she'd failed to notice Chester humping her leg.

'Fuck's sake, Chester-Chops.' Estelle pushed him away. 'That's Henry's job, not yours.' She glanced at her brother, a cheeky grin on her face. 'Your girlfriend's in heat. Want to nip off to a field for a quick roll in the hay?'

Henry froze, as did Libby. Heat moved up his neck as her cheeks turned from pink to red.

Estelle jammed her hands on her hips. 'Seriously? What *is* it with you two? Henry, you look like you're about to be shot.

Lighten the fuck up! Jesus Christ. I think Eveline's more up for it than you two, and she's the bloody vicar.' Estelle started striding towards the group by the lake. 'Come and get some Pimms in you. And if that doesn't loosen you up, I'll nick you some Viagra off Dad.'

❧ 19 ☙

Libby concentrated on breathing slowly in and out, trying to calm herself. This was a difficult task when Henry's pert backside was swaying on Duke's back in front of her.

'Go on then,' said Estelle. 'Top five Austen fantasies.'

'What?'

Estelle took her arm. 'Indulge me. They don't have to be in any particular order.'

Libby bit her lip.

'Oh, come on! Look, if you tell me, I promise I'll save you from Rupert or Julian if they get too close.'

Libby giggled. 'Okay, but you have to promise not to tell Henry.'

Estelle looked at her askance. 'Why not? Surely this is the basis of your entire sexual relationship?'

She shook her head.

Estelle was frowning as if she couldn't work out what her problem was.

'Only if you don't tell Henry,' she repeated.

'Okay, okay. I won't tell him. Right. Is one of them a man riding a horse?'

She nodded.

'Go on then, I can't bloody mind-read.'

Libby felt naughty and excited all rolled into one. Telling Estelle made all her Henry-specific fantasies real.

'Have you ever seen the TV series of *Pride and Prejudice* with Colin Firth as Mr Darcy?'

Estelle shook her head. 'I haven't, but I would bet my bottom dollar that one of your fantasies involves Henry walking out of a lake in a very wet white shirt.'

Libby blushed and Estelle shrieked, causing people to look up.

'Knew it! He's wearing a white shirt today. Want me to push him in?'

Omg yes! 'No!'

'You're no fun. Okay, go on, what else?'

Libby sighed happily. 'Dancing at a ball, spraining my ankle and having to be carried by him, taking tea in the parlour and trying to figure out a way to be alone, going for a carriage ride, being caught kissing in a garden and him duelling over my honour.'

'Holy shit.'

'And beautiful dresses,' she added. 'It's all about the frocks.'

They entered one of the gazebos and Estelle handed her a tumbler of Pimms.

'Right,' she said out of the corner of her mouth. 'Here's the plan. Have a couple of these, then I'll push you over. Henry will challenge me to a duel, and I'll punch him. He'll manfully recover, lift you up, stagger back to the Manor and kiss you in a hedge. Will that do for starters?'

Libby was still laughing when Henry joined them.

He glanced cautiously between them. 'Having fun?'

'Oh yes,' his sister replied. 'I've just been looking inside Libby's head and it's a very interesting place, I can tell you. Can you dance a cotillion?'

'A what?'

'Estelle,' said Libby, with what she hoped was a warning tone.

'Nothing,' she replied. 'Finn should be coming along later. Fancy being beaten in the Foxbrooke boat race another year?'

'He beat me because you were in the boat with him. Two against one is hardly fair.'

His sister shrugged. 'You're meant to be the rowing champ. I think you've just lost your touch. Right, I'm going to ring Eveline and see where the arse she is. You two go and have fun.'

She strode off.

LIBBY AND HENRY HELPED THEMSELVES TO PLATES OF FOOD and were about to sit on a picnic blanket to eat, when Gram-Gram waved them over. She was holding court at a table in a gazebo with her daughter, Charlotte, and Charlotte's large family. Libby was immediately on edge. To an extent, she could relax around Henry's parents and siblings. Despite their wealth and eccentricities they were friendly, and she didn't spend all her time feeling socially inferior.

This branch of the family was a completely different matter. Henry's aunt, Lady Charlotte Hatton-Blythe, and her husband, Sir Humphrey, oozed posh from every pore. If Charlotte resembled a horse, Humphrey was a walrus, with his enormous jowls and habit of loudly exhaling before he said anything. Their three children and spouses were regarding Libby as one might an exotic new specimen encountered at a zoo.

'Are you enjoying Foxbrooke, Elizabeth?' Charlotte asked, a cucumber sandwich in her hand, her pinkie finger extended.

'Yes, thank you,' she replied. 'It has been lovely.'

'Play your cards right and you'll be living here one day,' Rupert brayed from further down the table.

'Roo-Roo!' hissed Cecily at him.

Libby popped a blini heaped with smoked salmon and caviar in her mouth. If she was eating, maybe they would leave her in peace?

'Elizabeth,' Gram-Gram began.

'*Libby*,' Henry interrupted.

'Ah, yes, *Libby*. Do tell me more about your family.'

'I—' She hastily swallowed and a bit went down the wrong way. 'Excuse me... hang on—'

Henry passed her a glass of water and rubbed her back whilst she coughed.

The rest of his family watched her as if waiting to see her next move. She could feel Henry tense beside her.

Libby wiped the corners of her eyes and took a breath. She'd prepared for this moment, but the lies still stuck in her throat.

'I was born in Hollywood, just south of Birmingham, but was brought up in Surrey where my family still lives. My father is a lawyer, and my mother is a legal secretary.'

Silence.

She continued with the lies, basing as much of it as she could on India's family, and feeling sicker with every word that came out of her mouth.

'And why Henry?' Rupert interrupted. 'Apart from the title and all of this?'

'Rupert!' Gram-Gram barked.

Henry pushed his chair back, ready to confront his cousin.

Libby put her hand on his arm, guiding him back down.

Rupert shrugged. 'Innocent question. As far as we know, Henry's never had a girlfriend. We all thought he was a—'

'Roo-Roo! For heaven's sake!' Cecily snapped.

Julian hooted with laughter. 'We assumed he'd paid you to be his girlfriend.'

'Ah! There you are,' cried Estelle, entering the gazebo. 'You promised you'd come boating with me.' She hauled Libby to her feet and dragged her away. 'Just borrowing her for half an hour,' she called over her shoulder before lowering her voice and muttering in Libby's ear. 'Or the rest of the weekend...'

'Thank you,' she whispered back. 'They're terrifying.'

'Don't let them get to you.' Estelle squeezed her arm. 'They're a once-a-year endurance.'

Henry joined them and his sister frowned at him.

'Fat lot of good you were being back there, little brother.'

'I—'

'Henry was doing his best,' Libby said.

'I didn't see a shotgun,' Estelle replied. 'Or a bullwhip. That's the very least Rupert and Julian need. Seriously, did that ballbag suggest Henry bloody *paid* you to pretend to be his girl-friend?' She shook her head. 'Arseholes.'

A jetty extended out into the lake, with two rowing boats tied to it.

'Right, Henry, go and impress Libby with your rowing skills. Added bonus, the numpties can't get to you out there.'

Henry gazed at Libby, concern creasing his brow. 'You don't have to.'

'I want to.' She wanted to get far away from all of his family. Even Estelle was starting to stress her out.

His face relaxed. He led her onto the jetty and helped her into the back of one of the rowing boats that had cushions on a wooden seat. He sat opposite and rolled his shirt sleeves up.

Libby stared at his arms.

'Do you want a tissue for that drool?' Estelle asked as she pushed the side of the boat away from the jetty.

Libby ignored her.

'I said—'

'No thank you, Estelle,' she replied through gritted teeth. 'Everything's fine.'

As the boat cut through the water, Libby looked at the lake rather than at Henry in an attempt to keep her cheeks from bursting into flames or her underwear melting.

'I'm sorry about earlier,' he said. 'I didn't know when to step in.'

She risked a glance at him, then immediately regretted it. The top two buttons of his tailored white shirt were undone, and the rolled-up sleeves revealed his muscular forearms. Seeing so much of his skin felt positively indecent. No wonder young ladies used to swoon at such a sight. *Hold it the fuck together*.

'A conversation like that was to be expected. We've had an easy ride of it so far,' she replied, staring at his feet. In her peripheral vision she could still see the movement of his arms.

'True, but I'd still rather you didn't have to endure it.'

He rowed towards the centre of the lake.

'Henry...'

'Yes?'

He stowed the oars, his focus now entirely on her.

Libby swallowed and risked meeting his eyes. Henry was a magnet, drawing her in, and it was becoming harder and harder to stay away. He'd gone from gorgeous to utterly irresistible.

'I feel extremely guilty about taking more money from you.'

The shock on his face suggested she'd just asked him to remove the rest of his clothes, throw her to the bottom of the boat and rut her like a stag.

'What? Why?'

She couldn't tell him how her feelings for him had changed, but she could be truthful about everything else.

'Henry, most of the time this has been fun, not a job. I'm being treated like a princess and it's not costing me anything. You've been more than generous in so many ways, and it feels wrong to take any more of your money.'

He leaned forward, resting his elbows on his knees and steepling his fingers.

'Libby, may I speak frankly?'

Uh oh. She nodded.

'When we return to London, where are you going to live?'

The Foxbrooke bubble burst. In a couple of days, she would leave a fairy-tale four-poster bed for a sofa in the house of a newborn.

Henry waited, as still as a statue.

'Um, I'm going to stay with Claire until I can find another flatshare.'

'Do you have the money for a deposit?'

Fuck! Her cheeks flamed. No, she didn't. She didn't have enough money for anything because all of her savings had gone to Lucas.

Henry was frighteningly calm. 'Now that Claire's given birth, what's your business strategy going forward?'

'I'll sort something out.'

'Is there a plan in place?'

She shrugged, hiding how utterly mortified she felt. Henry was a successful City broker, and she was an arty-farty fuck-up. A gulf deeper than the Grand Canyon lay between them, and with every truth he stated, it got bigger. Memories of Giles flashed into her mind.

Your hobby job isn't exactly covering the increase in utility bills since you moved in.

'Libby. I picked you up from Claire's flat, so I know your sleeping choices are the sofa or the floor space between a cot and a changing table. Without a deposit, you won't be able to secure alternative accommodation, and without a job you won't get a deposit. Do you honestly think, in all good conscience, I can subject you to four days of my family then leave you high and dry when we return to London?'

She glanced at him, then away again. He was deadly serious.

'What kind of a person would I be if I treated you like that?' His voice was low and tight. 'Enduring a five-minute conversation with most members of my family should qualify for a bonus.'

She bit the inside of her cheek to keep the emotion at bay. Once again, she was a charity case.

He threw his hands up. 'Jesus, Libby. I'd give you all the money in my bank account if you'd let me. I was dreading this weekend, but you've made it enjoyable. You have no idea how much you've done for me.' He crossed his arms. 'And you signed a contract.'

That *bloody* contract again.

'Libby?' his voice was softer. 'Please look at me?'

She shook her head.

'Fuck!' He exhaled. 'I'm sorry. I shouldn't have spoken so harshly.'

Out of the bottom of her blurry eyes, she saw his fingers extend towards hers. This time he didn't stop, clasping her hands in his.

She raised her head. If she was in pain, he looked in agony.

'Libby, I couldn't live with myself if I didn't pay you for everything you've done. Please let me?'

'Cooee!'

Their heads snapped up. Estelle was rowing towards them.

Henry let go of Libby's hands. She wiped her eyes and put on a smile.

'Hey, lovebirds, I've come to race you.' Estelle drew nearer. 'Henry, have you got your phone on you?'

'No, it's back at the house. Why?'

'I can't get in touch with Eveline, so I thought I'd try from yours.'

Libby gazed at the bank where a figure with long, deep red hair was strolling towards the group.

'Isn't that Eveline?'

Estelle turned her head. 'Ah, yes, so it is.' She stood, holding an oar over her head and waving it. 'Eveline!' Her boat wobbled.

'Estelle, sit down,' Henry called out. 'What are you doing?'

Her boat started to tip.

'Fuck!' Estelle yelled, her arms flailing.

'Estelle! Sit down!'

She threw the oar away, dropping to the bottom of the boat and placing her hands on the sides. The oar floated away.

'Henry!'

He sighed. 'I'll get it. Hang on.'

He manoeuvred their boat to reach the oar, pulled it out of the water, then rowed back to his sister.

He tried to pass one end to her, but she was standing again and making her boat rock.

'Fuck's sake, Estelle. Why are you being such a muppet? You've been in these things a million times.'

She snorted. 'I may have had a bit too much Pimms.'

Henry stood, his footing sure, holding out the oar for his sister.

She took the other end in both hands.

'Thanks!' She yanked it towards her, pulling an unsuspecting Henry straight into the water with a loud splash.

'Oh my god!' Libby stared at Estelle in shock. Estelle responded with a wink.

Henry spluttered as he re-surfaced. 'What the fuck, Estelle!'

'Shit! I'm so sorry,' she replied. 'I didn't know that would happen. Thank god you didn't have your phone on you.'

Henry swam to the side of their boat and Libby held out her hand.

He shook his head. 'You'll capsize us if you help me. Go to the other side and lean over to counterbalance the weight.'

She did and he hauled himself back in.

They both glanced over at Estelle, who was already halfway back to the bank.

'I don't know why she did that,' Henry said. 'She's mental.'

'I'm afraid it's my fault,' Libby replied, quietly.

'How?'

'I told her my favourite bit from the first Pride and Prejudice TV series was when Mr Darcy swam in a lake and met Lizzie wearing a wet white shirt.' She stared at her feet. 'I think Estelle tried to make my fantasy come true.'

Silence.

Eventually Henry cleared his throat. 'Ah.'

More silence. Her mortification was complete.

'Do you mind helping me navigate back to the jetty?' he asked. 'I need to get out of these clothes.'

Gah! She kept her eyes on the bottom of the boat. 'What do you want me to do?' she mumbled.

'Well, my back is to the bank, so I need you to look at me and tell me whether to go left or right.' His voice was mild.

Oh god. She slowly raised her eyes, then wished she hadn't. His wet shirt clung to him. He pulled on the oars and his muscles rippled in response.

Oh bloody fucking hell. She stared at his body, her intellect taking a break from operations as her animal brain prepared to pounce.

'Am I going the right way?' he asked.

She looked up. They were not.

'Um, more to your right.'

She gazed back at her feet, trying to control her breathing as her heart ran double time.

'Libby?'

'Hmm?'

'I really need you to look at me. I can't do this without you.'

She glanced up to see that he was still rowing in the wrong direction. *I thought he was meant to be some kind of pro at this?*

By now the boat had turned so that Henry was facing the side of the lake populated by people.

'See?' he said. 'We'll never get back to the bank unless you help out.'

Libby stared at him. Henry may have been wet, but her pants were soaked. *Hang on*... Was that a tiny smirk? Was he doing this on purpose? Did he want to indulge her? *Oh. My. God.* This was going to fuel her fantasies till the day she died.

She swallowed. 'Yes, of course. Erm, hard about, and, ahem, put your back into it.'

❧ 20 ❧

Jeers from the shore washed over Henry. In the past, he'd never put less than one hundred per cent effort into his rowing, and today was no exception. However, this time, the effort was focussed on crap technique and absolutely zero sense of direction. If Libby wanted to stare at his body like an ice cream she was desperate to lick, he was determined to make their journey back to shore last as long as possible.

He didn't know if his physique had ever been so openly appreciated outside of discussions between his aunt and her husband about him modelling for their fashion house. But whereas their gazes had made him uncomfortable, Libby's made him feel like the sexiest man alive.

When the criticism from the bank became too much, and as Libby became more and more flustered, Henry pulled alongside the jetty. He'd been adamant about changing his clothes, but now made excuses about the distance back to the Manor and undressed down to his boxers, laying his clothes on the grass to dry in the sunshine.

Libby sat on the picnic blanket next to him, her spine

straight as she pretended to watch his cousin's kids swimming with Summer, Jasmine, and Willow. Henry stretched out, enjoying the furtive glances she was sneaking his way.

The sun warmed him and he closed his eyes. The picnic blanket seemed to possess a family-repelling force field (or maybe it was the power of his twin sister) because they were left blissfully alone.

Estelle always had his back. He owed her so much, not least another difficult conversation about the estate. But that could wait for another day. This afternoon was about staying eight inches close to Libby Fletcher for as long as possible and dreaming that one day she might think of him the same way she'd thought about Lucas before he'd messed it up.

'Henry?'

'Hmm?'

'Are you still asleep?'

Huh? He opened his eyes. *Had* he been asleep? 'What time is it?'

'Five.'

He pushed to a seated position, glancing around. Everyone had gone and most of the gazebos and furniture had been loaded onto the back of a truck. He rubbed his face and looked at his watch. How had he slept for so long?

'I didn't want to wake you up. You seemed very tired.'

He took off his shades to look at her. Her gaze fell away and he remembered his state of undress.

He cleared his throat. 'Um, did I snore?'

Libby shook her head and got to her feet, her back to him. 'You were very peaceful. Do you want to go back to the Manor and get ready for tonight?'

Ah yes, the costume party. He quickly dressed and shook out the picnic blanket. 'Are you going to tell me what my options are?'

She turned with a cheeky grin. 'Not yet, but I adore both of them.'

'A squirrel,' Henry stated.

Libby giggled. 'It doesn't reveal more than five per cent of your body, and your parents definitely wouldn't approve. Since your dad wants to shoot all the squirrels on the estate, I've ticked both boxes with this one.'

He ran his hand over his face to try and hide his smile. 'Okay, clever-clogs, what's option number two?'

Her cheeks coloured as she lifted a garment hanger from the wardrobe door. She unzipped it and revealed the outfit with a flourish.

'Mr Darcy?'

'Or Bingley, or Knightly, or Wickham,' she said hurriedly. 'Or you could just be your great-great-great-grandfather?'

'Which outfit do *you* think I should wear?'

Libby picked at the Regency suit in her hands. 'Well, from a purely practical perspective, this one would be preferable.'

Henry crossed his arms, pretending he needed convincing. 'In what way?'

'Well, erm, you wouldn't get so hot in this one, and if you did, you could remove your, er...' She swallowed. 'Jacket.'

'And?'

Her eyes widened. 'And?'

'Why else is that outfit more practical?'

Her free hand gestured to the top of the trousers. 'If you needed to, erm, go to the toilet, this has an easier, ahem, system, for access to your, er...'

'Okay, I've made up my mind.'

'You have? Which one are you going to wear?'

He smiled. 'You'll have to wait and see.'

. . .

LIBBY LEFT SHORTLY AFTERWARDS FOR SUMMER'S ROOM, arranging to meet Henry downstairs after the first gong. His youngest sister had insisted she wanted to do Libby's hair, and Henry didn't know whether to be worried or pleased another of his siblings was taking an interest in his fake girlfriend. Libby assured him she would be fine, so he let it go and went to take a shower and get dressed.

Looking at his reflection in the mirror, Henry decided he liked what he saw. He liked the structured and subtle formality of the clothes, the tightness of the cravat and the way the tail-coat jacket nipped in at the waist. The knee-high boots completed the outfit. Maybe he was more of a vain dandy than he claimed.

He glanced at his watch, impatient to see Libby again. He'd known she was special the first time they'd met, but now he craved her presence. She was sweet, kind, funny, and effortlessly beautiful. He thought of Lucas and his hand instinctively formed into a fist. That prick didn't deserve her love. And the way he'd kissed her... A slap across the face with a wet fish had more finesse.

But if I ever had the chance to kiss her, it would be with my heart and soul.

The contract lay on top of a chest of drawers, reminding him that his thoughts as well as his deeds should be gentlemanly.

Fuck's sake.

He hid it out of sight in his bag and went downstairs.

'IMPATIENT TO SEE YOUR LADY LOVE?' CONNOR ASKED AS Henry's gaze flicked to the door for the umpteenth time.

The first gong had rung, but Libby was yet to appear.

'Is it that obvious?'

'In the words of Mammy, "t'be sure, t'be sure",' Connor replied in an Irish accent.

Henry grinned. 'I like the effort you've put into your costume.'

Connor was dressed in his nurse's uniform. 'Hey, I came straight from work. And anyway, this is the first time you haven't come as a City boy.'

'That's true.'

'I'm really happy for you, Henry. Libby is lovely. You're a very lucky man.'

Henry's smile stuck halfway. He would have been the luck-iest man in the world if any of this were true.

The door opened and his throat tightened. Libby was breathtaking. Her eyes sought out his, her expression nervous as if wanting his approval.

'Well, well, well, and what fine lady do we have here?' Julian advanced like a toad overdosed on erectile dysfunction medication.

Henry and his brother moved as one, Connor steering Julian away, and Henry coming to Libby's side. He wanted to take her hand, but instead gave her a short bow. 'You are utterly beautiful, Libby. In every way.'

Her breath quickened, the low bodice of her yellow Regency dress pushing her breasts up high. For a supposedly conservative dress, it was utterly indecent, and each time she inhaled and her breasts rose, so did his dick. He placed his hands in front to hide the bulge.

'Shall we go into the dining room?' he asked.

She nodded, seeming at a loss for words.

Henry inclined his head for Libby to go first, then followed her, imagining Cousin Rupert, Julian and James Hunter-Savage naked and mud wrestling each other in an attempt to get his body back in line.

THE WAITING STAFF CLEARED HENRY'S PLATE FOR THE seventh course. How were his parents funding such extravagance? In addition to all the other events and the remodelling of his bedroom and former playroom, the weekend must have cost a fortune. Had his mom's work footed the bill?

Henry had promised himself he wouldn't get involved and, so far, he'd avoided conversations about the estate. But asking any questions would send him down the slippery slope that always ended in unpleasantness when he reiterated his intention to keep his life in London. As long as Libby remained next to him, he hoped the subject could wait until the last day of their stay.

And he wanted her close. He wanted to talk more, but the questions he really wished to ask were about the real her—not the fictitious Libby Bennet. So, he kept quiet and listened instead.

Estelle had ensured they were again seated at the opposite end of the table from Aunt Charlotte's socially dissonant family, so everyone seemed more relaxed.

After dinner they moved to the largest drawing room where a string quartet was playing. Libby stood to one side, swaying gently to the music as she chatted to Eveline.

'Ask her to dance, you twat,' Estelle hissed in his ear.

Henry sighed and gazed at his sister. She may have been dressed as Lara Croft, but in true Estelle style, she was more tooled up than Rambo.

'These guns are loaded,' she said. 'I was waiting for an excuse to use them on Jupert, but you're now pushing to the top of the queue.'

'Jupert?'

'Come on, brain of Britain, I thought you graduated with a double first? Jupert sounded better than Rulian.'

'Rupertulian?'

'Yeah, that works, but I'm not wasting extra syllables on those morons.' She slapped his shoulder. 'Don't distract me. You need to ask Libby to dance.'

'Why? No-one else is dancing.'

His sister growled and pinched his arm.

He yanked it away. 'Fuck's sake!'

'Because it's one of her fantasies! And it would make her happy. Fuck my life, you are inept sometimes.'

Libby turned around to look at them, raising her eyebrows in question.

'Go on, boyfriend of the year,' Estelle whispered out of the corner of her mouth.

Henry squared his shoulders. As he approached Libby, his sister drew Eveline away.

He bowed. 'Elizabeth Bennet, if your card is not already full, would you do me the honour of a dance?'

Her pink lips parted and her hand flew to her chest. 'It would, um, be, yes please.'

He held out his hand and she took it. 'I'm afraid I don't know any steps,' he said.

'Er, maybe we could slow dance?'

Henry nodded and drew her to his chest. *This is in public. It's okay. It's just an act.* He suppressed a sigh. Libby fitted into his arms perfectly. His heart thudded faster and faster as he swayed with her. He closed his eyes, wishing the rest of the world would disappear. Wishing this moment could be private. Wishing what they were faking could be real.

The musicians played on, and they didn't stop dancing. Henry had never experienced such blissful contentment before. As the piece came to an end, everyone clapped. He glanced up to see they were at the edge of the room, behind everyone. No-one was looking their way.

He gazed down. Libby's eyes were bright and her lips were parted. Her tongue slipped out to wet them and he stifled a groan.

'Libby...'

She brought her face closer to his.

'Yes?'

God, he wanted to kiss her. Did she want to kiss him?

Henry cupped the back of her head and she gasped, moving closer.

Her lips were millimetres away and he could feel the fast puffs of her breath.

Desire rushed through him, urging him to bridge the gap and bring his lips to hers.

She moved her hand to the back of his neck, clutching his cravat.

Holy shit. She *did* want to kiss him.

This was it.

'Jesus Christ, get on with it,' Julian barked. 'I've got twenty quid riding on this.'

Henry broke away from Libby in shock. Julian was staring at them, and Rupert was eyeing his watch.

Estelle yanked a bullwhip from her back. 'I will fucking *end* you!'

Julian hid behind his wife. 'The bet was Rupert's idea.'

Rupert laughed. 'And you just lost!'

Estelle shoved Rupert, pushing him backwards. 'You fucking twat! You ruined it.'

'What's going on?' Arthur asked, entering the room. He was dressed as a centaur and, thankfully, his genitals were covered.

'Henry and Libby were having a moment, and Rupert and Julian ruined it!' Estelle yelled.

'Is that all? Deary me, I thought the house was falling down.' Arthur turned to them. 'You two carry on. Don't mind us.'

Henry glanced at Libby. She looked mortified.

He took her hand. 'Come on, let's get out of here.'

$$\text{❧ 21 ❧}$$

Henry led Libby through the Manor at breakneck speed. She had to jog to keep up with his stride, struggling to breathe against the tight bodice of the dress. She was too flustered to ask where they were going.

He'd nearly kissed her.

Libby was sure she'd died and gone to heaven dancing in Henry's arms. But then the music stopped and so did her heart. His eyes had darkened and he'd brought his lips towards hers.

He'd nearly *kissed* her.

Had she imagined it? Was it wishful thinking on her part?

Her feet pattered along the corridor towards his bedroom. Henry flung open the door, led her inside and dropped her hand, clutching the sides of his head as if trying to stop it splitting in half.

Libby closed the door behind them and propped a chair against it to prevent it re-opening.

Henry paced. Was he angry? Embarrassed? Frustrated? Whatever he was feeling, it didn't look good.

Perching on the end of the bed, she traced the embroidered flowers on her dress.

His breathing was harsh, like he was trying to hold back a tsunami of emotion, his coat tails whipping around him with every abrupt turn.

'Henry—'

'I cannot bear it any longer.'

He stopped on the other side of the room, his hands clenched into fists.

'I cannot suppress my feelings any longer even though they are abhorrent.'

What?

He resumed pacing, addressing the carpet beneath his boots. 'From the moment we first met, Libby, I admired you. And this admiration has only grown despite my struggles against it.' He rubbed his head as if to scrub away his feelings. 'My passion for you has overcome all rational objections.' He stopped and lowered his head. 'In declaring myself, I'm aware that I'm going against my conscience, my word and my own better judgement.' He paused. 'And the difference between our families is the most mortifying part.'

Her jaw was quivering. Her family and background were mortifying to him? Having any sort of feelings for her was *abhorrent?*? At least Giles left her family out of his criticisms.

'Henry?'

He glanced up, his expression desperate. 'Yes?'

'Did you mean to channel Mr Darcy so completely just now?'

'Er, what? No?'

'You can't have read the book since I only gave it to you yesterday, so have you watched the TV series? A film?'

He looked utterly flummoxed. 'No. Why?'

'Because I don't think you could have been any more

appropriately offensive considering how you are dressed right now.'

He gazed at his outfit. 'I don't understand.'

'Clearly.'

He started towards her. 'Libby—'

'Stop,' she said, raising her hand.

He did.

She stood, lifting her chin, fighting the tears trying to come to the surface. Henry Foxbrooke had deceived her. She'd believed wholeheartedly that he was a good and decent man. That he liked her. But his true feelings...

'Libby—'

'Henry. What *exactly* are your feelings towards me?'

'I just told you. Erm, admiration, regard—'

'You like me?'

'Like? It's more than like, Libby. I can't stop thinking about you. I hunger for you. I burn for you. My passion—'

'And these feelings are abhorrent to you?'

'No! Yes! Fuck!'

A tear spilled down her cheek and she swiped it angrily away.

'Libby—'

'So, let me get this absolutely straight.' Her voice was cold despite the sharp heat of her anger. 'You have "struggled" against feelings towards me, which are "abhorrent". Your passion has overcome "all rational objections", and by declaring yourself, you're going against your conscience, your word, and your better judgement?'

His eyes widened.

'And the worst part of all,' she yelled, 'is that my lower-class family is not good enough to associate with the Foxbrookes. Any "possible connection" with the Fletchers would be mortifying?'

Her gulping breaths filled the silence.

'You are mistaken,' he finally replied.

'Am I?' she whispered.

Henry nodded, his face creased as if in pain.

'Am I?' she shouted.

'Yes! God, Libby, yes!'

He strode towards her, stopping when she held her hand up again.

'It is abhorrent to me to have these feelings when I promised not to. I gave my word I would behave in a proper and respectful manner, and yet here I am, telling you how I feel because not doing so is causing me untold agony.'

He pulled the contract from his bag and held it out.

'My word is my bond, but in my imagination and now in my actions, I've broken it at every turn. My feelings for you are rational, but to declare them is not. My better judgement would have been to keep quiet.' He let out a hollow laugh. 'And as for your family? Jesus Christ, Libby. It's not *your* family I'm mortified by, it's *mine*. How could I ever convince your parents and your siblings that I'm good enough for you when my father has two wives and can't keep his clothes on?'

'You're not embarrassed to be associated with me or my family?'

'Fucking hell, no. Not in a million years.'

'And you're upset because you like me but think you shouldn't.'

He nodded. 'Our relationship is supposed to be fake, but my feelings for you are very real.'

She blinked. *Oh. My. God.*

His gaze was desperate, clutching the contract as if it were his last link to sanity.

She crossed the distance between them and took it from

him, turning the pages until she found what she was searching for.

She read aloud. "'I, Henry Foxbrooke will remain at least eight inches away from Libby Fletcher at all times, in accordance with paragraph four, clause nine, and appendix one.'"

He stepped back to maintain the appropriate space between them. She hooked her finger inside the top of his trousers, pulling him back.

'Paragraph four.' She pointed. 'Any acts that involve bodily contact will be initiated solely by Libby Fletcher.' She looked up, trying to keep her voice steady. 'So, Henry. If I initiate acts that involve bodily contact, are you happy that we're still working within the letter of this contract?'

He swallowed.

She raised an eyebrow.

He nodded.

She dropped the contract to the floor and touched the back of his neck. He inhaled sharply, his plump lips parting, his pupils dilating until the irises disappeared into velvet pools of darkness. Her other hand pulled on his trousers to bring his body flush with hers. She sucked in a breath as she felt the thickness of his cock pushing against the thin cotton of her dress.

'Libby.' His voice was a caress, sending a shiver trembling through her.

She clutched his cravat, bringing his mouth to hers until their lips touched with a spark. Her heart was tripping over itself in a rush to propel her closer, but she forced herself to move slowly, brushing her lips with his as his breath became faster and his cock harder against her stomach.

'Henry,' she whispered.

'Yes?'

'Kiss me.'

His restraint dissolved with a groan and his arms encircled her tightly, his hot lips pressed to hers. His kisses were intense, his tongue sweeping into her mouth and sending tingles to the tips of her toes. One hand cradled the back of her head, the other bunched up the fabric of her dress to grip her backside and keep her pressed tight against him. His lips were fire, his desire explosive. It was as if he were a condemned man and worshipping her was the only thing that would save his life.

A whirlwind of fractured thoughts and pleasure spun through her. Despite her frequent fantasies, nothing had prepared her for the desperate passion that the controlled and contained Henry Foxbrooke was unleashing.

His tongue licked flames into her mouth. They flickered through her, lighting fires that burned brighter with his every touch. It was too much to keep track of. Her body was no longer hers; it had utterly and completely bent to his will.

Her knees gave way and he caught her, carrying her to the bed and placing her down gently. He raised his head and gazed at her, his cheeks flushed, his eyes unfocused.

'God, Libby,' he whispered.

She stroked his face. His gaze was so reverent. As if she was the only woman in the whole of existence.

'Libby, Libby, Libby.' He punctuated each murmured word with his lips, kissing, licking and nipping down her neck as she writhed beneath him.

'Oh god, Libby.' He reached the heaving plumpness of her breasts, pushed up by the bodice of her dress, and buried his face in her cleavage with a groan.

She twisted beneath him, freeing her left leg and wriggling until he lay between her thighs, his cock just where she wanted it. His mouth fell on hers again and she clutched him to her, grinding her swollen pussy against him. Spots flashed on and off behind her eyes as she struggled to get enough air.

She ripped her head from his. 'Henry, I can't breathe.'

In an instant he leapt off and flipped her onto her front, flicking open the tiny buttons on the back of her dress. As soon as the first few were released, she gasped, but it didn't calm her desire. She was desperate to have him on top of her again, his hard weight pressing her into the mattress, his mouth making her body sing.

She whimpered and he straddled her, rocking his length into the crease of her bottom. One hand undid the buttons, the other stroked the side of her face, running a finger across her lower lip. She sucked it into her mouth and nipped the end, bucking against his cock as he continued to drive it backwards and forwards.

'Libby,' he growled, pulling the top of the dress off her arms and down to her waist. She was only wearing a thin cotton slip underneath. He turned her onto her back then straddled her again, pinning her thighs between his and devouring her with his eyes. The slip was almost transparent and her nipples were poking through, aching to be touched.

He traced the shape of her breasts through the material and she arched up to him, her breath coming faster. He rubbed her nipples between his fingers and thumbs and electricity shot through her body, straight to her clit.

'Oh my god! Henry, don't stop.'

His thighs tightened around hers as he touched and tugged, rocketing her up to heaven.

Just as she thought she couldn't go higher, his hot mouth was on her breast, sucking her nipple through the thin cotton. She cried out with pleasure and he sucked harder.

'Henry, Henry,' she moaned, holding his head tight to her chest.

She was caught beneath him, imprisoned in sensation that multiplied and collided with every stroke of his tongue.

Shifting his body to the side, he ran his fingers up the inside of her thigh underneath her dress as he sucked on her nipple. She opened herself to him, desperate to have him touch the centre of her pleasure.

As he reached the apex of her thighs, his head jerked up. 'Fuck! Libby!'

Holding his breath, he pressed his forehead against her breast as his fingers brushed through her wetness. Wanting to stay true to Regency fashion, she hadn't worn underwear. Henry panted as he regained control, then circled her clit and tugged on her nipple.

She was panting now, her body trembling with the promise of an orgasm so powerful she was almost afraid to embrace it. Fire built deep in her core, the pressure rising as her temperature went from orange, to red, to white hot. Without warning, everything went nuclear, the release shooting up her body and knocking out her breath in a silent scream.

Her body was buffeted, lost to his touch as blinding waves of light rolled and crashed through her. She moaned as her breath returned, her hips circling up into his fingers, eking out every last flicker of pleasure.

Henry kissed his way up her neck to her cheek as she breathed. Who knew such bliss was possible? It was utterly overwhelming. And who could have guessed just how wild and passionate he truly was?

He kissed below her ear. 'You're so beautiful.' The vibrations from his voice made her shiver.

'Henry,' she managed. 'That was unbelievable.'

She felt him smile against her neck and his fingers slip free. He raised his head and she watched, her breath quickening, as he brought his wet fingers to his mouth, licking and sucking them.

He slid down the bed, bunching the skirts of her dress up to her waist and laying her completely open.

'So beautiful,' he murmured again.

He knelt on the floor, pulling her legs towards him and hooking them over his shoulders.

'Henry,' she cried as he parted her curls and licked up her length.

He groaned into her pussy.

'Henry, oh god!'

His tongue flicked against her clit. She was already so swollen, her body primed for more, a second orgasm was already almost there. He locked her hips to the bed as he licked in steady strokes.

'Henry, Henry, Henry...'

She held his head, her back arched, her eyes squeezed tight as she raced towards the white light of another climax.

He licked faster and faster.

'Oh my god, I'm coming!'

Libby screamed as she hit the wall of pleasure at maximum velocity. Henry vibrated his tongue against her and she held on for dear life, buffeted by feelings as they collided inside her, smashing through every cell.

'Oh my god, oh my god, oh my god,' she gasped, her chest heaving to draw in enough air to keep her conscious.

He moved to lie next to her, stroking her hair, and staring at her as if she was the dawn of creation herself.

A shocked laugh escaped her, and he smiled.

He was so beautiful. So utterly perfect. Even after giving her the two most spectacular orgasms of her life, he wasn't smug about his skill or eager to fulfil his own pleasure.

But she wanted to make him feel as good as he'd made her. She wanted him to lose control and cry her name.

She reached down and held the stiffness of his cock through his trousers.

His breath hitched.

'Do you have a condom?' she asked.

'No. Do you?'

She shook her head. 'This situation was not exactly on my radar.'

He huffed. 'Nor mine.'

She stroked his thickness, and he took another sharp breath.

'Well, Henry. Until Foxbrooke Pharmacy opens tomorrow morning, we're going to have to think of another way to relieve your affliction.'

'Affliction?'

She gave his cock a tug. 'You do appear to be in some discomfort. I think I need to take a closer look.' Libby sat and rolled Henry onto his back. She'd always dreamed of undoing a man's Regency trousers, but didn't quite know how it all worked, so decided to simply undo as many buttons as she found. Underneath, he was wearing boxers, the front damp from precum. She pulled out his shaft and stared.

If Henry was beautiful, then his cock was spectacular. She was suddenly shy, not knowing how to approach such a beast.

'What do you want?' he asked, his voice low and scratchy.

She swallowed. 'I want you to show me how you like to be touched.'

He sat up, his face inches from hers as he gripped the base of his cock and tugged upwards. His gaze was on her, but she stared at his hand, her arousal building again as she imagined him burying himself inside her.

Her breath quickened with his as she watched him spread the slickness of his precum over the swollen head, then stroke again from base to tip. His hand moved faster, twisting up the length.

'Libby,' he whispered. 'Will you touch me?'

Shaking, she replaced his hand with hers and copied the movements she'd seen him make.

'Tighter,' he gasped. 'Harder.'

She did and he groaned, his forehead touching hers.

'Oh god, Libby. Yes, just like that. Oh god.'

His trembling lips sought hers and he kissed her with a desperate, blistering intensity. As she stroked, his hand found her breast and he thumbed her nipple.

She could feel how close he was, his body stiff and starting to shake, his breath ragged and uneven. She moved her hand faster, giving more attention to the head as his mouth broke from hers, his jaw clenched, his breath hissing in and out.

'Christ! Libby!' His climax cracked him open with a cry, his body shuddering as his release spilled out.

She continued stroking, pulling out his pleasure as he shook, whispering her name over and over like an invocation.

Then he kissed her again, his emotions pouring into her with such feeling that her heart wanted to weep. How lucky was she to have experienced this man in this way?

He pulled back, staring at the mess all over his costume. 'Ah.'

Libby snorted with laughter and wiped her hands on his trousers. 'These are going to need a bit of a wash before Estelle returns them.'

'I, ahem, got a little carried away.'

She kissed him. 'We both did. And it was unbelievable.'

'That it was,' he replied softly. 'You're something else, Libby Fletcher. I've never met anyone quite like you before.'

'And I've never met anyone quite like you, Henry Foxbrooke.'

He looked suddenly unsure. 'Libby, would you be okay if we didn't have the pillow wall between us tonight, and, er, maybe I could perhaps get under the covers with you?'

She leapt off the bed.

'Libby?'

She picked up the contract and took it to the chest of drawers where a pen lay.

'What are you doing?'

'Amending the contract. Pillow walls are banned and under the cover snuggling is mandatory,' she replied with a grin.

22

A drum pounded a war beat through the door. A hunting horn joined in the cacophony. The castle was under siege. *What the...?* Princess Libby woke with a start.

'Fuck's sake!' Prince Charming grumbled, throwing back the covers.

Libby had a mouth-watering view of Henry's backside before he hid it inside a pair of boxer shorts and stalked to the door. Up against it was the largest wardrobe in the room.

'Hang on!' he called out as he pushed the wardrobe out of the way.

The door opened and his father ducked to enter the room. He had an enormous pair of antlers on his head, and pieces of ratty old brown fur covered his genitals. An ancient looking drum was hanging around his neck and a huge ram's horn was pressed to his lips. He blew into it and the windows rattled.

'Happy Midsummer's Eve!' he declared. 'No tea this morning as I don't have three arms. However, I do have three legs. Ha, ha ha!' He beat the drum as he danced in a circle, then backed out of the room. 'Toodle-pip, young'uns. Don't forget to search for the magic fern at midnight!'

He pranced off down the corridor, blowing his horn. Henry shut the door and put a chair against it. He looked uncertainly at her as if worried this latest development would finally have her packing her bags and running for the hills.

'Well.' Libby shook her head. 'No tea in bed and not even a glimpse of your father's sausage this morning? I'm afraid that's cost you at least one star on my TripAdvisor review.'

The relief on Henry's face was palpable. 'Are you sure I can't get you to change your mind?' He advanced slowly towards her. 'Maybe management can find a way to make it up to you?'

She knelt on the bed. 'Well, I've heard a rumour there's a far superior sausage on offer?'

He raised an eyebrow. 'I'm afraid that's available only to Ms Libby Fletcher.' He brought his lips to her ear. 'If she still wants it.'

She sucked in a breath. 'Oh yes. Very, very much.'

Henry nipped her earlobe and she shivered, running her fingers over the hard planes of his chest. She still couldn't believe what had happened last night.

'Libby.' He cupped her chin, bringing his lips to hers.

She whimpered as he kissed her, liquid desire pooling in her abdomen. His tongue flicked into her mouth and a sharp, sweet sensation darted down inside her. She clung to him, pressing her body to his, rubbing against his hardness.

The door opened with a crash and the chair fell over.

'Morning, kiddies!'

They broke apart. Henry grabbed a pillow and chucked it in his lap.

Dervla entered the room carrying a tray with two mugs of

tea balancing on it. She was wearing her outfit of scarves and a crown of ivy sat on her head.

'Did you think we'd forgotten?' she asked Libby, placing the tray on the bedside table and sitting on the bed. 'We're so pleased you're here for today. And tonight. And tomorrow.'

'Er, what's going on?' Libby asked.

Dervla clapped her hands. 'Singing and dancing, feasting and fire-jumping. You're going to love it!'

'Fire-jumping?'

'Yes. For the harvest. And to stop bad luck. Or you can stamp on the embers with your bare feet.' She shrugged. 'It's up to you, darling.'

By the time Henry's mammy had finished describing in detail the Midsummer celebrations in at least twenty different countries, the rest of the house was awake and any thought of intimacy with Henry had been put on hold. Dervla took their now empty mugs of tea with her as she left, promising to see them later.

'Can we go and stay with your family now?' Henry asked.

Libby laughed. 'You've never even met them before, how do you know it wouldn't be worse?'

He raised an eyebrow as if her question were ridiculous.

'A tiny house with two adults, six kids and us?' she continued. 'Can you imagine how loud and cramped that is?'

Toots and bangs from the horn and drum drifted in from outside, accompanied by an instrument that sounded like a set of bagpipes being murdered.

'Is there any of that?'

'No.'

'Then I'm sold. South Birmingham? If we get a move on, we'll be there by lunchtime.'

She giggled. 'I'm not missing out on the once-a-year chance to find a magic fern.'

'Okay, if you insist...' He cleared his throat. 'I did have an idea I wanted to run by you.'

Yes! To all of them! 'Hmm?'

'Astronomically speaking, this is one of the most important times of the year and pivotal in biodynamic farming.'

Whuut?

'The sun is at its zenith and nature is thought to be at its most fecund.'

Yes, Henry, I will 'fecund' you outside. Many, many times. 'Mmm?'

'So, I thought we could take some flour and water into the estate and create Serafina mark two?'

Her train of thought stopped in its tracks as the field of flowers came to mind, the warm air filled with unseen life.

'The flour is biodynamic and from here, and the water would be from the spring, so it's as natural as possible,' he continued. 'It wouldn't be exactly the same as Serafina, but hopefully it would still work.'

Libby thought back to when she'd first created her sourdough starter in a cramped London flat. The wild yeasts were dirty gangsters compared to what she might hope to capture at Foxbrooke.

Her throat was suddenly tight at Henry's thoughtfulness. *You're amazing.* She was determined to stay in this bubble with him until real life dragged her kicking and screaming away.

'Thank you, Henry. That sounds perfect.'

Lucas: Lib-Lob, you there?

Lucas: I know you're still alive...

Lucas: [Screenshot from Summer's Instagram account of Libby in her Regency dress and Summer looking like a samba dancer from the Rio Carnival]

Lucas: We need to talk x

Lucas: I hope Foxy isn't taking advantage of my girl?

Lucas: Do you need rescuing, babe?

Libby: I'm fine.

Lucas: There she is!

Libby: I can't talk now. There's too much going on.

Lucas: When you back? Today?

Libby: No, tomorrow.

Lucas: Dinner?

Lucas: Tomorrow night?

Lucas: I could murder one of your curries.

Libby: Not possible. I no longer have a place to live.

Lucas: What happened with Claire's place?

Libby: Nothing.

Lucas: Then we're golden. I haven't seen Claire in ages. And I can meet the baby.

Libby: No. They're exhausted.

Libby: I need my money back.

Libby: I have nothing left.

Lucas: What about the five grand from this job?

Libby: Half has already gone on my debts.

Lucas: Well, you've still got two and half left?

Libby: I'm not taking it.

Lucas: Why the fuck not?

Libby: Henry's already paid me more than enough.

Lucas: Seriously, Lib-Lob? He's fucking loaded.

Libby: He's not.

Lucas: You're so naive, babe. He's taking advantage of you.

Libby: No, he's not.

Lucas: It's just more upper-class bullshit. Give me his number and I'll speak to him.

Lucas: Where is he now?

Libby: He just popped into the village.

Lucas: Give me his number, Lib-Lob.

Libby: NO! Lucas, it's fine. Henry and his family are nice.

Lucas: Nice? They're nobs AND nutters.

Lucas: They're not trying any weird shit with
you, are they?

Libby: Christ, Lucas, NO!!!

Lucas: Okay, calm down. I'm just looking out
for you, babe.

Libby: I need you to pay me back.

Lucas: Let's talk when you get home.

❧

HENRY HUMMED THE TUNE THE QUARTET HAD PLAYED AT THE party the previous night as he strolled past Foxbrooke Primary School. Memories flitted through his mind. When was the last time he'd been this happy? Maybe during his early years when he, Connor and Estelle had toddled around the Manor. Or when they'd started at this place. Back then he'd been blissfully unaware of the unusual nature of his family. Until that fateful day when they'd been dragged from their screaming parents by the police. Henry stopped humming, his happiness fading, and picked up his pace.

After that moment, everything had changed. Primary school was manageable, but the low-level anxiety that rumbled away in the background increased to a roar when they moved to Foxbrooke Secondary. Starting Eton should have been a reprieve. But even though he was a Viscount and his father the Duke of Somerset, polyamory and sex parties were not acceptable, no matter what social class you were in.

Henry's plan had always been to make enough money to support his younger siblings in their education. But now his obligations to Summer were over, what would he do? And did he even have a job to go back to? He swallowed a wave of nausea. He'd been suspended for at least two weeks, after which the 'situation would be assessed'. So much depended on whether James decided to press charges or not.

Stop thinking about it. He tapped the packet of condoms in his pocket and a smile spread across his face. Being with Libby was an ongoing surprise party with him as the honoured guest. His previous girlfriends had been pleasant but unsurprising. They may have found him dull, but that was the life he wanted, where everything proceeded according to plan. But last night with Libby was the hottest experience of his life, and he wanted her back in his arms.

His phone rang. It was the Dower House.

'Gram-Gram?'

'Hello, Henry, it's Marie here. Are you and Elizabeth available to visit your grandmother today?'

Elizabeth. The fake name was a reminder that he was lying to his family. And now he'd crossed a line with Libby he never wanted to uncross. He didn't know what his future held, but he was going to do his best to ensure it contained her. In a few short days she'd shown him how happy it was possible to be. But if their relationship continued, how long could they keep the Elizabeth Bennet lie going?

'Henry?'

'Sorry, Marie, I was miles away. Yes, I'm sure we can pop in later.'

'Splendid, I'll let her know to expect you both.'

He ended the call, his happy mood soured. As long as Libby still wanted to be with him, at some point they would have to explain why she no longer worked in publishing and that her surname was Fletcher, not Bennet. The first was relatively easy to deal with. The second, not so much.

'Henry!'

His heart lifted. Libby was outside the Manor's front entrance, a large ceramic bowl in her arms.

'Look at this! Perry says it's at least two hundred years old!'

He looked dubiously at the hairline cracks in the glaze. 'That's a good thing?'

'Yes! This starter is going to be living history.'

'Which part? Smallpox?'

'Ha ha. Only the tastiest bits.'

His gaze flicked to her lips and she blushed.

She glanced around as if to check they were alone. 'Was your, erm, shopping trip a success?' she whispered.

He nodded.

'Jolly good. Um, excellent shopping skills. Ten out of ten.' Her cheeks went a darker red.

He leaned forward until his mouth was by her ear. 'Are you going to mark my performance out of ten later?'

She squeaked and lost her grip on the bowl. He caught it before it smashed on the ground.

'Shit! Thank you, I, er, thank you.'

He smiled. 'I've decided that making you flustered is my second favourite thing to do.'

'Oh.' She licked her lips. 'And, er, what's your, erm, first favourite thing to do?'

He paused, holding her gaze. 'Making you come.'

Libby chattered the entire way to the field of flowers. Very little input was required from Henry. All he had to do was catch her eye during a lull in her monologue, raise an eyebrow and imagine all the different ways he wanted to pleasure her body.

Without fail, her mouth would open and a new stream of

delightful commentary would burst forth. He hoped this was confirmation that she liked him. He'd decided to ask her to stay with him when they got back to London. It may have seemed a crazy decision to anyone looking dispassionately at how long they'd known each other, but to him, it was crazier still for Libby to live with Claire and Ritchie and their new baby when she didn't even have her own room.

The thought of her struggling made him feel ill. At his, she could have her own space if she wished and come and go as she pleased. And he wanted to have her around. Libby brought light and joy to everything in his life, even his bonkers family.

But how would she react to this suggestion? Would she even want to see him again when they got back to London? Was this weekend simply 'faking with benefits' for her?

'Henry, is everything okay? You look unhappy.'

He managed a smile. 'I'm fine. Gram-Gram wants us to visit, so once we've got the bowl in place, we could wander over there? If that's okay with you?'

'Yes, sure. I'm going to cover it with a muslin cloth so we can leave it outside overnight. You promise you won't leave me alone with your grandmother?'

He shook his head. 'Never.'

23

'Bttt where's Marie? Why can't she go?' Henry demanded.

Libby's stomach knotted as Gram-Gram's lips thinned.

'My dear boy, she can't be expected to be on call any hour of the day or night.'

'Yes, she can. That's *exactly* her job. And when she takes time off, the agency supplies cover for her.'

Gram-Gram waved her hand dismissively. 'I never know what I'm going to get with temporary staff and I knew you were coming. I don't quite see what the problem is.'

Libby perched stock still on the edge of a chintz sofa. This visit was not going according to plan. They'd been in the drawing room of the Dower House less than a minute, and Henry's grandmother was asking her grandson to leave.

'Gram-Gram, forgive me, but I don't understand why Marie has left it until the last possible moment to collect your prescription. Surely a nurse would ensure you had at least a couple of weeks in reserve?'

'Oh, don't blame Marie, it's not her fault. There was a mix-up at the surgery.'

Henry ran his hands over his face as he looked at Libby.

'Can it wait until later? Tomorrow?'

His grandmother peered at him over the top of her glasses. 'No, it cannot.'

'Okay, we'll nip into the village now.'

Gram-Gram extended her cane across Libby's lap, like a bar locking her into the seat of a roller coaster. 'Elizabeth will remain here.'

'But—'

'It's okay, Henry,' Libby interrupted. 'I'm sure you won't be long, and I promise to be on my best behaviour.'

He glanced from her to his grandmother as Gram-Gram's eyes glinted with the light of victory. All three of them knew it wasn't Libby who was at risk of behaving badly.

THE SOUND OF THE FRONT DOOR SLAMMING WAS THE CUE for the start of the verbal assault.

'So, *Elizabeth*, we were rudely interrupted yesterday, just when you were telling me all about how you got started in publishing.'

'Libby, please call me Libby, my lady.'

'Well, if we are to converse in such informal terms, are you now intending to refer to me as Gram-Gram?'

Libby bit the inside of her cheek. 'Conversing' with the Dowager Duchess of Somerset was like trying to navigate a crocodile-infested swamp whilst defusing a bomb.

'I'll address you in whatever way makes you feel most comfortable.'

Gram-Gram sniffed. '"My lady" will suffice for now.'

Thought so. 'Of course, my lady.'

There was a pause as Gram-Gram eyed her, as if waiting for her to crack. Libby kept as still as a statue, her spine straight. As long as she pretended she was on stage and this was a performance, she could get through it. She was praying that Henry was currently sprinting a four-minute mile to Foxbrooke Pharmacy and back.

'Where were we?' Gram-Gram asked. 'Ah, yes, your publishing journey.'

Libby smiled as she continued to weave her story of fact and fiction based on India's sister's career. Whilst her speech was perfect, complete with little asides and personal touches, behind her calm countenance, she was crying into a pillow. What she'd begun with Henry the previous night could go nowhere. How could they have any future when she'd lied so completely and utterly to his family? Even if they both came clean with the truth, it would tarnish their opinion of her forever.

'And what is your favourite Polly Hart book?' Gram-Gram asked. 'I have them all.'

She pointed her cane at a bookshelf where every title was displayed in publication order.

Fuck. Libby hadn't read any of them. Buying time, she crossed to the bookshelf, selecting a couple and quickly skimming the blurbs on the back covers.

'This one, I think.' She held it out. '*Christmas Sparkles and Homely Hedgehogs at the Tiny Village School on Bluebell Bay.* It was the first in her Bluebell Bay series, and I think her best.'

'Hmm... I loved Daisy Spring and Wolf Redwood's wedding scene. Absolutely charming, don't you think?'

Libby knew how to read people, and Henry's granny looked like she was readying to push her inside a roasting hot oven and shut the door.

She gazed at the book and frowned. 'I didn't think their wedding took place in this one?'

The light dimmed slightly in Gram-Gram's eyes and her lips thinned. 'Ah yes, of course. You are correct.' She gave a brittle smile. 'My memory isn't quite what it was.'

Libby replaced the book on the shelf and sat, knowing full well Gram-Gram's mind was sharper than a box of tacks.

'I have to say, *Libby*, I'm glad my grandson has chosen you as a partner.'

'You are?'

'Yes. He needs a woman who can compensate for his lassitude.'

Excuse me? 'Er, lassitude?'

'General weakness in character. He's like his father. But whereas my son squanders his energy on acts of moral turpitude, Henry simply fails to fulfil the most basic of his responsibilities.'

'I don't understand.'

'He has no drive or ambition. Even Cousin Rupert is moving into politics. Henry lacks sufficient moral fibre, that's why he's still in London and not here where he belongs.'

'I thought you considered Henry thoughtful, polite, sensible, and kind?'

Gram-Gram gave a dainty laugh. 'Well, one needs to find *something* positive to say about the heir to the Foxbrooke estate. But those are hardly virtues one looks for in the future Duke of Somerset.'

'Clearly. And how do you believe I can remedy these character defects?'

'My dear, there's no need to take that tone with me. Your job is to persuade him his life belongs here. He needs to stop being so selfish and self-absorbed. If not, he'll end up like his good-for-nothing father.'

Fuck it. They were leaving for London tomorrow. Today was the last time Libby would ever set foot in Foxbrooke and the last time she would see Henry's grandmother. She was going out in a blaze of glory.

'My lady, you are mistaken.'

'Hardly.'

'Yes, you are. Henry and his father are not self-absorbed. *You* are.'

'I beg your pardon?'

'Henry's father has been nothing but welcoming and kind to me. His love for his son is deep and self-evident. While his marriages may be unconventional, I've seen more support and affection between Henry's parents than I have witnessed in most relationships.'

'Have you now?'

'And as for Henry, I've never before met a man so deeply caring and committed to the well-being of others at the expense of himself. Yes, he's not yet willing to move back home, but it appears the rest of the family have the estate well in hand. He has worked for years to support his youngest sister's education and for that he should be applauded. Henry is the most moral, upright, kind and generous man I have ever had the fortune to meet, and you should be incredibly proud of the man he has become.'

Her heart was roaring in her ears, her chest heaving with every breath. How fucking *dare* she criticise him like that?

The two women stared at each other as Henry burst into the room holding a paper bag. 'Here you are,' he wheezed.

Gram-Gram peered at the clock on the mantelpiece. 'That was faster than I expected.'

Henry looked at Libby, frowning. 'Is everything okay?'

She plastered on a smile. 'Yes, we were just discussing your many, *many* virtues.' She levelled a death stare at his grand-mother. 'Weren't we, my lady?'

Gram-Gram reached for her cane, and Henry helped her up.

'Thank you, dear, I'll see you out.' She looked at Libby. 'You run along. I require a moment alone with my grandson.'

Libby gave her a curt nod and strode out of the room, seething.

She exited the house and drew in lungfuls of sweet summer air. Gram-Gram had just acted like the worst of her class. Like Giles, and the kind of person Lucas criticised all the time.

Henry stepped out of the front door and closed it behind him. 'What happened?'

She turned on her heel, marching down the drive towards the Manor.

He caught her up. 'What did you say to her?'

'The truth. Whether she wanted to hear it or not.' *Fuck.* She'd really blown it. She sneaked a glance at Henry. He looked relaxed and happy. 'What did she just say to you?'

He smiled. 'She said you were perfect, and that if I let you go, there would be hell to pay.'

Libby stopped. 'She said *what*?'

His forehead creased. 'Why would she say otherwise?'

Her mouth hung open. 'I don't know. But I think I've just been played by your granny.'

Henry grinned. 'You wouldn't be the first. She's the wiliest fox in Foxbrooke.'

THAT AFTERNOON THE FAMILY DECAMPED TO THE RIVERBANK where a bonfire had been set up for the evening. The Foxbrooke river was fairly small and meandering, but there was a weir that had created a natural pool behind it. Stone steps led down into the water and further up the bank, there was a platform and a rope swing for leaping into the deepest part of the water. Libby borrowed a swimming costume from Willow and swam with Henry before lazing on a lilo as he pushed her up and down the small stretch of river under the canopy of trees.

'Is it always like this?' she asked, as she watched the green leaves sparkle in the sunshine.

He hesitated before replying. 'No.'

She raised her head to look at him. He was holding onto the end of the lilo, looking like a water god. 'What makes this different?'

'You.'

'Really?'

He smiled. 'The weather certainly helps. And I suppose this is the first time in years that I've been home for more than a night. But you do make the difference. No-one wants to argue in front of you.'

It was all so perfect she never wanted to leave. She would stay in the countryside with Henry forever if she could. But tomorrow they returned to London. Tomorrow this would all be over.

He frowned. Was he thinking the same?

'Aren't you cold?' she asked. 'You've been pushing me up and down like Lady Muck for ages.'

He leant forward and kissed her.

'Henry, you're freezing! We need to get you out and rubbed down.'

He raised an eyebrow.

'Henry!'

'Yes, Libby?'

She pulled his head closer and kissed him again, slipping her tongue through his parted lips and being rewarded with a groan.

Shrieks of laughter broke them apart as Minty and Monty barrelled into the water a couple of feet away.

'Little brats,' he murmured, pushing her back downstream.

'Do people stay here the whole night?'

'Yes, there's bedding and camping mats. But we don't have to if you don't want to. I haven't done it since I was a kid.'

Libby couldn't think of a better end to the weekend than spending the night with Henry in the middle of nature. Just not surrounded by the whole of his family.

'Could we possibly do it in the field of flowers? That way we can bring Serafina mark two back with us in the morning?'

His smile was wicked as he replied. 'Yes, Libby, we can definitely "do it" there.'

THE SUN WASN'T DUE TO SET UNTIL NEARLY HALF PAST NINE, so they ate around the bonfire with the family and Libby wove another flower garland with Summer and Willow. Henry brought his car down and they loaded it with bedding before driving it through the narrow lanes to the field.

Henry made up a bed under the oak tree and lit a small fire as Libby walked her new starter through the flowers, trying to gather as many wild yeasts as she could. Then she sat back in his arms, listening to the crackling flames, the chirp of crickets, and the trills of birdsong as the sun sank towards the horizon.

'Libby?'

'Yes?'

'I want to ask you something, but I don't want you to take it the wrong way.'

Her heart rate spiked. She shifted to look at him. 'What's wrong?'

'Nothing! Nothing at all, I just wanted to talk to you about what's going to happen when we go back to London.'

Oh. She returned her focus to the view as the sky darkened behind the golden glow of fire. This was it, the moment he drew a line on their time spent together and they went back to their very different lives.

With her back against his chest, she felt each breath he took. He kept inhaling as if to start a sentence, but stopped short each time.

'It's okay, Henry, just say whatever you need to.' Her stomach was knotted, waiting for the inevitable speech that would tie the strands of tension tighter.

'Libby, I've been increasingly concerned as to your living situation. And I wanted to offer you the use of my flat for as long as you need it.'

What?

'I don't want you to take my offer the wrong way. You would have your own room and bathroom.'

Was he offering because he felt sorry for her?

She swallowed. 'How much... What would you charge for rent and bills?'

His body tensed behind her. 'Nothing. Jesus, Libby, I wouldn't charge you a thing.'

So, she *was* a charity case. She couldn't take advantage of him like that. She'd been burned by Giles and had had enough of wanting Lucas without reciprocation. She didn't want to move in with someone she had feelings for, especially if they were moving on with their own lives now their arrangement was over.

'Thank you, Henry,' she eventually replied. 'But I'll be fine at Claire's.'

He was silent. Surely if he really wanted her there, he would ask if she was sure? Plead his case? Tell her he wanted their fledgling relationship to keep growing when they returned to London? But he didn't say anything.

Eventually, he stirred. 'I forgot the hot chocolate.' He got to his feet. 'I'll just go and get it from the car.'

He jogged off before she could protest, and his shadowy form disappeared down the side of the hill.

※ 24 ※

'Fuck!' Libby muttered, throwing herself back onto the blankets and staring at the blackness of the tree canopy above her. Should she have said yes? No matter how much she loved Claire, the thought of returning to their sofa and zero privacy for god knows how long filled her with dread. If she couldn't get her money back from Lucas, it would be months before she'd be able to afford a deposit on a new flatshare. Money didn't buy you happiness, but it made life a hell of a lot more comfortable.

These past few days at Foxbrooke had been a dream. She'd stuffed herself with the most amazing food and never once had to make do with a jam sandwich or whatever she could afford from the bargain basement section of the supermarket. She was tired of walking for hours every day because she couldn't afford the bus. Tired of always saying no to social occasions because she didn't want to appear cheap. Tired of the constant fucking struggle.

Saying yes to Henry would be the easiest thing in the world. But he was asking out of the goodness of his heart. And if she took advantage of his good nature, she'd be no better than Lucas.

Conscious of time passing, she stood and stared down the slope. Where was he? How long did it take to look for a flask? Had he left her there? Just as she was about to go searching for him, he reappeared.

'Sorry, I must be losing my mind. I couldn't find it anywhere. It must be here after all.' He rummaged in a bag. 'Here we are. Fancy some?'

The evening was taking a weird turn. Rather than a wild night of passion, Henry was acting as if they were at Scout camp.

'Yeah, sure.'

He poured her a mug, then one for himself, sitting next to her on the blanket. Gone was their intimacy, and she had no idea what to say or do to get it back. This was it. She should be grateful for a few days in the country and the two best orgasms of her life.

Suck it up, Fletcher. She sipped her hot chocolate and stifled a moan. Of course, it was the best in the world. It was made from biodynamic raw Jersey cow milk. She wouldn't have been surprised if the beans had been hand roasted by Perry. Why did everything in Foxbrooke have to be so bloody delicious? She sneaked a glance at Henry. *Especially* him.

He rolled his sleeves up.

'Are you hot?' she asked.

He didn't look at her. 'Yes. I should have lit the fire a little further away. Do you mind if I take my shirt off?'

Fuck no! 'Not at all, I don't want you to be at the wrong temperature.' *Seriously, Libby! 'Wrong temperature'?*

He slowly undid the buttons, then faced away from her and took it off. She drank him in. The firelight flickered across his broad shoulders and danced down his spine. She wanted to lick him like a lollipop.

When he turned back, she was staring at the fire again.

'Any better?' she asked.

Out of the corner of her eye, she saw him shrug. 'Not much.'

He took off his shoes and socks and she gulped her hot chocolate.

'Are you still too, er, warm?' She kept her tone as innocent as possible.

He sighed. 'Yeah. I'd like to lose the trousers, but I don't want to make you uncomfortable.'

Off! Off! Off! 'Makes no difference to me,' she replied casually, trying not to squirm with anticipation.

He stood and unbuttoned his trousers. *Fucking hell.* All she needed to do was kneel, turn right and his cock would be *right there*.

The trousers dropped to the floor, and Henry stepped out of them. Libby kept her eyes glued to the fire whilst her peripheral vision took in everything it could.

'Better?' she peeped.

'Getting there. How are you doing?'

Not very well, actually, I need to have sex with you right now.

She shrugged. 'I think I hurt my shoulder earlier, jumping from the rope swing.'

'You did? Are you in pain? Do you need to see a doctor?'

She forced herself to not roll her eyes. Henry was too sweet for his own good.

'I'm fine.' She brought a hand to her shoulder, trying to rub her back. 'I just think the muscles need loosening.'

'Would, er, you like me to have a go?'

Keeping her gaze on the fire, she attempted extreme nonchalance. 'If you don't mind.'

'Not at all. I'd do anything—' He cleared his throat. 'Not at all.'

She turned her back, her heart jumping up into her throat and undid the buttons on the front of her dress. 'I think it might be more effective if my dress wasn't in the way.'

'Yes,' he instantly agreed. 'It would be much better.'

Before she could second guess herself, she lifted the dress over her head and tossed it to the ground. She took off her bra, trying not to gasp as the cool night air touched her breasts, then lay on her front, her head facing away from him.

'Does that work for you?' she asked.

He didn't reply, but placed his warm hands on the small of her back, sweeping up either side of her spine and massaging her shoulders.

Oh god. She bit her lip to stop a moan escaping.

His strokes were firm and confident, easing out knots she didn't even know she had and turning her insides to honey. A throbbing beat of pleasure pulsed deep within her and she had to force herself to stay still. She'd never felt so drunk on desire before, so close to spreading her legs and begging him to thrust his cock inside her and make her come.

'How does that feel, Libby,' he asked, his voice low.

'Amazing,' she breathed. 'Please, don't stop.'

His hands continued to move over her skin, lower and lower until they grazed under the top of her underwear and kneaded the flesh of her bottom. She bit down on her fist as she moaned.

He hooked his finger under the fabric of her pants. 'Should we lose these?'

'Yes,' she whimpered. 'They're in the way.'

He drew them down her legs and off, leaving her completely naked before him.

His hands returned to her skin, kneading her calves with

firm, sure strokes. She inched her legs apart a fraction and his breath hitched. She couldn't tell what he could see in the firelight, but she wanted him to see all of her. She wanted him to want her as much as she wanted him.

His hands moved higher, his thumbs moving up her inner thighs, getting closer and closer to her aching centre.

She spread her legs a little more, arching her bottom up.

'Libby.' His voice was raw and rough. 'Where do you need it?'

Trembling, she opened her legs wider. 'Higher,' she whispered.

She felt one hand massaging up her back and she almost cried out in frustration, but then his other was between her legs, his fingers stroking through her wetness.

'Yes, yes,' she cried, all pretence gone. His touch was fire as he circled her clit, sending sharp shocks of pleasure through her. His breath was as ragged as hers, and that only made everything hotter.

He pressed down between her shoulder blades and pushed two fingers inside her. She cried out and thrust into his hand.

'Yes, yes, yes...'

His fingers were thick as they pumped in and out. Her orgasm was whipping inside her, desperate for an escape. She wriggled into his hand, trying to find the friction she needed.

He lay beside her, hooking his left arm under her neck and moving her onto her side, her back against his chest. He lifted her right leg up and over his, then brought his hand back to her pussy, his fingers thrusting as his thumb rubbed against her clit.

She turned her head and his lips found hers, kissing her with an intensity that took her breath away. His other hand found her breast, tugging on the nipple as she shook in his arms.

She was so close, but didn't want to come unless he was inside her. If this was their last night together, she wanted the wave of her pleasure to break around the hardness of his cock.

She dragged her mouth away from his. 'Please, Henry. I need you inside me.'

His fingers pulled out of her and he grabbed his jeans, rummaging in the pocket. He tore open a condom packet with his teeth and rolled it onto himself with one hand.

Then his fingers were back against her clit, the fat head of his cock at her entrance. He nipped up her neck, his arm locked around her torso as he tweaked and tugged her nipple.

She could feel his size, but he was entering her in millimetre increments and driving her to the point of insanity. She tried to push herself onto him but he held her in place, biting and sucking her neck as his fingers thrummed against her clit.

Her breath was frantic, her heart pounding. The touch-paper of her orgasm had been lit and she could do nothing but give herself over to him as the fire of pleasure burned faster and faster, brighter and brighter, racing her forward.

He thrust completely into her, and she detonated with a scream. He held her tightly, his fingers working her as his cock thrust deeply, again and again. Everything contracted within her, then exploded out in ever-expanding waves of pleasure. Nothing had ever been so earth-shattering before.

As she floated back down to an earth that was utterly changed, he slowed but didn't stop. She opened her eyes, the corners damp as she looked down her body with him behind her; his large hand cupping the weight of her pale breast, his cock disappearing deep inside her, the tips of his fingers gently rubbing her swollen clit.

'You're so fucking hot,' he growled in her ear, each word punctuated by a deep thrust.

A shiver ran through her and she angled her head back to pull his mouth to hers. He kissed her as if giving her his soul. His tongue, fingers and cock relentlessly drew out her pleasure, demanding she come again. His power was complete and she had no desire to fight it. She was molten gold, being forged anew in the fires of his passion. As the threads of her orgasm spun together, he worked her higher, stealing the breath from her lungs until she broke the kiss, crying out into the night, again and again.

He held her to him, his movements erratic as he thrust. A third orgasm was wrenched from her as he roared with his release.

'Libby, Libby, Libby,' he whispered, as if lost in darkness and trying to find her.

She brought his hand to her lips, kissing it as she would a holy relic. If this was indeed the end, she was going to spend the rest of their final night together worshipping him.

$\maltese$ *25* $\maltese$

The sun rose just after half past four, but the dawn chorus had started an hour before that and sleep was impossible. Henry lay with Libby in his arms as birds chattered and squabbled above them. The nervous anxiety that always hummed at the edges of his consciousness was starting to march inwards like an army seeking to regain territory.

She doesn't want to move in with you equals she doesn't like you.

No, it doesn't. There could be loads of other reasons why she turned you down.

Like... she wants the arrangement to end as per the contract when you go back to London?

Shut up.

She obviously doesn't like you enough.

You don't know that. I'm not giving up on the chance of us being together.

Ah yes, your 'cunning plan'...

She can't sofa-surf at Claire's. It's not fair on her, or Claire and Ritchie.

So, you're going to fix it?

'What did you say?' he asked, suddenly aware that Libby had been speaking.

'I was just saying,' she shouted, 'I had no idea nature was so bloody loud.'

He laughed. 'Did you sleep at all?'

'A bit. Although it's nowhere near as comfortable as your bed.'

'Want to head to the Manor for a power nap before we return to London?'

She paused, her expression unreadable. 'Yeah, sure.' She climbed out of their nest of covers. 'Although I have to do one thing first.'

'Obey the call of nature?'

She smiled. 'Yes, but more importantly I have to wash my face in dew to make me beautiful.'

'You're already beautiful.'

Her cheeks pinked. 'More beautiful then,' she replied with a grin.

THEY GOT BACK TO THE MANOR AT FIVE A.M. AND CRASHED for a few hours. Henry awoke to find Libby awake and packing. His heart sank. He'd been summoning the courage to ask her to stay with him in Foxbrooke longer, but she was obviously keen to get back. He had a quick and lonely shower, then threw his things into his bag.

He couldn't think of anything to say, and it seemed neither could she. His hand lingered on their fake relationship contract. So much had changed since he'd first showed it to her. Could he persuade her to sign another one? A *real* relationship contract? He dismissed the idea. He was losing his mind.

'We can leave these here and come back for them after breakfast,' he said, indicating their bags.

She nodded, placing the yellow dress she'd worn to the costume party in its garment bag. The dress seemed to shine with memories, and when she zipped the bag up, it felt like clouds covering the sun.

Henry opened the bedroom door for Libby and they walked in silence down the corridor. Voices murmured in the distance, a strident one rising above them all. *Estelle.*

The entrance to the Manor was filled with people. Most were in their sixties or older, but there were also younger people from a variety of nationalities. This was obviously the once-a-month day when the Manor was opened to visitors.

None of them looked very happy. Some were arguing with Estelle, who was standing a few steps up on the stairs, some were on their phones, and the rest stood wearing their most fearsome faces, lips pressed tightly together as they edited in their heads the scathing reviews they were going to leave online.

'Look,' his sister shouted. 'I apologise, but your guide will be along any minute. Please bear with me.'

'What's going on?' Henry asked her in a low voice.

Estelle turned to him, her confident face collapsing.

'Our fucking useless arse of a father failed to book the tour guide,' she muttered. 'Perry rang me when this lot showed up. I contacted the guides we usually use, but they're booked on another job at Stonehenge, and our parents can't do it as they're probably still shagging by the river. I can't either, as I've got to be back at the livery this morning for a meeting.'

She looked at him, hope in her eyes. He took a step back, panicked at the thought of having to remember details about the house and put on a polite face when someone asked him about his parent's marriage.

'How long does the tour normally last?' Libby asked.

Estelle pulled a face. 'At least a couple of hours.'

'Anywhere you don't allow visitors?'

'Some of the bedrooms. There's a tiny red dot on the top of any door we don't want them to see. Why?'

Libby squeezed her hand. 'I'll do it.'

'*You'll* do it? But you don't know anything about the Manor.'

'I did my homework when I was researching this jo— researching Henry's home, and I think I remember a lot of it. If I'm no good, either of you can stop me and take over.'

Libby's eyes were alight. Henry recognised the same spark from the improv workshop and comedy night.

His sister's face was a mix of uncertainty and cautious relief. 'If you're sure?'

'Libby will be amazing,' he said.

Estelle gave him a look. 'Loving the confidence, Romeo, but have you ever seen her guide a group of pissed off punters around a stately home?'

He hesitated before shaking his head. 'No, but if anyone can rescue this situation, it's her.'

Estelle shrugged and sighed. 'Okay then, Libby, they're all yours.'

'Can you hold them at bay for five minutes? she asked. 'I just need to change.'

His sister glanced at her outfit. 'What's wrong with that?'

She squeezed her hand again. 'Trust me?'

Estelle nodded.

Libby turned to him. 'Come on, I need your help.'

She sprinted back up the stairs and he followed.

'What's your plan?' he asked as they ran down the corridor.

She'd already pulled off her dress by the time they reached

his room. She threw it on the bed and unzipped the garment bag.

'Living history,' she replied. 'But I can't get this on without help.'

She shimmied out of her bra and he tried not to stare.

'Come on, Henry! Give me a hand.'

He started doing up the top buttons on the back of the dress as she fiddled with the ones at the bottom.

'What do you need me to do once you start?' he asked.

'Get Perry to bake a batch of biscuits and have the ingredients ready for the group to make a load more. See if she can find a Regency recipe online.' She pulled on a pair of long white gloves and moved to the door. 'You don't have to dress up, but if you do, I want you to channel Mr Darcy.'

He followed her down the corridor. 'I haven't started the book yet or watched it on TV.'

She stopped just before the stairs and put her hands on his shoulders.

'Can you channel aloof and grumpy?'

He raised an eyebrow. 'Aren't those my default settings?'

She grinned. 'Not at all. You're a sweet ray of sunshine hidden inside a sharp suit.'

She kissed him quickly, turned and ran down the stairs until she got to the first landing. He watched as she drew back her shoulders.

'Ladies and gentlemen...' Her voice rang out as clear as a bell.

The murmurs from the crowd abruptly stopped.

'My name is Elizabeth Bennet, and I am delighted to welcome you all to Foxbrooke Manor.'

Her posture was regal as she continued slowly down the stairs, her gloved hand sliding down the dark wood banister.

'I appreciate you may not associate me with the Manor,

however the Gardiners, relatives on my mother's side of the family, have a close connection with the Duke and Duchess of Somerset. Indeed, I have spent many a happy hour perambulating the estate grounds and losing myself in a book from their well-appointed library.'

Estelle's mouth was hanging open as she stared at her.

'As such, they have tasked me with escorting you around the house this fine morning,' Libby continued. 'And giving you a taste of what life was like here across the ages.'

She stopped a few steps from Estelle and swept her arm wide.

'Let us travel back in time to Midsummer's Day, nine hundred and seventy-eight, as the King of Wessex wakes, after a night spent celebrating the solstice.'

Estelle crept up the stairs and met him at the top. They moved a few feet down the corridor.

'Fuck me,' she whispered. 'Did you know she could do this?'

Henry shrugged. 'She's very clever.'

'Yeah, but it's one thing being clever and another being able to improvise like that on the fly.' She frowned. 'Maybe all they do at Winterblossom Press is role play Jane Austen?'

He didn't reply.

'Look, I've got to run. I should be back by the time she finishes. Can you help her out if she needs?'

He nodded.

'Thanks. I'll take the servant's stairs back down.'

'I'll come with you,' he replied. 'I need to speak to Perry about making Regency biscuits.'

HALF AN HOUR LATER, THE FIRST BATCH OF BISCUITS WAS out of the oven, and Henry was retying his cravat. Thankfully the trousers had been cleaned and had no lasting stains.

That wouldn't have been a good look for the Manor's visitors.

He followed his ears to the ballroom and peeked through the half open door in search of Libby. She was teaching some sort of dance.

'Splendid form, ladies and gentlemen. Now, let's ask our musicians to play for us so we may showcase our quadrille.'

She pulled her phone from a small silk reticule that hung over her shoulder. After a few seconds, music sounded. She turned the volume up and put the phone back in her bag.

'And, let us begin!' she cried. 'Couple number one, bow... Now cross the circle to each other's places—'

He watched in awe as she directed the groups. Older people dressed in anoraks and beige trousers danced with young tourists, and everyone was smiling and laughing. Libby noticed him watching through the crack in the door and winked.

As the dance finished, she led a round of applause.

'I must say, that was a bravura performance. I'm quite certain all of you are ready to attend the ball at Pemberley next week. Now, let us perform it one more time for luck, then we'll proceed to the library where, I believe, if we are lucky we might encounter a very famous gentleman.'

Henry stepped back from the door. This was obviously his cue. He went to the library and selected an hour of piano music on his phone. He hid the phone behind framed photos on top of the grand piano, selected a leather-backed book from one of the bookshelves and sat down, pretending to read.

A few minutes later, he heard Libby outside.

'Ladies and gentlemen, we must be extremely quiet, because I do believe the Manor has a visitor.'

He glanced up as she opened the door and peeked in. He grinned at her and she smiled back so brightly his heart sang.

'Now, this gentleman and I have had a difficult acquaintance so far,' she continued from the other side of the door. 'However, I do believe he is actually a hedgehog. His prickly exterior is merely protection for his kind and generous heart.'

She opened the door.

'Ladies and gentlemen, allow me to present Mr Fitzwilliam Darcy.'

Henry stood as the crowds entered, snapping his heels together and bowing his head.

'Forgive me,' he began, as officiously as he could manage. 'I was not expecting visitors.'

Libby advanced on him, trying to contain her grin as many of the guests sighed with appreciation behind her.

She dropped a curtsey. 'We apologise for the intrusion, sir, however these honoured guests have come many miles to view such an impressive collection.'

'Ah, yes.' He held up the book in his hand. 'Cicero. He once said "a room without books is like a body without a soul". May I welcome you all to the soul and, I believe, *heart* of Foxbrooke Manor.'

LUCKILY HENRY KNEW WHERE ALL THE BEST BOOKS IN THE library were and brought out the huge atlases, which contained fantastical drawings and descriptions of mermaids and sea monsters. Being Mr Darcy was easy. All he had to do was retreat behind a wall of indifference and let Libby lead the conversation.

The tour had already been going for two hours and no-one seemed to be flagging. The final stop was the kitchen, where Perry had discovered a mob cap and paired it with a vintage white apron. She taught the group how to make sugar biscuits, passing around old wooden stampers, each one containing a few nails embedded in the design to punch holes in the biscuits and stop them bubbling up when being cooked. Once the biscuits were in the oven, she passed around the batch she'd produced earlier and an enormous pot of tea.

It was midday by the time they led the party back to the entrance hall where Estelle was waiting.

Libby took their praise and thanks in her stride, but Henry was mute, relying on firm handshakes and nodding to convey his pleasure. She appeared energised by the performance, while he needed a stiff drink and a lie down.

He glanced to his right as his parents wandered around the corner. His father was bleary eyed and dishevelled, the antlers and furs still intact, his mom and mammy equally worse for wear. Henry caught Estelle's eye and she moved the tourists on whilst he dashed to cut their parents off.

Arthur scratched his hairy belly as he approached. 'What's all this then?'

'The monthly tour.'

'Already? Time bally flies these days.'

'Dad, you forgot to book the tour guide.'

'I did?' His father pulled a face. 'I can't be expected to remember everything at my age.'

Henry's patience was wearing thin. 'Dad. You're fifty-four, not ninety-four. Put it in your diary.'

The last cars were moving down the drive. Libby remained by the entrance, waving, as Estelle stormed over.

'I don't even know where to fucking start,' she screamed.

Henry took a step backwards, as did all three of his parents.

His sister was vibrating with anger, her hands shaking, her lips pale.

She gestured at the house behind her. 'Do you like this place?'

'Er—' Arthur began.

'Well start saying your goodbyes, because thanks to you bunch of idiots, we're going to lose it.'

'What?' Vivienne looked at her husband. 'Arthur?'

His dad shrugged in response. 'Don't know what Estelle's talking about, darling.'

'Wanna know why the last estate manager left?' Estelle fumed. 'Well, no fucking surprise it was the same reason we lost the one before that and the one before that. It's because you never listen. Any of you. You change your mind at the drop of a hat, turn down ideas that might actually make money, and embrace ones that never will.'

'The parties make a tidy profit,' Arthur protested.

'Oh yes,' replied Estelle sarcastically, her hand on her hip. 'Just about enough to compensate for the abject failure of naked yoga classes, naked country-dancing and naked body-painting.'

'I thought that last one went rather well.'

'Did you even see the bill to clean up the mess?' Estelle yelled. 'But that's the tip of the fucking iceberg. I've just had an emergency meeting with our lawyer because we're being sued.'

'What on earth for?' Vivienne asked.

'At the last party there was an accident in the "lube room". A water blaster filled with peach flavoured lube got wedged up someone's arse.'

Arthur chortled. 'That was a bit of fun. He was absolutely fine.'

'Well, he's changed his mind and is taking us to court. But that's not the biggest problem. A week before the event, *someone* cancelled our insurance policy saying, and I quote, "I'm not paying that bally much. It's health and safety gone mad".' Estelle eyeballed their father. 'Ring any bells, Dad?'

Arthur looked at the ground, scuffing the gravel with his sandals. 'It'll all blow over.'

'Will it? When did you last look at the bank accounts? I told you we shouldn't spend all this money on our birthday weekend. We can't afford it.'

'Honey.' Vivienne inched towards Estelle as if approaching an enraged tiger. 'We've still got my money.'

'No, Mom, we don't. It all went on the remodelling of Henry's bedroom.'

'It can't have. It doesn't cost that much to do up a couple of rooms.'

Estelle threw her hands in the air. 'Yes, it does. That bloody bed alone cost eighty thousand pounds!'

Henry heard Libby gasp behind him. He hadn't realised she'd walked over. If his family had seemed eccentric before, now they were also flash gits with more money than sense.

'And that didn't include the ten grand for the mattress,' his sister continued. 'Six grand on bedding and nearly a hundred-fucking-grand on the bathroom! Mom, go look at the accounts. There's almost nothing left.'

Dervla started crying and Vivienne went to her side, drawing her close.

'We'll be okay,' she murmured. 'I promise.'

The fight seemed to leave Estelle and she sagged like a deflating balloon.

'I can't run the livery and the estate on my own,' she said. 'I'm working over a hundred hours a week and it's breaking me. This weekend was the first time I haven't worked a sixteen-hour day in nearly nine months. I can't do it anymore, and I can't work with you, Dad. It's impossible.'

'What about Henry?' Arthur asked. 'Now he's met Libby, he can finally come home.'

Out of the corner of his eye, Henry saw Libby stiffen.

He opened his mouth to speak but Estelle got there first, puffing back up.

'Seriously? Do you think Libby wants to leave her dream job in publishing and her entire fucking life in London for this shit show?' She shook her head. 'And leave Henry out of this. I'm not going to force him to do what he doesn't want to. I understand why he's made the decisions he has. Let him lead his own life.'

He felt a huge rush of love for his twin with an even bigger swell of guilt following behind. He had no idea things had got this bad. Would his family really lose the Manor?

'Estelle,' he began.

She turned to him. He could see the sadness in her eyes and the dark circles under them.

'Henry, just go. Take Libby back to London. She doesn't need to see any more of the Foxbrooke family circus. We can speak in the next couple of days.'

He nodded and looked at Libby. Her face was white.

Fuck.

$$\text{❧ 26 ❧}$$

Henry was silent all the way to Stonehenge and Libby didn't know what to say. She'd gone from the absolute high of the impromptu living history tour to the shock of seeing behind the upper-class curtains at Foxbrooke Manor.

Eighty thousand pounds on a *bed?* You could buy a house for that in some parts of the country. She couldn't wrap her head around such excess when to her, every penny mattered. She was on her way back to Claire's sofa and the task of running improv nights and workshops without her best friend and business partner. The enormity of it all sat like a weight in her chest.

She loved the spontaneity of improv, the way her brain threw her into a flow state running at warp speed. But it was the other side of the business, the admin and marketing, that she wasn't good at. She'd joined Claire's business, rather than the two of them setting it up from scratch. As such, her friend had always done those jobs. But now it was down to her and she didn't know where to start.

'Do you like animals?' Henry asked.

She lifted an eyebrow. 'To eat, or just in general?'

He smirked. 'As a *pet*. Have you ever wanted one?'

'One day, maybe. Probably a cat. Why?'

He cleared his throat. 'My other best friend, Jack, the one who lives abroad, needs a cat-sitter.'

'Where? In the south of France?'

'Oh no. At his flat in London.'

Libby stared across at him, utterly confused. 'He lives in France but keeps a house *and* a cat in London?'

'He comes back occasionally so uses the flat as a bolt hole.'

'And the cat?'

He shrugged. 'I think he likes the company.'

'And he *pays* someone to what, go in and feed it twice a day?'

'Er, no. He pays people to stay in the flat when he's not there.'

'Seriously? Is he like Dr Evil levels of rich and insane?'

Henry laughed. 'I don't know about the money, but he's not nuts.'

'What's his job?'

His forehead creased. 'Something to do with the hospitality industry? Putting on big events and parties? I think that's it.'

'He's your best friend and you don't know what he does to afford a flat and live-in cat sitter?'

'Well, in fairness, I don't think he knows what I do either. If you asked him, he'd probably just say I'm a City wanker.'

She grinned. 'So, why are you telling me this?'

He cleared his throat again. 'He rang the other day and asked if I would do it. He usually uses an agency but the person they'd lined up pulled out. I was thinking I could recommend you for the job instead.'

'Me?'

'Yes. You'd be paid to live in his flat. You could come and go as you please, so you'd be able to work as normal.'

Oh my god. Somewhere to live and a *wage* for doing so?

'Where's the flat?'

'Soho.'

Oh my god, oh my god, oh my god! Was this for real?

'What's the catch?'

'Um, I don't know.'

'Can I speak to him about it? Jack?'

There was a pause before Henry replied. 'Um... I suppose so?'

'You *suppose* so?'

He looked away. 'He's out all the time and is really difficult to get hold of, but I could ask him?'

'Okay. So, when would he want me to start?'

'Er, tomorrow if you can? His current house-sitter is leaving then.'

Her head was in a whirl. This was a lifeline. A way of being able to stay in London and work. She couldn't take advantage of Henry's charity and move in with him, but she could do this. She could pay off her debts and start to build her savings back up. Finally, there was light at the end of the tunnel.

HENRY CARRIED LIBBY'S BAGS TO CLAIRE'S FRONT DOOR. Her friend flung it open, a devilish smile on her face.

'How did it go?' she asked.

There was a brief but excruciating silence as the two of them froze, before Libby recovered.

'Fine! Great! We, um, I had a lovely time.'

'Marvellous. So glad it was a success. Henry, do you want to come in for a cup of tea?'

He took a step back. 'Thank you, but I should get going.'

'Oh. Okay, no worries.' She lifted Libby's bags. 'I'll take these in and leave you to say your goodbyes.'

As Claire disappeared, Henry stepped forward, hands in his pockets.

Libby waited for him to speak, but it appeared he was struggling to find the words.

'Henry—'

'Can I see you again?' he blurted. 'Dinner maybe?'

Her heart raced off the blocks. His cheeks were darker, his gaze intense. Maybe he *did* want what they had to grow?

She nodded, suddenly unable to find her own words.

His shoulders relaxed. 'Tomorrow? After you've settled into Jack's place?'

She nodded. 'But should I really leave the cat alone on our first night together? I know nothing about looking after them.'

'We can get take-out.'

She smiled. 'Thank you, Henry. For everything.'

He shook his head. 'The thanks are all for you, Libby. You were... It was—' He broke off, staring at the pavement. 'Amazing.'

She put her arms around him and squeezed. He took his hands out of his pockets and held her tightly back.

She kissed his cheek. 'Tomorrow?'

He nodded. 'Can't wait.'

'Well?'

Claire was waiting inside with a huge mug of tea and an even bigger smirk.

'Where's Harper?'

'At the park with Ritchie. Come on! Tell me everything!' She patted the sofa cushions next to her and Libby sat, her cheeks on fire. 'So then, just how foxy *is* Henry Foxbrooke?'

'Extremely,' she mumbled.

Claire shrieked and kicked her legs like a spider unexpectedly encountering two hundred and forty volts of electricity.

'Knew it! Knew it! Knew it!'

Libby grabbed a cushion and hid her face in it, waiting for her friend's excitement to fade.

Claire pulled it away from her.

'Libby, this is the best news ever. He's so nice. We both saw it at the workshop. He's a genuinely decent bloke and clearly thinks the world of you.'

She shrugged, embarrassment and excitement battling inside her.

'Also, being shallower than a puddle here, he's also fit as fuck.'

Libby fanned herself as red-hot memories scorched her cheeks.

'And, by the look on your face, he clearly knows what to do with what God gave him,' Claire continued.

Libby stood, pacing the room, trying to shake off the heat and nervous energy.

Claire slumped back onto the sofa. 'Wow. Henry Foxbrooke really rocked your world.'

She nodded. 'It was—he was—' She broke off and sighed, her hands clasped to her chest. 'Amazing.'

'Aw, love! That's the best! When are you seeing him again?'

'Tomorrow!' she squealed.

Claire clapped. 'Thank fuckity fuck for that. Now you can draw a big fat line under Lucas.'

Libby sat on the sofa and picked up her mug of tea.

'He got in touch with me,' Claire continued. 'Wanted Henry's number.'

Libby choked and put the mug down, coughing. 'Don't give it to him!'

Claire rubbed her on the back. 'Course not. He's a slimy little star-fucker.'

Libby nodded.

'What? You're not going to contradict me?'

She shook her head.

'I think hell just froze over. What made you do such a one-eighty? Vulvagate, or Henry?'

Libby stared at her mug on the coffee table. It felt bigger than she did right now.

'Claire, I need to tell you something, and I want you to promise not to freak out.'

'Oh my god, what's happened? Did you sleep with Lucas? Did he give you an STD? Are you pregnant with his baby? Fuck, fuck, fuck!'

She stared at her friend. 'That is the exact definition of freaking out, and to answer those questions, no, no and no.'

'Oh my Christ,' Claire exhaled, her hand on her heart.

Libby raised an eyebrow at the theatrics.

Claire put her hands in her lap. 'Sorry. I am now calm and centred. Please continue.'

Libby's gaze returned to the mug of tea. 'You might have noticed the last few months I've been a little short of money.'

'No shit—' Claire stopped herself. 'Yes, I have been aware. And concerned.'

Misery seeped into her every cell. She'd been a fool *and* she'd made her friends worry.

'The, er, situation is very bad. All of my savings are gone and I'm over ten grand in debt.'

Claire gasped.

'Well, seven and a half grand after Henry paid half the fee upfront.'

'And he'll pay you the rest?'

'I'm not going to accept it.'

'What? Why not?'

'Claire, I can't *possibly* accept it! We're having sex now! If I took it, then it would be like I was a...'

'Jesus, Libby!'

She sneaked a glance at her friend and Claire mimed zipping her lips shut.

'Anyway.' She sighed. 'I'm in the shit because—' She gulped in a breath. 'I've been paying the rent on Lucas's studio for over six months.'

Silence.

'How much?'

'Nearly twelve grand,' she muttered.

'And when is he planning on paying you back?' Claire's voice was ominously quiet.

'He's not,' she whispered.

CLAIRE'S PROMISE NOT TO FREAK OUT LASTED THE AMOUNT of time needed for her to draw breath. Libby huddled in the corner of the sofa, her knees to her chest while her best friend paced the room screaming obscenities and making incredibly detailed plans for how she was going to cause Lucas extreme physical pain.

'I knew something was wrong. I fucking *knew* it!' she yelled. 'Cock-sucking son-of-a-bitch! Stringing you along, taking your food and your heart. Mother-fucker! I'm going to cut his arty-farty fuckboy dick off one centimetre at a time. With a rusty spoon! Then I'm going to shove his paintbrushes up his arse and sell his organs to get you your money back. Bastard!'

The door opened and Ritchie entered, Harper strapped to his chest.

'Everything okay?' he asked.

Claire burst into tears and ran to him. 'Oh Ritchie, I'm so

grateful to have you. I love you, baby.' She peppered kisses over him and their daughter. 'And you too, my sweet girl. I'm never going to let anything bad happen to you, ever.'

Ritchie looked over her shoulder at Libby, his eyes wide.

'It's okay,' she said. 'I'm the problem here.'

Claire's head whipped around.

'No, you're not!' she sobbed. 'You're never a problem. It's that arseclown, Lucas.'

Libby got up and put her arms around her friend so she was held from every side.

She kissed the side of Claire's head. 'I'm going to be okay.'

'How? It's such a lot of money,' she wailed.

'I've got a new job.'

Claire lifted her tearstained face. 'You have? What is it?'

She smiled. 'I'm going to be a cat lady.'

27

From: Libby Fletcher
To: Jack Newton
Subject: Flat sitting
Hi Jack!
Thanks so much for the opportunity! Do you have any special instructions? I want to make sure I do the right thing.
Best wishes,
Libby

FROM: JACK NEWTON
To: Libby Fletcher
Subject: Re: Flat sitting
Hi Libby,
My work schedule is extremely busy, so please can you arrange everything with Henry? You'll be fine.
Best,
Jack

. . .

HENRY MET LIBBY AT CLAIRE'S THE NEXT AFTERNOON TO help her move into Jack's flat. He was immaculately dressed as always, and she had to swallow at how deliciously his shoulders filled out his tailored white shirt. He glanced at her boots and her tummy tightened with anxiety.

'I'm glad to see you back in them,' he said with a smile. 'It reminds me you're the kind of person to kick ass and take names.'

She snorted with laughter and relief. 'As if.'

He grinned. 'That's what you and Claire did at Conqueror, just so subtly that none of us noticed.' He glanced at her bags. 'Have you got everything?'

She nodded, suddenly drenched with memories of the flood. 'I don't have much stuff left.'

A muscle in his jaw twitched, but he hid it behind a smile. 'Okay, let's get you settled in.'

AS THEY DROVE SOUTH TOWARDS SOHO, THE ROADS GOT busier. Libby clutched the tupperware box containing her new starter like a comfort blanket, as if trying to hold onto a piece of the countryside. Somerset seemed very far away.

Henry glanced at it. 'Have you decided on a name for Sera-fina mark two yet?'

'Yep. She's called "Sunny", which is short for "Sunnestanden". It's the old English word for solstice. It literally means the sun standing still. I know it's a bit poncey, but...' She shrugged.

'I think it's perfect. Have you tried to make a loaf yet?'

She shook her head. 'She's still growing. I'll try in a couple of days.'

. . .

THE FLAT WAS ON A BUSY STREET IN THE HEART OF SOHO, UP two flights of stairs. A key safe box was attached to the wall outside the door.

'Jack has this for the cleaner or anyone else if they need to get in,' Henry said. 'I've made you an extra set of keys, so you won't need to use it.'

'What's the code, just in case?'

He looked embarrassed. 'Sixty-nine, sixty-nine.'

Libby raised an eyebrow. 'Is he a bit of a joker?'

Henry frowned. 'Not normally. Although he did say that if the combination had only been three numbers, he would have chosen six-six-six.'

'Ah, so a devil-worshipper then.'

He grinned. 'Maybe that's what his actual job is.' He passed her a set of keys. 'Go on, it's all yours.'

She opened the door and entered the flat, not quite knowing what to expect. It was modern, light and airy, with high ceilings and exposed brickwork painted white. The bedroom and bathroom were to the left, to the right a lounge, and up ahead a large kitchen diner.

'It used to be part of a factory,' Henry said. 'That's why the rooms are larger than you'd expect and the ceilings so high.'

'It's amazing. But very, very white.'

The flat looked like a show-home for angels. There wasn't a mark on any of the walls. The rug in the lounge didn't look like it had ever been walked on, and the white leather sofa appeared never to have met a backside before. It must have been cleaned recently, as there wasn't a single cat hair to be seen.

An enormous cat crate stood on the white marble countertop in the kitchen. A pair of amber eyes peered out through the black grille.

'Why is it in a crate?' she asked.

'Er, I picked him up earlier from an old people's home. He moonlights as a therapy cat.'

'Aww, that's lovely!' She leaned closer. 'Hello, sweetie. Shall we get you out of there now?'

The cat growled.

Henry lifted the crate to the floor. 'He can be a bit, erm, energetic.'

She stared at the backs of his hands. It looked as if he'd lost a fight with a barbed wire fence. How had she missed this?

'Holy shit, Henry! What happened!'

'Nothing, it's fine. I think I startled him earlier.'

'And he's a *therapy* cat? How? Is he dangerous?'

'I don't *think* so.' He sounded far from convinced. 'I think it just might be me he doesn't like? I'll open the door and we can see what happens.'

She glanced around the kitchen. There was a litter tray, scratching post, feeding station, bed, a selection of toys, and the most astonishing structure she'd ever seen. It was over six feet high and looked like a cat adventure playground.

'What the bloody hell is that?'

'Er, apparently, it's called a "cat tree". It's for stimulation and because cats like to be up high and look down on people.'

She grinned. 'Sounds about right.'

This cat looked like it had everything it might need, but it all appeared unused.

Henry opened the crate door and they both stepped back.

Nothing happened.

Libby took a toy and held it out.

'Here, kitty kitty.' She looked at Henry. 'What's its name?'

His mouth opened. 'Um...' he began, his eyes wide as if he'd forgotten its name.

She looked back at the cat, shaking the toy. 'Here, puss puss, want to play with my—'

'Pussy!'

She stared at him. 'What?'

He swallowed. 'Pussy,' he repeated.

'Jack called him "*Pussy*"?'

He tugged his collar away from his neck. 'Um, it's actually "Mr Pussy".'

'Oh. Well, I see Jack's sense of humour extends to his pet,' she said. 'Here, Mr Pussy, want to come and play?'

The cat stalked out of the box and swiped the toy from her hand. Instinctively she moved back. It was bloody huge. She'd never seen a cat this size before, or this fluffy. It had long fur in shades of blacks and browns and paws like furry dinner plates with talons. It turned its back on the two of them, lifted its tail and started to produce a size-appropriate poo. Straight onto the white tiled floor.

'Shit!' Henry grabbed the cat and attempted to move it towards the litter tray.

It responded by screeching and swiping across the back of his hand, drawing blood.

'Fuck!'

He dropped Mr Pussy, who finished defecating then leapt to the top of the cat tree, where he sat, licking the blood off his claws and staring at Henry.

Henry stared back, an already blood-stained handkerchief pressed to the back of his hand.

'Jesus, are you okay?' Libby asked as she opened drawers and cupboards to find something to clean up the mess.

'I'm fine. I'm just not sure he likes men.'

'Well, he must like Jack? What about the ones at the old folks' home?'

'Er, there aren't any. It's only women.'

'Maybe he ate the men?'

'What?' Henry looked completely flustered.

'It's a joke! Look, I think it's understandable for Mr Pussy to be scared of new people. I'm sure he'll get used to us soon enough.'

Mr Pussy stayed at the top of the cat tree as Libby unpacked. Jack's flat was like a hotel and she alternated between feeling terribly grown-up and scared to touch anything in case she left fingerprints behind. How the flat remained so immaculate with a cat that large and hairy was a mystery to her. She would need to make sure he was brushed every day.

'Does Mr Pussy have a grooming kit?' she called out from the bedroom.

'Yes, he does. Hang on.' Henry returned with a large white tin containing brushes, clippers, scissors and tools she couldn't name.

'Are these brand new? I can't see a single hair.'

'Er, yes. His old brush was looking a bit tatty, so I bought this for him.'

'Aww, Henry, that's so sweet! Did you buy him the toys as well?'

He blushed and nodded.

'And the cat tree? And the bed? I swear to god, everything he has looks like it's never been used before.'

He looked away, rubbing the back of his neck. 'I wanted him to have the best.'

She stood and wrapped her arms around him.

'You're the best, Henry. Mr Pussy and I are extremely grateful.'

He kissed the top of her head. 'Libby—'

There was a plaintive *miaow* from the kitchen, and she broke away.

'We'd better check he's okay.'

MR PUSSY WAS SITTING ON THE KITCHEN FLOOR, HIS DRIED food scattered like marbles around him. He looked at her and mewed again.

She crouched down. 'Oh dear. Would you rather eat something else?'

Mr Pussy stalked over and purred against her knee.

She tentatively reached out and stroked his head.

The purr got louder.

'Thank fuck,' breathed Henry behind her.

The purring stopped. Mr Pussy raised his head and growled.

'It's okay,' she said, in what she hoped was her most soothing voice. 'Don't be scared of Henry, Mr Pussy. He's a big ole puddy-cat just like you.'

⚜

HENRY TRAIPSED BACK TO THE FLAT THROUGH SOHO, LADEN with take-out boxes of chicken and lamb kebabs, ribs, sushi, and two dirty burgers just in case. He hoped he would get to have some of it, but it had been bought in the vain attempt to get Mr Pussy to eat.

After turning his nose up at the dried food, the cat had cried and cried forcing Henry to run to a local shop to buy a tin of wet food. Mr Pussy didn't want any of that either, so Henry was now walking the streets looking like a food delivery guy who'd lost his moped.

He shook his head. He'd tried to live within the lines, but since meeting Libby he'd gone so far off-road he was totally lost.

What the fuck had he been thinking with the bloody cat? He sighed. He knew exactly what he'd been doing. He knew Libby was unlikely to buy the flat-sitting lie without a bigger reason behind it. Hence Mr Pussy, who he'd bought that morning from an online ad. The cat had belonged to a woman who'd just died and her son couldn't wait to be shot of him, referring to him as 'Evil Bastard'. Jack was going to go batshit when he found out. It was one thing to give the okay for Henry to move Libby in and pay her 'wages' via Jack. It was another to bring a pet with her.

And didn't Jack hate cats? He couldn't remember. *Shit*. He just had to hope his friend continued to stay away from the UK long enough for him to convince Libby to move in with him. He sprinted up the stairs to the flat and opened the door cautiously in case Mr Pussy was lying in wait.

'In the kitchen,' Libby called out.

He entered with the bags to see her on the floor with Mr Pussy in her lap.

'He's calmed down a bit,' she said, as the cat stood and prowled towards the enticing smells, his tail twitching.

Miaow.

She stood. 'Oh my god, Henry, how much did you get?'

'It'll keep if you don't mind eating leftovers?'

'But the cost? I should give you some money—'

'No, absolutely not.'

'But Henry—'

MIAOW.

'Look, let's discuss this later,' he said. 'Let's get Mr Pussy— Ow! What the fuck!'

The cat had clearly decided their conversation should come to an end and ensured this happened by using Henry's leg as a scratching post.

'Oh my god!' Libby pulled the cat's claws from his trousers. 'Are you alright?'

'Yep, all good.' He grimaced. Was he going to have to get some kind of shot after today? Rabies?

He quickly opened the food cartons and Libby held them under Mr Pussy's nose one at a time.

It would appear the cat had expensive tastes, preferring the sashimi and rarest cuts of beef. It also turned out that he would only eat if Libby hand fed him. Fucking hell, this was a nightmare. Cats were meant to be easy. He should have got a bloody horse instead.

'Cats are carnivores, right?' she asked. 'So surely we should just be feeding him raw meat?'

He bit back a sigh. 'I'll nip back out and get some minced steak.'

'We don't need to get any now. I think there's more than enough here to satisfy him for the night. I can pick some up in the morning.'

Henry opened cupboards until he found plates. 'Are you hungry? All the blood loss has made me starving.'

She giggled. 'Yes, I am. And it smells divine.'

After the cat had eaten enough to feed a ravenous teenager, it staggered to the cat tree to sleep. Henry and Libby piled their plates with food and sat at the breakfast bar, facing him in case of an unexpected attack.

Despite his injuries, Henry was happy. Libby may not have wanted to move in with him but he'd secured her accommodation and pay. The fact that he'd had to lie to achieve this sat uncomfortably with him, but he justified it with the knowledge that his solution was better than a sofa in a house with a newborn.

After spending so much money on Summer over the years, he wasn't rich, but now the obligation to his sister was over, he had enough to help Libby. And he wanted to. She was never going to make enough money doing improv compared to what he made as a broker.

And why should she have to struggle to do what she loved? Helping her out made him happy. She didn't need to know that the money for the flat-sitting was coming from him, and he wanted nothing in return. He smiled to himself. He was back in London where, cats withstanding, everything was under his control.

'Henry?'

'Yes?'

'I checked my bank account this morning. You paid me the rest of the money.'

'Uh-huh.'

'Why?'

'Um, because I said I would?'

'But I told you I couldn't accept it.'

He put his cutlery down. 'And I said I'd give you all the money in my bank account if you'd let me. I asked you to come with me, Libby. I told you how much I was going to pay you, and you agreed. I would be a callous bastard if I went back on that.'

She twisted her hands together. 'But Henry, things changed.'

'That doesn't matter to me.'

'It matters to me.'

He sighed. 'I actually wanted to talk to you this evening about your fee for the living history tour.'

'My fee? What?'

'Your payment for staging a three-hour interactive performance, which saved my family's arse.'

'But I don't want any money for that. It was fun.'

'I'm pleased it was fun for you, because it was also brilliant.

Do you think I could have pulled that off? Estelle? My *parents*? None of us could. And anyway, this is your job. You should be paid for it. Do you think plumbers show up and work for free just because they enjoy it? If you hadn't stepped in, not only would we have had to refund people's money from bank accounts you now know are empty, but we would have been slaughtered on review sites. You saved us, Libby.'

She was silent. How could he get through to her? He hated money sometimes. It bought you freedom but it also led to conversations like this, plus guilt, unhappiness and a feeling of obligation. As long as he could feed himself and pay his bills, he didn't give a shit if she had all his money. Using what he had to make her happy made him infinitely happier than the thought of spending it on himself.

He rubbed his hands over his face, then dropped them to his lap.

'Libby, do you appreciate what I'm saying? If I came and saved your family from public shame and a bill they couldn't afford by doing my job, wouldn't you want to pay me?'

She was still silent, but understanding flashed across her face.

'My parents can't afford to pay you, but I can. If you won't accept the second half of the money for being my fake girl-friend, then will you at least accept it for the awe-inspiring job you did on the tour?'

This time he let the question hang in silence and waited for her response.

'Thank you, Henry,' she said, her voice low.

Halle-fucking-lujah. His shoulders relaxed.

'But...'

'Yes?'

'I want to pay for dinner.'

No fucking way. He'd spent over a hundred pounds on this feast. He wasn't letting her foot the bill.

He cleared his throat. 'I didn't get any receipts and have no idea how much it was. Why don't you buy the next one? Or...'

'Or what?'

'You said you liked cooking?'

She nodded.

'Would you cook for me sometime?'

Her smile lit up her face. 'I'd love to. When?'

'Tomorrow?'

Her cheeks flushed. 'Which meal?'

He got off his stool and moved closer. She turned to him, pressing her delicious breasts into his chest as he reached his arms around her. Her face was lifted towards his, her pink lips parted. She was utterly irresistible. He kissed her and she whimpered.

'How about we start with breakfast?' he murmured.

'Sounds like a plan,' she whispered, before pulling his mouth back down to hers.

28

Libby navigated herself out of dreamland the next morning, directed towards consciousness by a deep rumbling snore.

Henry?

She opened her eyes to a hot purring wall of fur.

'Good morning, Mr Pussy,' she mumbled.

Lying next to her and still asleep, Henry rolled over.

'Shh,' she whispered to the cat. 'I'm going to make him breakfast.'

Mr Pussy lay down in the warm spot she'd just vacated, stretched and closed his eyes.

Libby grinned at the two new men in her life. She couldn't believe her luck. Life was perfect. She tiptoed out of the bedroom and almost straight into another monster cat poo. This one was runny and leaking through the fibres of the formerly pristine sisal rug.

'Fuck, fuck, fuck!' she muttered, dashing to the kitchen for cleaning supplies.

Ten minutes later the rug was rolled up and condemned to

be thrown out. No matter how much she scrubbed, it was trashed. She'd find a replacement later, and hopefully Jack would never know. She put the kettle on and went to the fridge to see what she could make for breakfast.

Two seconds later a yell came from the bedroom. She ran down the corridor to find Henry in a three-way fight with the duvet and Mr Pussy. The cat had its claws in both the duvet and him and was hissing and snarling like a tiger.

She ran forward and pulled the cat off him. It ran out of the room.

'Henry!'

He was wide-eyed, his chest covered in deep scratches. He looked as if he'd woken from a nightmare, only to find reality was far worse.

'Jesus Christ,' he finally said, sitting down on the bed with a thump.

She pulled tissues from a box by the bed and dabbed at his wounds.

He shook his head. 'I thought I was waking up next to you.'

Libby giggled. 'But that was not the pussy you were looking for?'

'Good god, no.' He smiled and stroked the side of her face. 'You're beyond amazing, Libby. Last night was out of this world.'

Her cheeks heated under his touch.

'I was trying to make you breakfast. But I'm afraid I had to deal with another little present from Mr Pussy.'

He dropped his hand. 'Where is it? I'll clean it up.'

'Don't worry, it's sorted, but I'm going to have to buy a new rug for the hall.'

'No, Libby, I'll replace it.'

'But he's my responsibility.'

His mouth opened, then shut again.

'Okay?'

He nodded. 'But I wouldn't tell Jack if I were you.'

Shitsticks. She couldn't lose this job.

'I won't tell him. But only if we can find an exact match for the rug. If we can't, then I'll have to fess up.'

'We can go looking today if you have any time?'

'Yes. I don't have anything in the diary until next Tuesday for the improv night, although I should be doing more to find work. What about you? Don't you have to get back to the office?'

He hesitated, then shook his head. 'I haven't taken any leave for a while, so I'm taking a few weeks off.'

'Oh. What are you going to do? Go on holiday?'

He looked away. 'I was wondering if you'd like to, er, hang out? If you can spare the time?'

'Kind of like a staycation?'

He smiled and nodded.

'And what did you have in mind?' she asked, her tummy turning over with excitement.

'Well, when I wrote the contract, I did lots of research on date ideas, so I thought we could go on some of them?'

'I am not swimming with sharks at the Sea Life Centre.'

He grinned. 'But would you be up for a spin on the London Eye?'

'Only if you hold my hand.'

His fingers found hers and he squeezed. 'Deal.'

OVER THE NEXT WEEK, LIBBY SPENT ALMOST EVERY MOMENT with Henry. He took her on dates, claiming it was a subsidiary clause of their contract, and also delivered multiple orgasms each day, which had most decidedly not been in the small print.

On the flip side, she'd struggled to find anyone to replace Claire for their Tuesday improv night and was relying on a total stranger for the next performance. Lucas was hassling her to meet up while ignoring her money-back requests, and Mr Pussy was a literal shit show.

'I don't understand,' she cried as the cat rubbed against her, the deep purrs vibrating up her leg.

Libby was standing in the living room, her phone in her hand as she stared at an armchair. How could one animal inflict this amount of damage? *In an hour?*

Henry poked the stuffing back in the gaping holes as if that might fix the problem, his face lined with worry.

'According to Google,' she continued. 'Mr Pussy is really happy.'

Henry raised an eyebrow, a deep scratch visible over it.

'I think he's warming to you?' she said, hopefully.

He stared at Mr Pussy.

The cat growled back.

'At least he's using the litter tray now,' she said, trying to find any positives.

'I think that's because he ran out of rugs.'

She bit the inside of her cheek and glanced around the room. Everything between three feet and ground level was scratched, and all soft furnishings, from the curtains to the sofa and armchairs, had been mauled.

'Does he do this at the old people's home?' she asked, looking back at her phone to search for a local upholsterer.

'Huh?'

'Where he's a therapy cat? Do I need to take him there?'

'Er—not at the moment.'

'Let me guess? They're refurbishing after his last visit?' She lifted her phone. 'I've found a professional to sort out some of this mess.'

'Lib—'

'No, Henry, you can't pay for this. It's not your fault.'

'But—'

'Look, I'm clearly the problem here. Mr Pussy has lived here for—what, *years* in this beautiful flat without any issue, and now I'm here and he's tearing the place up. I've never had a cat before so it must be something I'm doing wrong.' She waved her hand at the wounded armchair. 'This is my problem to fix.'

She wanted to shut the conversation down before it grew legs again and crawled uncomfortably over her skin. No matter how much Henry insisted, she couldn't take any more money from him. So, she'd dipped further into her overdraft to fix or replace everything Mr Pussy had destroyed.

Henry opened his mouth to argue but was interrupted by a ping from his phone. He took it out and stared at the screen, his face impassive.

It rang.

He declined the call and put it back in his pocket.

Libby knew what was coming next. She looked away and braced as if preparing for an electric shock.

Sure enough, her phone buzzed with an incoming message.

> Dervla: Hello darling, how are you today? Do you have any idea when you're coming back up? Henry's been too busy with work to let us know. XXX

It buzzed again.

> Dervla: Any luck with getting Gram-Gram and Eveline signed copies of Polly Hart's books? Doesn't matter which ones. You must have a couple spare around the office? XXX

And again.

> Estelle: Give your boyfriend a kick up his arse
> and tell him to reply to his messages. Hope
> you can make it back up here soon, with or
> without my brother. And if you can get signed
> Ploppy Fart books for Eveline and Gram-
> Gram I will owe you FOR LIFE. Love from
> your new friend (whether you like it or not) xxx

Libby put her phone down, suddenly nauseous. No matter how her relationship had changed with Henry since they'd first arrived in Foxbrooke, their initial lie sat in her stomach like an undigested meal, refusing to go away. She was falling head over heels in love with him, but how long could they keep this charade with his family going?

And did Henry even consider a future with her? No matter how wonderfully he was treating her, was she his girlfriend? What would happen once he went back to work? Was this just a holiday fling for him?

She glanced across the room as Mr Pussy rubbed against her leg. Henry was staring out of the window, his face strained. She had to be brave and ask the awkward 'us' question to know if she needed to start the process of disengaging from him and closing down her heart just as it was opening.

She took a breath.

He turned, abruptly. 'Libby. I need to talk to you about something.'

Oh god. Here it comes.

He rubbed a hand over his head. 'I haven't been truthful.'

She let her breath out slowly, trying to stay calm.

'I need to tell you something, but I'm worried you'll think less of me.'

Her mind raced. 'You can tell me anything, Henry.'

She perched on one end of the sofa, her knees pressed

together. Mr Pussy leapt onto her lap, turned in a circle, then collapsed in a furry heap and started purring.

Henry sat at the other end of the sofa, his hands interlocked.

Digging her nails into her palms, she waited.

He cleared his throat. 'I told you I had extra leave days I had to take, which is true, but not the whole story. I, I've been suspended.'

What? She stared blankly at him, struggling to process his words.

'I punched James Hunter-Savage. Three times.'

She wanted to laugh. This was ridiculous. She couldn't imagine Henry hitting anyone.

'The guy who left the workshop early?'

He nodded, rubbing his knuckles as if remembering the blows.

'Why?'

He sighed. 'We've got a long history, but he lied to Elizabeth, the woman I was dating, and manipulated her into thinking he was a better option. He then stole my work and my biggest client, losing me the commission. The last straw was when I found him flirting with Summer. I'm afraid I lost the plot.'

So, James had taken Henry's girlfriend... Was Libby a stopgap? A placeholder until he could get Elizabeth back?

'I've got a meeting with HR next week to see what action will be taken against me. I could lose my job. And I could be prosecuted for assault.'

Oh my god.

He looked stricken. 'I'm sorry to put this on you, Libby. I've done my best to put it out of my mind, but I've been so stressed about it, and you're so... comforting and easy to talk to.'

Was this what she was? A shoulder to cry on, with benefits? She swallowed and managed what she hoped was a reassuring smile.

'I'm sure it will be okay, Henry.'

He shrugged, looking miserable. 'It's the not knowing that's eating me up. I didn't want to tell you, but I also didn't want you wondering why I've been a little on edge.'

She bit the inside of her cheek to keep a hysterical laugh from escaping. This revelation aside, they were still dealing with Mr Pussy destroying Jack's flat and Henry's family hassling him to return to Somerset with his publishing guru girlfriend, Elizabeth Bennet. One of those situations was enough to bring her to the edge. The other was about to push her off it.

Her heart ached for him. She couldn't burden him further by bringing up the state of their fledgling relationship. It could wait until after his meeting with HR.

Careful not to disturb Mr Pussy, she reached across and took his hand.

'I'm always here for you.'

He squeezed it. 'Thank you. You're amazing, Libby.' His eyes widened slightly. 'And I'm holding you up. Aren't you meant to be meeting your new improv partner in half an hour?'

She nodded and carefully transferred Mr Pussy from her lap to the sofa.

'I'll leave you to it,' he said. 'And come along later to help you set up.'

'Thank you, Henry.'

'You sure I can't do anything else?'

She tensed but managed to smile as she shook her head. Her search for more work was not going well. Despite being sick and exhausted with a tummy bug, Claire had given her pointers on approaching companies, but so far Libby had drawn a blank. Henry kept offering to help with some of his City contacts, but she turned him down each time. How could she accept any more help? She was already too indebted to him. She would make it work by herself, starting with tonight.

TWO HOURS LATER, LIBBY WASN'T SO SURE.

'No, a fanny describes a woman's, er, genitals,' she said. 'What you've got there is called a bum bag, although this might make a good gag between us about how we can't understand each other?'

Brandon, a friend of an old improv colleague, had flown in from New York a couple of days ago. It was his first time in the UK, and although he had the requisite levels of enthusiasm and his own ukulele, he didn't yet understand British words and cultural references.

He pulled his red braces away from his plaid shirt. 'And these aren't suspenders?'

'Er, no. Suspenders are what hold up women's tights. You call them "stays" I think?'

'Gotcha. And a wife-beater is a vest?'

'Yes, but we should probably keep any reference to domestic abuse out of the show?'

He nodded. 'And if I'm pissed, then I'm drunk?'

'Yes, except when you're pissed off, which *does* mean you're cross.'

His forehead furrowed. 'Man, I need to write this down. I think I'm still jet lagged.'

'Don't worry. We'll be fine,' she said, feeling anything but. 'Let's go upstairs and set up.'

Brandon put his hand on his stomach. 'I'll join you in a bit. I just need to visit the bathroom.'

Libby went upstairs and started setting up the space. It was so familiar, yet without Claire it felt wrong. Her friend had promised to be back within six months but it seemed unlikely. Motherhood looked exhausting and Claire was wiped out from the lack of sleep and the bug, which didn't seem to want to leave her.

Libby thought back to the living history tours she saw in Bath and the one she ran at the Manor. Was she crazy to think of getting work in Somerset? What would happen if Henry lost his job at Conqueror? Would he get another one in the City or might he return to Foxbrooke?

'Libby!'

Henry was at the top of the stairs, his arms open.

She ran into his hug. 'I missed you.'

His face was alight as he smiled at her. 'I missed you too. Two and a half hours away from you is two and a half hours too much.'

He cradled her head and brushed his lips against hers. Desire roared to life and she grabbed the back of his collar to pull him closer, her tongue slipping out to dance with his. Each time they kissed it felt more potent than the last, more charged with energy, feeling and meaning.

The sound of a throat being cleared broke them apart.

Lucas was standing at the top of the stairs.

A supercilious smile spread across his face as he gave them both a slow hand clap and a little bow.

'Very impressive. You're getting very method there with my girlfriend, Henry.'

Henry's hold on her tightened.

'Lucas.' Libby's heart hammered as she faced him. 'I told Henry that you and I were not together.'

Lucas raised an eyebrow then looked around the empty space. 'So, who is this particular show for then?'

'No-one.' Henry's tone was even, but it was underpinned

with steel. Libby bit back a whimper at the authority in his voice.

'So, you two...?'

'Libby is my girlfriend.'

She bit the inside of her mouth to stop herself shrieking with excitement.

Lucas looked at her sceptically. She nodded.

He sniffed. 'Well, do you mind if I borrow *your* girlfriend for a moment?'

Henry stiffened. '*Borrow?*'

She gave Henry's hand a squeeze. 'I've got a few minutes before people start arriving. It's fine.'

Lucas stalked to the end of the room and stood by the grimy window, his arms crossed.

Libby followed, making sure there was enough space between them to reassure Henry her feelings for Lucas had changed.

'Lib-Lob,' he whispered. 'What the fuck? Did he pay you extra to shag him?'

His words were like knives of ice to the heart. This was what everyone would think if they knew their relationship was fake from the start.

'No, of course, he didn't,' she hissed back.

'Then what the fuck is all that?' Lucas gestured angrily towards Henry, who stood watching them.

'Things changed.'

Lucas ran his hands through his greasy hair. It flopped straight back over his eyes.

He tutted. '*You've* changed.'

'What is that supposed to mean?'

'You know, Lib-Lob. You've crossed over. You're hanging out on the other side of the fence. But they'll never accept you as one of their own. Don't think this is going to end with you as Lady of the Manor.'

Her stomach heaved at his words. It was like the break-up with Giles. Neither he nor his family wanted someone like her. Lucas had just articulated her deepest fears about her relationship with Henry.

She swallowed the bile in her throat. 'What are you doing here, Lucas?'

He looked at her askance. 'Is that how you speak to your friends now?'

She stared at him, full of fury, but her heart still breaking. She couldn't believe how much she'd loved this man and how much he'd taken from her. She peered at his face. The skin around his left eye looked different.

'Are you wearing make-up?'

He glanced away and she could see the left side of his face was slightly swollen.

'What happened to you?'

'I was attacked.'

Her hand automatically shot out to his arm. 'Oh my god, by who?'

He shrugged. 'One of the owners of the gallery.'

She dropped her hand, realising what must have happened. 'Saphy's husband?'

He stared at her in shock. 'Do you know him?'

She shook her head.

'Why did he hit you?' she asked, already knowing the real answer.

'Because the fucker's got no taste. He wouldn't know art if it smacked him in the nuts.' He sighed. 'Lib-Lob, I need your help.'

'What kind of help?'

'The show's been cancelled. He's blacklisted me, and a load of the buyers have pulled out.'

Her heart sank. Now she'd never get her money back.

'And what can I do about it?' She tried to keep her voice even.

'You're my best friend, Lib-Lob. I've got nowhere else to turn. I need a bit more help to get me back on my feet.'

'I don't have any money, Lucas,' she hissed. 'I gave it all to you, remember?'

'But what about the money you got from Foxy?'

'That hasn't paid off all my debts.'

'But you're not paying rent anymore.'

'And I'm not exactly raking it in doing improv, either! It's going to take me months to get back into the black and even longer to build up my savings. You have to pay me back.'

'I will, I promise, Lib-Lob. Just help me out for a couple more months and I'll find a way.'

'What's your plan? Are you going to take up that teaching job you were offered at the college?'

He screwed up his face as if she'd just suggested he roll about in dog shit.

'Jesus, Libby. Teaching is for professional failures. I just need time to reach out to my models, get them to buy their pictures off me. Then I'll be able to pay you back.'

She crossed her arms, trying to keep her emotion tied up inside. 'I can't help you.'

'You'll think of something,' he said with a smile. 'You always do.'

He kissed her on the cheek before she could stop him, then quickly walked to the stairs and jogged down them without a backwards glance.

❧ 29 ❧

Lorna Ferguson met Henry in reception and buzzed him through security.

She handed him a visitor's pass on a lanyard. 'Nice to see you again. Come on through.'

After his attack on James, they'd revoked his access to the Conqueror building. The pass hung around his neck like a sign announcing his fall from grace.

Lorna beckoned. 'This way.'

Henry made an effort to appear relaxed. He needed this job and the money that came with it. But he wasn't excited about returning to work. The enforced holiday had finally put the brakes on the never-ending train ride of his life, and now that it had stopped, he didn't know how to start it back up again. He didn't want to spend twelve hours a day in front of a computer screen and his nights schmoozing clients in bars. He wanted to be with Libby.

He was drowning in his feelings for her, but did she want or need him? Her insistence on paying for the damage to Jack's flat was like a knife twisting in his guts. He'd caused this mess, but she was paying for it. And when she turned down his offer of help finding her work with other City firms, it felt like she was turning *him* down. She hadn't contradicted him when he'd told Lucas he was her boyfriend, but she hadn't agreed with him either. *Fuck's sake!* He hadn't known this level of insecurity since secondary school.

He flexed his fingers to stop them tightening into fists at the thought of Lucas. Was there really any reason to hate him so viscerally? Technically, he hadn't done anything wrong. He was one of Libby's friends and had stepped in to check Henry wasn't taking advantage of her.

But there was just something about Lucas that made his skin crawl. The way he'd kissed her in the coffee house? Or how he didn't seem to care about her even as a friend? Maybe because his art was based on painting women's vaginas? Or because Libby had been in love with him?

Upstairs, a man was waiting for them in a small conference room with glass walls. He stood as they entered.

'Henry Foxbrooke?'

He nodded.

'I'm Mike Richards. I work alongside Lorna. She's asked me to sit in on this meeting.'

Mike was enormous. He looked like he should be playing tighthead prop on a rugby team. Did Lorna think she needed a bodyguard in case Henry kicked off?

'Please, Henry, take a seat.' Lorna slid into the one next to Mike.

Henry sat on the other side of the table, taking slow breaths. He felt like he was back at school, knowing he was in trouble but not sure what the punishment was going to be.

'So, Henry,' Lorna began. 'How was your time off?'

I paid someone to be my fake girlfriend. I turned thirty. I fell in love.

The revelation hit him like a punch to the chest. Was he in love with Libby? The smile spread across his face. Of course, he was.

'Henry?'

'Oh, yes, it was fine, thank you.'

'And how are you feeling?'

'Fine.'

'So, I thought we'd start by informing you that Mr Hunter-Savage will not be pressing charges.'

The tightness in his chest eased. He hadn't realised how much the threat of prosecution had been weighing him down until it had gone.

'We're keen to see you back at work,' Lorna continued.

Okay, this is good.

'However, we would like you to attend therapy with a focus on anger management.'

'Is that necessary?'

'It's a mandatory condition for you returning to the workplace.'

'When can I start?'

'Let's see how the first session goes, shall we?'

HENRY STRODE OUT THE CONQUEROR offices and bumped into Carl smoking a cigarette.

'Foxy!' Carl slapped him on the back. 'It's been weird as fuck not having you around. How was your birthday?

He smiled. 'Almost as expected.'

'Almost?'

He had the sudden urge to tell Carl more about himself than he'd ever done before.

'I got a girlfriend.'

Carl's mouth fell open. 'What, as a present? I know your dad's a bit wild. But...'

Henry smiled and shook his head. 'No. I managed to get this one all by myself.'

'Fair play, mate. What's her name?'

'Libby,' he replied without thinking.

'Hmm. Like that chick who did that improv thing with us?'

'Yeah.'

Carl looked at him through narrowed eyes and took a deep drag of his cigarette.

'Does she look the same as well?'

Henry nodded, failing to stop his smile.

Carl slapped him on the back. 'Sweet. She's the killer combination.'

'Huh?'

'Hot *and* nice,' Carl replied. 'And you don't have to worry about Hunter-Savage nicking her.'

'Why? What's happened to him?'

Carl exhaled a plume of smoke. 'Left.'

'Where did he go?'

He shrugged. 'No clue. Middle of last week he told Gaz he was off and he didn't show the next day.'

'Oh.' *Good.* James was someone who'd been in his life far too long. He was glad to finally see the back of him.

Estelle: Hey bro, I know I haven't returned your calls, but we do need to talk. I'm coming up to town Tuesday. Can we meet early evening? Then see Libby after? Xxx

Henry: Libby's got other plans on Tuesday evening, but I can meet you. Just let me know where X

. . .

THE LATE AFTERNOON SUN WARMED HENRY'S FACE AS HE SAT on the bench in Regent's Park. In front of him, pedalos drifted across the boating lake. He imagined bringing one to Foxbrooke. No doubt his dad would think it hilarious and Gram-Gram would have a fit.

'This is all very clandestine,' a voice said to his right. 'Should I be wearing a bowler hat and carrying a copy of Pravda?'

He stood as Claire approached, pushing a pram. She was smiling, but her skin was grey.

'Thanks so much for coming,' he said. 'How is, erm, motherhood going?'

Claire sat on the bench and blew out her cheeks. 'Honestly, I would murder the last panda left on earth with my bare hands to stop feeling like shit and get a good night's sleep.'

'I'm sorry, would you rather just go home?'

She shook her head. 'To be honest, it feels good to get out for a bit, and the vitamin D is good.' She swivelled to face him. 'Okay then, Henry. What's this all about?'

He cleared his throat. 'You're Libby's best friend, and you know her better than I do. I wanted to ask your advice.'

'Go on.'

'She hasn't been particularly, er, *successful* at setting up workshops—'

'I bloody knew it.'

'And I want to help her. I've got some contacts in the City I could approach, but...'

'She said no?'

He nodded. 'I know she's uncomfortable if I spend any money on her, but I want to. And I want to help her find work. I want to make her life easier. It makes me happy.'

'And you want me to talk to her?'

He shrugged. 'Maybe? I don't know. I want to help, but I don't want to cock it up.'

'Because you're head-over-heels in love with her?' Claire asked with a smirk.

He gave a rueful smile. 'That pretty much sums it up.'

She stamped her feet on the ground and clapped her hands. 'Knew it! Oh Henry, I can't tell you how happy that makes me after the last two years of bullshit with—'

'Lucas?'

She nodded.

'I have been worried she still holds a torch for him.'

Claire raised her eyebrows. 'After what that arsehole did?'

His blood ran cold. 'What did he do?'

She sighed. 'Fucked her over good and proper.'

IT WAS ONLY A HALF HOUR WALK FROM REGENT'S PARK TO Paddington station, but that wasn't enough time to bring Henry's boiling rage down to a simmer. Claire had made him promise not to say anything to Libby, and in return she promised not to tell her about their meeting.

Was Libby even over Lucas? Henry hadn't heard their conversation the other night, but Lucas had still kissed her on the cheek. Maybe a love that strong didn't go away so easily.

AN ENORMOUS HUG ALMOST BOWLED HENRY OVER JUST AS HE was about to enter the pub.

'Thanks, Bro,' Estelle said. 'I appreciate this.'

He shook his head. 'You know as well as I do any thanks between us should come from me.'

'Well,' she replied, raising her eyebrows. 'Let's see if you still think that after you've heard what I've got to say.'

They ordered food and took a table in the corner of the pub. Tall and stunning with the voice of a foghorn, his sister usually filled any space she was in. But today she seemed smaller and more subdued.

'You never told me what happened after we left,' he began.

She let go of a breath with a whoosh and shrugged. 'Just more of the usual bollocks. Same same, but different.'

'But the guy who's suing?'

'A few years ago, I made a list of things we could sell to raise capital in case we needed to,' she replied. 'I've been meeting with auction houses today to see which items would give us the most bang for our buck. The trouble is, this is the third time we've had to do this already.'

'What?'

'Nearly half the paintings at the Manor are reproductions. I pay an artist to recreate them so no-one will know.'

'You're *forging* paintings?' he spluttered.

His sister rolled her eyes. 'No, dummy, I'm reproducing them. It would only be a forgery if I tried to pass one of them off as the original.'

'Does Dad know? Mom? Mammy, *Gram-Gram?*'

'Gram-Gram doesn't. Jesus Christ, can you imagine the shit that would go down if she found out? The only ones who know are our folks, you and me.'

He rubbed his forehead. 'I had no idea it was this bad.'

She shrugged. 'Well, it is. I've tried for nearly ten years to fix it, and I can't. This latest clusterfuck was the last straw. I'm going to have to walk away and try and split the livery from the estate before I lose that as well.'

'But how can I make a difference if you can't?'

She held his gaze. 'You can *be there*. No matter how Dad

wangs on about worshipping the divine feminine, the patriarchy runs deep in him. Fuck, it runs deep in all of us. Even Mom, who's as badass American as they come, still defers to him when push comes to shove. He doesn't fucking listen to me, and even if he does, he still goes and does exactly what the fuck he wants. If I had a penis, we wouldn't be having this conversation. But I don't, so we are.'

'Seriously, Estelle, you think he would listen to me just because I have a dick?'

'Yes. The only way he's going to get into any sort of line is if you come home. For good.'

'But—'

'I mean, fuck's sake, look at the sodding redesign of your bedroom and bathroom. Has he ever done that for any of us?'

'I don't know.'

'Well, I'm telling you, he hasn't. You're the prodigal son, Henry. That's why he let Mom pay for you to leave Foxbrooke Secondary and go to Eton.'

'What do you mean, he "let" Mom? It was her money.'

'Yes, it was, but she didn't pay for me when I asked her to go to the Royal High.'

He sat back, his head pounding. 'You asked her to pay for you to go to private school?'

'Yep.'

'I had no idea.'

'I know.'

'What about Connor? Leo? Willow?'

Her laugh was hollow. 'Connor didn't bother after it didn't work for me. Leo and Willow were the same. And it wasn't like Mammy had any money.'

'Fuck. Estelle, I'm so sorry.'

'It's not your fault.'

'But if I'd have known, maybe I could have—'

'Changed Dad's mind? Maybe, but unlikely. If Mom couldn't change his mind, I doubt a thirteen year old could have. I was so mad at the time, but I just sucked it up and got on with it.'

'I'm so sorry.'

She shrugged. 'What's done is done, but now we need you back in Somerset. Look, I know Libby complicates things, but maybe Winterblossom Press can let her work remotely for at least part of the week? And if that doesn't work, there are several publishing companies in Bath she could approach.'

He didn't know what to say. He couldn't ask Libby to give up her whole world in London for him. And was he ready to throw away *his* life just when he'd finally got it how he wanted?

'Henry,' Estelle began. 'One day, Foxbrooke is going to be yours whether you like it or not, and at this rate the only thing left of our family home will be a conference centre or an old peoples' home. Neither of which you would own. You need to make a decision. Come home, or accept the consequences.'

30

Footsteps sounded on the stairs and Libby caught Brandon's eye with a frown. An early punter must have ignored the rope across the stairwell. She put down the chair she was carrying and straightened with a smile.

The smile froze as Lucas appeared.

Her heart ran double time. He wouldn't accept that she had no more money to give, so she'd stopped answering his texts altogether. Despite the summer heat, she shivered.

'Sorry, Brandon, this is a friend of mine. I'm just going to have a quick chat with him, okay?'

Brandon looked uncertainly between her and Lucas. 'Yeah... Yeah, sure. I'll be over there, warming up.'

Libby started across the room to the window, wishing Henry were here rather than across town with Estelle.

Lucas followed. As they faced each other, she crossed her arms.

'Oh, Lib-Lob, don't be like that.' He gave her a hug.

She tensed. Everything about him now felt off.

330

'Lucas,' she said as he disengaged. 'I've told you, I don't have any more money. I can't magic it out of thin air.'

He ran his hands through his lank hair. She used to think the move was sexy. Now it made her shudder.

'Lib-Lob, for someone who does improv for a living, you're not very creative.'

What the fuck?

He smiled like a patient teacher about to explain the blatantly obvious to a dimwit student.

'You've got Henry at your disposal now.'

'At my "disposal"?' she replied in disgust. 'He's not a cash machine.'

He laughed. 'Babe, think outside the box. His dad's a collector *and* a connoisseur of the female form. Foxbrooke Manor is stuffed with art. You can get me an in.'

The thought of introducing Lucas to Henry's family as her friend made her stomach roll.

She shook her head. 'No way, Lucas, I won't do it.'

'Jesus, Lib-Lob, why not?'

If she couldn't bear the thought of Lucas at Foxbrooke Manor, the thought of his art hanging on the walls she liked even less.

'I'm not using Henry or his family.'

'Don't you want your money back?'

'Yes, of course I do! But taking it from them is not the answer!'

'But they're a perfect fucking fit!' he hissed. 'The Duke is all about the "divine feminine". If you could just get me in front of him, I could persuade him to commission me to paint both his wives. Think of the money in that!'

'Paint *them* or their bits?'

'*Vulvas*, Libby, *vulvas*. Don't be such a prude when it comes to the beauty and mystery of the female form.'

She swallowed to stop the rising bile shooting up from her stomach. Even though the image was the last thing she wanted crossing her mind, it still conjured up Dervla and Vivienne, their legs spread as Lucas held up his paintbrush and stared.

'No, Lucas. I'm saying no.'

'Well, then. If you won't, I'm going to give your new "boyfriend" a piece I've been working on.'

'What piece?'

His eyes were pale, his smile sly and thin. 'It's of you.'

'But you've never painted me before.'

He shrugged, as if that fact were irrelevant. 'And it's also of *me...*'

'What?'

He tapped the side of his head. 'Unlike you, I've got imagination, and I've been putting it to work. This piece may be life-size, but it's very intimate. Probably best hung in the bedroom... I've titled it "The Submission of Liberty". I think Foxy will like it. Might give him some fresh ideas for what he can do with you,' he sneered.

She stumbled back. 'You wouldn't,' she whispered.

'Everything okay over there?' Brandon called over.

Lucas turned. 'Yeah, bud, no drama.' He looked back at her. 'My life is in the shitter and I'm trying to get out. As a friend you should be there for me.'

Her heart was hammering so hard she couldn't reply.

'Get me in with the Foxbrookes or I give Henry the painting,' he said, before walking away.

'Calm down, Libby, I can't understand a word you're saying!' Claire yelled, her voice shrill on the phone.

Libby was huddled in one of the stalls in the pub's toilets, shaking and crying.

'Are you in immediate physical danger?'

'No,' she gulped.

'Has anyone died?'

'No, it's, it's worse than that.'

'Okay, take a big breath, in and out. Come on, Libby, you've got this. Tell Auntie Claire what the fuck is going on.'

In between heaving sobs she told Claire what Lucas had said. She expected her best friend's response to be volcanic, but it was the opposite.

'Libby, you need to contact the police.'

'What? Why?'

'He's blackmailing you. I think he's been inhaling too many paint fumes. That or he's started eating it from the tubes. The man's lost his fucking mind and you cannot do what he says.'

'But if he sent a picture like that to Henry—'

'And you need to tell him as well.'

'Tell who?'

'Henry. He needs to know.'

'No, Claire. I can't. No way.'

'Why not?'

'Because compared to him, I'm a total fuck-up at life. If I told him about Lucas, I'd have to tell him *everything* about Lucas. Henry's got his shit together. He's got a good job, he owns a flat in Canary Wharf for chrissakes and he's a fucking Lord! I'm just plain old Libby Fletcher. I've given away what little money I had to an arsehole, and I can't even find work on my own. Why the hell he's still with me, god only knows.'

'He loves you.'

'Yeah right. The moment he goes back to work and his normal life, the scales will fall from his eyes and he'll see me for who I really am. It'll be just like Giles all over again.'

'Bullshit!' Claire shouted. 'Giles was a tosser. Henry loves you, and rightly so. You're fucking amazing.'

'I don't feel particularly amazing right now.'

'I know, love, but we'll get you through this, I promise. Message Lucas and say you need to meet up in a couple of days to work out the best plan. Then you're going to record him and take it to the police. Okay?'

'That sounds risky.'

'It's either that or tell the police now.'

'But I have to work out what to say, or won't it be seen as entrapment?'

'Don't worry about it. In between throwing up, I'll do the research.'

'Oh my god, are you still sick?'

'Yeah, it sucks but it's usually only once a day, so when it's done, I feel better.'

'Have you been to the doctor?'

'Nah, waiting lists are two weeks plus. I'll ring them if it doesn't go by the weekend and make an appointment.'

LIBBY DREW ON ALL HER RESERVES TO MAKE IT THROUGH THE evening's performance. Brandon didn't pry, instead channelling his energy into the ukulele, playing it as if he was rocking out at Madison Square Garden. She felt a stab of guilt that she wasn't more grateful for him. After the show she thanked him profusely then checked her phone.

> Henry: Estelle's just got on the train back to Bath. I can meet you wherever you like. Hope it went well and sorry I couldn't be there X

> Libby: Shame I missed her. I'm on my way back to the flat. I'm really tired and just want to crash xxx

Henry: No worries, see you later X

She then sent a text to Lucas.

Libby: I need to think about how to make
what you suggested happen. Can you meet
me in a couple of days to discuss?

Lucas: Sure babe x

Back at the flat, Libby got Sunny out to make a new loaf of sourdough. Kneading and pummelling the dough was therapeutic. She didn't want Lucas's bad energy going into her beautiful bread, so she closed her eyes and took her mind back to the field of flowers and making love with Henry under the stars.

'Hi, only me,' Henry called through as the front door opened.

Mr Pussy ran out to meet him.

'Incoming!' she yelled.

But for once there was no screeching or yelling.

'Are you alive?' she called into the silence.

Henry entered the kitchen carrying Mr Pussy, who was purring into his neck. He looked as shocked as she felt.

'Um,' she began.

'I don't know what I've done differently. But my relationship with Mr Pussy has definitely turned a corner.'

She giggled. 'Should I be jealous?'

'Never.' He carefully kissed the top of her head. 'The only reason I'm not coming any closer is that I don't want any cat hair ruining Sunny.'

She grinned. 'I'll be done in a bit.'

'How did the show go?'

She took a big breath. She was not going to be a fuck-up

anymore. She was going to project the person she wanted to become: confident, successful and going places.

'Great!' she replied enthusiastically. 'Much better than last week. Brandon's got some fantastic ideas, and I'm going to meet up with him in a couple of days for a brainstorm. I really think this new partnership is going somewhere.'

He smiled, but something about it was off.

'How did it go with Estelle?'

He carried Mr Pussy to the cat tree.

'Fine.'

She bit her bottom lip. Based on her picture-imperfect departure from Foxbrooke, she highly doubted it.

'Henry?'

'Mmm?' He was still holding onto Mr Pussy and staring out the window.

'Do you need to go back to Foxbrooke? Permanently?'

He transferred the cat to the top platform and faced her, his smile still in place.

'Not at all, Estelle has everything well in hand. I want to be here with you, cheering from the sidelines as you take over the improv world.'

If Libby had wild fantasies about moving to Somerset and spending her days dressed as Lizzie Bennet, entertaining tourists at the Jane Austen Museum, Henry's words had shown her dreams the door. And they were just dreams. Her world was in London. Her friends were in London. Her job was in London, as was Henry's now his situation with Conqueror had been resolved.

In a couple of months Claire would be back and they could pick up where they left off. And even if Claire were delayed, she'd find a way to make it work with Brandon. Respond, adapt, change. That's what improv was all about. She'd had it easy with Claire. Running improv sessions and workshops with Brandon was going to be a new challenge and a fun one. She'd make sure of it.

She'd arranged to meet Lucas at Regent's Park on Friday. It was close to Claire's, so they could practice what she would say before she met him and review the recording afterwards.

ON FRIDAY MORNING SHE WAS SICK WITH NERVES AND SHE could tell Henry was worried. Each time he asked if she was okay and she denied it, the tension between them increased. She knew he was frustrated, but she had no intention of telling him anything. She was playing the part of successful improv artist and entrepreneur, not a broke wannabe undercover agent.

'So, you'll be back from Claire's around six?' he asked as she prepared to leave.

'Yep.'

'Anything in particular you want for dinner?'

'Not fussed. Whatever you want.'

'You don't think you might have caught that sickness bug from Claire?'

'Huh?'

'You've hardly eaten anything all day. How are you feeling?'

'Fine. I'm fine, honestly. I think it's the heat. I'm not that hungry.'

His phone rang but he didn't move to answer it.

'Henry, I'm fine!' She checked the contents of her bag. 'Go answer it. It might be important.'

He hesitated, then went to pick it up.

She had to get away before he asked her any more questions. As he took the call, she opened the front door. Closing it quietly behind her, she took a deep breath and started jogging down the stairs. She could do this. She was a badass who was going to take Lucas down.

'Libby!' Henry was yelling from the flat.

She turned and ran back up the stairs. 'What is it?'

He was at the door, his face ashen.

'It's Gram-Gram. She's dying. I need to go back to Foxbrooke right now.'

❧ 31 ☙

Libby: There's been an emergency and I have
to reschedule. I'll text you when I'm back.

Lucas: WTF? I need that money, Lib-Lob. You
can't do a runner on me.

Libby: I'm not. Henry's grandmother has been
taken ill and we're on our way back to
Foxbrooke now.

Lucas: Cool. You can talk to the Duke about
my art in person! When will you be back?

Libby: By Tuesday for the improv night.

Libby held Henry's hand tightly as the train ran through the suburbs of west London into the countryside. With his car across town at his flat in Canary Wharf, it was quicker to take public transport. They'd packed overnight bags and Brandon had agreed to housesit for Mr Pussy.

Libby's heart raced. There had been very little news on Gram-Gram's condition, only that she'd taken to her bed the previous day and had gone downhill fast. Libby would have accompanied Henry back to Somerset had he asked, but his grandmother had already insisted she return with him to Foxbrooke. Libby couldn't understand why. She'd only known the family a few weeks.

Henry didn't talk, just occasionally checked his phone, his face set with tension.

At Bath Spa, Henry and Libby took a taxi straight to the Dower House. Connor met them at the door and pulled them in for a hug.

'What's going on?' Henry asked.

His brother frowned. 'She won't let me check her vitals, and Marie won't share them with me. She looks terrible to be honest, but unless she talks to me or lets the doctor tell us what's going on, I can't make any kind of accurate assessment.'

'How's everyone else?'

'A mess. Dad's the worst, of course. He's up there now with Mammy and Mom. I'd better take you straight up.'

Libby held back as Connor and Henry started towards the stairs.

Connor turned. 'And you, Libby. She wants you there too.'

'Why?' she whispered.

He shrugged. 'You're family.'

Henry reached out his hand and she took it. He squeezed to reassure her, then followed Connor up the stairs.

. . .

Gram-Gram's room was large, but the light was dim. The chintz curtains had been pulled across the windows, allowing only a sliver of sunshine to enter. Arthur, Vivienne and Dervla rushed to embrace them.

'My dear girl,' cried Arthur, kissing Libby's forehead. His face was puffy and his eyes red-rimmed.

'Is that Henry?' a tremulous voice sounded from the bed.

'Yes, Gram-Gram,' said Connor.

'And Libby?'

'I'm here too,' she replied.

'Come here, child,' Gram-Gram said, her voice wavering.

Libby swallowed her anxiety and followed Henry to the bed. He sat on the edge and took his grandmother's hand.

'I'm here, Gram-Gram,' he said softly. 'How are you feeling?'

Her face was papery white, her features sunken. Her hair, which Libby had only ever seen immaculately coiffed, was now a grey squall around her head. She was unrecognisable from the imperious dragon Libby had met a few weeks before. Gram-Gram's free hand crept across the quilt towards hers as she stood by the bedside, then clasped it with surprising force.

'You're here,' Gram-Gram whispered.

'Yes,' Henry replied. 'We're both here.'

'Good,' she exhaled, her eyes closing.

Everyone else in the room took a sharp intake of breath.

'Gram-Gram?'

Her eyes flickered open. 'I'm dying.'

'No, you're not,' Henry replied. 'You'll be up and about again soon enough.'

She slowly shook her head. 'I don't have much time left.'

'What do you mean?' Arthur cried. 'What's wrong with you?'

She ignored him, her rheumy eyes fixed on Libby and Henry.

'You must promise me,' she said, her voice getting weaker.

'Yes, anything,' Henry said. 'Whatever you want.'

Gram-Gram stared directly at Libby. 'Both of you.'

Libby's heart was pounding. What was going on? She nodded at Gram-Gram.

'Good,' Gram-Gram sighed and closed her eyes as if the matter were now settled.

Henry glanced at Libby and pulled a questioning face.

She shrugged, as bewildered as he was.

'Gram-Gram?' Henry asked, tentatively.

Her eyes re-opened.

'What can we do for you?'

She coughed. It sounded like a death rattle.

'Before I die,' Gram-Gram began, her gaze sharper than her voice. 'I want to see you both married.'

Silence.

Oh my god. Libby couldn't breathe.

'Promise me.' Gram-Gram gripped their hands tighter. 'Promise me.'

Henry glanced at Libby, wild-eyed with panic.

'Henry?' Gram-Gram croaked.

Henry had frozen.

What the fuck could they say?

Improvise!

'Yes, of course,' she said to Gram-Gram. 'We will make that happen.'

A collective gasp of relief ran around the room.

'Somebody fetch Eveline,' Gram-Gram said. 'We need to start making the arrangements.'

. . .

LIBBY STUMBLED THROUGH THE NEXT HALF HOUR ON autopilot, smiling and agreeing with everything anyone said like she was a nodding dog on the dashboard of a car. Luckily, Eveline wasn't answering at the rectory, so they agreed to find her the next day and left Gram-Gram with a subdued Marie.

On the walk back to the Manor, Henry's parents alternated between concern over Gram-Gram's condition, and excitement at the prospect of Henry and Libby getting married.

Henry was mute.

All Libby wanted to do was speak to him in private, to apologise and let him off the hook. Seeing how decrepit Gram-Gram was, she'd panicked and given the Dowager Duchess the answer she wanted. But Henry's shocked silence clearly said her save was the opposite of what he wanted.

Nearing the grounds, she spotted Duke running free in the park.

'Must have slipped the bally stables,' said Arthur. 'Henry, can you go and fetch him?'

Henry looked at Libby. 'Can you tell Estelle?'

She nodded and took his bag, following his parents into the house as he went after the horse. She couldn't face the whole family, so dropped their bags by the front door, sent Estelle a text and wandered to the kitchen, hoping she might be there.

Estelle was sitting on the centre worktable, her phone in one hand and a Chelsea bun in the other. She looked up as Libby entered.

'I woff wus exxing oo,' she said, her mouth full of pastry.

She hopped off the table, put the phone and bun down and drew Libby into a hug.

London disappeared in a puff of smoke as she smelled the familiar scents of Foxbrooke on Estelle. It felt like home. She swallowed her emotion as Estelle swallowed her mouthful of Chelsea bun.

'God, I'm glad you're here.' Estelle said. 'How is she? I saw her earlier and she looked fucking awful.'

'She didn't look good. I'm so sorry.'

Estelle swiped at her eyes. 'This is what I hate about old people. They never tell you what's really going on. And posh old people are the bloody worst. It's all "How impertinent for you to ask about details of my health. I don't even talk to my doctor about that!"'

Libby smiled. 'I know what you mean. My nana once tripped over my grandad's walking stick and broke her ankle. She refused to see the doctor for three weeks and didn't tell anyone what had happened. It was only when my mum demanded a proof-of-life visit that she fessed up.'

Estelle snorted. 'Jesus, I hope I never end up that pig-headed.'

Libby gave her a sly look. 'I think that ship may have already sailed.'

Estelle threw her head back and roared with laughter. 'Thank you for that, Libby Bennet. For the laugh, and for making me remember why I like you so much.' She held out the tray of Chelsea buns. 'Want one? Perry made them to help me cope with the current crisis, and even I can't eat them all.'

'Thank you, I haven't eaten much today.' Biting into one, Libby was hit with another sensory wave of longing for a life she could never have. She'd lied about who she was and now Henry was about to break up with her because of her impulsive mouth.

Estelle picked at the edge of the table. 'I never got a chance to thank you in person for what you did to save the tour. You were outstanding. We got the best reviews we've ever had.'

Libby smiled, but inside guilt ate at her.

'Honestly, if you wanted a job doing that, I'd employ you in a heartbeat.'

'You would?'

Estelle glanced up. 'God yes, but I know you'd never leave your fancy job in publishing to be a tour guide for a small and infamous stately home.'

Libby thought that sounded like her perfect job. Swanning around all day pretending to be in an Austen novel and waiting for Henry to ride in on his horse.

'Oh, I forgot to tell you, Duke got out just now. Henry's gone to bring him in.'

Estelle bashed her forehead with her hand. 'Fuck's sake. I need to fix the latch on the stable door. That's the second time he's got out this week.'

She smiled. 'I feel your pain. Mr Pussy keeps trying to make a bid for freedom every time I come back to the flat.'

Estelle snorted. 'Excuse me? Mr Pussy?'

'Yes, Jack's cat. I've been flat-and cat-sitting for him in London. Didn't Henry tell you?'

She looked confused. 'Jack?'

'Jack Newton, Henry's friend? He pays someone to live in his flat and look after his cat when he's abroad.'

'His cat?'

'Yes, Mr Pussy. Although despite the fact he's meant to be a therapy cat, I don't think he's used to having new people around. We've had to replace all the rugs after he crapped on them, and he's scratched everything he could get his claws into.'

Estelle was frowning. 'I don't understand.'

'Understand what?'

'Why Jack would keep a cat when he's in London only once a year, if at all?'

'Oh.'

'And he's allergic to them.'

'Allergic?'

'Yeah. When we were kids, we visited Dervla's aunt who lived in the village. She had one. Within five minutes, Jack's eyes puffed up so much he couldn't see. It was terrifying and hilarious all at the same time.'

Libby couldn't speak. Pieces of a puzzle she didn't know existed were starting to fall into place, creating a picture she couldn't bear to look at.

'Is it one of those weird hairless cats?' Estelle asked.

The door opened and Henry entered.

'I knew I should look for you here first,' he said, hugging his sister. 'Duke's back in his stall.'

'Thanks, little brother. How was Gram-Gram?'

He hesitated, glancing at Libby. She shook her head.

'Er, not great to be honest, but it's difficult to tell when she refuses to tell us what's really going on.'

Estelle raised her eyebrows at Libby. 'See? That's belligerent bloody old people for you.' She handed Henry the tray of Chelsea buns. 'Want one?'

Summer entered the kitchen. Without make-up and her usual perkiness, she looked young and fragile.

'Thought I would find you here,' she said. 'Has Perry been making you buns behind our backs?'

Estelle moved in front of the table to hide the tray. 'Nope.'

Summer rolled her eyes. 'Whatevs.' She turned to Libby. 'Your friend's arrived.'

Her mind went blank. 'What friend?'

Summer shrugged. 'Some artist dude? Luke? He's talking to Dad in the second lounge, the one with all the Holbeins.'

LIBBY RACED OUT OF THE KITCHEN, HENRY FOLLOWING behind. She knew enough of the Manor to know the room

Summer was talking about. She pushed open the door and entered.

'Ah, there she is!' said Arthur. 'Libby! It's your friend Lucas. You didn't tell me he was in the area.'

She glanced around the room, counting everyone off: Vivienne, Dervla, Connor, Leo, Willow. Estelle and Summer had entered after Henry. Every member of the Foxbrooke family was there.

'And he's an artist who works with the divine feminine!' Arthur continued. 'We've got so much in common!'

The family's eyes flitted from her to Lucas and back as if waiting to see which of them would drop the ball first.

'Lucas,' she stammered. 'What are you doing here?'

Concern oozed from his face. 'I was passing by and wanted to see how you were holding up under the very difficult circumstances.'

Arthur patted his shoulder. 'Much obliged, Lucas, much obliged.'

'And I knew I would find a kindred spirit in the Duke here.' Lucas gave Arthur a smile. 'Both a lover of art and of the goddess-nature found within all women.'

'See?' said Arthur to the room. 'A true connoisseur, just like me!'

Willow was curled up in the corner of a sofa, twisting a strand of blue hair around one of her fingers and looking warily at Lucas. 'How do you know Libby?' she asked.

'We met at her improv night a couple of years ago,' he replied. 'And have been best friends ever since. She may not be able to draw or paint, but she's an artist in her own right.'

'Improv?'

'Yeah, Libby runs a regular night on a Tuesday in Covent Garden and workshops for City firms who need to fulfil their "touchy-feely" quota for the year. That's how she met Henry. Libby's a very talented actress.'

The room was deathly quiet, but Lucas had failed to notice the changing mood. Libby's heart was trying to exit her body through her ribs.

'Lucas—' she began.

'Libby Bennet?' Willow interrupted.

Lucas frowned. 'Bennet? No, Fletcher.' He glanced around the room, then laughed and rolled his eyes. 'Bennet is just a persona Lib-Lob created for this job. Although—' He raised his arms, gesturing to her and Henry. 'As you can see, what was fictitious really has had a happy ending.'

'Fictitious?' Arthur asked.

Lucas hesitated and looked around, finally realising he'd brought a bad penny into the room and dropped it.

'Erm, in the best possible way,' he continued. 'Totally above board. Henry had a contract drawn up and everything. I saw it myself. Paid her properly, too. And, erm, happy-ever-after and all that?'

Libby fled.

She made it to the front door before Henry caught her up.

'Wait!'

She grabbed her bag.

'Libby!'

She was shaking so hard she could hardly speak. 'I need to get out of here.'

She didn't wait to hear his reply, wrenching the door open and running down the drive towards Foxbrooke.

He sprinted after her. 'Please!'

She didn't stop running until she was out of sight of the house. Out of breath, she slowed to a fast walk, heading for the high street.

'Please don't go. It's going to be okay. I'll fix it.'

She ignored him, powering her feet forwards until she got to the bus stop for Bath.

'Libby, *please*. Let's talk about this.'

Every cell in her body wanted to throw up until there was nothing left inside. In all her worst nightmares about how her fake relationship with Henry would play out, none came close to the excruciating horror of what she'd just experienced. The image of his family looking at her was a tableau that would live in her soul forever, the sharp edges scratching and drawing blood, continually reminding her of its presence.

A bus in the distance was moving slowly down the high street towards them.

'How long were you going to keep lying to me?' Her voice shook as she struggled to breathe.

'About what?'

'Jack's flat. The money for house-sitting. The cat?'

His face paled. 'How—'

'Jack's never there and is so allergic to cats they make him blind within five minutes.' She choked back a sob. 'You've been lying to me. Giving me money so that I can watch a "therapy cat" trash his flat.'

'Yes.'

'Why?'

'Because I wanted to help you, but you wouldn't accept it. I wasn't going to stand back and watch you struggle at Claire and Ritchie's. There isn't even room for a blow-up mattress in the nursery. Every night you'd have to wait until they went to bed before you could sleep on their sofa, which isn't long enough, even for you.'

'So, you've been paying me to live at Jack's?'

'Yes. I want to make your life easier. Why can't I do that?'

The bus was getting closer.

'Because it's too much, Henry!'

'Why is it "too much" for me to give you a few hundred quid, but you can happily hand over your life savings to Lucas?'

Her mouth opened. 'What?'

'Twelve grand, wasn't it? You gave that fucking arsehole twelve grand and you won't let me give you anything? How the fuck is that fair?'

'I'm not a charity case.'

'Of course you're not. But you're in a difficult situation and I want to help you out. Just as you wanted to help Lucas. Tell me, Libby. How is this different?'

The bus drew up and the doors opened with a hiss.

'You lied to me,' she whispered.

Henry shrugged. 'And you're still in love with Lucas.' His face was etched with pain. 'I don't want you to go, but I can't stop you. I'm going to try and fix things with my family.'

He stood, waiting for her decision.

Libby got on the bus and the doors closed behind her. As it pulled away, she didn't look back.

❧ 32 ❧

The bus disappeared around the corner, taking Henry's heart with it. As a child, he'd known paralysing fear and misery, but never pain as raw as this. He swallowed back a lump of emotion. Was this it?

When Gram-Gram had suggested they get married, he was shocked, then excited. And when Libby had agreed with his grandmother's edict, he thought his heart would fly out of his chest.

But as soon as Gram-Gram looked away, Libby's face fell into an expression of abject horror. She smiled and nodded at everything his parents said, but he could see the panic in her eyes. Then before he could talk to her, Lucas had arrived.

Henry stood for a few moments longer, staring up the high street, hoping Libby might change her mind, then turned on his heels, resigned to facing the music back at the Manor.

As he passed through the main gate, Lucas was ahead, walking briskly away from the front door. *Little fucker.* Adrenaline roared through his blood, spiking his heart rate as his body prepared for battle. His mind fought back. *Play the long game*. He might have lost Libby forever, but he could still try and get her money back.

Lucas noticed him and slowed his pace, his gaze wary.

Henry gave him a friendly wave.

Lucas stopped.

'You off back to London?' Henry asked, as pleasantly as he could manage with the dogs of war in his belly snarling to be let off the leash.

'Uh, yeah, I thought I'd better leave you to it,' Lucas replied. 'What with your granny ill and everything.'

Henry nodded. 'I thought I could chat to my father about your work. I'm sorry I couldn't come to your show opening last month.'

Lucas shrugged. 'I've left Balbis. I've got more freedom without a gallery taking fifty per cent for doing fuck-all. Means I can offer you a better deal, too.'

'Hmm. Let me take your number and I'll give you a call next week.'

Lucas's eyes lit up. He read it out and Henry added the number to his contacts.

'Cheers, Foxy.'

Henry nodded again, desperate to get away before he obeyed the call of his fists.

'Er,' Lucas began. 'Are things cool with Libby?'

'She'll be fine. Just give her some space, eh?'

He nodded and held out his hand. 'See you at the studio next week?'

Henry took it, forcing himself not to crush it to dust. 'I'll be in touch.'

. . .

HENRY DIDN'T PAUSE TO COLLECT HIS THOUGHTS AS HE strode back to the drawing room. The flurry of voices competing for airtime ceased the moment he entered.

'Is Libby with you?' Estelle demanded.

He shook his head.

'Fuck's sake! I thought you were going after her?'

'I did. But I can't force her to stay.'

His sister crossed her arms, her silence acknowledging the truth in his words, whilst her body language argued that he should have brought her back flung over his shoulder.

'Honey,' Vivienne said. 'Please tell us what's going on.'

'Isn't it clear enough?' he replied bitterly. 'I had to pay someone to pretend to be my girlfriend to get you all off my back.'

'But...' Arthur looked utterly confused. 'You were intimate with her. We all thought it was a fox on Midsummer's eve making all that noise before we put two and two together.'

'Dad!' he yelled as Willow and Summer put their hands over their ears.

'What? It's clear how much you love each other.'

Henry shook his head. 'I love her, and she might have grown to love me if I hadn't utterly fucked it up.'

'Honey, you haven't, I promise,' said Vivienne.

'And she *does* love you,' Dervla added. 'It's as clear as the nose on the end of my face.'

'*How* have you fucked it up?' Estelle asked. 'Unlike our parents, I'm positive you've fucked it up, but unless you tell us what you've done, we can't help you fix it.'

FROM: LIBBY FLETCHER
To: Jack Newton

Subject: Apologies

Hi Jack,

I've just found out Henry's been giving you money so you can pay me to live in your flat. I've also discovered you're seriously allergic to cats so I presume Mr Pussy does not belong to you?

Please send me your bank details so I can refund what you've sent. I'll find somewhere else to live in the next couple of days.

I'm so sorry,

Libby

FROM: JACK NEWTON

To: Libby Fletcher

Subject: Re: Apologies

Hi Libby,

You are correct, 'Mr Pussy' is not mine, however that is a truly splendid name for a cat. None of this is your fault. I've just spoken to Henry, and he agrees the blame for everything lies with him, not you.

Please do not refund the money. I don't want or need it, and apparently most of it has already gone on replacing soft furnishings and patching skirting boards after Mr Pussy put his mark on them. Also, please continue to stay at the flat for as long as you need. I have no intention of returning to the UK any time soon. If you don't use it, it will only lie empty.

I've known Henry all my life, and despite this error of judgement on his part and his hilarious inability to come up with a better name for a cat on the spot, he is the very best of men. I sincerely hope you can forgive him.

My very best wishes,

Jack

Ps - Please stay in the flat, even if just for Mr Pussy who seems to quite like it there. Also, I will be mortally offended if you offer to pay rent, so please don't.

Pps - I very much hope to meet you one day, although I will need to remain at least twenty feet away from your feline friend at all times.

Henry: I'm so sorry. I've spoken to Jack, and he wants you to stay in the flat. Please can we talk?

Libby: Where is Mr Pussy from? Do I need to take him back somewhere?

Henry: I got him from an ad online. He belonged to an old lady but when she died, her son didn't want to keep him. Do you want me to rehome him for you?

Libby: No.

Henry: Can I ring you? Please?

Libby: I only want to hear how your grandmother is.

Henry: Okay. I'll message you in the morning after I've seen her.

Henry: I'm so sorry, Libby. For everything.

THE NEXT MORNING HENRY AWOKE TO FIND HIS FATHER sitting on the edge of his bed holding a mug of tea.

'Morning, m'boy.' Arthur put the mug on the bedside table.

Henry sat and rubbed the sleep off his face.

'Morning, Dad.'

His father cleared his throat. 'I'm sorry, son.'

'What for?'

'Putting you under pressure to find someone. I've just had so much joy from your mothers and you and your brothers and sisters. I wanted you to have the same.'

Henry sighed. 'I think you were lucky to meet Mom and Mammy so young. Until Libby, I hadn't met anyone I really connected with.'

'She's such a lovely girl. Your mom is tickled pink that she's really an actress. I do hope you can win her back.'

He shrugged. 'I doubt it. And what are we going to tell Gram-Gram?'

His father raised his arms as if to summon divine intervention. 'I spoke to Marie this morning to give her the heads up and told her not to tell Mater. She rang back half an hour ago and said that you should go around there as soon as you're up.'

'How is Gram-Gram doing?'

'Must be a little better, or we'd all have been summoned. You can give us a full report when you're back.'

He took a gulp of tea to fortify himself.

'Dad?'

'Yes, Henry?'

'Have you ever spoken to Estelle to explain why you didn't let her go to private school when you let me?'

His father's eyes widened, then he hung his head, the toes of his carpet slippers scuffing the floor.

'No,' he eventually replied.

'You should.'

He shrugged. 'Seems such a long time ago now.'

'It doesn't seem that way to her.'

Arthur nodded then stood, heading for the door.

'Come find us the moment you're back from the Dower House,' he said before shuffling out of the room.

The perfect weather taunted Henry mercilessly as he crossed the park to his grandmother's house. Little white fluffy clouds hung high in the brilliant blue sky and the July sun bathed the countryside in a golden glow. Birds sang their joy at being alive and leaves rustled in agreement. Every sight, sound, smell and feeling reminded him of Libby, and his heart ached for her. The depths of his misery were equal to the depths of his love.

He rang the bell and knocked even though he knew the door to the Dower House would be open.

Marie answered it with a smile. 'Thank you for coming, Henry.'

'How is she?'

She hesitated, her cheeks colouring. 'Er, she is much improved.'

He started towards the stairs.

'She's in the drawing room,' Marie said, indicating one of the doors off the hall.

Henry paused, confused, then followed her through the house.

Outside the room, she stopped.

'Be gentle with her,' she whispered, before walking quickly away.

Worry spiked his heart. How bad *was* she? He knocked tentatively on the door.

'Come in,' came his grandmother's voice from inside.

He opened the door and froze.

'Gram-Gram?' he croaked.

'Yes? Do you not recognise me? Is a visit to the optician in order?'

His grandmother was sitting in her favourite chair, her spine ramrod straight, her hair and make-up immaculate enough to pose for a portrait.

She lifted her cane and pointed to the chair next to hers.

What the fuck? He sat before his knees gave way.

'You're better,' was all he could manage.

'Yes. A good night's sleep has worked wonders.'

He stared at her. What the hell was going on? *She hasn't asked about Libby...*

'You know,' he stated.

'For weeks.'

'What? How?'

His grandmother lowered her head a fraction to give him one of her hardest stares. The steely glares were designed to remind you of your pecking order in the family, which was always beneath her in every way.

'On your first night back, you didn't sleep in your room. I saw you through my binoculars. And I know what kind of girls work for publishing houses like Winterblossom. They're sweet young things and dream of being the next Polly Hart. Libby's not like them in the slightest. It only took one phone call to discover she didn't work there.'

He shook his head. She'd known. All this time?

'So, then I had to determine who she was and where you found her,' Gram-Gram continued. She lowered her head another inch to give him the full force of her glare. 'It took me less than a minute.'

'How?'

'Using the world wide web, of course,' she replied. 'When

your name and hers didn't produce a result, I searched for "Conqueror" and "Libby". It delivered me her website and a photograph from the workshop she ran at your company.' She paused. 'I hadn't seen you smile like that since you were a child.'

'But why didn't you say anything?'

'Because I wanted to observe the two of you, to deduce why you chose her for this ridiculous scheme, and why she accepted.'

'And yesterday? Your sudden "illness"? What on earth was that all about?'

'Do not take that tone with me, Henry.'

'Fucking hell, Gram-Gram!' he exploded. 'We've been worried sick!'

'Humph.'

'Why? Why did you do it?'

She rapped her cane sharply on the floor. 'To force you to take action. To marry the girl and finally come home.'

'What?'

'I don't know enough about what is going on at the Manor, but I know the situation is precarious. If your father is not kept in check, the estate will fall. Estelle has done her best, but Arthur does not take heed, and I will not see the Foxbrooke legacy destroyed in my lifetime. As for Libby, it was clear you both had strong feelings for each other. She's got the spark you need in a partner.'

'But marriage, Gram-Gram? We've only known each other a few months.'

She sniffed. 'Longer than I knew your grandfather before we were married. I know that girl is right for you even if you don't.'

'But her life is in London.' He rubbed the back of his neck. 'And I've messed it up with her anyway.'

'Everything is surmountable. The preferred outcome is the two of you back here permanently. However, if I must, I will accept either you returning on your own or continuing your present life in London, but with her.'

'You'd accept it if I didn't come back to Foxbrooke, but stayed in London with Libby?'

'If it means you are happy, then yes,' she replied testily. 'I'm not completely heartless.'

❧

Henry: Gram-Gram has made a full recovery.

Libby: Oh, I'm so relieved. Thank you for letting me know.

Libby: What was wrong with her?

Henry: Nothing. She was faking it to try and force us to get married.

Libby: What?!!!!!

Henry: I'm sorry for putting you through that. I'm sorry for everything my family and I have done to you.

Libby: Why would she do that?!

Henry: Because she wants me to move back to Foxbrooke.

Libby: And what's that got to do with me?

Henry: She believes you are the right person for me.

Libby: But she doesn't even know who I really am!

Henry: She does. She knew you were Libby Fletcher by eleven a.m. the morning after we arrived.

Libby: How?

Henry: Apparently, you're not like the kind of girls who work for Winterblossom Press so she googled you and found the photo from the Conqueror workshop.

Libby: Oh.

Henry: Look, I know I've fucked up and my family is mental, but you don't have to go back to Foxbrooke ever again. I promise. I start back at work next week. Please can I see you?

Libby: I'm sorry, Henry, I just can't right now.

❧ 33 ❧

Estelle: Please forgive my brother for being a
dick and my entire family for being, well, you
know… You're my favourite person Henry's
ever brought home.

> Libby: I'm the only person he's ever brought
> home.

Estelle: Not true. He brought some chinless
wonder called Crispin back from Eton once.

> Libby: I'm sorry for lying to you.

Estelle: You didn't. Not about the important
stuff.

Estelle: I'm going to stop hassling you but
please stay in touch. You're awesome. Xxx

Dervla: Hello Libby darling, it's Mammy again.
None of this is Henry's fault, it's ours. Big
hugs to you xxxx

Arthur: I've decided to buy a tandoor oven. Going to send you some links. Appreciate your thoughts as you're the curry expert in the family.

Arthur: After me, of course. Ha ha ha! (Laugh out loud!)

Vivienne: May I come to your show next week? Vivienne XO

Libby: I'm sorry, I would find it too difficult to perform if you did. I'm so sorry for lying to you all.

Vivienne: Honey, stop with that. Everything's fine. We all love you XO

Claire: I know you feel like the world has ended, but I promise you it hasn't. Please come over so I can give you a hug xxx

After a weekend curled up with Mr Pussy and a tub of ice cream, Libby dragged herself out of Jack's flat to visit Claire. Henry had finally stopped texting, but his family hadn't. She knew they meant well, but each time a new message arrived, memories flooded back of the shame and humiliation, and the anxiety made her want to throw up.

If Henry's family had bombarded her with communications, Lucas hadn't been in touch at all. Maybe he'd got what he wanted? She'd reconciled herself to never getting her money back from him.

Even though she didn't want to stay rent-free in Jack's flat, she had Mr Pussy to think of. She could no longer stay with Claire and there was no room back with her parents in

Birmingham. Last week she felt like her life had taken two steps forward. Now she was back at the starting line once more.

'COME HERE.' CLAIRE DREW LIBBY IN FOR A HUG AS SOON AS the front door opened.

'You feeling better?'

Claire disengaged and pulled a face. 'Fuck no. I've just been sick again. But the doctor says it's not contagious.'

'What's wrong with you then?'

'Let's have a cuppa and we can chat. Harper's down for a nap and Ritchie's out shopping, so we've got time to catch up.'

Libby looked across a sea of toys, blankets, rockers and a baby gym in the living room. Henry was right. There was no way she could have stayed here.

'Have you talked to Henry?' Claire asked.

She shook her head.

'You're still that angry?'

Libby nodded.

'Are you angry at him for helping or because you didn't know?'

'Both.'

'But if he did tell you, you wouldn't have accepted it.'

She was silent. Claire was right. If Henry hadn't done what he did, she'd have spent the last few weeks tripping over baby toys, sleeping on a lumpy sofa and losing her mind.

'What's so wrong with your boyfriend helping you out when you're in need?'

Libby shrugged. She couldn't articulate why it had upset her so much. It just seemed so unequal. She had nothing to contribute in return.

'If I was homeless with debts up to my eyeballs,' Claire

continued. 'And you had an extremely well-paid job, would you offer to help me out?'

'Of course I would! But it's different.'

'How?'

'Because you're my friend!'

'So, if I was homeless with debts up to my eyeballs, and *Ritchie* had an extremely well-paid job, would it be wrong of him to help me?'

'No, of course not.'

'What's the difference?'

'Ritchie's your husband. Henry's just...'

'Your fuck buddy?'

'Jesus, Claire, no!'

'You know what I think, Libby?'

'No, but I'm about to find out,' she replied morosely.

'You don't like not being in control.'

'Come again?'

'You're quite happy to be in love with Lucas for years, because deep down, in your heart of hearts, you knew it was never going to happen.'

'That's not true.'

'It bloody well is. Unrequited love is safe because only a small amount of your heart is at stake. Remember, before you met Lucas, who you were in love with?'

She stared at the floor, refusing to give Claire an answer.

'Kyle. Gorgeous, funny and so gay he never even kissed a girl to experiment when he was a teenager. Again, completely and utterly safe because nothing was ever going to fucking happen!'

Libby didn't want to acknowledge a word Claire was saying, because her gut said she was probably right.

'Giving all your money to Lucas was also about you being in control. It meant he owed you. Even if he never ended up as your boyfriend, you would always have a special relationship with him that no-one else could have. But with Henry, it's different. He actually wants you back. So, it's now too scary for you to handle. You only feel safe in your love life when you are in control, and loving Henry isn't safe because you've given him the whole of your heart. You know, Libby, you're fearless on stage. But in your love life, you're meeker than a mouse.'

Claire sat back and closed her eyes. She looked completely exhausted.

'Can I get you anything?' Libby asked.

Claire shook her head. 'I know this insecurity comes from what happened with Giles,' she said, her eyes still closed. 'He was a posh twat who didn't think you were good enough and thought he could mould you into his mother. Henry's not like that. He loves you, Libby, and he wants you to be happy.'

'You don't know that.'

'Yes, I do. He told me.'

'What? When?'

Claire opened her eyes and sighed.

'He wanted to talk to me to find out how he could help you without pissing you off. Apparently, you'd refused his help to get workshop gigs in the City.'

Libby stood, furious that once again the people closest to her were going behind her back.

'Did you know he was paying me to stay in Jack's flat?'

'No, but I told him you'd given all your money to Lucas.'

'Why?'

'Because he was convinced you were still in love with that twat, and he also needed to know you were in serious financial shit.'

Libby threw her arms in the air. 'Anything else I don't know?'

'Yes,' Claire replied. 'I'm pregnant again.'

✦

Henry closed his eyes. Birdsong, the melodious bubbling of a stream, and the distant sound of panpipes drifted through the air.

'Now, take a deep breath in through your nose,' a man's voice intoned. 'And out through your mouth. Ahhhhh.'

Henry did as instructed.

'Fantastic, Henry. You're doing really well. Immerse yourself in the sounds of nature.'

Behind the water, birds and panpipes, he heard honks of car horns and a distant police siren. The therapy room overlooked a busy London street and the soundproofing was not up to spec.

'Feel a sense of deep peace and stillness moving through your body.'

The man's voice was getting progressively louder as he tried to drown out the approaching siren.

'You are calm, you are centred, you are in control!'

Henry was most definitely none of those things. Libby was refusing to talk to him and he was in enforced therapy. In addition, in a few short hours he was leaving the country. His plan for getting her money back from Lucas involved stepping so far out of his comfort zone, a swim in the shark tank at the Sea Life Centre after smearing himself in fish paste seemed preferable.

'Now, think of somewhere you feel relaxed and content.'

People were shouting at each other in the street. Right now, London was definitely not his happy place.

'Imagine everything you can see, smell, feel, hear, touch and taste.'

His mind took him back to the field of flowers, sitting

under the oak tree with Libby as she weaved a flower garland for her hair.

'Feel how happy and at ease you are.'

His senses were filled with the memory of sunshine and smiles, of how full his heart was with Libby by his side. He remembered walking down the country lane, the hedges on either side of them bursting with life. He saw the old thatched cottage, the rose clambering up it, the look in Libby's eyes as if she'd just found a piece of heaven on earth.

Libby was his happy place.

But would she ever forgive him? He shouldn't have gone behind her back to give her money. But how else could he have helped her without making it seem like charity?

'Okay, we've got a bit of a frown coming on there. Shall we try and turn it upside down?'

Henry bit back a sigh. Was returning to Conqueror really worth all of this?

❦

LIBBY ZIGZAGGED THROUGH PUDDLES ON HER WAY TO Covent Garden to meet Brandon for their improv night. Every year the newspapers would fearmonger about droughts and hosepipe bans, and each summer the weather would stick two fingers up at their pronouncements and piss all over Britain. What would the countryside be like in the rain? A mud bath? Or just as beautiful as it had been in the sunshine?

Claire's announcement about her surprise second pregnancy had thrown Libby for a loop. There was no way her friend would be able to return to work for at least a year and a half. And even if she felt up to it after that, with the current crisis in childcare could she find someone to look after two babies whilst she ran workshops?

Libby leapt back just in time to miss the spray from a passing bus. She was trapped in limbo. She couldn't keep taking advantage of Jack's flat, but didn't have enough money to pay rent somewhere else. Her attempts to set up more workshops were yet to yield results, and the improv night didn't bring in enough money to live on. She'd googled living history tours in Somerset and drafted emails to the Roman Baths and Jane Austen Centre about possible work opportunities, but without any funds for a deposit on a house share, how could she afford to move her life to Somerset? And anyway, did she want to be there when Henry was still in London?

Henry. She missed him terribly.

Claire's words stung. *Was* she scared of losing control? She was used to living out of a small room in India's flat. Her friends were actors and artists. Could she live in a mansion? Maybe one day be the Duchess of Somerset? The thoughts were an Austen-inspired fantasy, but the reality threw her so far out of her comfort zone she felt stomach-churning anxiety instead of excitement.

After her whirlwind romance with Giles, it had turned out he didn't want her after all, and neither did his family. Henry and his family didn't seem to care about her humble roots, but part of her did. She was comfortable with his parents and siblings, but what would happen if she had to go to a society ball? Would she be laughed at for using the wrong knife?

Get over yourself! These things don't matter! You love him! Maybe she *had* overreacted and now put him off for good.

She stopped under a shop awning, pulled out her phone and rang him before she could second-guess herself. The dial tone was different. He was abroad? It went to voicemail and she hung up not knowing what to say.

She attempted a text.

Libby: Can we talk?

Libby: I'm sorry I went so mental at you.

Libby: Hey! Funny story! Claire's pregnant again!

Libby: I want to move to Somerset even though I know you don't want to.

She pocketed the phone without hitting send and made her way to the pub, striding angrily through the puddles as if they were responsible for her own ineptitude in love.

BRANDON HELPED HYPE LIBBY UP BEFORE THE SHOW AND kept her energy high throughout. But it was tough going as a large section of the audience were drunk tourists. Every suggestion for a scene was related to sex. After 'pornstar', 'double-headed dildo', 'anal', 'wank' and 'horny nuns' had debuted, Brandon brought out his ukulele and she improvised a song consisting entirely of swear words back-to-back. It brought the house down.

When the performance ended, the crowd drifted downstairs calling for more alcohol. As the room emptied, Libby noticed a familiar face sitting in a corner at the back.

Estelle stood and crossed the room.

'You were fucking amazing!' she cried. 'Even with all those dickwads in the audience.'

She froze as Estelle lifted her off the floor in an overly enthusiastic hug.

'What are you doing here?'

Estelle let her back down. 'Come to see you of course. Have you got five mins?'

Libby glanced at Brandon.

'I'm just going downstairs to grab a drink,' he said. 'Either of you want one?'

They shook their heads and he nodded and disappeared.

Estelle sat at one of the tables and kicked a chair out.

'Take a seat. How are you doing?'

Libby wasn't sure how to answer. Should she be truthful? She sat. 'Not great, to be honest.'

'I'm sorry, Libby. For everything.'

She shook her head. 'I'm the one at fault.'

'Bollocks. And that's the last word on the matter. I'm bloody over the moon you don't publish Polly Hart books. That shoots you right up in my estimation.' She paused. 'Have you even read any of them?'

Libby grinned. 'I finally read one the other day.'

'Scarred for life, were you?'

A giggle escaped. 'Her books are insanely popular you know?'

'Yeah, yeah, all read by old gits like Gram-Gram or hopeless romantics like Eveline, who keep wishing that someone called Gerald Buttwad—with floppy hair, corduroy trousers and a Labrador called Bunty—will turn up at church one Sunday and sweep her off her feet.'

Libby snorted. 'After she accidentally knocked him off his bicycle with her Morris Minor.'

'Into a field of buttercups and daisies.'

'On her way to deliver homemade pork pies to the Foxbrooke wedding fayre.'

'Holy shit, Libby,' Estelle laughed. 'You should be writing these.'

Libby shook her head.

There was a pause as the women smiled at each other. Even though she hadn't known Estelle long, Libby didn't want to lose her as a friend.

'Are you free this Thursday?' Estelle asked. 'Day after tomorrow?'

She nodded. 'Why?'

'My muppet of a father booked another tour after your brilliant performance and thinks he can pull it off.'

'A living history one?'

Estelle nodded. 'But unless he's going to play mad King George, wear a straightjacket and stick a gag in his gob, it's not going to happen.'

'Is he employing any actors to help?'

Estelle gave her a look of disbelief that said, *You think?*

'And you want me...?'

'To run the tour for us, of course. Please, Libby. I don't trust Dad further than I could throw him. We can't do this without you. I've re-hired the dress you wore the other week, just in case. You could take the train up in the morning, either stay the night at the Manor or at the livery with me, or travel back to London the same evening. I can pick you up from Bath and take you back.'

'Will Henry be there?'

Estelle hesitated, then shook her head. 'He's abroad for work at the moment.'

Libby desperately wanted to see him, but maybe he didn't want to see her.

'What about the rest of your family?' she asked.

Estelle shrugged. 'If it would seal the deal, I can make sure they bugger off out of your way?'

She held her breath. Could she return to Foxbrooke if Henry and his family weren't there? One final goodbye to her fantasy home?

Estelle took her hand and squeezed. 'Please, Libby. Please say yes.'

❀ 34 ❀

nergy fizzed through Libby's veins as the train pulled out of Paddington station. Brandon had agreed to stay at Jack's to keep an eye on Mr Pussy, so she'd packed an overnight bag just in case the day wasn't a complete disaster and she spent the night at Estelle's.

Her heart ached for Henry. Less than a week ago she'd taken this journey with him as they dashed to the bedside of a supposedly dying Gram-Gram. What grandmother went to such lengths to get what she wanted? Did she really believe Libby was the right person for her grandson?

Since the comedy night, she'd received only one text from him.

> Henry: I'm sorry I missed your call. I'm abroad for work, and the hours are really long. Please can I see you at the end of the week when I'm back?

She'd replied with just one word: **yes.**

After that there had been no more exchanges between

them, both seemingly too scared to jinx the tentative move towards reconciliation. Still, it didn't stop her checking for new messages every couple of minutes.

Her phone vibrated on the table and she grabbed it.

Lucas: Hey babe, go check your bank account…

What? She opened the app and blinked to assure herself the numbers were correct. She was no longer in the red. She was very much back in the black.

Lucas: Told you I'd pay you back! And with interest, cos I'm nice like that X

She tried to do calculations in her head whilst simultaneously checking she hadn't lost her mind. Lucas had paid her back everything he owed, plus about… *Twenty per cent?*

A tiny thought of refunding him the interest assaulted her, but she threw it away. If Lucas was returning her money with extras, it meant he'd got his big payday and the amount he owed her was now a drop in the ocean. Had Henry's father bought his work? The thought made her feel sick.

Libby: Did you sell a painting?

Lucas: I sold ALL of them…

Libby braced herself against the table as a tidal wave of nausea crashed through her. How could Arthur afford that when the estate was in trouble? She tried to control her breathing. The thought of the Manor filled with all those vulva paintings was too much to bear.

Libby: Who to?

Lucas: Dubois. The fashion house in Paris.

Henry's aunt? Why?

Lucas: It's a sign, Lib-Lob. I've got to move to
France. London's too small for someone
like me.

Libby: You're moving to Paris?

Lucas: Yep. The paintings got shipped there
an hour ago after the final legal bullshit was
sorted.

Libby: When?

Lucas: Dunno? This week? I think I'm just
gonna skip. My landlord's an arsehole
anyway. He doesn't deserve any more of my
hard-earned cash for his piece of shit studio.

She didn't know what to say. Lucas's behaviour wasn't any different to how it had been before. How had she ever thought so highly of him?

Lucas: Wish me luck babe X

Libby: How did Dubois get in touch with you?
Why did they want to buy all of them?

He didn't reply.

ESTELLE WAS WAITING AROUND THE BACK OF BATH SPA station with her Land Rover Defender. All the mud had been washed off the exterior.

She pulled Libby in for a hug. 'I cleaned her up for you.

And covered the passenger seat, so I promise you won't get dirty.'

Chester and Joy were in the back, barking with excitement.

Libby smiled. She'd even missed the family's pets.

'Are they really that excited to see me?'

Estelle wiggled her eyebrows. 'Maybe it's because you smell of pussy.'

She snorted. 'He's called *Mr* Pussy.'

'Well, at least we all know what passes through my little brother's mind every time he looks at you.'

'*Estelle!*' She glanced around the small car park to check no-one was around.

'What?'

Libby rolled her eyes. 'Do you want me to do this tour or not?'

'Yes, yes, yes.' Estelle opened the passenger door and shoved her in.

AS THEY PARKED OUTSIDE THE MANOR, LIBBY COULDN'T help but feel a crushing sense of disappointment that Henry's car wasn't there. Even though she knew he was still abroad, she wanted to dream that he'd cut his trip short and come home to find her.

'You might as well dump your bag in Henry's room,' Estelle said. 'I've laid your costume out there, and I'll help you into it before I head back to the livery.'

'You're not staying?' she asked, suddenly worried about being left all alone in the Manor.

Estelle pulled a face. 'No, sorry, I've got too much to do. I'll be back by the end though.' She passed Libby a piece of paper with notes scrawled on one side. 'Based on what you did last time, I think this itinerary will take about three hours. Perry will be in the kitchen making biscuits, and I've set up croquet on the back lawns so you can finish with everyone there.'

'Croquet wasn't invented in Jane Austen's time.'

Estelle huffed. 'Okay, Ms Pedantic, called it "Pall Mall, the Foxbrooke Edition".'

She grinned. 'Okay. The room order you've given me makes sense. How long have I got?'

Estelle glanced at her watch. 'Forty minutes, and we're going to need all of that time just to do up those bastard buttons.'

HENRY'S BEDROOM WAS EMPTY AND QUIET, THE COVERS drawn across the bed. It looked as if it had been put to sleep for a hundred years. Estelle chattered away about horses as she helped Libby dress, which enabled her to zone out and try and get into character. She'd decided to keep being Elizabeth Bennet, but unfortunately this time, Mr Darcy would not be making an appearance.

Estelle fixed the last clip into Libby's hair. 'You look absolutely perfect. I'm going to go and herd the cats into the entrance hall, so you just follow me down when you're ready.' She checked the time again, then dashed out of the door.

Libby stepped away from the bed and over to the window, her heart full of memories. Her gaze ran from the parkland on one side to the large area in front of the Manor where a coach was currently disgorging passengers.

True to her word, Estelle had removed the rest of her family from the house and the building seemed unnaturally quiet as she made her way down the corridor towards the main stairs.

Come on, Libby. You can do this!

She stepped into view.

'Ladies and gentlemen,' she began loudly, before noticing some children amongst the party. 'Girls and boys. My name is Elizabeth Bennet and I am delighted to welcome you all to Foxbrooke Manor.'

Libby smiled at the expressions on people's faces. She may not have had Henry at her side, but what she was doing made her happy. She continued gliding down the stairs, her posture straight out of Gram-Gram's school for deportment.

'I appreciate you may not associate me with the Manor, however the Gardiners, relatives on my mother's side of the family, have a close connection with the Duke and Duchess of Somerset, and I have been a regular visitor here since arriving in Bath.'

Estelle stood behind the group. She gave Libby two thumbs up, then disappeared out the front door.

'The Duke and Duchess have tasked me with escorting you around their home this afternoon and giving you a taste of what life was like here across the ages, but in particular during the Georgian era.' She swept her arm wide. 'First, let us travel back in time to nine hundred and seventy-eight as the King of Wessex enjoys the delights of his summer palace here at Foxbrooke Manor.'

After explaining the early history of the building, Libby moved through the ground floor, stopping in the picture gallery and the dining room. In the distance, music was playing. Had Estelle put it on? She paused outside the library doors. The sound quality was incredible. She turned the handle and peeked inside, blinking at the sight before her.

Playing the piano, wearing a pink Regency dress and with her blue hair curled into ringlets, was Willow. Standing beside her was Connor, dressed as a Regency gentleman. He noticed Libby and waved, holding up a piece of sheet music and miming the song.

She turned to the crowds clustered behind her, her heart pitter-pattering.

'Ladies and gentlemen, girls and boys,' she began. 'Today, we have an extra special surprise for you.'

She flung open the library's double doors.

'May I present Miss Jane Fairfax and Mr Frank Churchill.'

There were gasps as people filed into the library. When everyone was in, Connor bowed.

'It is my great honour to meet you all today at Foxbrooke Manor,' he said. 'I have been given a great task to accomplish this morning, namely, singing a song for Libby here on behalf of my brother who is presently detained abroad.'

All eyes turned to Libby, and her cheeks heated. Had Henry organised this?

Connor cleared his throat. 'This is an old English folk song titled "My Sweetheart's Like Venus".'

Willow played the introduction.

'My sweetheart's like Venus, she's lovely and fair. There's no one like her from far or from near...'

Libby clutched the fabric of her dress as she listened. Had Henry chosen this song?

'Her form has the beauty of tall summer trees. Her hair's like the wheat that is stirred by the breeze. Her cheeks are like apples, her heart is so pure. If only she'd love me, I'd ask nothing more.'

Connor's voice was a rich baritone that filled the air like the scent of mulled wine and spices. When he finished, the room broke out in rapturous applause. He gave a short bow, then took a pile of papers off the top of the piano and handed them out.

'My brother believes that my voice may not be powerful enough to convey the sentiment of this song to the lovely Libby, so he asked if you would be so kind as to help me sing it again?'

She caught Willow's eye and mouthed, '*What's going on?*'.

Willow grinned in return and began playing.

Connor led everyone in two more renditions of the song. When it finally finished, people stamped their feet, clapping and cheering.

Libby didn't know what to say.

'Thank you, ladies and gentlemen,' said Willow. 'I believe Libby is now going to escort you through to the private parlour where Mr Wickham is taking tea with his sister.'

Libby covered her astonishment with a gentle incline of her head. 'Indeed. Do follow me.'

She tried to keep her feet steady as words overflowed in her mind like a flooding river. Was this Henry's idea or his family's? Were they doing it for him or for themselves?

Raised voices carried through the open door to the parlour.

'I say!' cried Leo. 'Dash it all! I'm a man and if I want to fight for king and country then I bally well will!'

Libby led everyone into the large room where, at the other end, stood Leo and Summer. Leo was dressed as if about to head off to the Napoleonic wars, and Summer was wearing a ball gown.

'But brother dearest,' Summer cried, 'you might never return! How can you do this to Mama and me?'

Leo strode up and down, his sword slapping against his thigh. 'It is my sense of honour. My sense of duty.'

Summer put her hand on her hip. 'But you didn't possess honour when you seduced Georgiana Darcy, brother.'

'Slander!' Leo thundered. 'I did nothing of the sort. And now I must leave the country. Forthwith!'

'Is there nothing that will persuade you to stay?' wailed Summer. 'I fear I may swoon.'

Leo stopped pacing and ran a hand through his hair. 'There is only one thing that could induce me to remain here, rather than throw myself in front of the French cavalry.'

Every member of the tour took a breath and leaned forward.

'What is it, brother. Tell us!'

Leo broke the fourth wall and looked directly at Libby. He raised his hand dramatically, his fingers shaking like Poirot finally revealing the murderer at the end of an Agatha Christie novel.

'I will not travel to Waterloo if Libby forgives our family, in particular Grandmama and our beloved older brother, Henry Fitzwilliam Darcy.'

All heads swivelled to look at her.

'Er...'

'Libby!' Summer cried, the back of her hand against her forehead. She stumbled forward. 'Say yes!' she managed before dramatically falling to the floor.

Libby rushed to her side. 'Oh my god, Summer! Are you okay?'

Summer opened one of her eyes. 'Of course, I am,' she whispered, before crying out. 'I have swooned!'

Leo bit down on one fist and shook the other one at the ceiling.

'Good god, love,' said an older man on the tour. 'Forgive them, please.'

Libby glanced at Summer, who was chewing on her lower lip, her brow furrowed. She'd already decided to forgive Henry and apologise to him, but the thought that his family were so desperate for her to pardon him that they'd gone to these extremes made her heart well up. She nodded at Summer, who recovered from her swoon immediately and threw her arms around Libby's neck.

'Thank you,' she whispered.

'Praise be to god!' Leo cried, leading a round of applause. 'I think this calls for a celebration! Who here is up for learning a quadrille in the ballroom?'

Everyone cheered.

'Libby?' Leo extended his arms to help her and Summer off the floor. 'Would you like to lead the way?'

❧ 35 ❧

Libby wasn't sure what to expect as she led the way to the ballroom. This tour was like waking up one summer morning to discover Christmas had come early. Each new room contained an unexpected present and she was unwrapping each one by opening the door.

'Darling Libby!' Arthur cried. He stood in the centre of the ballroom next to Vivienne. Both were dressed in Regency fashion, but it seemed they'd become competitive about the size of their wigs. Vivienne's contained artificial birds and flowers, and Arthur's was decorated with more baubles than a Christmas tree. Vivienne's wig was taller than her husband's, however he'd gained the overall height advantage by wearing a pair of high heeled satin shoes.

The audience filled the space, gawping and pulling out their phones to take pictures.

Libby cleared her throat. 'May I present... Er—'

'Mr and Mrs Bennet,' Vivienne supplied, curtseying to the group. 'We are busy preparing for the upcoming ball at Netherfield where I hope my daughter will catch the eye of a certain gentleman. My husband and I were wondering if you would care to join us in learning a quadrille?' She turned to Libby. 'My darling, could you lead us in the correct steps?'

'It would be my pleasure, Mama,' she replied, as Arthur went to a sideboard where a stereo system was hidden behind a row of potted plants. She addressed the group. 'Now, let us begin.'

TWENTY MINUTES LATER, LIBBY HAD TAUGHT EVERYONE A quadrille, a cotillion and a jig, and most people had tried on Arthur's wig. Even though she was having the time of her life, she was still trying to process what Henry's family was up to and hoping that he would be in the next room.

But as they finished in the ballroom and moved to the kitchen, her hope died.

'Good afternoon, all,' Dervla said in her lilting Irish accent as Libby led everyone in. 'My name is Lady Catherine de Bourgh and my esteemed housekeeper here, Perry the Magnificent, is going to show you how to make Regency love biscuits.'

Love biscuits?

'That's right,' Perry continued. 'Made with love and a sprinkle of Foxbrooke magic to help young sweethearts find their way back to each other.' She winked at Libby. 'Now then, if you'd like to join in, please wash your hands and avail yourself of one of my pinnies.'

WHEN THE DOUGH HAD BEEN MIXED AND ROLLED, DERVLA unwrapped a wooden stamper.

'Ladies and gentlemen, girls and boys, this has been made especially for today.'

Libby tried to see the design but couldn't make it out.

'Carved by Foxbrooke's resident carpenter, Finn Oakley, this has been created to celebrate reconciliation and love,' Dervla caught Libby's eye. 'Why don't you show everyone how to use it?

Libby stepped forward, took the stamper from Dervla and pressed it into the dough. When she removed it, she saw what Finn had carved. It was a heart with her and Henry's names inside.

'Perfect!' said Dervla. 'Carry on, we've plenty more to make and everyone needs to get the message.'

After the biscuits had been put into the oven, Perry produced a batch she'd made earlier and handed the first one to Libby.

'What do you think?' she asked.

Libby took a bite. 'Sweet and delicious.'

'And that's the taste of love,' Dervla cried. 'Now, who else wants to see how perfectly Libby goes with Henry?'

She couldn't help but smile. Henry's family may have been different from the norm, but their hearts were huge. They were doing everything they possibly could to bring about a reconciliation between her and Henry, and to also show how much they cared for her.

After copious amounts of love biscuits and strong tea, Dervla clapped her hands.

'Now, if you follow the lovely Libby into the gardens, we have a game of Croquet set up for you.'

Was this the moment that Henry might arrive? Or was he still abroad? When Perry was instructing people in biscuit making, she'd dashed into the larder to ring him, but the call had gone straight to voicemail.

'Indeed,' she said loudly. 'Please follow me.'

. . .

Libby followed the sound of voices to the lawns at the very back of the grounds. The far side looked out over the parkland and ended with a ha-ha, the edge of the lawn dropping vertically into a dry ditch that slowly sloped back up on the other side, giving the illusion of the garden continuing out into the wider estate. Croquet hoops had been set up and Arthur and Vivienne, Connor, Willow, Leo and Summer were already playing.

'Aha!' Arthur cried. 'There's our darling girl with the guests. Want to split 'em up into teams?'

Libby bit back her disappointment. The scene was almost perfect, but it was clear Henry wasn't coming. She put on a smile, divided the tour members, and put each group with one of the Foxbrooke family before explaining the rules and how the game of Pall Mall evolved into croquet. Dervla arrived with plates of biscuits as the game continued, with Arthur, Leo and Summer crying foul the moment things weren't going their way.

Happy that the tour was exceeding everyone's expectations, Libby strolled to the edge of the ha-ha and gazed across the parkland. The ancient oak trees stood like sentinels in the landscape and in the distance the surface of the lake glittered in the summer sun. Skylarks swooped through the air hunting insects and high in the sky, a buzzard soared on the thermals. The version of the countryside she'd loved in Jane Austen novels was in front of her, more visceral and more beautiful than she could ever have imagined.

In the far distance, two specks of black shimmered on the horizon. Were they horses? Within a minute she could see two of them galloping at full tilt in the direction of the Manor, their riders low on their backs and urging them on. Was one of them Estelle?

They were still a few hundred yards out when one of the riders waved, her long curly black hair streaming behind her. But if that one was Estelle, who was the—

Henry.

Relief, joy and emotion bubbled out of her and she gulped a breath, tears spilling down her cheeks.

'Stand back, everyone!' Arthur yelled. 'Incoming!'

The horses weren't slowing down. Surely, they weren't going to jump from the park onto the lawn over the ha-ha?

Estelle was whooping as they drew near, urging Duke to overtake her brother. Everyone moved to the side as the two horses leapt onto the garden. Henry circled his horse to a stop. He looked uncertain as he gazed at Libby, his forehead furrowing when he noticed her tears.

'Henry!' Estelle yelled. He turned instinctively towards his sister as she aimed a weapons-grade water blaster at his chest and pulled the trigger.

He shook his head and dismounted once she'd emptied it.

'There we go, Libby,' Estelle said with a grin. 'He's all yours now.' She took the reins from Henry's horse and led it away.

Henry stepped towards her, his wet shirt clinging indecently to his body.

'Libby,' he began, uncertainly.

Fresh tears ran down her cheeks. 'You're here,' she whispered.

He wiped her tears away with his thumbs, then took her hands. 'I'm so sorry, Libby. If your feelings are still what they were last week, tell me at once. My affections for you are unchanged. I love you with my heart and soul.'

'You love me?'

He nodded. 'I am yours. Forever, if you'll have me?'

Her heart pounded, her mind rearranging itself as it struggled to comprehend what he was saying.

'If you won't have 'im, I bloody will!'

Libby glanced around with a gasp. She'd completely forgotten they were surrounded by people. People who, until that moment, had been silent.

Some of the members of the tour were filming; the rest, like his family, were standing as still as statues, anxiously waiting for her answer.

She turned back to him and blinked her blurry eyes clear. 'Yes, of course I will,' she replied. 'I love you. I love you so very much.'

The tension dissolved from his face and she reached up and brushed her lips against his, only vaguely aware of the shouts and cheers around them.

He wrapped his arms around her with a groan, his mouth pressed to hers as he kissed her with the passion and intensity of a man brought back from the brink.

Libby clung to him. Now, in his arms, the love she felt only amplified how bereft she'd been without him by her side. She had to find a way to make this work. He was too precious to lose.

His lips broke from hers and he lifted her off the ground. She held around the back of his neck, positive she was only seconds away from swooning.

'Where are we going?' she asked, breathlessly as he strode towards the house.

'Anywhere they're not.'

'I thought you were abroad?'

'I was. I got back this morning and legged it to Somerset to be here in time.'

'Was this your idea?'

He pushed open one of the side doors to the Manor with his shoulder then carefully carried her through.

'It was Estelle's. She said I had less chance of you turning me down if I were Mr Darcy.'

She shook her head. 'I don't want Mr Darcy anymore. I only want you.'

He stopped walking, his dark eyes fixed on her. 'Are you sure?'

She nodded. 'But...'

He looked panicked. 'What?'

'Lucas paid me my money back this morning. With interest. He said your aunt's fashion house had bought all his paintings.'

Henry nodded.

'But how? Was this your doing?'

'Libby, I would have taken out another credit card and paid him ten times over if it meant you got your money. But I knew, if you took me back, it would always hang between us. So I found another way.'

'What did you do?'

He glanced down, seemingly embarrassed. 'I, er.' He cleared his throat and looked at her directly. 'My aunt has always wanted me to model for her, but I've always refused. I contacted her and said that I would do it if she agreed to buy the entirety of Lucas's collection.'

'Oh my god! That must have been such a lot of money!'

He shook his head. 'It wasn't what Lucas wanted, but he'd run out of other options and was about to be arrested for blackmailing his models. Part of the deal was that he paid you back with interest.'

She swallowed. 'So, are the paintings going to be displayed around the fashion house and their shops?'

Henry smiled. 'The other part of the deal was that the paintings are to be exhibited in room SS14 only.'

'And where is that?' she asked, imagining the worst.

'SS14 stands for "Sous-Sol Quatorze", and "Sous-Sol" is French for basement. Room fourteen is the one at the very back. It doesn't even have the privilege of containing cleaning products or box files.'

Libby felt guilty for the laugh that escaped. 'Does Lucas know?'

He shrugged. 'Don't know and don't care. All I care about is you and making sure he doesn't screw over any of the women who posed for him.'

Love rushed through her and she smoothed away the lines in his forehead.

'You're the best of men, Henry. Thank you.'

His cheeks darkened. 'It means you have your freedom back. You can go wherever you want.'

'I want to be wherever you are. I just want to be with you.'

He swallowed. 'Libby, I need to tell you something. I'm leaving Conqueror. I have to help Estelle save Foxbrooke.'

'Oh!'

'We can find a way to make it work,' he replied hurriedly. 'I can work from London part of the week or commute every day by train. I can't abandon my family, but I will always put you first, I promise.'

'You need to come home? For good?'

'Libby, home is wherever you are. And I'd never ask you to compromise your career or your dreams.'

She laughed, even as tears filled her eyes.

'Oh god, Libby, I'm sorry. Please believe me, we'll find a way to make this work.'

She kissed him. 'Henry, I want to move to Somerset. Claire's pregnant again, and our lives are changing whether we want them to or not. There are opportunities here that excite me more than doing the same thing in London without my best friend by my side. That chapter of my life is coming to an end and a new one is starting. Here, with you.'

'You'd be happy to move to Foxbrooke with me?'

She nodded. 'I've fallen in love with the countryside almost as much as I've fallen in love with you. This is where my dreams are now.'

He hesitated. 'You know it's not always summer here?'

'I'll adapt. As long as I can have a pair of yellow wellies, I'll be more than happy.'

He grinned. 'Deal.'

'Although...'

'Yes?'

'I'm afraid I won't be moving in with you on my own.'

His eyes widened.

'Mr Pussy.' She giggled. 'We can't leave him behind.'

He rested his forehead on hers. 'Am I ever going to live that name down?'

She snorted. 'Nope.'

'You sure we can't rename him?' he asked hopefully. 'I could ask very, very politely?'

Her heart fluttered. 'And how might you ask impolitely?'

He held her gaze, his eyes darkening.

'Let me show you,' he replied, striding in the direction of the stairs.

❧ 36 ❧

Libby wasn't sure her heart could withstand the excitement of being carried through the Manor by Henry. But when he kicked open the door of his bedroom with his riding boot, strode in and deposited her onto the bed, she was convinced she'd had a mini orgasm.

He tugged off his boots and socks then went to the door.

'What are you doing?' She was struggling to breathe against the confines of her bodice.

He raised an eyebrow, hung one of his socks on the handle outside, then closed the door and pushed a wardrobe up against it.

His eyes were on her as he approached the bed. He undid the buttons of his sodden shirt, then tugged it off and tossed it to the floor. Her mouth was dry, her breath stuttering. He unfastened the drapes attached to one of the four posters and tossed the silk ties onto her lap.

She glanced at them and swallowed.

When he finished with the final tie, the fabric fluttered into place, encasing her in a silken prison. He parted the curtain and crawled onto the bed, kneeling above her, his cravat in one hand and one of the ties in the other.

His eyes glittered with intent. 'You once suggested we add some items to our contract. How do you feel about a little light bondage?'

A thrill of adrenaline rushed through her and she clenched her thighs with excitement. She'd never been restrained during sex before but trusted Henry implicitly.

She nodded. 'Yes please.'

His gaze heated. 'If you want me to stop at any moment, just say and I will.'

'It's not going to hurt?'

He shook his head. 'Never.' He leaned forward until his mouth was by her ear. 'Although I do want to make you scream.'

Her heart pounded, her breath stuck in her throat. He stroked the side of her face with the silk tie, his lips hovering above hers.

'Breathe, Libby.'

She drew in a shuddering breath, stealing it from him as he pressed soft kisses to her face. The energy sparking between them felt unbearably intense.

He folded the cravat into a wide band, placed it over her eyes and fastened it behind her head.

'Okay?' he murmured.

'Yes.'

'Good.'

She'd never felt such anticipation before, but there was no time to process the feelings as suddenly she was flipped onto her stomach, his body pressing against hers, his mouth by her ear.

'Shall we lose the dress?'

'Yes, yes, yes.'

His weight shifted as he straddled her. Tracing a finger down her spine, he flicked open the first button and rocked his cock into the crease of her bottom. She gasped, feeling how hard he was through his trousers. Each time he undid a button, he thrust.

With half of the bodice undone, he helped her arms out of the sleeves, then pulled it to her waist. He kissed and nipped the hypersensitive skin of her neck as he worked a hand underneath her body to her breasts. He found her hardened nipple, rubbing it between his fingers and thumb. She moaned, bucking against his cock.

He pressed her body into the mattress, biting and sucking her neck, his hips thrusting and his fingers tweaking her nipple each time he popped another button free.

Then his weight was gone. She took a breath but before she could call his name, her dress was tugged off, followed by her ballet pumps and stockings. She shivered as he hooked his thumbs underneath the top of her knickers, pulling them down over her bottom. He pressed a soft kiss to each cheek.

'I fear I may be breaking the letter of our contract,' he murmured.

She giggled. 'You did specify "face cheek only" for kissing.'

'Hmm... But then you mentioned that no-one had ever kissed your beautiful backside before, so I wanted to be the first.'

And the last. She reached back to find his hand and squeezed tightly, trying to convey her hopes for their future.

He covered her body with his again, stroking her back and nuzzling her hair.

'And the last,' he whispered.

She turned her head towards him and he captured her mouth in a blistering kiss. Shocks of pleasure pulsed through every nerve, all shooting south to burn deep in her core. His tongue was electric fire, sweeping into her mouth and setting everything alight. He ran a finger down her spine, following the curve of her bottom, then slid it inside her wet pussy.

He wrenched his mouth from hers. 'God, Libby.'

She pushed against his hand and he eased another finger in, slowly pumping.

'Libby, Libby, Libby...'

She panted, squirming to get closer as the swells of her orgasm built. Sensations whipped higher and higher and she clenched around his fingers, dragging her climax forward.

But then his fingers were gone, and before she could complain she was flipped onto her back and one of the silk ties was secured around her ankle. She couldn't see anything; all she could do was feel as he spread her legs wider to fasten the other ankle. Had this been anyone else she might have felt vulnerable and exposed, but with Henry she felt like a goddess to be worshipped.

He tied her wrists and she gently pulled against the restraints. She couldn't move more than an inch. Desire spiralled through her limbs. He wasn't touching her, but she felt his heat covering every inch of her skin.

'Okay?' he whispered, brushing his lips down her throat.

She shivered. 'God, yes. Please Henry, kiss me.'

His mouth found hers, his lips firm and possessive, his tongue claiming her. She opened to him, arching her back, trying to get closer, but the ties held her in place. She wanted to feel his weight on her, the hard length of his cock rubbing where she needed it the most, but his mouth was the only point of contact. Just as she felt she might go mad with need, he squeezed her nipple. Sensation scorched down to her clit.

'Yes, oh god, yes!' she cried, breaking the kiss.

Then his hot, wet mouth was on her other nipple, sucking

and tugging, vibrating the tip of his tongue against the end as stars danced in the blackness of her vision.

She moaned. Nothing had ever felt so good. Nerves fired and misfired, setting off chain reactions that split and multiplied her pleasure. His other hand found her clit and she screamed his name. Her climax was now a mighty wave that swelled bigger and bigger as it waited to break.

She held her breath, preparing to be wiped out—

He stopped.

'Henry!' Her chest was heaving. 'Keep going.'

His mouth and fingers returned, but they were leisurely. She wriggled against him, her body urging him to go faster.

The wave picked up momentum again, her release building once more. The wave reached its apex and—

He stopped again.

'What are you doing?' she gasped.

'Do you remember what else you suggested we add to the contract?' he whispered in her ear.

Her mind was scattered, tossing and turning in a storm of pleasure. She doubted she could even remember her own name right now.

'What? What did I suggest?'

'After "a little light bondage", you suggested "orgasm denial".'

'Nooooooo!' she wailed. 'We can call Mr Pussy whatever you like. Just touch me again and make me come. Please!'

He chuckled. 'No.'

'W—what?'

'You're not going to come on my fingers.' He licked just below her ear. 'You're going to come on my tongue.'

Oh my god, oh my god, oh my god.

He traced patterns and promises over her skin, the tip of his tongue circling, pressing, vibrating.

'When?' Frustration ached in every cell.

He nibbled the lobe of her ear. 'Are you going to beg?'

She could hear the smile in his voice and tugged against the restraints.

'Yes!' she cried. 'Right now I'll confess to every major unsolved crime from the last ten years if you'll just move your magical tongue two feet lower.'

He chuckled. 'You don't want it here?' He rolled the peaks of her nipples between his fingers and thumbs.

'Aah!' She bucked on the bed, the pleasure shooting down to her clit with the message that relief was coming soon.

'Well,' she panted. 'You could take the scenic route.'

'Two delightful diversions off the O road?'

Her laugh was huge and unrestrained. 'That's brilliant. I love you, Henry.'

His hand stroked her face, and he kissed her as if she was the most precious gift in all the world.

'I love you too.' His voice was soft and full of wonder.

Her heart overflowed. 'I didn't know it was possible to be this happy.'

He kissed her again. 'Well, let's see if Lord Henry Foxbrooke's Grand Tour of Libby-a can improve your current state?'

She giggled. 'Do I need to buy a ticket?'

'You've got a lifetime pass.' He trailed his kisses lower, then sucked a nipple hard into his mouth.

She cried out as sensation shot through her, and again when his hand covered her other breast, his fingers and thumb rolling and tugging the nipple as if in competition with his mouth to see which breast might spontaneously orgasm first.

Her hips bucked against nothing, desperate for the release he had so far denied her.

'Henry!'

Then his mouth was gone, and in a heartbeat arrived exactly where she needed it.

Now there was nothing leisurely about his touch. He licked and sucked her clit with an urgency that took her breath away. She was back in the ocean swell as it moved with unstoppable power towards land. His tongue moved faster, driving it on, until it finally broke.

She stiffened as the full force of her climax hit, crashing and thundering through her. She convulsed on the bed, rolling and tumbling in the blinding white surf of indescribable pleasure.

Shaking and gasping as her breathing returned, her body floated in the shallows of bliss. But Henry didn't let her stumble to dry land. He eased two fingers inside her, rubbing the tips against the top wall of her channel as if beckoning another orgasm forward, whilst his tongue dragged her back out to sea.

'Oh, oh, oh, oh,' she gasped, her arms and legs tensing against the restraints as every muscle in her body strained to hold her together. Her skin was fizzing, unable to contain or control the pleasure that rioted through every cell. She let go, surrendering to the wild nature of her body, giving herself over to him as he lifted her onto a wave of sweetness and she rode it to shore, her core contracting around his fingers with sharp spikes of pleasure.

Aftershocks flickered across her skin, but her limbs were lead. She was suddenly aware that he was gone.

But then he was back between her legs, his clothes removed, the hard head of his cock at her entrance. She angled her hips to meet him and he thrust deep with a growl. The awareness of being stretched by him, filled by him, took her breath away. This was it. They were two separate beings, but in their love and in this moment, they were one.

He braced on his elbows above her, his hot weight covering her. His mouth devoured hers as he slowly withdrew then buried himself deep inside her again with a grunt.

The blindfold on, all she had were the sounds of their passion, the scent of him that drove her wild, and the feel of his body on her, inside her, possessing her.

His thrusts became faster and he circled his hips each time he sank home, sparking a new fire in her clit that radiated out, building to another release.

She broke their kiss. 'Yes, yes, there, don't stop,' she panted.

His own breath was ragged, but he continued with utter precision and dedication as if rowing for the line and taking her with him. He seemed to know he had the perfect angle and wasn't going to stop until he'd gifted her the gold medal of orgasms.

Her pussy was the centre of the storm. Each time he pumped deep, she was shocked with another bolt of pleasure until every part of her was trembling. He must have sensed how close she was as he pounded faster, then reached his mouth to her nipple and bit down.

Showers of light rained through her and she threw back her head with a scream as she shattered around his cock.

'Libby, Libby,' he cried, his thrusts getting faster, magnifying her pleasure until she realised that she was going to climax again.

He drove her on, only allowing his own release when he'd pushed her over the edge of hers. He cried her name, shuddering above her as she squeezed around him, drawing out every ounce of pleasure.

As she was trying to make sense of what planet she was currently on, he undid the silk ties, ripped off the blindfold and covered her body with his.

'I love you, I love you, I love you,' he said between kisses.

She clung to him. 'Henry,' she whispered. 'Oh my god, will it always be like that?'

He lifted his head, his eyes shining.

'No,' he replied with a smile. 'It's going to be better.'

❧ 37 ❧

Cocooned inside the silk tent with Henry, Libby was in heaven. No longer fearful of the future, she wanted to run towards it with open arms.

He stroked her back as she snuggled against his chest. 'Are you happy to live here until we can find somewhere else?' he asked.

'It is a bit small.' She sighed. 'But I suppose the Manor will have to do until we can find something a bit bigger.'

She felt his grin against her cheek. 'Rest assured I'm going to fix the door, so we don't have to push a wardrobe against it every time we want privacy.'

'Oh, I don't know. The sock seems to have done the trick.'

There was a sharp rap at the door.

'Yoo hoo!' Arthur called from the corridor.

Henry raised his head to give her a look. 'You were saying?'

'We *have* been up here a while...'

'Dinner's on the table in half an hour,' Arthur shouted. 'So you've got time for one more round before the gong. Henry, I'm leaving your bag outside the door. Toodle-pip!'

Henry's head fell back to the pillow. 'Please don't change your mind about all of this. I'm begging you.'

She kissed him. 'Never. Although I can't believe I'm about to move in with your family and you haven't even met mine yet.'

'We can visit them on the weekend? If you think I'd make the grade?'

'Oh, you'll make the grade alright.' She giggled. 'My mum will think you're royalty.'

'And your dad?'

'He'll use you as an example of what kind of boyfriend Chloe and Paige should be looking for. Seriously, compared to some of the blokes they've brought home, you're like the best bits of Einstein, James Bond, and the Dalai Lama.'

He grinned. 'They can't be *that* bad, surely?'

She raised her eyebrows. 'Chloe's ex-boyfriend got drunk last year and tried it on with Paige, claiming it was a scientific experiment into shagging twins. He then projectile vomited all over the hall as Chloe was kicking him out. After spending hours cleaning it up, we discovered he'd emptied my dad's wallet and nicked his Christmas whisky.'

'Ah,' he replied. 'I see how high the bar is now.'

'Exactly. You won't even notice when you step over it.'

THEY SHOWERED TOGETHER, DRESSED, AND WENT downstairs to the dining room hand-in-hand. Estelle was the first to greet them, pulling Libby in for a hug strong enough to uproot a tree.

'Thank you for taking him back,' she said as she squeezed. 'Finally, one of us has found someone.'

'Speak for yourself,' said Leo. 'I'm rather popular with the ladies of the West Country.'

Summer and Willow started *baaing* like sheep and everyone laughed.

'Fuck off,' said Leo. 'Not sheep.'

Summer and Willow changed their *baa's* to *moos*.

'Libby, darling.' Dervla pulled out a chair. 'Come sit next to me and Vivi.'

Henry kept hold of her hand as if he never wanted to let go and sat on her other side.

'Tonight's normally curry night,' Dervla continued. 'But Arthur's been busy with far more important matters today.' She paused and winked at her. 'So we're having shepherd's pie instead.'

'Which one of your girlfriends are we eating tonight?' Summer asked Leo. 'Dolly or Baa-braa?'

He flipped her the bird in response as Perry and Arthur carried in trays of food and placed them on the table.

'There she is!' said Arthur as he spotted Libby. 'What an exciting day we've had, all thanks to you, my dear.' He took a seat at the table and gestured at the food. 'Help yourself, everyone.' He turned back to Libby. 'You know, I think I'm going to buy my wig. It's absolutely splendid. It's built on a frame and one can fit all kinds of things under it. It could be a man-bag for my head.'

'A head bag?' she suggested.

'Capital name.' He clapped his hands. 'And terribly handy for parties. That's the trouble when you're naked, there's just nowhere to put the essentials.'

'Dad—' Henry began.

'And I've banned bum bags from Foxbrooke. Revolting things. What do you call them in the States again, Vivienne?'

'Fanny packs.'

Arthur hooted. 'That's right, but we all know that fanny means—'

'DAD!' Henry shouted along with the rest of his siblings.

Arthur dolloped shepherd's pie on his plate. 'What?'

'Henry has *just* persuaded Libby to take him back,' Estelle replied curtly. 'But if you don't rein it in, there's every chance she'll change her mind.'

Arthur looked at Libby, his eyes widening. 'Would you?'

She squeezed Henry's hand and shook her head. 'Never.'

Arthur turned to Estelle. 'There you go. Straight from the horse's mouth.'

'Dad!' said Henry. 'Please don't liken Libby to a horse.'

'Why not? Beautiful creatures. Your sister would marry one given half the chance. Wouldn't you, Estelle?'

Estelle ignored her father. 'Dare we ask what your plans are going forward?' she asked Libby.

Libby hesitated and looked at Henry. Her stomach flipped over as he smiled and nodded.

'I'm going to hand over the improv nights to a guy called Brandon and not run workshops anymore,' she began, 'or at least until Claire's ready again. And Henry's leaving Conqueror. We're moving to Foxbrooke.'

There was stunned silence, then the table erupted with cheers and stamping of feet.

Estelle's posture relaxed. '*Thank you*,' she mouthed.

'This calls for a celebration!' Vivienne leapt up. 'Where did we hide the last of Simone's champagne?'

Arthur pushed his chair back. 'Priest's hole?'

'Isn't it under our bed?' Dervla asked.

As Henry's parents left the table in search of booze, Estelle turned back to him and Libby. 'Do you have any idea when you're moving?'

Henry glanced at Libby with such love in his eyes, she lost all her words.

'Well?'

'As soon as possible,' he replied. I don't need to work out my notice, as I've got plenty of leave accrued. The only thing we have to sort out is fixing Jack's flat after Mr—the cat tried to destroy it.'

'And are you bringing Mr Pussy with you?' Estelle continued.

Henry cleared his throat. 'Yes, he will be coming with us. However, from here on, he has been renamed "Mr P".'

Estelle sniggered. 'For "pussy".'

'He's actually named after Henry,' Libby said.

'What? Mr Penis?'

'No,' she grinned. 'Mr Perfect.'

AFTER THE MEAL, LIBBY STROLLED WITH HENRY OUT OF THE gardens into the parkland. It wasn't yet fully dark and the horizon glowed with the echoes of the sun. Apart from the swishing of their feet through the grass, everything was quiet, the world at the still point between day and night.

'Look,' he said.

A small, black shape fluttered above them.

'Is it a bird?'

'It's a bat.'

'Oh my god,' she whispered. 'I've never seen one in real life before.'

She clutched his hand tightly, needing reassurance she wasn't dreaming. There was a hoot in the distance.

'Henry! It's an owl!'

His smile was shining in the twilight. 'You'll soon be wishing they'd shut up.'

'Never. Anything's better than traffic, sirens and other people's televisions. I mean look.' She gestured upwards. 'You can actually see the stars here.'

His laugh was soft. 'Yes, you can.'

'Are you sure you want to make this move?' she asked. 'I don't want to take you away from London if you're happy there.'

He brushed his lips over hers. 'Libby, I'm happy if I'm with you. And yes, I do want to come back to Foxbrooke. Seeing everything through your eyes makes me remember how beautiful it all is. It's like you've woken me from a dream.'

He drew her closer, his lips pressing against hers, and she melted into the heat of his body. His kiss seared straight to her soul, a soul that would now, forever, be bound to this landscape and this incredible man. Libby had found her place in the world and it was here, with Henry.

EPILOGUE

India: Holy shit Libby-Lou, have you seen this month's Vogue???

Libby: Not yet. Why?

India: I might have accidentally had an orgasm while perving over your boyfriend…

Libby: Lol. Henry told me the campaign would be starting soon, but I haven't seen any of the pictures yet.

India: OMG are you serious? It's like he's bringing all your fantasies to life.

Libby: What?!

India: Hang on, I'll take some pics of Foxy Mr Darcy…

India: [Close-up photo of Henry in a starched white collar]

India: [Photo of Henry, shirtless, sitting on the edge of a bed and holding a riding crop]

India: [Photo of Henry from the back, naked under a waterfall]

Libby: Oh my god!!!

India: I KNOW, RIGHT??????

India: I've no idea what they're advertising, but fuck me, I'm buying one of everything.

Libby: Lolol. He's really embarrassed about the whole thing. That's why he hasn't let me see the test shots.

India: Well, you need to find somewhere to hide him, because he's the hottest thing on the interweb right now, and women are going to come looking for a big, long, hard piece of Foxy…

Libby: India!

India: I can't believe you get to fuck him. He's got two brothers, right? Are they fit? Single?

Libby: I don't think they're your type.

India: Bugger.

Libby: I've got to go. See you in a few weeks?

India: Yeah, yeah, I know exactly where you've got to go.

India: Off to ride your hot AF boyfriend.

India: Is that riding crop his?

India: And is that waterfall in Somerset?

India: I need to know these things.

India: Libby???

⚛

Henry strolled down Foxbrooke high street to meet Libby and Estelle, a contented smile on his face. Despite the continued difficulties managing the estate and his father, his heart had never felt so light. The financial hole they were in was deep, but he was confident that he and Estelle could save the Manor and turn things around.

Libby's living history tours were bringing in more money than his dad's sex parties. She'd taken the idea and run with it, talking to local schools about working with them and organising whole days devoted to period specific clothing, food and architecture. She was desperate to do a day on medicines with Dervla, although so far Connor had talked her out of using arsenic, lead and leeches.

Since the campaign for Simone's fashion house, Henry had rarely stepped foot into the village. Foxbrooke was small, but it would take a while for the fuss to die down. It was mortifying what people yelled at him, but it had been worth it. First, for being able to get Libby's money back, and second, for the effect the photos seemed to have on her. He was a sex god in her eyes and he was only too happy to prove her right.

However, last night she'd turned the tables on him, tying him to the four-poster bed and driving him insane. When she finally allowed him to come, the release was so powerful he was convinced he'd blacked out. Life was more than good, it was perfect.

He ducked his head to enter the café, spotting Libby with

Estelle at a table near the back. His sister was on a mission to show her all the delights of the village, keeping up the hard sell to stop Libby getting bored and running back to London. He grinned as he crossed the room to join them. That wasn't going to happen any time soon.

'Oh my god, Henry!' Libby squealed. 'Guess what Estelle and I were just discussing!'

'Um—'

'She wants me to run a Jane Austen festival at the Manor!' Libby was bouncing up and down in her chair.

Estelle was grinning from ear to ear. 'You're going to have to get out your Mr Darcy costume again, little brother.'

He raised an eyebrow. 'Really?'

Libby's hand was on her chest. 'Oh. My. God. Yes!' She was practically hyperventilating with excitement. 'And people with VIP tickets get to watch you walking out of the lake.'

'What?'

'And we can auction off your shirt afterwards!'

'Er—'

'Ooh! Or, if we sell enough tickets to men, we could have a wet dress shirt competition,' she continued, clearly on a roll.

He crossed his arms and glared at his sister. She shrugged and smirked back.

TEN MINUTES LATER THEY STARTED BACK TOWARDS THE Manor and Libby still hadn't paused for breath.

'We can have a bonnet-making workshop and maybe a reticule-making one, too. And at least one ball. Maybe a swooning competition? But only if we have crash mats, I don't want anyone getting hurt. Maybe we could borrow the ones your dad uses for his parties? Well, after a thorough clean of course. Oh look! Isn't that the guy you used to work with?'

Huh? Henry was only just keeping up with Libby's stream of consciousness, but the end of her monologue didn't quite fit.

He looked up. Walking towards them, staring at his phone, was James Hunter-Savage.

Henry stopped dead.

James glanced up just before he ran into them. 'Foxy?' he asked, looking surprised.

'What the fuck are you doing here?'

'Henry!' Libby hissed. She turned to James, extending her arm. 'James, right? You probably don't remember me, but I did a workshop with you a few months ago at Conqueror.'

Recognition dawned on his face and he shook her hand. 'Yes, I remember. What are you doing in Foxbrooke?'

'None of your business,' Henry snapped. 'More to the point, what are *you* doing here?'

Libby grabbed his arm. 'Henry! Please!'

'I live here,' James said.

'No, you don't,' Henry replied, his blood boiling.

James smiled, but he didn't look happy. 'My family bought the estate on the other side of the river.'

Everything Henry wanted to say would upset Libby so he kept his mouth clamped shut.

James extended his hand to Estelle. 'You must be Henry's sister? I'm James.'

Estelle crossed her arms, her expression closed and hard. 'I know exactly who you are. And if you know what's good for you, you'll stay away from my family.'

James's hand dropped to his side and a slow grin spread across his face. 'I can't promise that, foxy lady.'

Henry's mouth opened at the same time as his sister's, but before either of them could let rip, Libby forcibly dragged them away, back towards the Manor.

'What is wrong with you two?'

'Wrong?' Estelle spat. 'That "person" has been the bane of Henry's life ever since school. Not to mention stealing his biggest client and trying to get into Summer's pants.'

'Maybe it was a misunderstanding? I know he comes across as a bit of a lad, but I'm sure it's just because he's insecure.'

'I don't think he even knows that word exists,' Henry said. 'Given half the chance, Hunter-Savage would make every nun in a convent pregnant.'

Libby snorted. 'Well, Summer has left for Paris to stay with your aunt, so you don't need to worry about her. And I can't see Willow giving him the time of day.'

Henry knew that was true, but it wouldn't stop James from trying.

'So that only leaves Estelle.' Libby turned to his sister. 'Do you feel capable of repelling an amorous advance from the gentleman we just met?'

Estelle cracked her knuckles. 'I welcome the opportunity.'

'Then we're all good,' said Libby. 'I highly doubt we'll ever see him again. And if he decides to attend one of your dad's parties, you can block his application.' She smiled. 'See, nothing to worry about.'

'Are you always this sunny?' Estelle grumbled.

She sighed, happily. 'It's the Somerset air. That, and being head over heels in love with your brother.'

His heart swelled whilst his sister pretended to throw up.

'I have to show Libby something,' he said to Estelle. 'See you later at dinner?'

She nodded. 'Just remember to avoid being anywhere near a public footpath when you show Libby your "something". I don't want to have to bail you out if you're arrested for public indecency.'

He rolled his eyes. 'It's not that.'

'Henry?' Libby said. 'I thought we were just going for a walk?'

Estelle winked at her and headed through the Manor gates. 'Enjoy being shown "something" on your "walk".'

'See you later,' he said as he led Libby towards the park.

As soon as they were out of earshot of his sister, questions bubbled out of Libby like champagne from a shaken bottle.

'So, we're not just going for a walk? What are you going to show me? Is it something I've seen before? Something new? Will I like it? Can I eat it? Should I be excited? Am I being too excited? How long will it take to get there? Are we nearly there yet?'

Henry smiled and mimed zipping his mouth closed. Her excitement was infectious, but there was also the possibility that she wouldn't like his surprise.

They strolled through the park, then cut through a hedge onto a single-track road.

'Oh, I know where we're going,' she said confidently. 'We're going to the field of flowers.' She stopped, her hand to her chest. 'Have the cows been through already? Are the flowers all gone?'

'I don't think they're being moved until next week,' he replied. 'And don't forget, it's their poo that makes it so beautiful.'

She wrinkled her nose. 'I forgot how essential dung is for the proper functioning of the countryside.'

He grinned and squeezed her hand. 'Come on, it's not far.'

They walked another hundred yards or two up the road and came to a natural halt.

'Oh Henry, look! Someone's moving into the cottage.'

He allowed her to pull him towards it. The scaffolding was already erected around the building and a man was on the roof.

'Is that Finn?'

Finn turned and waved. 'Give me ten minutes, and I'll be with you,' he called.

'Is he moving in?' she asked.

Henry took a breath. 'No, but I thought *we* could.'

'But, but how?'

'There was a lot of money left over from my modelling fee after Simone's company paid Lucas off. So I thought I'd use it to pay Finn to make the cottage habitable again. We don't have to live here if you don't want to. I just thought you might like the idea?'

Her face was frozen with shock, but then it cracked and she leapt into his arms with a squeal, clinging to him like a love-limpet.

'Oh my god, it's too perfect for words! I love it! I love you! Thank you, Henry!'

He laughed as she peppered kisses over his face. 'The work's just begun, so you can decide exactly how you want it.'

'Wood-burning stove, rug, you naked,' she replied, still attempting to kiss every part of him she could reach.

'I'll make sure it's in the contract.'

She looked at him and raised an eyebrow. 'You love a good contract.'

He kissed the end of her nose. 'I love you more.'

Her face was sunshine and smiles. 'I love you more too. Thank you, Henry. This is just incredible.' She turned to gaze at the cottage. 'This is the cherry on top of the icing on top of my perfect Henry-cake.'

'I'm a cake?'

'Yes,' she grinned, looking back at him. 'You're sweet and

utterly moreish.' She nipped at his bottom lip. 'And one bite is never enough.'

THE END

☙❧

Thank you so much for reading Love ad Lib! Want more of Henry and Libby? Read their fiery and romantic extended epilogue by joining my newsletter list at **www.eviealexanderauthor.com/subscribe**

☙❧

Jack and Eveline's story is up next in An Unholy Affair…

Gorgeous Jack Newton has fallen in love. But Eveline Shaw's a vicar dreaming of marriage and kids, and he's a male escort on his way out of town… **Winner in the Romance category** in the 2024 NYC Big Book Awards, An Unholy Affair is a steamy romcom which will steal your heart and make you swoon!

Get An Unholy Affair in print, audio, or eBook format at www.eviealexanderbooks.com

REVIEW LOVE AD LIB
WRITE A REVIEW & MAKE MY DAY!

Thank you so much for reading Love ad Lib! I hope you enjoyed reading it as much as I enjoyed writing it!

Even if just a few lines (or star rating), writing a review is the most amazing thing you can do! It helps people find my books, and lets them know what you loved about them.

You can review Love ad Lib at:
Apple
Amazon
Kobo
Barnes & Noble
Google Play
Goodreads
Bookbub

And any other storefront or platform you use!

And, if you want to share more about Love ad Lib on social media or your blog, please help yourself to our library of graphics, elements and more by going to **www.eviealexanderauthor.com/love-ad-lib/**

Thank you!

Evie ♡

READ AN UNHOLY AFFAIR

**Next up is Jack and Eveline's story!
Eveline's about to learn things that definitely aren't
taught at Sunday school…**

**AN UNHOLY AFFAIR
Her perfect man isn't supposed to be a male escort.**

Vicar Eveline Shaw has always dreamed of finding 'the one',
but her job keeps getting in the way. Only one person has ever
made her soul sing – a perfect stranger who walked away
without a second glance.

Jack Newton has a talent few men have, but his job's a dirty
secret, and as his bank account gets bigger, his heart gets
smaller. He left his one chance at happiness at a bar and didn't
look back.

Dragged back to Somerset after a family crisis, Jack discovers his dream woman living in Foxbrooke. But Eveline wants forever, and he's an escort with no plans to stick around.

As the sparks flying between them ignite into an explosive affair, Jack's past catches up with him. Now he has to choose: keep running, or risk everything for love?

An Unholy Affair *is a wickedly funny, super-steamy, standalone romcom. No cheating, no cliffhanger – just pure, fiery chemistry and a heavenly happy ending!*

Get An Unholy Affair in all formats from www.eviealexanderbooks.com

NEWSLETTER SIGN-UP

Want to read Henry and Libby's fiery and romantic extended epilogue? Sign up to my newsletter to get it today, plus so much more...

In my newsletter you get Evie news before anyone else, as well as exclusive content and goodies.

Newsletter subscribers are my extra special friends, and get everything from bonus epilogues, 19,000 words of deleted sex scenes, free stories, free audiobooks, extracts from my current work-in-progress, and exclusive offers and giveaways.

Sign up now!

http://www.eviealexanderauthor.com/subscribe/

SEX INDEX
(AKA THE GOOD BITS)

There have been many great contributions to the world of literature. Gutenberg invented the printing press, Shakespeare invented romantic comedy, and J K Rowling invented Harry Potter. However, all of these achievements pale into insignificance compared to my contribution – the sex index.

Using this sex index, you can easily find the steamier moments from Love ad Lib. Enjoy...

Page 241 – Oh! Mr Darcy!
Page 271 – Al fresco nighttime nookie
Page 392 – A little light bondage

And if that wasn't enough, don't forget I've got nineteen thousand words of super-hot deleted sex scenes from Highland and Hollywood Games as well as Henry and Libby's extended epilogue available exclusively for newsletter subscribers.

ACKNOWLEDGMENTS

Yay! Here's the place I get to thank all the amazing people (and animals) who have helped me get this book to publication!

This book is dedicated to the real Chester and Joy—fifty per cent Toy Poodle, twenty-five per cent Jack Russell Terrier, twenty-five per cent Border Terrier, and one hundred per cent daft. They may not be as intelligent, beautiful or useful as Estelle's Chester and Joy, but they are very loved, and as I write these words, Joy is asleep on the chair behind me, keeping my lower back toasty warm.

In terms of thanks due to Homo sapiens, first up is one of my oldest friends - Joe Samuel. He's a classically trained musician who specialised in musical improv and now teaches people all over the world. My first real experience of improvisational comedy was with Joe and his 'work wife' Heather (who Libby is based on). I had NO idea I was about to take part in an improv workshop and it was fucking terrifying. It was also the first time I'd ever met Heather and she bounded up to me with more energy, enthusiasm, and kindness than Libby and Claire combined, helping to turn fear into fun.

Find Joe and Heather via their website! www.openyourmouthandsing.co.uk/

Thanks as ever go to my alpha reader, Pash Baker, and Margaret Amatt for reading the first draft and being able to help so much with fine-tuning Love ad Lib. Thank you also to the lovely Andrea Hopkins who sensitivity read for me.

Thank you to Aanchal Jain for editing this story and to Margaret Amatt and Mike AF for their additional input. Thank you to Matt Wellstead for designing this wonderful cover and Mark Karasick for taking such fabulous photos of me.

My team at Emlin Press: Victoria, Mandy, and Liezl. Thank you for doing everything I can't, won't, or don't have time for. Thank you for tolerating my foul mouth, laughing at my unfunny jokes and sticking around.

Thank you to my husband—the best decision I've ever made, and to my daughter—the best luck I've ever had. I love you both to the ends of the multiverse and back.

And last, but by no means least, I want to thank my fabulous ARC team, the incredible online community of book lovers and YOU, the reader! Thank you for your continued support and for reading the first full length book of the Foxbrooke series! Each time you read my books, write me a review and recommend me in countless different ways, my heart gets a little fuller. Thank you!

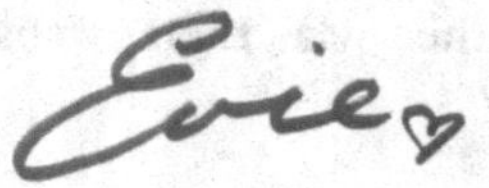

Ps - I love love LOVE hearing from my readers so please get in touch via email or social media to ask me anything or just tell me about your day!

ALSO BY EVIE ALEXANDER

Get all of Evie's books in print, audio, or eBook format, as well as special offers, early releases, and exclusive deals at www.eviealexanderbooks.com

THE KINLOCH SERIES

HIGHLAND GAMES

Zoe's given up everything for a ramshackle cabin in Scotland. She wants a new life, but her scorching hot neighbour wants her out. As their worlds collide, will Rory succeed in destroying her dream? Or has he finally met his match? Let the games begin...

Tropes

Small Town, Enemies-to-Lovers, Grumpy/Sunshine, Fish-out-of-Water, Opposites Attract, Forced Proximity

HOLLYWOOD GAMES

In a last-ditch attempt to save Kinloch castle, new lovers Rory and Zoe throw open the doors to a Hollywood superstar. But when it all goes south, it's up to them to rewrite the script, save the castle's future, and find their own happy ending.

Tropes

Small Town, Soulmates, Grumpy/Sunshine, Fish-out-of-Water

KISSING GAMES

Bodyguard Charlie has a new mission: teach workaholic Hollywood actress Valentina how to play, one wild adventure at a time. But when no-strings fun turns into something more, they have to face some hard truths. Can they find a future together, or will their love remain a Highland fling?

<u>Tropes</u>

Small Town, Dark Secrets, Bodyguard/Actress, Forced Proximity, Alpha-roll hero, Dating Game

MUSICAL GAMES

After lying to a Hollywood megastar, Sam needs Jamie to write an album with her in just ten days He's got the voice of an angel and the body of a god, but fame is the last thing on his mind. Will he help make her dreams come true?

<u>Tropes</u>

Small Town, Grumpy/Sunshine, Male Virgin, Cinnamon Roll Hero, Opposites Attract, Fish-out-of-Water, Forced Proximity

WEDDING GAMES

Rory and Zoe want to get married. Not easy when their mothers are mortal enemies and Rory's step-father is a Hollywood star with a death wish. Can they unravel the tangles in time to tie the knot, or is eloping the only answer? Get ready for Scotland's wedding of the year!

<u>Tropes</u>

Small Town, Grumpy/Sunshine, Opposites Attract, Soulmates, Fish-out-of-Water

CHRISTMAS GAMES

Having a baby's easy, right? Until wayward in-laws, an out-of-control cow and mad Santa get in the way. All Rory and Zoe want is a relaxing Christmas before their baby arrives, but straightforward is not their style...

<u>Tropes</u>

Small Town, Grumpy/Sunshine, Opposites Attract, Soulmates, Fish-

✦

THE FOXBROOKE SERIES

ONE NIGHT IN FOXBROOKE

When chef Ben 'Kenobi' Walker gets the call to help save a VIP dinner at Foxbrooke Manor, he doesn't expect to run into old flame Leia Perry. She's all grown up and even more attractive than when they were teenagers – but she hasn't forgotten what happened ten years ago, and she *definitely* hasn't forgiven him. Will one night give Ben the second chance he needs to prove himself and win back Leia's heart?

<u>Tropes</u>

Small Town, Second Chance, Return to Hometown, Enemies-to-Lovers, Bet, Brother's Best Friend, Work Colleagues, Forced Proximity, First Love, Reverse Grumpy-Sunshine, Opposites Attract

LOVE AD LIB

Shy and reserved Lord Henry Foxbrooke needs a fake girlfriend. Free-spirited actress Libby Fletcher needs a job. But when they arrive in Somerset for Henry's birthday celebrations, neither are prepared for their reception. As friendship blurs and faking it starts to feel a little too real, disaster strikes. Can Libby and Henry stick to the script, or has their entire act just bombed?

<u>Tropes</u>

Small Town, Fake Dating, Grumpy/Sunshine, Opposites Attract, One Bed, Different Worlds, Fish-out-of-Water

AN UNHOLY AFFAIR

Gorgeous Jack Newton has fallen in love with Eveline Shaw. But she's a female vicar dreaming of marriage and kids, and he's a male escort heading out of town. Can Jack show Eveline heaven and keep his secret safe, or are they both headed straight for hell?

Tropes

Small Town, Forbidden Love, Love at First Sight, Sworn off a Relationship, Priest, Different Worlds, Opposites Attract, Dark Secret

THE UPPER CRUSH

James Hunter-Savage is a cocky city boy who isn't used to anyone else taking the reins. Lady Estelle Foxbrooke is a fiery country girl who's about to show him who's boss. Can they learn to fight for love rather than with each other, or will their love hate relationship destroy everything they're working for?

Tropes

Small Town, Enemies-to-Lovers, Alpha Hero, Love/Hate, Playboy in Love, Different Worlds, Workplace Romance, Fake Dating

THE LOVE POSITION

Beautiful academic, Sophia Hunter-Savage, has run away to an ashram to reinvent herself. Hot yoga teacher, Isaac Hayward, has left town to avoid the only woman able to tempt him off the spiritual path.

But karma sucks.

Now Isaac's teaching Sophia and they're finding themselves in all kinds of unexpected positions. Will their forbidden love bring inner peace and happiness, or end in a tangled mess?

Tropes

Forbidden Love, Opposites Attract, Teacher/Student, Sworn off a Relationship, Forced Proximity, Love at First Sight, Different Worlds, Fish-out-of-Water

CHRISTMAS OFF SCRIPT

Best friends, Leo Foxbrooke and Ella Chamberlain, have never been single at the same time. Until now... Playing Cinderella and Prince Charming in the Christmas pantomime, their on-stage chemistry kindles an unexpected spark behind the scenes. Can they rewrite their friendship this festive season and finally unwrap true love?

Tropes

Small Town, Friends-to-Lovers, Best Friend's Ex, Oblivious to Love, Unrequited Love, Fake Relationship

ONE NIGHT ONLY

Pop star Avery Taylor craves a break from her public life, and a one-night stand with a stranger feels like the perfect escape. A year later, while recovering from an injury, she's stunned to find her nurse is Connor Foxbrooke, the man who touched her soul that night. Avery is ready to break the rules for love, but Connor, who values his quiet life, fears heartbreak. With Avery set to return to the spotlight as soon as she's recovered, can they bridge their worlds and turn their one night into forever?

Tropes

Second-Chance, Mistaken Identity, One Night Stand, Different Worlds, Opposites Attract, Injury, Forced Proximity, Fish-out-of-Water, Celebrity, Pop Star, Small Town

RIGHTING MR WRONG

Mooning a party of nuns is bad for anyone, but for TV star Aiden Wilder, it's catastrophic. Enter Willow Foxbrooke, a quiet PR worker who's tasked with saving his reputation through a fake relationship. As Willow teaches him how to recover his image, they start to fall for each other. But how can true love grow from something that was never real to begin with?

Tropes

Small Town, Fake Dating, Grumpy/Sunshine, Celebrity, Opposites Attract, Different Worlds, Fish-out-of-Water

UNDER THE INFLUENCER

Sunny Summer Foxbrooke's career as an Influencer is over. Now she's forced to work with grumpy Finn Oakley, the man who's avoided her for years. Will Finn finally return her love, or will she always just be his best friend's little sister?

<u>Tropes</u>

Brother's best friend, Grumpy/Sunshine, Beauty and the Beast, Age Gap, Unrequited Love, Rivals, Different Worlds, All Grown Up, Small Town

❖

Get Evie's books in all formats as well as special offers, early releases, and exclusive deals direct from her website:

www.eviealexanderbooks.com

ABOUT THE AUTHOR

Evie Alexander is a multi-award-winning author of sexy romantic comedies, blending snort-laugh humour and panty-melting chemistry into unputdownable stories that will steal your heart.

When she's not dreaming up swoony heroes and relatable heroines, Evie can be found in the beautiful West Country of the UK, where she lives with her ridiculously patient husband, miracle daughter, and two dogs who think they run the show.

eviealexanderbooks.com

www.eviealexanderauthor.com

- instagram.com/eviealexanderauthor
- facebook.com/eviealexanderauthor
- x.com/Evie_author
- bookbub.com/authors/evie-alexander
- amazon.com/Evie-Alexander/e/B08ZJGLP29?ref=sr_ntt_s-rch_lnk_1&qid=1630667484&sr=8-1
- pinterest.com/eviealexanderauthor

www.ingramcontent.com/pod-product-compliance
Lightning Source LLC
Chambersburg PA
CBHW010535170726
48285CB00008B/2628